RICKARD A.

ALSO BY SOL YURICK:

RICHARD A.

A NOVEL BY
SOL YURICK

ARBOR HOUSE
New York

6/1982
gen'l

Library of Congress Catalog Card Number: 80-66497

ISBN: 0-87795-272-8

Manufactured in the United States of America
by The Haddon Craftsmen

10 9 8 7 6 5 4 3 2 1

ACKNOWLEDGMENTS

I would like to acknowledge the invaluable help of Theodore Conant, Robert Osband, Martin Elton, and especially Bert Cowlan and Steve Kindel.

PROLOGUE

IT was a night for memories. Every October, for the last twenty years, was a bitter anniversary for Richard A . . . Each year he vowed that *this* would be the year in which he would celebrate that anniversary. He had brought himself to the point of readiness five years ago, but somehow his courage had failed. But this October, 1982, twenty years later, he might bring himself to act, finally. If he didn't, how much longer could he keep the others together?

Richard entered a large room in the back of his house. The house stood on a cliff in northern California; the back overlooked the Pacific Ocean. The nearest house was twenty-five miles away. Tonight the ocean was calm, streaked with moonlight. The beach below shone, white and narrow. It should have been a night for peaceful memories, but he had no peaceful memories. It was a night for destruction.

The room was full of electronic equipment: transmitters, terminals, monitors, computers, disc and tape drives, high-speed printers, receivers, teletypes . . . it all looked jumbled together. But it was one of the best systems in the world, as good as any system of IBM's, Bell's, Citibank's.

He was a tall man, hair beginning to go gray. He exuded a sense of tension, power, violence, all held under terrific control. To tell the truth, he would rather hit or shoot someone. At least you had

7

the person you hated in front of you. He did something evil to you; you paid back the debt directly. Your fingers pulled the trigger; the body jerked across the room. He hadn't done anything like that for twenty years now. He paced around the room, smoking, restless, nervous . . . scared . . . yes, he was scared.

He sat down in front of a console and his hand stroked buttons, keys, switches. He stood up and paced again, smoking cigarette after cigarette. Small lights glowed and gleaming sine-waves undulated across the screens. Everything was ready . . . except him. He inhaled deeply. He shook his head and started to walk out the door.

He stepped onto the patio, facing toward the ocean. How calm. He walked to the railing, turned and leaned against it. He looked up at the sky. On his roof, like a mock black shadow moon, a large disc antenna tracked the satellite he would be penetrating. Invisible tentacles, radio waves, would reach up, twenty-two thousand miles. The waves were frailer than a baby's fists, yet they affected the lives of billions, and for five years he and the others had sucked those waves downward, stealing the information that was in them.

Beyond the dark disc was the real moon, surprisingly big. A harvest moon. They had sown; all right, he would harvest. The features on the moon were obscure enough for him to imagine faces on it, as he used to do when he was a kid. He saw the faces of women he had once loved twenty years ago. Laura, Carol, were dead . . . or worse. He threw the cigarette over the railing. He watched it arc down over the edge, down, finally disappearing. All things moved down into darkness. The darkness swallowed up all things, all light, all humans . . . but that darkness that was *in* humans was a darkness deeper than the blackness between the stars.

He went in again. He lit another cigarette and sat down in front of the console keyboard. His hands were together, almost as if praying. His hands spread and his fingers turned and tensed downward—like a concert pianist, poised, ready to play, trembling. The audience, invisible, scattered all over the world, didn't know they were about to hear the most dissonant composition mankind had ever heard. The trembling was almost a shaking; he might hit the wrong keys.

8

He remembered the moon. He remembered the faces of the women. He began to tap some of the keys and the shaking stopped. He had started. In about twenty minutes he has activated a network of thirty people around the world: in Bonn, in New York, in Tokyo, in Riyadh, in Paris, in Moscow, in Hong Kong, in the Bahamas, in Rio de Janeiro . . . He was ready to go. They were ready to go.

Twenty years ago, Ziggy, a blind genius now dead, had told him, "The time is coming soon when the whole world will be nerved up. *Everything's* going to depend on telecommunications. And when that happens, that's going to be our time. We'll be stronger than armies, more explosive than atom bombs, richer than . . ." That time had come.

Out there in the world, there is a bank. You wouldn't know of it. It does business only with central banks, national reserve systems, national treasuries. In the United States it has a German name. In Germany it has a Japanese name. In England it has a Chinese name. And somewhere in the center of that bank, there is a man, a director, a key officer. A man who had once used the name of Keats. It was that man Richard was after. He was going to penetrate that bank's radio network. In about an hour, chaos would begin all over the world. Funds in the major world's banks would begin to ooze, hemorrhage credit from one country to another, flow into that bank, and then begin to evaporate into thin air, automatically drained by the computer programs Richard and the others had developed. Central and clearing banks around the world would begin to report that there was a sudden and tremendous escalation in the world's monetary supplies. Inflation would rise to astronomical proportions. Some countries would find that their treasuries had been drained in an instant. Other countries, with low standards of living, with barely any trade at all and no visible means of support, would suddenly have too much money and choke from the overglut. They would frantically try to lay it off and find that the lines were mysteriously blocked. Real and false orders on the stock and bond markets would make a hash of everyone's system of accounting. The accounting of thousands and thousands of small savers, those who had a few hundred, a few thousand dollars, would suddenly grow

9

rich. The internal revenue systems of many countries would begin to disburse billions in refunds. It would work. It would work. Their experiment in 1979 with the Federal Reserve system had proved that. It would be a war of electronic gold against real gold.

And in response, from somewhere at the center of that vast web of finance and communication, Keats, the man Richard was after, would get his message and begin to move outward, outward, into visibility . . . emerging once again to hunt him down. And Richard would be waiting for him.

And in a few days governments would begin to topple.

Richard A had begun to get revenge for what was done to him twenty years ago. . . .

PART 1

CHAPTER 1

"YOU mean he's listening to me every time I pick up the phone?"

How like Holcomb to personalize it, Keats thought. It was a beautiful spring evening in 1962 and Keats wished he were elsewhere. It was going to be a long night. "Not quite . . . not every time."

"How did Aquilino penetrate *here?* How did he even think to find us? No one knows about us."

"It was probably an accident. I think he—"

"There are no accidents in this business, Keats. You know that," Holcomb said. His huge left hand held a sheaf of papers and, improbably, a .45. "What the fuck are you waiting for? Look at this shit." Holcomb waved Keat's report back at its author.

Keats hoped the safety was on.

"Bring him in."

Keats controlled himself. He hated Holcomb. A real primitive. A leftover from the old days when the sides were clean . . . or appeared to be . . . the good guys and the bad guys. Keats leaned away from Holcomb's littered desk. "I don't think we should rush to do that. Sir."

Evening brought a stillness to Richard Aquilino's loft and softened the sound of the perpetual traffic's rumble outside, on Canal

Street. The darkness inside was lit only by the streetlights filtering in through the unwashed windows. The darkness joined the piles of magazines—technical journals, science fiction, telephone operations manuals stolen from Bell Telephone, the wiring, the circuits mounted on their boards, speakers, papers, bed, refrigerator, posters on the wall—into indistinct blocks. Everything seemed to fuse. It might have been the interior of a space ship.

A speaker played music. Rock and roll. Not too loud. The songs were of lost loves, loves never consummated, loves that didn't lead to marriage and happy endings, lovers drifted apart, missed opportunities. He couldn't forget Laura.

It was finally working. It would take some fine tuning, it didn't work all the time, but it was working. He had made a breakthrough. Richard was seated in front of a table on which was mounted a huge upright sheet of plastic. The whole rig was about six feet high and ten feet long. As it grew darker, the intricate wiring behind the sheet, leading through the plastic's little holes, faded, leaving only the little lights attached to the sheet, gleaming, blinking, as circuits all over the country, circuits he had plugged into, connected and disconnected. As it got darker, the lights seemed to float in space. Each one marked an ongoing conversation. Sometimes, when it was completely dark, he would watch the lights blinking on the board and imagine they were stars, galaxies. He was in a space ship, journeying across the void to planets with strange exotic populations, who talked strange exotic languages. True, now and then he had heard languages other than English, but even what he heard spoken in English was difficult to understand. The lights, each one of which represented a telephone connection into which he had penetrated— and now his rig made the hookups for him automatically—were individuals. Each of them led, branched out into complexes of other individuals, groupings, populations, all leading lives that were mysterious to Richard. He wondered about those people and, for over more than two years, he was beginning to understand what it was most people thought about.

Every time a light went on, a connection was made, a conversation was held. Instead of holding a receiver to his ear, Richard had rigged up a speaker which allowed him to listen comfortably. It left his hands free to make notes. The man who was speaking

14

now was a lawyer in Washington, some man named Acheson, talking to someone in New York, probably another lawyer. "Edward, I don't like what happened in Berlin in June. I don't think that an embargo will be a strong enough measure by far. The people who are around him manage to keep us away from him. I think, frankly, that they're socialists, or worse, academics with no experience in the real world. Frankly, they are selling this country down the river. I think that they and they alone must bear the responsibility for what happened at *Bahia de los Cochinos.* We could have ended it all there, in one fell swoop. And now, with Allen gone from the Company . . ."

". . . what do you suggest . . . ?"

The sound wasn't clear. Richard suspected a loose connection. The descrambler was working well. He was proud of it. He had designed it himself.

". . . We should get together a committee. People like ourselves. Very senior. A lot of people from banking and industry . . ."

"Very senior? Don't depress me, Dean. Who'll carry on when we're too old, or gone?"

"I'll be talking to the President later. He's put me off just about as long as he politely could. In the meantime I'm going to have some papers hand-delivered to you. I think that Tom Dodd, Ken Keating and Ev Dirksen, to start, should get copies. It'll put them in the picture. You know the list. We should aim for October. Late October. The perfect time before the election. Timing is important, I don't have to tell you. They really have to know what's going on down there. Later, we can supplement our initial presentation with some pictures . . ."

"Are there pictures?"

"There will be . . ."

Richard didn't really pay attention. He didn't know what they were talking about. This talk about Berlin, Cuba, the Congo . . . His interest had fallen off since Laura stopped using her phone.

Richard had listened to Laura talk to some young man in Connecticut. Was it one of her boy friends? He should listen in to her. It depressed him; the people she knew; the worlds she lived in, so different now from his own. The man in Connecticut had

15

talked to a woman in Baltimore, a new contact, and the machine had registered it. The woman in Baltimore had made an assignation with someone who seemed to be her lover, a general in Washington. Their talk made him squirm. She was choosing a time to meet the general when her husband would not be around. The lover, the general, had talked to someone in Florida, some kind of military man, but without any rank, at least none had been used. The talk was of landing craft, tanks, and infantry, and strikes. The man in Florida had spoken to this lawyer in Washington, Acheson, who ... Except for Laura, and the general and his woman, none of it really interested him. What *did* interest him was how well the switching system worked and how each new connection was permanently registered in his machine. It was all operating beautifully.

Richard flicked a switch. The room was filled with a vast, murmuring babble. All of the voices at the same time, filtering in to his listening post. He liked to do that now and then. It mixed with the music nicely and allowed him to dream of Laura ... Laura ... sometimes unrequited love spurs genius. Would she love him again if he sold it all to Bell?

After a while he turned it off. He was going out. Ziggy would want to know about the breakthrough.

Richard's system of taps and intercepts led, accidentally, into two realms, one visible, the other invisible. The New York Richard lived in was in the visible realm, the ordinary city of ordinary people. The other New York had everything to make it one of the great underground intelligence battlefields, right up there with London, Zurich, Moscow, Berlin, Istanbul, Washington, Athens, Paris, Teheran, Tokyo, Hong Kong. New York had the UN—filled to overflowing with operatives from the Soviet Union and the United States—airports, the great multinational corporate headquarters, the great law firms that were not household words, the major international public relations and advertising firms; New York was *the* communications center, with great banks, major foundations, libraries, great universities (which were part public and part underground); and it had cellars, lots of cellars, and cellars under cellars, and, under those even deeper cellars.

Surely the temptation of Jesus must have taken place in such an atmosphere.

Agents of all countries come here to these invisible realms. They fight one another silently. They make and break, form and reform, shifting alliances. They betray and are betrayed. Some have the ability to change sides in the middle of a sentence. Others remain fiercely loyal, willing to die for their countries. Part of the invisible city Richard had inadvertently stumbled into had begun to listen back.

In the basement of Richard's loft building, voice-activated tape recorders plugged into Richard's telephone line. Every two days someone came into the basement, collected the filled-up tapes and took them away. They were delivered uptown to the Coffin Foundation. Most of the Coffin Foundation was in the visible world, albeit a very expensive part of the visible world. There it stood, in the forties, down the street from the UN. Anyone could go into the front door and reach any of its offices . . . if he had business there. Once inside the front door, there were two channels, although one of them couldn't be seen. One led into the invisible realm, although a very visible elevator took you there —a small part of the Coffin could not be reached directly. The tapes were brought in through the delivery entrance. They were brought upstairs—or maybe it was downstairs—and turned over to a typist-stenographer who transcribed them.

It was a game of small moves played out by two men who hated one another. Holcomb threw down the report on his littered desk. Holcomb hated being a desk man; he had always been a field man. Even in the New York City Police Department, the FBI, the CIA—all of which Holcomb had served in—he was known as a wild man. Of all the uncontrollables, Holcomb had a unique reputation. He was loath to follow orders he thought were stupid, or stupidly worked out. He was known to go off on his own and run his own operation. He took chances and frequently produced results that few others did. Keats had just come back from a CIA assignment in the Congo, the province of Katanga, but it was his first overseas assignment. This blond faggot Keats, Holcomb thought, hadn't learned a thing. "Go on, Keats, tell me.

Give me some of that college analysis."

Keats wondered: how drunk was Holcomb? Big, almost 250 pounds. Big wrists, big neck, big crew-cut head, big ass. Fast moving . . . at least in a straight line. But if he was big and brutal, his mind was not. It was the mind of a small, shifty-eyed man, the mind of a man who cannot stay still. Holcomb had that old-time policeman's instinct, the smell for things. Keats had learned about the smell from witch doctors in the Congo. Keats put a little of the bureaucrat's whine into his tone; he knew how much Holcomb hated paper pushers and it would throw him a little. "In the first place, Mr. Holcomb, we're not even sure . . ." Holcomb's fat fingers were tightening on the gun.

Keats smiled faintly.

"The penetrator's one of theirs," Holcomb said. "I feel it. I taste it. My balls tingle and the hair on the back of my head . . . sure signs, buddy."

No doubt Mr. Angleton, head of CIA counterintelligence, would be glad to put these signs into a training manual, Keats thought. That was the way Mr. Angleton worked too . . . on instinct. "There's a whole missing dimension—"

"What's the missing dimension?"

"The connection. There is none. To whom does Aquilino's take, if there is any, go? If there's a who, it would lead to how and what, which would lead us to why." Someday, Keats thought, I may indulge myself and make Holcomb the first person I kill for personal reasons. "It doesn't make sense. It's not the Soviet *modus operandi.*"

Holcomb noted that Keats said "Soviet" and not communist. It counted against him. "Because the other ways aren't working. Listen, when it comes to those godless S.O.B.'s . . ."

To Keats, Holcomb was a dangerous dinosaur in a changing world of faster-moving political animals, unable to adapt. Here it comes, Holcomb's lecture on the monstrousness, the cunning, the evil, the endless craftiness of those instrumentalities of The Night and Satan, the Commies. Times were changing, and sometimes the patriots were worse than the Russians, who had problems with their own Holcombs. For instance, the man they called El Supremo, Vassili Oprichnik's KGB boss . . . Keats and Vassili

18

had covertly fought their employers, both KGB and CIA, in Katanga . . . and lost. For the time being. They had lost in the Congo and were ordered to take the battle toward the center of power by their real boss. To here, to the unit under Coffin Foundation cover.

It is said that battles begun in St. Petersburg more than forty-five years ago, in the turmoil of the Russian Revolution, are continued (or finished off) in the streets, hotel rooms, cellars and offices of New York, sometimes carried on by the grandchildren of the original combatants. There are some, if they can be persuaded to talk, who will say that the battles are of even more ancient origin, perhaps even two thousand years old. Small, covert wars that began in Rome and Jerusalem, raged through all the cities of Asia Minor, spread into Europe, and were continued down to these days. Battles not to be found in history books or in the Bible. Maybe they started when the Roman Secret Police, the *Frumentori*—who were also sorcerers—infiltrated a small group of zealots in the ancient and perpetually troubled land of Canaan. Others will say that the Frumentori set up that small group in the first place. Its aim? To overthrow the Hebrew hierarchy, or maybe it was to overthrow Rome. It worked, but in a way no one had anticipated.

Her job was boring. She was young. Twenty-two. She wasn't even allowed to listen to a portable radio. She had red hair and thought a lot about clothes. She spent her time looking into store windows. She sat all day and typed reports, transcribed dictation and sometimes tapes. This set of tapes was particularly dull. Maybe if she could have seen the whole scene . . .

Two men, she figured, were sitting, talking over coffee, in Ferdi's restaurant across the street from the UN. One was short, skinny, excited; he talked so fast he tended to stutter. He wore an expensive, three-button jacket, charcoal gray. Slim maroon tie. Ivy League. But he wore his suit sloppily. The jacket was pressed but the pants had long failed to hold their crease. The frames of his glasses were bent and they kept sliding down his nose. He kept nervously pushing the frames up with his thumb and it looked as if he were thumbing his nose at the person he

19

was talking to. He was very nervous; he plucked at his clothes, arranging and rearranging the silverware, the cups and plates. His name was Abromowitz.

The other was tall, blond, aristocratic. He had almost blank gray eyes. His name was Carstairs and he was very calm. His calmness, his repose, made him hard to remember, even though he was very handsome. They became friends at Harvard, but in some way they didn't really like one another. Maybe the dislike came from the genes. Carstairs had always thought Abromowitz was a pushy Jewish boy genius; the brightest-boy-in-class syndrome. Abromowitz thought Carstairs was an insolent and empty-headed goy. Abromowitz was a junior officer working for the National Security Council. Carstairs was also connected with government, but not in the way Abromowitz thought.

Abromowitz was talking about the 1962 round of disarmament talks that had just adjourned in Europe without any real results. He had left—or been forced to leave—prematurely before January 29th. Talks were absolutely deadlocked and Abromowitz was explaining why. "I THOUGHT THE NEGOTIATORS WERE JUST BEING STUPID AND SENILE. THEY COULDN'T SEE WHAT WAS RIGHT IN FRONT OF THEIR EYES. I THOUGHT THAT THEIR NICKEL-AND-DIMING WAS GOING TO BRING ON THE WAR . . . THEY WERE TESTING OUT THEIR MANHOOD . . . PLAYING NUCLEAR CHICKEN. BUT NO." Abromowitz and his opposite number, a junior Russian bureaucrat, had worked out a perfectly simple formula for disarmament. They had almost completed the plan when their superiors found out what they were doing. The Russian was whisked off to heaven knows where, probably the cellars of the Lubianka. Abromowitz was flown home on a military plane and chewed out by John F. Kennedy personally for one humiliating quarter-hour. That had been followed up by Robert Kennedy's tongue-lashing. After that, Dean Rusk was nothing.

"I WOULD SAY THAT'S QUITE AN HONOR TO BESTOW ON A JUNIOR OFFICER, WOULDN'T YOU?" Carstairs said. The red-headed girl typed it, missing the irony. Probably you had to see the face . . .

"SOME HONOR. THAT'S NO LANGUAGE FOR A PRESIDENT TO USE. 'WHAT THE FUCK DID YOU THINK YOU

20

WERE DOING? MAKING FUCKIN' FOREIGN POLICY BY YOURSELF?' " Abromowitz imitated the Boston accent perfectly. "NO MAN SHOULD HAVE TO EAT SHIT LIKE THAT. OH NO. YOU KNOW WHAT I REALIZED, CARSTAIRS? *THEY DIDN'T WANT A DISARMAMENT PLAN.*"

Carstairs nodded and shrugged. He remained impassive. "MAYBE YOU'RE BEING A LITTLE PARANOID." Welcome to the real world, he thought. The less Abromowitz understood, the better.

There was just one trouble. Every table in the restaurant was bugged. By late afternoon, the conversation was retailed to Americans, Germans, British, French, Russians and Israelis, by phone. It was known in the Chase Bank and at Lazard Frères. The transmission had been picked up by Richard. That night, Abromowitz was dead. Carstairs was still alive because that wasn't his real name.

Of course the red-headed typist missed the nuances. She didn't have the training. Still, the part about the President was interesting.

"Look, bring this Richard Aquilino in," Holcomb was saying. "A couple alongside the head, one or two in the balls should start him singing—"

"Or scare him to death."

"Keats, he's a professional. We can do business with him. He's going to expect a display of strength . . . it's a part of the *händling.*" The Yiddish word sounded strange in Holcomb's mouth. "He'll be disappointed if we don't put it to him that way . . ."

"What if he's not a professional?"

"He's gotta be. Just look at this shit . . ." Holcomb hated this effete, slender blond snake. Always showing off his Ivy League education . . . always giving you the "on the one hand" and "on the other hand . . ." Always working toward *"détente"* . . . wanting to work with the Russians . . .

Be careful, Keats thought. Holcomb was one of the old breed, got his law degree at night and went on to join the FBI. But he was uncontrollable. He was kicked out of the FBI by Mr. Hoover personally, for drinking, womanizing and, finally, calling Mr. Hoover a faggot to his face. A distinguished record did not help.

21

Holcomb, who had intelligence experience in the FBI in Latin America and combatting Nazis during the early part of the Second World War, moved on to the CIA. It was in the CIA he had his greatest triumph . . . for about two years under William King Harvey. The Berlin Tunnel operation. Then Holcomb had worked Cuba and, after the Bay of Pigs operation, had come on here, to the Coffin Foundation to set up a counterintelligence operation. It was not clear why Holcomb had been edged out. It had something to do with his paranoia about Russians. Holcomb had heard something in Berlin, assumed it was a Commie operation, made a nuisance of himself, threatened to blow a delicate, subtle, long-range operation.

The Aquilino transcripts went from the typist up to Morrison. Morrison was supposed to distill all the take into a manageable report. It was not easy to do. In most eavesdropping operations, most of the talk was to the point, but here there was a lot of irrelevancy. An odd mixture of important and unimportant people. For example, the military stuff . . . why was there no consistency and followup? He was shocked at the sensitivity of some of the material. Highly classified. The kid had penetrated it with ease. Yet, able to listen into all this, why didn't he just keep on listening? There were a lot of conversations with a woman named Laura; in fact, she was the one person listened into the most. Why? Who was she? Of course Morrison was surprised at the contacts she had. She got around. The President . . . And, of course, as he had always suspected, the man played around. Jesus, who was minding the store? Morrison whistled at some of the big names: congressmen, cabinet members, industrialists, bankers . . . movie stars, sports figures, football. That talk, for instance, of moving the New York Giants out West . . .

It was as if the kid was impatient. He couldn't sit still to listen to one set of people. As if he was searching for something or someone. A four-way conversation between two Americans, a Frenchman and an Englishman discussing events in the Congo . . . Just as it got interesting, it seemed to get boring for Aquilino. The notes to himself; they didn't make sense. Was it a code, a scrawl, or what? A surprising amount of it was unclear. A chain of phone calls about something that was going to happen sometime in the near future. "The pernicious doctrine of small wars . . . whoever heard of three and a half wars . . . I vote a strike . . . before the power becomes entrenched and unmoveable . . ."

Morrison decided to prepare two reports. The first was to his immediate superior, Keats. It was, as much as he could do, a summary of activities, an estimation of what was going on and an emphasis on the most sustained threads. The second report, informal and for Holcomb's eyes only, was his own estimate of what this was all about. Morrison didn't trust Keats any more than Holcomb did.

Everything about them was different. Background. Temperament. Looks. Education. But be careful. Fat and fool, or not, Holcomb had that witch doctor's sense of smell. Dangerous. You couldn't control him directly, and if he couldn't get satisfaction from a higher source, he was just as likely to kill you as not. Keats had planned his moves. The only thing that could spoil it was impatience. He looked mildly, innocently, a little insolently at the pistol pointing his way . . . the tautening finger on the trigger. What was he supposed to do, shit in his pants? He began. "Aquilino is not an agent."

"He's spook all the way. He's a whole Berlin Tunnel operation by himself. Do I have to go through this with you again?"

What if this fool pulled the trigger accidentally?

". . . the President of the U S of A, where there is no higher than . . ."

There was a "higher than," Keats thought. In fact there were a number of "higher thans" and one of them was right here, on the twenty-first floor—Edward Kelley. Aquilino was going to help Keats get up there . . . right up into the empyrean. "Aquilino is just a kid playing games. He's listened in to people who have absolutely nothing to do with national security. If he's a spy, where's he bringing the take? There is absolutely no connection . . ."

"Come on, Keats, what did they teach you in training? That's his legend, the hobby nut. 'Who me? I was just having fun.' Well, we'll see if this innocent hobbyist can take one or two in the balls."

"None of it sounds right, sir. The more channels you penetrate,

23

the more chances there are of getting caught."

"Keats, your trouble is that you spooks are overeducated. And what do they teach you people in college? Freud, literature, and everything has a thousand different interpretations and nothing can mean what it is. You come out of that education shadow-crazy. You think the Russians are just shadows and dreams? You haven't been touched by them yet, beaten, had your balls squeezed. Russians have subverted half the country. Why can't you accept the fact that this Aquilino kid is an agent?"

"Because he's probably not."

"Well, we'll find that out."

"And if he's not?"

Holcomb pointed the gun at Keats's head. "This's real, right?"

Keats nodded.

"What's in it is real, right?"

Keats nodded.

"And if I pull the trigger, what happens to your head's real, right?"

Keats kept nodding, but he knew that the days of daring, of swift, poorly thought-out operations were over. It was the time of the analyst now. The last gasp of the action-faction was the Bay of Pigs, and they'd fouled everything up. Now it was a war of attrition, of small moves, little killings, limited wars, and of changing sides. Straightforward chess had mutated into *Gō*, an infinitely subtler game. The real war was between two antagonistic populations: the old guard of all countries, who wanted to keep things the way they were, and the new guard—neither Russian nor American but international.

"Aquilino is an innocent. He's a case for the FCC, not us."

"You're going to stick by that?"

"Yes, sir."

"And if I order you to bring him in?"

"I'll bring him in, of course, but—"

"You'll register your protest in channels. Cover yourself. Right?"

"I don't think I have a choice."

The finger tightened and whitened around the trigger. "What if I ask you to rewrite that report?"

24

Keats shrugged.

"You know I have the final word. Besides, you'd end up with a bad performance rating. I could go further, you know I could. You know the agency is riddled with moles. I can give you some uncomfortable days and nights. And someone might get the idea that you're not worth the trouble of an investigation."

Again Keats shrugged. "If we go around doing what 'they' do, we end up like 'them.' "

"Oh, that's cute, Keats. Is that the way you operated in the Congo? Is that why the niggers are taking over the world?"

"I've seen the real world, Mr. Holcomb. You've read my file. What *is* interesting about this Aquilino is the way his mind works, how he managed to do what he did."

Holcomb, who at least understood bureaucratic infighting, the war of tiny moves, as much as he hated it, now understood. Keats wanted Aquilino for himself.

To make an executive summary for Holcomb was an arduous, daily task. Keats had to go through the already summarized material submitted by Morrison and others. Scanning a summarized transcripted version of a conversation is always peculiar. There are no rounded sentences, only fragments of conversation. To the outsider it might sound like gibberish. Seen in print, you don't know where the inflections and emphases go. The sense of speaking is missing.

Suddenly Keats recognized something. His reaction was alarm, panic. He sent for the full transcripts and began to read them. He had almost missed it. But there it was: a transcript of himself, talking to people. To Mr. Kelley. To Laura. To Vassili Oprichnik. To Abromowitz. No real names, true, but now he had to listen to the complete tapes themselves—a time-consuming exercise, but Keats forced himself to go through it. When he was finished, he knew. He was almost blown. His voice could be identified from the tapes, possibly even from the full transcript. Keats's first thought was: two people know . . . the typist and Morrison. His second thought was that he had signed the full transcripts and the tapes out . . . his name was logged in. He had to keep the tapes from Holcomb.

"Supposing, for the sake of argument," Keats told Holcomb, "Aquilino is . . . well, a kind of agent. But also, supposing he doesn't know he's an agent."

There it was, Holcomb thought, the endless series of Chinese boxes all the younger agents were addicted to. "And?"

"Then he wouldn't know who his contact is and he wouldn't know who his control is, would he?"

"I'm listening."

"Maybe it has to do with the new science of control, mind control . . ."

A red-headed girl was walking down the sunny streets of New York, window shopping. She looked like a secretary on her lunch break; that's what she was. She worked in the underground city, for the CIA unit under cover of the Coffin Foundation. She had been typing all morning, making transcripts of tapes.

She started to cross the street. There was a store she particularly wanted to see before she got back to work. An expensive store, fashionable. An exclusive store. Styles six months ahead of *Vogue* and *Cosmopolitan*. Never be able to afford them. Still . . . As she crossed, a car started moving, shot through the light, almost crashing into other cars. The car flicked sideways, almost as if it were a human. It caught her and hit her and lifted her. Her red hair flashed in the sunlight. She was tossed to the side, over other cars and into the window of the store she was going to look at. Her body smashed into the plate glass. Her skin erupted suddenly in slashes and punctures. But she was dead before she hit the glass. Her body came to rest among the dresses, the belts, the suits she wanted to buy so badly. Mannequins of icy hauteur didn't change their expression as they teetered, fell, collapsed on top of her.

The car kept moving before anyone could react. As people began to walk, run, the car turned the corner a block away. There it pulled up before the only free space, in front of a hydrant. The driver got out and walked away. A passerby turned and called after the back of the man: "This is a fire-hydrant. You'll get a ticket."

26

CHRPTER 2

IT began this way:

Maybe, if it were merely a technical problem alone, or if it were only a matter of love, Richard Aquilino might never have gone as far as he did. Love for a Laura who had disappeared. But perhaps technology and love went together. Add to it the feeling that he was different, odd, a total outsider. He never had believed what his mirror told him. Tall, black hair, wide-shouldered . . . that's not what his eyes saw. He never knew the right thing to say. All he ever wanted to talk about was radio, telephony, the world of the future, a universe connected, many individual minds united, on this and other planets, into a sort of supermind. Ultimately, electromagnetic telepathy, a kind of love and understanding in which spoken words didn't get in the way. All of that drove Richard into an obsession that ultimately carried him, without leaving his loft, into the lives of hundreds of people.

Laura had disappeared, or gone with someone. Where? You start looking.

A small accident. One day you pick up the phone and dial someone. It's a friend, or a loved one. But something's wrong. Nothing special. It happens all the time. There are other voices on the line. Annoying. You talk but you hear the other voices. Crossed wires? Faulty switches? You might even say, could you please get off the line. But, somehow or other, the speakers don't

27

hear you say that. And that's fascinating because you can hear *them*. Maybe it's gossip, or a business deal, or something more important. There's talk of trading Roger Maris. You talk and listen at the same time and somehow it's not as satisfying as if you could pay complete attention to what they are saying. Your own interests are overridden. Then their conversation ends and you are left hanging. What happened? What was the resolution? Did she believe him, or he her? You think that maybe if you telephone your friend, or the loved one, you might blunder into that conversation again. But it doesn't happen again. Why not? You're curious.

If you're an ordinary person, it's only an idle thought; you say that the telephone company has screwed up and I'm paying too much for such lousy service. But if you know something, you think, what if you could find some way of listening in to these people at will? Some way of crossing the wires, leaving that faulty switch directing conversations in a multiplicity of directions, or find some way of duplicating the faultiness. And if there's a way to do that, then there is certainly a way to be able to find and listen in to the loved one who doesn't love you anymore and won't give you a reason why she stopped loving you and disappeared so suddenly.

Richard Aquilino knew something. He was a ham radio operator. He had begun in grade school, over the objections of his parents who wanted him to do better. When he met Ziggy—who was crippled and legally but not totally blind—buying equipment, he learned how to make his transmitters and receivers more powerful, and how to listen all the way out to extraordinary wavelengths. Ziggy also had something marvelous: a complete list of secret and secure frequencies. In order to hear these frequencies—Defense, Air Force, CIA, FBI, Secret Service channels for instance—it was necessary not only to erect a bigger antenna, but to redesign the receiver, since you couldn't buy such a receiver commercially. Child's play. A lot of fun. A problem which kept his mind off other problems. He and Ziggy had a good time together, doing it. In the process, he met some of Ziggy's friends, particularly Tarzan (who was Ziggy's arms and legs) and Marvin, who was a walking memory machine, and a whole circle of people, all fanatics about communications technology, and most of them, like himself, science fiction nuts, too.

But, unlike radio, whose airwaves were available to anyone who could build the proper equipment to receive the bandwidths, the telephone system was different. It went over wires. Somewhere you had to connect. Each conversation was coded for some degree of privacy. If you could afford it, or were important, or powerful enough, the degree of privacy increased—unlisted numbers; classified numbers; TOP-SECRET numbers; channels which led to trap-switching centers with an electromechanical (and recently electronic) guardian, before they were put through to their destination. Sometimes they went halfway around the country before they connected two people a few blocks apart. But what if you could find a way to hook into a call so you could overhear what was being said, without being suspected. Not tapping in the ordinary way, in which you hooked right into the wire or intercepted the electromagnetic waves surrounding the wire, but from *inside* the system? How could it be done?

Richard decided that it was time he abandoned his little business of repairing radio and television sets (a job he had taken to escape the nagging of his parents and his two sisters, and their husbands) and get a straight job. He went to work for the telephone company. Where else could you learn, but from the competition? Most of all, he wanted to find a way to listen in to Laura, and that meant tapping her parents. He heard more than he wanted to; it upset him, horrified him, but he couldn't stop.

Bell Telephone was the first to pick up the penetration—complaints of bad service from valued customers, strange echoes, interruptions, hollow sounds. The security services of various enterprises complained to Bell that they suspected their secure lines might be penetrated. Other subscribers said that a voice had broken in on their conversations. The Maras, owners of the New York Football Giants, were particularly concerned that someone might have overheard certain particularly delicate negotiations which, if leaked to the press . . . About what? No comment. Bell investigated a number of lines and found that someone was intercepting. The more they searched, the more penetrations they found.

If things had been done routinely, Richard Aquilino's case

29

might never have come into the CIA unit operating under Coffin Foundation cover. Bell might simply have had Richard Aquilino —an ex-employee—arrested. But, considering some of the people Aquilino was tapping, and the extent of his penetrations, there might be espionage aspects to the case.

The first thing Malrowe, who was in charge of Bell's security, did was to assess whether this was a problem Bell wanted to handle alone. Many Bell interests were threatened. The technical aspects of what this person had done were staggering. How had he, alone (alone? Unbelievable . . . maybe not alone) solved some message-traffic, routing and switching problems that were still vexing Bell Labs? What if the competition, who were trying to get business away from Bell, got hold of the kid—Siemens, Erricssen . . . ITT? Malrowe was shocked at how high a level this kid, Aquilino, had reached, apparently with bits of wire and jury-rigged switches.

A policy discussion was held. Did Bell want to arrest the kid? Did they want to offer him a job, or what? Perhaps he could be used to make a point to the government which Bell had been unsuccessfully trying to make for years: The government—the military, executive and intelligence communities in particular— needed a completely secure, dedicated, enclosed system, with a satellite. It was a disgrace how the civilian and government systems connected. One could blunder (or something more insidious than blundering) from the public sector into the national security sector. AT&T had wanted the satellite for themselves and had been defeated. They had to settle for Comsat, a joint venture. Perhaps as always, the government had to have dramatic examples before they could or would move. One had to be able to convince budget-minded and technically illiterate congressmen of the gravity of the situation. Maybe Aquilino should have a little help . . . help he need never know he was getting.

Bell assisted Richard Aquilino in making some more interconnects he probably would never have made by himself . . . to Allen Dulles's own secure home line. They would have helped Aquilino reach the President, but Aquilino had by himself gotten into Kennedy's line, the one that bypassed the White House switchboard. Did Bell want to take a chance that the government would learn some of Aquilino's secrets before Bell did?

30

After another discussion, it was decided to pass the case on to someone Bell could trust and work with, someone who understood their needs and could make their case to the government. Malrowe had an extensive list of contacts in the Defense Department, the CIA, the NSA and the FBI. Holcomb, for one. Malrowe had worked with Harvey Holcomb and Braunstein, an old Nazi, on the Berlin Tunnel operation from 1954 to 1956.

They had tunneled to East Berlin and penetrated the central telephone exchange. For more than a year they had intercepted all the phone traffic back to Moscow. Malrowe and Holcomb took incredible intelligence out of there in 1956, as well as a lot of good gossip. They began to hear the first themes of a new and cacophonous symphony emerging out of the complicated traffic, gossip about Stalin's crimes, something no one had dared talk about before. Khrushchev's speech, to be made before the Twentieth Party Congress, was being sent up as a trial balloon. An internal, secret and informal debate was raging. Should such a speech be made? Should this can of worms be opened? Would it rend the fabric of Russian society? Or could it be a wiping clean of the slate; a new beginning? What would the effect be on Poland, Hungary, Rumania, Czechoslovakia? On the other hand, could the speech convince the West of the Soviet Union's good intentions, its basic commitment to peace?

Strange music. A red symphony fading to a pink coda before coming to a white end. King, Holcomb, Malrowe and Braunstein tried to trace the discussants. Holcomb, at Braunstein's prompting, began to suspect that Khrushchev's developing speech denouncing Stalin and the slave camps was not Khrushchev's. And by now he was sure that Khrushchev had never made such a speech. In that case, who had? Had the speech been prepared in Washington, delivered to "Russia," planted in order to be stolen and brought back to the West, there to be released to the media? Holcomb glimpsed a flash of a deep, long-range operation underneath, something codenamed the Parvus Game.

Braunstein went wild. He had been tracing Parvus for years. His section had a task force devoted to nothing else but this Parvus, said to be the man who in 1917 had persuaded the German General Staff to make sure that Lenin got to Russia in time to participate in the Revolution. Perhaps, Malrowe thought, that's when Holcomb's paranoia—or rather his understanding of the complicated, devious and half-Asian Russian mind—began. And that's when he started to see that the current unrest in the United States—the fight for Civil Rights and Fair Play for Cuba, with all the prestigious hangers-on—was all about. It was the Russians weakening the West.

They also overheard the Hungarian uprising developing, and the Suez Crisis which almost broke up NATO. The British, French and Israelis vs. Egypt and the United States, but with the Soviet Union curiously quiescent, seeming to miss a golden opportunity. Was there some unannounced complicity between elements in the United States and Russia? Were there moles in America? They heard it all developing before the crises flamed into existence. Some of the Moscow–East Berlin traffic was remarkably prescient, as if a forecaster knew just what was going to happen. And how did these events connect to Khrushchev's speech; was the Grand Alliance breaking up, or *being broken up?*

The Russians discovered the East Berlin intercept. How long could you conceal something like that? The Russians began to plant items for the Americans to hear. It was six months before the Americans discovered that their operation was blown. The Americans, in turn, pretended they didn't know the Russians had caught on. Holcomb, who was an uncomplicated man, was not happy with the operation; he was used to more direct action. Anything that couldn't be solved with a gun was probably not worth solving . . .

Maybe Malrowe remembered that, and maybe not, but he decided on Holcomb anyway.

When Keats found out he was on the verge of being blown, he began to think what he had to do. He didn't let himself panic. Some intelligence theoretician had calculated that for every minute of action, there were (or should be) three hours of thought, reading, research, search through the labyrinthine dossiers. The James Bonds were few and far between and most of them were very quickly dead. Yet his boss, Holcomb, even though he looked nothing like James Bond, was in the flesh a man of pure action. How he had survived this long, Keats did not know, and he was determined to overcome the already skewed law of averages by helping Holcomb to his demise at the proper time. Holcomb's marvelous instinct protected him. Where the analytic type would have to go through the tapes and the transcripts and the names and the numbers time and time again to make out the pattern, someone like Holcomb could frequently just feel what was wrong in a second, and that instinct might lead him directly to the crucial points in the glut of raw data—to Mr. Kelley, and to himself. Dimly, he began to work to a way of deflecting Holcomb . . .

The first thing Keats had to consider, now that the typist was dead, was how to cover up the trail of memoranda that connected him to the tapes.

The second thing to consider was how to get rid of the sound of his voice on those tapes . . . as well as the sound of others. He would need backup, lots of it.

The third thing was, how was he going to make use of Richard?

Should he go upstairs to Mr. Kelley, the fabled and barely known-of Mr. Kelley, with the news? Should he go through channels, or try to reach Mr. Kelley directly? Should he begin to act and come to Mr. Kelley with a *fait accompli?* Dangerous, if Mr. Kelley didn't like what he did. Keats made a decision. He began to plan and write.

He contacted certain actors he knew . . . out-of-work actors. He gave them certain scripts he had written up and some partial tapes of certain characters Richard had overheard. All the actors had to do was to talk to one another on certain phones, using a variety of voices. Richard would be sure to listen in and, well, at least catch some of it.

Malrowe found that his cold-wartime buddy Holcomb had ostensibly left the CIA and moved on to the Coffin Foundation. No doubt a cover. Well, no matter, Malrowe thought; it must still be a Company operation. They had dinner together. Malrowe watched Holcomb load up on spaghetti and red clam sauce, and drink a lot of scotch. "Load up, load up. Guy who owns the place owes me from the Big War," Holcomb said.

"No one owes anyone that much."

"It was a big favor. I helped some of his *paisanos* in Sicily."

Malrowe briefed Holcomb about Aquilino's penetration, its

33

extent, its technical ramifications. Not everything, but whatever Bell felt Holcomb needed to know. If Holcomb wanted to pass the news on to one of his old outfits, that was fine. But no. As Malrowe expected, Holcomb said he would use the information himself.

"It's delicate, Holcomb, I don't have to tell you. I mean, we want certain things to come out of this."

"I didn't think you were giving this to me out of the goodness of your heart, Malrowe."

"You know, you people are one of the penetratees."

"Who, Coffin?"

"Not so much Coffin. One of its officers."

"Who?"

"A Mr. Kelley."

"The counsel. Well, at least it isn't us. What is it you want?"

"The technical data. How this kid does it. I'll give you some backup."

"Sure."

"And—"

"There has to be an and." Holcomb chewed and spoke. "How do you like the food?"

"Really superb." Malrowe looked around. There was only one other pair of men eating there.

Holcomb saw the look. "It's that kind of place."

"Is he working for, say, our competition?"

"ITT, RCA, GTE . . . that kind of competition? Don't the Russians interest you too?"

"Only insofar as they want to buy our equipment."

"Shit, Malrowe."

"You don't think the cold war is going to go on forever do you?"

"Till the end of time, Malrowe. You know their song, don't you? 'Tis the final struggle . . .' "

"Listen, Holcomb, while you people are fighting these Stone-Age ideological fights, ITT got Cuba's business."

"And if the U.S. makes friends with the spics, you'll get that business?"

"You can do business with anyone. Business cools the revolutionary ardor."

"Not the Commies?"

"There's another 'and.' "

"Yeah? How come you don't drink as much as you used to? Want to get laid when we finish?"

"I'm slowing up. I think that certain people in high places have to understand that national-security issues are involved here. I mean, when any kid can walk in off the street and get into the Joint Chiefs' pants—"

"With a little help?"

"Maybe."

"A lot of heavy help?"

"Here's the report. Judge for yourself."

The Coffin Foundation was good cover. The Foundation was devoted to funding research studies on what they called communecology, all leading to developing worldwide communications links. The social, psychological and neurological effects of new and massive communications and information systems, and how to bring such changes on line. And, since intelligence is all about communications and information, albeit stolen, what better cover?

The Foundation had been funded by a consortium of American corporations to help development of research in what they called, at that time, politneurons. This was done in 1943 when Washington was already planning the Cold War after the Second World War. After the war, the founding American corporations had been joined by corporations of other countries as they recovered from the war. All would work to foster international relations and diminish tension between nations. Good communications dissolved ideological rigidities, a first step toward dissolving nations. When the CIA was established in 1947 it set up a unit, using the Coffin as a front and a conduit for passing money to sensitive ventures that required laundered funds.

The structure of the Coffin paralleled the structure of such organizations as the CIA or State Department. Operations were divided by countries and regions, assigned to funding officers. Global planning and coordination was done at the top, which was actually in the basement, where the situation room was.

In 1953, after Stalin's death, the world business and banking community expected that an opening to the Russians would be made when the regime changed. This had not happened. The other Western allies began to grow restive under American control. A number of American firms, wanting to go truly international, to do business with the Soviet Union, found that America's policy began to grate.

In the Coffin, there were a series of high level and highly secret meetings that ran from 1953 to 1956. What to do? New strategies were devised; new initiatives were tried out. The first struggle became the Suez Crisis, ostensibly mounted against Egypt by France, England and Israel. That was cooled down by the Americans.

There were other operations. Bit by bit the operatives working for the CIA unit inside of the Coffin Foundation were replaced by people more loyal to the people who ran the Coffin—the corporations who had set it up. The fight was still going on in 1962. Holcomb was employed by the CIA, but he had to report through channels, which meant that the chain of command went upstairs to Coffin directors before being transmitted to Langley.

In truth it was no longer even the corporations who had provided the funds to set up the Coffin who ran it. It was now run by directors who no longer always followed the desires of certain American, British, French, West German, Japanese, Swedish firms. Under direction of Mr. Edward Kelley, the legal counsel to the Coffin, they had taken off secretly in their own direction and had brought in some high-level Russians discontented with their country's perpetual containment, its stagnation. These Russians were determined to fight their own hard-line ideologues. Certain Americans and certain Russians had turned against their own countries and were at war with them both.

When "civil war" broke out in the Congo over the secession of the mineral-rich province of Katanga, there were those who suspected that Americans fought Americans. A peculiar war, they said. Union Minière (minerals: copper, cobalt, chrome, uranium), Forminière (diamonds), Société Générale (a holding company and loan source)—all Belgian—united with Anglo-American (diamonds and minerals), Englehard (an American minerals firm), several Belgian, French, American, British merchant bankers, together with Northern Rhodesia and South Africa into a minia-

36

ture Grand Alliance *opposing* UN forces backed by the United States.

It was to the Congo that Keats was sent by the CIA. Keats received one set of instructions in Langley. But on his way to Africa, he received a message and stopped over in New York. Keats had been double-recruited in college.

In New York, he had an interview with a Mr. Kelley, a lawyer for the Coffin. There he was given another set of instructions and provided with laundered funds to support Katanga's battle for independence, contrary to the instructions he had received from the CIA. In Katanga Keats linked up with Vassili Oprichnik, who ostensibly worked for the KGB. Together, they had arranged for Godefroid Munongo, Katanga's minister of the interior, to kill the rebel leader Patrice Lumumba. They had difficulty in persuading Munongo not to eat his rival and so ingest his spirit . . . as his grandfather used to do. They needed the body for evidence. When the war was all but over in November of 1961 and the independence movement had failed, Keats had come back and been assigned to the CIA intelligence unit in the Coffin, to replace an agent who had a sudden and unexpected heart attack. A few months later, Oprichnik was assigned to the United States by the KGB.

By 1962, the Coffin and its agency undercover were ready for a major test of strength. So was Keats.

The next step Keats took was to get in touch with Vassili. This he did, using a Russian transmitter with a dedicated channel to Vassili. They arranged to meet. Keats explained the position to Vassili and the actions he had taken.

"Did you consult with our masters?"

"I thought that they would be more amenable to that which is already done."

Vassili whistled. "You're living dangerously."

Keats explained what he had in mind.

"Chancy. Ambitious. We're lots simpler in our country."

"There's such a thing as sounding too Brooklyn, Vassili."

"Listen, some of us trained in the Kansas City *gubernia,* others in L.A. Me, I got assigned to Brooklyn, USSR. You went to Harvard. Good grammar is your legend, not mine. Anyway how do you want this joker? It's going to be expensive. I don't know . . ."

"Come on, Vassili. You owe me a favor. Leave it at that."

"Quid pro quo. Actually, friend, I owe you one rubout, rather than what you're suggesting. It will cost me some of El Supremo's manpower and money, to say nothing of risk, which is more expensive still."

"God will provide . . . as soon as what's done is explained."

"If we have learned anything from you people, it's cost efficiency, I'm sad to say. The whole apparatus is being taken over by accountants. The point is, a killing is easier than a tail with all the safeguards for what you want to do."

"Vassili, after this we're even, and I'll throw in a great French dinner."

"Not so. In fact you will owe *me.*"

"How do you mean?"

"You neglected to tell me that this person had also somehow gotten into *our* embassy's communications and heard much that was of interest. For instance, who was fucking who and who was listening in to who . . ."

It was Keats's turn to whistle. "Whom, Vassili."

"Who. I'm from Brooklyn, remember. And perhaps he heard the embassy listening to those who shouldn't be listened to. Get what I mean?"

"I'll square it. Believe me."

"State secrets we can part with, but scandals are another matter. I believe you. Who else is there to trust? But it's these little imbalances that can get out of hand and bring on the final struggle. After all, not everyone is civilized the way you and I are."

"We'll connect soon," Keats said.

When Holcomb had first received Bell Telephone's dossier on Aquilino from Malrowe, he should have passed it on, formally or informally, to his colleagues in the CIA, but he no longer trusted them. He was sure they were penetrated; rotten to the core. The whole country was penetrated. He had decided to keep the matter of Aquilino under his own control. And anyway, since it was the Coffin Aquilino had penetrated, he felt he was within his rights investigating the case himself. The matter was routed to his second in command, Keats. Keats in turn had assigned a routine investigation to one of his subordinates, Morrison. Morrison began, in turn, to look into every facet of the penetrator's life: one Richard Aquilino, twenty-five, who lived in a loft on Canal Street, right off Sixth Avenue, very close to one of the big telephone centers.

Morrison did the usual things. An investigation of Aquilino's family, friends, school records . . . A black-bag job on Aquilino's loft. A bug planted in the loft, a tap on Aquilino's phone line. Without upsetting anything, a complete survey of all the paper in Aquilino's possession. Lots of technical journals, science fiction, some reams of scribbled notes on overheard conversations in some kind of scrawl—code or encryption?—technical drawings and schematics. Everything was photographed.

At first Keats decided Richard Aquilino was that most ridiculous of creatures, the pure technician, the quintessential tinkerer and problem solver possessed by the demon, technology. Gradually he began to sense that Aquilino's mind, his unconscious out of which flowed his interests and his expertise, bordered on the genius. The second fascinating thing was the catholicity of Aquilino's voyeuristic taste. He was interested in everyone and everything. This confirmed, for Keats, that Aquilino's unconscious was fascinating. Was his unconscious *his own,* or was it *outside* of him? That was to say, was someone running him? No sign of a control. *Was someone running him without his knowledge?* Possibly. Possibly. Doubtful. But that was going to be the legend Keats invented for Aquilino, to maneuver Holcomb. And Vassili was going to implement that control.

Keats undertook to create a pattern out of the variety of Aquilino's intercepts, based on the telephone company's reconstruction. Where names had not been spoken, the phone numbers had been used to trace to the names: Group 1.) A lot of men and women who seemed utterly unimportant, about fifty scattered all over the country. Group 2.) People of some minor prominence . . . lower and higher levels of organized crime, politicians, local and national. Group 3.) Higher-level politicians, senators and congressmen, especially on key committees. Group 4.) Athletes and movie stars, rock and roll stars. Group 5.) Key business executives, for instance the president of AT&T, Frederick Kappel. Harold Geneen of ITT at home and at work. Group 6.) Such people as Dean Acheson, George Ball, Robert Lovett, John J. McCloy, Mr. Edward Kelley (Keats whistled), McGeorge Bundy, John McCone, Theodore Sorensen, Robert F. Kennedy and John F. Kennedy, Douglas Dillon, Foy Kohler, Nelson *and* David Rockefeller . . . G. Mennen Williams, Edward R. Murrow, Ralph Bunche, André Meyer (Aha! The Congo), Robert S. McNamara, Roswell Gilpatric, General Curtis LeMay, General Maxwell Taylor, Admiral Arleigh Burke, Edwin Lansdale . . . Group 7.) Women: Marilyn Monroe . . . Laura . . . and who was Judith Exner? . . .

The elements shifted, came together and dissolved and reformed in Keats's mind as he tried out pattern after pattern. Why so much attention to Laura . . . whom Keats had briefly met . . . Did Aquilino listen to them all? How long? What did their conversations mean to Aquilino? What did Mr. and Mrs. Harold Summerson on West Eighty-seventh Street have in common with Richard Helms? No matter. He would supply the connections and the patterns that Richard's unconscious must have made.

A few more steps were required to launch Keats's operation.

Keats arranged a lunch in the Coffin Foundation's lunchroom, with a man in the Domestic Section who ran psychological communications. Keats explained some needs and was told that the person to get in touch with was a Dr. Seymour Gottlieb, tied up with a Project MK Ultra. He did. Another lunch was required to explain another set of needs and he was given a list of four names. The most likely choice seemed to be a neurobiologist, Dr. Sidney Ficino, who was running a neuron-mapping program under the auspices of Columbia Presbyterian up on the West Side. He telephoned Dr. Ficino and announced that he was Mr. Barnstable of the Coffin Foundation, and that he had heard of the wonderful work Dr. Ficino was doing up there at Columbia Presbyterian, and could they have lunch together at the Harvard Club . . .

The next step was to call up Mr. Kelley. On the way to the Congo, Keats had been summoned by Kelley. Now, thanks to Richard Aquilino and Bell Telephone, he had Mr. Kelley's very private and highly classified number. Keats reviewed carefully what he was going to say. He would have to make his presentation quickly, catch Mr. Kelley in perhaps the first twenty-five words, and take the chance that he wouldn't be dead in twenty-four hours. The words should be calm, not alarming, not in the least threatening. After a while he thought he had it worked out.

Keats made the call. The voice at the other end was calm and measured. Do you shake a God? He would.

"Sir," Keats said. "My name is Keats. On June fifth, on the telephone, you deplored, to someone close to you, the policy of holding the price of gold, thus undoing what had been done at the Gate to Europe in the sixteenth century."

There was a little silence. A chuckle. No asking, "how did you get this number?"

"Sir. I would like to be able to tell you something of importance . . . in person."

"Keats? Ah. You had occasion, I believe, to meet the grandson of the head in the oil drum?" The grandson was Godefroid Munongo. The head was his grandfather's, sent back to Belgium. Mr. Kelley knew who he was. "Yes, let's do that. Perhaps next Monday. A dinner. That would be nice. We'll be in touch." The phone clicked off.

Now if Keats wasn't dead in the next twenty-four hours. . . . He noted, pleased, that he was not sweating, nor were his hands even trembling.

There was one final step to take, and that was to work a little on Holcomb.

Holcomb's gun was pointed again at Keats's head. The thick finger was whitening on the trigger. All the things by which Holcomb lived were being upset. Sides were dissolving and changing and he didn't understand what was happening. A new and crazy world was breaking out of the skin of the old. The fear of the changes made Holcomb dangerous. The business with the gun was a well-known out; still, it was rumored through the agency that he had killed his own men.

Holcomb, like some primitive beast, smelled a vast change in the global climate. The very act of smelling the change was the sensing of his own, and his species', doom. The theatre had

41

changed; the actors were taking on new roles on the global stage. The gun was a sort of magic wand to ward off the spell. What Holcomb saw as the encroachment of primeval anarchy, chaos, the ultimate Night, was to Keats the emergence of a new order. Holcomb didn't have the history to put all this into words but, Keats reminded himself, the history was in Holcomb's body, with its perfect instinct. The thing to do was to work Holcomb carefully . . . carefully . . . or he would be dead. It was Keats's second test in a day.

Keats was a magician of sorts. He had studied, along with literature and mythology, psychology and, later, along with economics, the gnostic crafts of the ancients. You weave your magic out of a person's lusts, fears, uncontrollable habits. To do that you had to know your target. He knew about Holcomb two ways. The first way of knowledge came out of dossiers; Keats had studied three sets of them . . . the Coffin Foundation dossier, the CIA dossier, and the KGB dossier. The second way of knowing had to come from within, for Keats too felt that he had *the feel,* and that allowed him to enter his subject's skin. He sensed the terror beneath the bravery.

Keats waited. The time seemed long, especially when he was having a gun pointed at his head. Timing was everything. He had to wait for that moment just before Holcomb was driven over the edge. Keats began to speak. The tone was soothing, almost hypnotic. Keats had learned a trick from a witch doctor in the Congo . . . how to make conversation and, at the same time, to emit a contrapuntal hum beneath the words, so low that it was barely heard but with enough vibratory power to affect the listener.

"Mr. Holcomb, in 1957 you had the misfortune to be captured by the Russians. I believe they gave you a very hard time for a month . . ."

"They beat the shit out of me. Only reason they didn't kill me was they needed something to trade."

"But was that all?"

"What do you mean?"

"You remember every minute of that month."

"Sure."

"You remember every minute of that month?"

"Stop playing games. This isn't *Darkness At Noon* . . ."

42

"Nor is it *The Manchurian Candidate,* but what if—I'm speaking hypothetically—what if they altered your mind and part of that altering was to forget what happened?"

"That's not what happened."

"That's not what happened, Mr. Holcomb, but if it happened, how would you know? You would have forgotten . . . and not the kind of forgotten where the hint of a memory plays around the outer edges of your consciousness either . . . Implanted suggestions, specifically directed amnesias, helped along with drugs, mild and targeted electroshock while drugged, and the event covered over with strong memories of physical abuse. There's a kind of brain damage to the temporal lobes which causes a condition called centerograde amnesia. This leads to an inability to retain new information, an inability to transfer new knowledge from the short-term to the long-term memory. But of course we're talking about brain damage, which is nonspecific, general, imprecise. What if such a damage had been made precise, or designed?

"If such a thing happened, or was caused to happen, every time you tried to remember and went over your experience again and again and again, all you would, or could remember was not the prison hospital with the white walls, and the intravenous dripping drugs into your arm and the white, enameled bed, with a piece in the shape of the map of France, black, missing from one of the bars on the bed, but rather the visual images, the suggestions of the dank cell, where they beat you, which your body remembers—or is it merely your mind which remembers? —a pain which never took place, forgetting the white walls, forgetting the man who leans over you and tells you . . ."

"You cocksucker, Keats." But Holcomb, half hypnotized, was sweating.

"Mr. Holcomb, you're a legend in the Company. You've stood up to a lot, and you're not afraid of anything . . . physical. But sometimes there are things that are stronger than a body, and sometimes they are stronger than that gun. Supposing the Russians, who are the most advanced in this art, have learned to 'damage' certain microscopically precise and relevant portions of the brain . . . to play with the brain's circuitry. Supposing they have learned to mimic the 'damage' with hallucinogenic drugs which bear structural resemblances to the neurotransmitters. So that you don't exactly forget, but cannot remember. I mean, *you* can't remember, but there's something, or someone, which can 'remember' for you . . . every time you can be made to place your intelligence in a kind of 'drop.' A cut-out in your brain.

"Memory, dreams, fantasies. In the brain they all get confused together. Memory is a chemical compound with a long life. Memory is a series of electrical signals which keeps on going on and on through the years. A complex molecule. Memories, emotions . . . *false or real* . . . clustered, linked, indissolubly bound . . . going along certain tracks, being switched from complexes of neurons to other complexes of neurons . . . associated with other memories in tight super-molecules, which are hard to sort out, hard to tear apart. Many memories," Keats lulled, *"real or false, false real* . . . which cannot be torn apart, because what you imagined or dreamed, or actually experienced, might scare you to death. Every time you try to remember, the attempt conflicts with your program, a conflict of instructions, the forgotten and the to-be-remembered is felt as an intolerable discomfort which you remember only as a dank prison in which the walls run with damp, and in which the pain of an induced schizophrenia is felt as a memory of someone, and then another, and then a third, who come in and beat you. And the remembrance of the beating is the emanation of your conflicting order which, in other people, is the same as the uncomfortable feel of indecision, but which in you is an actual memory implanted in you which hides the memory of the white room, the intravenous, the white, enamel bar with the peeled-off dark spot shaped like the map of France, and the man to whom a section of your brain swears allegiance . . . you will *not* remember, no, not even like a nightmare . . ."

"It's bullshit, Keats," Holcomb said, but his eyes were a little glazed.

"And you're wondering, aren't you, that maybe I'm right, and maybe I know something about you that you don't. And you know that you can stand up to any beating, but can you stand up to having had your mind invaded?

"And if I try and force you to remember what happened in that white room, I'll drive you crazy unless it's done in the right way.

44

And if it's done in the right way, you'll lead us back to the memory of that white room . . . and to your control."

Holcomb's hand was on the desk, loose around the gun. The body was slumped, but his eyes were dark and steady upon him.

"You think Aquilino . . ."

"No, Keats thought, but all that matters is that you think so. "Maybe. The Russians are very good. They invented this game. We're just come-lately's to this field, but we're making enormous progress.

"We Americans are a straight-thinking people. We're direct. We're impatient with all that European subtlety and that eastern sophistication and ancient wisdom. The operation you and Harvey worked on, the Berlin Tunnel, was simple, direct, brilliant. But it was conceived with a built-in mistake that caused it to fail, sooner or later: it went directly for the center of the action. Are we to suppose that the Russians didn't learn anything from that? Why wouldn't they want to get directly into *our* central switching systems? Only thing is is that our communications systems are not organized like the Europeans', like an organism with one brain, but something more primitive and more flexible, with many centers. Now supposing that someone could find a way to get to those centers and then penetrate into the other secure systems. Could one person do that alone? Not unless he had an operation as big as Bell itself. No one could handle the take. So supposing that there are many switchboards, many Aquilinos. And what this Aquilino misses, another gets. What then? And suppose that this Aquilino, and the other Aquilinos, don't even know what they are doing. They've forgotten. Like yourself— like the hypothetical yourself, Mr. Holcomb, like the imaginary yourself, Mr. Holcomb—they don't remember the white room and the white bed and the intravenous and the bars of the bed, one with a piece missing shaped like the map of France.

"And if we come to this Aquilino and beat him and say, who's your control, will the stiff remember? He *can't.* And if he tries hard enough, he'll go crazy, as you would too. Anybody would. And that body of yours won't protect you, nor will any bravery.

"When you think about it, every telephone in this country leads, one way or another, to every other one."

Holcomb was silent for a long time. Then his right hand left the gun on the desk. He reached for a drawer and pulled out a bottle. "Want a drink, Keats?"

"No thanks. It's too early."

"Whaddaya mean, early? It's four in the morning."

"Then it's too late."

"All right, whaddaya want to do? How're you going to run back this Aquilino? Draw up a plan . . ."

What if there really had been a white room when they held Holcomb for a month? Keats leaned forward and took great care not to show his triumph. Real or not, he had put Holcomb in touch with the white room. Everyone should have a taste of the white room. He, Keats, had been through it at Harvard. It was terrifying when you entered it, but when you left it, you were liberated and a little above ordinary mortal men.

"You want to go get laid, Keats?"

I just did, Keats thought.

CHAPTER 3

ANDRUSH Harkavy of ITT was sweating, but he knew the KGB man wasn't going to kill, kidnap or torture him, yet. He didn't ask the question most people would: "How did you ever find me?" Instead he asked the question any professional in a difficult position would: "How much will it pay?"

"Always the same question, Harkavy," Vassili Oprichnik said. "One would think you would have learned something; it was what got you in trouble in the first place. You sure belong in this country."

"That's why I came."

"The pay will be very good." It was understood what would happen should Harkavy refuse; not his employer, not even the United States could protect him—at least not forever. It didn't have to be spelled out. Harkavy was a professional.

Vassili outlined the problem, as he had been told it. He finished by saying, "I can run a transmitter . . . I can mount a tap . . . all those things we need to know. But spare me the arcane technical details."

They paid a visit to Richard Aquilino's loft when he was not there. Harkavy, ever the technician, was now interested in the problem for its own sake.

"Really," the man from ITT said, "it's fascinating." Harkavy was a Hungarian who had come over to the United States in 1956,

47

after the uprising. In Hungary he had worked for the AVO, the Secret Police; in America for ITT; for the CIA. He was a triple. He didn't like to be reminded, especially by the KGB.

"Don't get carried away by details. Paint me the broad strokes. What's he done?"

"I went up to his place and looked around. The boy knows his stuff. You have to respect the craftsman."

Craft, Vassili thought. Obsessions. Spy tradecraft. Communications craft. Bank tradecraft. Lawyer's tradecraft. They all think that they are at the center of the universe. "All right, Andrush, I respect him. How? What? Where? Why? Mostly, why?"

"From what you told me, I would say it's the game whose playing is its own reward."

And that was what Harkavy needed to know, Vassili thought. If Aquilino doesn't have a why, I can give him Keats's why. "How did he begin?"

"I can't answer that."

"A related question, then: *where* did he begin?"

"I can't answer that either. But remember, this is not Europe. People do things here for fun. It may be illegal, but it probably has no deeper purpose."

"So we begin *in medias res?*"

"What's that mean?"

"Craft talk from another technology."

"I'll have to go in there and look at the setup a few more times, but I have the idea of how it works. Good thing the kid isn't a spy."

He is now, Vassili thought. Keats wants him to be one . . . for Holcomb, wants him recruited so he doesn't know it.

"There are many ways to bug a system—"

"You're learning American, Andrush."

"Call me Andy. You can connect a wire directly to the wire you want to listen in to, but that causes a drop in current and can be detected. You can put a coil near the wire and read the electrical field around the wire. The tap picks up the signal, voice or whatever, and turns it into the voice, like a telephone. Harder to detect. But that's still a one-to-one system. You can connect to local or long distance trunk lines, pick out the wires you want, but in America that raises incredible problems since the conversation

48

is not necessarily confined to one wire, but is broken up, especially on the long lines, into bits and pieces, routed along many channels—the new microwave relays, or up to the new satellite —and especially the secret military satellites. The bits and pieces of talk are reassembled at the destination. Time-division switching, pulse-code modulation, multiplexing. Off the lines, what you get is babble, unless you have some way of picking out the conversation you want, put some sort of tracer on the speakers you are interested in. It can be done. NSA does it. Others do it. With help, of course, from Bell. So that means one has to get into the switching center and connect up there. If you're Signal Intelligence, NSA, or Bell, that's one thing; you have resources at your command. If you're just one person, that's a hell of a problem. This looks like the one-person problem, which is amazing, considering the amount of traffic."

"He did work for the phone company, a couple of years ago. But now he just does freelance work to make a living, like repairing radios and televisions."

"Well, he still has all the necessary manuals in his place, up to the minute. That tells us he has friends at Bell. He understands most of the whole system. The *whole* system. Look, you pick up the receiver to make a call. That's a signal to the system to begin working. It's an electrical request for service. And you get a dial tone. Now when you do that, if someone is on to you, then there should be a signal also at his place—a sound, a light. He can decide then if he wants to listen in or not. Aquilino's got a whole set of notes about the people he's listened to.

"Okay. When the target dials the number he wants, a scanner checks his lines and picks up the dial information, the directory number. The number translates into an equipment number which belongs to a particular subscriber in a particular place. The scanner then instructs the machinery to begin a search for a path to the person your target is calling. After all, lines get crowded and if the signal can't go one way, there should be another way —especially if you are important. Important people never get an overload signal. Now it gets complicated. It raises many technical, economic, historical and philosophical questions . . ."

"Philosophical? Come off it."

"No. Really. In Eastern Europe, the system is hierarchical with central controls . . . it's easier to listen in to people. In America the system is democratic; everyone gets fairly good service. In Europe, the further down the social scale you are, the worse the service is. But this 'democracy' raises other problems. It becomes easier for enterprising people in America to listen in to everyone else. In Europe, also, secrecy and surveillance are built into the design of the system. In America there are ways of getting around secrecy. All this is reflected in equipment design. Secrecy in this country consists of unlisted numbers, classified numbers, top-secret numbers—but they're all to be found in some directory or other. At the top there are directories locked in office safes. You can build in a lot of complications, identification codes, voice or electronic, but whoever has a phone can be reached. The military, for instance, has its own system, but it's still connected to the civilian system at one place or another.

"If you know what or who you're looking for, that's one problem. If you're just fooling around and don't care who you get, that's another question. So when he picks up a conversation, he probably doesn't know who he's listening to, unless names are used. If the phone isn't classified, he looks it up in the directories. If the phone is classified, that's something else again. Now let's say, for the sake of argument, the target has a direct line to the President. A line that bypasses the White House switchboard. You listen long enough, you're going to get the number. In fact, one could say that having a specific target makes the problem more difficult. Are you following me?"

"Like the hounds the stag."

"All right, now supposing instead of plugging in line-by-line, the kid figures out another way. Supposing he invents a parallel signal scanner and distributor and hooks it right into Bell's equipment? When you dial and the instruments give each other instructions, they also give *his* parallel scanner instructions and open up a line to his house at the same time, so that the conversation is routed two ways: to the person who talks, and to him. Actually he doesn't invent anything. He modifies the standard equipment. He probably got into local switching centers, and into trunk lines, and planted his modified circuit. He reinvented the kind of wheel the CIA, the FBI, NSA or the phone company uses. He worked for the phone company? He just keeps his pass,

50

or duplicates another, or has friends in the work force."

"What about the equipment?"

"That's the easiest, in this country. He can pick up a lot of good surplus army, navy, Signal Corps, even NSA equipment, tinker with it. With his mind, he goes shopping in the surplus stores, sees this or that, knows what it is. Or he can steal telephone equipment and play with it. All you have to know, or believe, is that it has been done, that it can be done. Belief is half the battle."

"You've turned into a mystic, Andy. Now I understand that it works locally, but how about long distance? Does he go to each city and get into the lines and switching centers in various places and do the same thing?"

"He doesn't have the money, does he?"

Vassili didn't answer.

"Does he have friends?"

"He has friends. In fact, you are going to make friends with his friends."

"Well I've got to figure the circuits out," Harkavy said. "We have a partial explanation."

"And that is?"

"A phone call to another city is made. You pick up the line. You can listen in and lift the number when it is dialed. But how would you automatically tune in when that person, there, say in Los Angeles, calls someone else? How would you arrange to have it done from here, say in New York?"

"All right, how?"

"I'm not sure yet. It's fascinating. I want to work on that."

"That's what we are arranging to do."

"There is a clue. Say you call up from here, New York, to there—"

"Los Angeles?"

"Yes. Well, say you have a test board. They have this board with two rows of six contacts arranged vertically. They are numbered in one row from one to five and the sixth contact is called KP. The second row is numbered from six to zero and the sixth button is called ST. It allows you to go through the lines manually. If you have troubles on the line, or perhaps with the equipment, you call up someone in the company in Los Angeles and say something like, I have troubles with my party and your party;

could you check on your end to see if everything is all right; hook me up to line and pair for area two-one-three and so forth. Someone checks you out on a verification circuit—that is to say, they call back and verify if you are the real thing or not. Now the kid has to figure out a way of holding and keeping the other line potentially open once the repairman on the other end helps him out, so he can add it to his network. We can rule friends out, because too many people would know and sooner or later the phone company would know."

"This is more or less what he did." Harkavy noticed that it was not a question.

"Now when I figure it all out and find out where he's planted his circuits, when I get a look at it, then we'll be in business. But it won't be easy. Why didn't *I* think of it? I could make a fortune."

"Or get yourself killed. When you find this out, will you be able to build a number of these devices?"

"I said it won't be easy."

"I have faith in you. Now let us pose a more hypothetical problem. If you figure out what he did—"

"What do you mean, if? It will be, as the Americans say, a piece of cake. *He* did all the serious work."

"I see you have the proper spirit. Could you rig up a device that plugs into *his* system and does for him what he's doing unto others, keeping in mind that he's under surveillance?"

"If you give me protection."

"You'll be covered. Don't worry. That's part A of the examination. Part B is this. I don't know if I'm going to phrase it right. Bear with us poor nontechnical people. Our boy listens to a lot of people he shouldn't be listening to. There are many switching centers, many lines, many phones, all over the landscape. It's bad for his health . . ." Aquilino would be getting sick soon, ". . . and we want to protect that health. Supposing we could, well, loop the lines in such a way that while he *thinks* he's connecting to and listening to certain people, in fact he's not. The connections *appear* to be going here and there, where he thinks they are going, but they are going somewhere else . . . places that are under our control."

"You mean he calls this party in L.A., and the pathway goes not to L.A. but to the local center where circuits have been installed

52

to double back to someone of your choice? The boy feels that he has listened to L.A., but he has not?"

"That's the general idea."

"Yes. It can be done." Harkavy forbore from asking if this wouldn't confuse those who were doing the surveillance.

"Now for part C. Can *we* continue to listen in to the people he was listening in to before, but can no longer hear? You will be provided with a list of who he will seem to be listening to and where they are."

"You're asking a lot. In principle it can be done, but I don't know if I can do it."

"You will be amply rewarded. You'll have backup. I'm going to give you the name of one of your superiors in ITT, a high-level person who will be delighted to give you every assistance, that is to say money and other considerations. I know your time is valuable. Do you understand what I'm telling you?"

Harkavy nodded. He was trapped. "It won't be easy. What if the boys at Bell catch me?"

"It will be handled. It's a matter of 'national security.' "

"I'll try."

"You'll do better than that. Since *I* believe it can be done, in your heart of hearts *you* believe it can be done."

"Yes, but you don't know equipment."

"Equipment is only the concrete manifestation of belief."

"What are you talking about?"

"Philosophy, Harkavy, philosophy. Anyway, are you going to let a mere boy outdo someone with your background?"

CHAPTER 4

RICHARD started to open the door of the cafe and backed off. He stood there in the street, not noticing the people around him. He had never been so depressed. Ziggy's truck was parked down the block from the coffeehouse on Bleecker and MacDougal Streets, which meant Ziggy was in his "office" in the Cafe Figaro. The truck had two cots and was also loaded with equipment: oscilloscopes, meters, wiring, phones, phone parts, jacks for plugging into street phones, short-wave radio receivers. Ziggy still liked to scan the short wave military frequencies: he knew most of them—even the most secret—and had monitored the military traffic from Cuba during the Bay of Pigs. Ordinarily Richard was eager to see Ziggy and the other friends, but tonight he didn't feel like going in.

What was wrong with him? The last few days he felt as if he were moving through mud. He was going nowhere. He was twenty-five already. He wanted to be like other people, regular people, ordinary people . . . Like his family? No, not like that; he couldn't stand the way they lived. A life lived for small business. Export-import; the junk business. He had just come from a family dinner at his sister Angela's in Queens. "Get married, Richie," his brother-in-law, Morris, said right in front of the whole family. The other brother-in-law, Benjamin, had guffawed, and his older sisters, Angela and Elizabeth, tried to protect him. They were growing fat, sort of like his mother, who wasn't fat but big-boned. His father had glanced at him. Sometimes Richard couldn't stand his father's perpetually commiserating look. His mother, however, had glared at her sons-in-law, silencing them.

Ziggy's truck was, he always said, also his body. Ziggy was crippled. He claimed that when he was plugged into his truck, it gave him the senses of a god. He could see what his eyes could not see, hear what his ears could not hear. One day he would feel what his body couldn't feel. Cyber. During the week, Ziggy, Tarzan and Marvin—and frequently Richard—sat at the back of the Figaro. They had their own table. Others would drift in and join them. Sometimes, when it was not too busy, they would pull up another table, chairs, and the air would be thick with cigarette smoke. Babble. They would sit there until closing time at one o'clock in the morning. Most of them wore surplus army clothes. On weekends they would have to go somewhere else because the Figaro was busy with tourists who came to stare at bohemians.

Snatches of song filled his head. "Are You Lonesome Tonight," Elvis Presley sang. Songs of loneliness. We parted, but someday we'll get together again. Driving rock and roll beat. Chuck Berry. The Twist . . . everyone was doing the Twist, even the President's wife, Jacqueline. Strange new dances, like African tribes . . . But lately, just in the past few days, he was uncomfortable listening to music; it was some hidden rhythm, some pitch in the music. "We'll Be Together Again . . ." Why had tonight's dinner in Queens been so different? Something had gotten into him to make him sad and depressed.

When are you going to get married? When are you going to get a job? When are you going to be like other people? He wanted to be like them and he hated the idea. What had made him different? Laura had, for a while. Laura was the only woman he had ever wanted to marry. But you can't have Laura . . . you can only listen in to her . . . and hear what you don't want to hear. Find another girl. "Listen, Richie. I don't understand what you do, but is there any money in it?" his brother-in-law, Morris, asked.

"There could be."

"Tell you what. I'll set you up in business. Open your own electrical plant."

"Electronic."

"Electronics. Whatever."

Richard hadn't been able to answer. He was tongue-tied. Instead he went into the other room and played with his nephews and nieces. He was good with kids, who seemed to sense something in him, that the adults didn't . . . He spun tales for the kids. "We'll play space voyage. Now the galactic empire is falling apart. A small band of people get in a space ship and flee from the empire's central planet, Morg, which is full of corruption—"

"What's corruption, Uncle Richard?"

"Corruption is like disease. Sickness." Prostitution. "Crookedness. Being a crook. They fly through space from world to world, landing and looking for a planet to live on. Because it takes so long to travel."

"How long?"

"Well, light travels at the rate of one hundred and eighty-six thousand miles a second."

"Around the world in a second?"

"Less. Faster. Maybe six or seven times in a second. Nothing travels anywhere near the speed of light, so there has to be a better way of getting around from sun to sun, or everyone on the space ship would die of old age, so they make jumps in space. They have many adventures, for on the planets there are many strange and weird beings." Could they be stranger or weirder than the people he listened in to? "There's lot of danger—"

"What kind of danger?"

"Plants that move around and eat human beings. Monsters."

"There's no such thing."

"Is there a princess in it?" Elissa asked.

"There is. You must be the princess." That's what Richard was doing with his life, searching for a different planet in which there were different kinds of people, right here on earth. There would be an evil king, and there would be a beautiful captive princess —Laura—whose mind had been put under a spell. He and his wonderful companions, journeying through space. "Great lizards living in perpetual snow and ice . . . killing thousand-mile-an-hour winds . . . but beneath the snow there are great ice caves, Antonio."

"Don't call me Antonio, Uncle Richard. Call me Tony."

56

"Tony. Inside the caves live all kinds of strange and wonderful plants. But there's also the great lizards. Dragons. And people. Now all you kids are the space cadets and you're wandering around in the cave, when the great dragon comes out . . . that's me." And he had gotten behind an easy chair and had come roaring out. The kids screamed. In the other room, the adults were sitting around the table. His sisters were preparing the meal. His brothers-in-law sat with his parents, his mother at the head of the table. She ran the business. "I have a head for the numbers, but no head for bargaining or sales," his father used to say. . . .

Richard looked through the window of the Figaro. The walls were lined with paintings. The artists and the musicians and the writers sat in their own clumps, students and bohemians nursing cups of coffee and talking, except for those who were stoned. They went into the bathroom and smoked the grass. Richard didn't approve.

Should he go in? He didn't really fit anywhere. When he was with his family, he hated the way they lived. Business. Business. *This* was his family, right here, but even when he was with Ziggy and the others, he got restless lately and dreamed of what life would be like, married, having a steady business, children—a place to come home to at night. Laura. He was an outsider, an eavesdropper, a spy on life, spying on love, looking for the secret of the way people lived in the conversations they had on the phone.

Ziggy was the crippled one. Siegfried. Strange name for a crippled man. "In the German legends, Siegfried can understand the twittering of the birds. I can understand the twittering of signals." Among the electronic angels, Ziggy was the oldest, in his middle thirties. Everyone else was young, some of them sixteen-year-olds. Hobbyists. Hams. Ziggy the mentor; Ziggy the cripple. Half blind. His legs had once been broken and badly set, so he could barely walk. He used canes, sometimes crutches, and when he was tired, Tarzan just carried him. Tarzan proudly said that he was Ziggy's automated wheelchair.

Ziggy spoke with a German accent. He had grown up in Germany and, as he told it, he was a genius with radio and telephony. He had been a communist in those days. He wasn't ashamed to

57

admit it. "We had a dream then, universal brotherhood, an end to exploitation and hunger, solving the world's problems through science and technology. My version of the dream was that everyone would be intimately connected together, by wires, by radio, brain to brain, soul to soul, sharing thoughts and talk, making everyone *feel* and understand one another. A real international, bypassing language barriers. The truly communist world had to be intercerebral. Cybernetic. Weren't we all, wasn't all matter, diffuse and solid forms of electromagnetism? It is a question of designing the proper modulation and demodulation devices to convert one form into another form, just like voice gets put out as a carrier wave, reaches the ear and gets converted into a sort of biological electromagnetism and chemistry. I used to think that's what would bring communism about, abolish nations. I learned better. No one wanted that."

They had sat around the table in Queens, the whole family, eating when the food was ready. Three times a year. The adults talked. The children played. He sat there: he was disconnected. He had been disconnected since he was a kid. He was still a kid among the adults; he was an adult among the kids.

What would it be like to have a family, to be a father, to be able to sit at the head of a table and talk so everyone would listen? But what about? Radio? Telephones? Circuits? Frequencies? He could talk about the voices he overheard, but he was ashamed. Listening in, snooping. How could he explain a thing like that? It was a terrible habit, a compulsion, dirty. Could he tell his family about the way actors, for instance, and actresses talked to one another . . . and to others. "Listen, I want you down here in half an hour, sucking my cock . . ." The terrible and intimate things he had heard. He didn't even tell Ziggy about that.

Ziggy knew he listened. They *all* listened in, but none of them as much as Richard did. Ziggy wouldn't approve of it. It was dangerous.

That time when Marilyn Monroe had been sobbing on the phone. A man had been yelling at her, using the vilest language. Whore . . . cunt . . . Something familiar about that voice. He had heard it before. Then the man had hung up on Marilyn Monroe before Richard could remember where he had heard that voice. But she didn't hang up. She kept talking, crying. Someone whom everyone loved and worshipped . . . she was so miserable. He couldn't help breaking in. No one should be that unhappy. It was true; the rich, the famous, were more unhappy. As he talked to her he closed his eyes and visualized her face from the movies. The way she moved, talked, the way her golden hair swirled . . . her body, her breasts, her smile. And they had started to talk before she realized the strangeness of the situation. Words of comfort . . . surprisingly they came easily, almost glibly, as long as he didn't have to face her. Who was he, she asked? Where had he come from?

He shouldn't have done that. He was lucky. Someone else, instead of being thankful, would have reported him to the FBI. The FBI would have started to track him down. He wouldn't give her his name, or tell her where he was calling from. "I'm near, no matter how far away I am," he told her. "You need someone," he said. You need me, he thought. "I'm just a friend. I want to help. I'll always be near when you need someone."

Was he in Los Angeles? "You're an angel," she told him. An angel! He wanted so badly to tell people. Guess who I talked to —Marilyn Monroe. Marilyn Monroe called me an angel. Me! Can you believe it? And then she had hung up and called someone else. He listened; it might be the police. No. Instead she placed a call to Washington and . . . she couldn't get through.

He turned suddenly. Was someone watching him? He thought he saw a movement. No one. People in the Greenwich Village streets. Inside, Ziggy's arms were moving. He was talking, holding the table's attention. Seven of them tonight.

During the Second World War—what was Ziggy then, sixteen? —he had worked for the Communist International, which was run by Moscow. He was in charge of communicating intelligence out of Berlin. That didn't sit well with those who were older and had experience running spies, but Ziggy was able to tap into the most secure Nazi lines. He had an instinctive sense for what was important. He was a combatant in what the British called the Wizard War. The trouble with radio communications was that sooner or later the enemy got your frequency and recognized your transmitting style, and then could triangulate you, and move in. And the Russians insisted on long transmissions. So he had made a breakthrough; designed a radio that broadcast a carrier wave that couldn't be tracked. It moved through hyperspace, he said. Non-Gaussian waves. Built the transmitters and receivers: two of each, one set for the Russians and one for himself. Set it up right inside the Alexanderplatz Prison in Berlin. Comrade had gotten him in. Who would think of looking for an "instrumentalist" in a prison? He kept the Russians informed. Troop movements; what divisions were going where, at what time, what armaments shipments. If the Communist International had another network, the Red Orchestra, supplying the Russians with superb intelligence, Ziggy was the infra-red orchestra, invisible to ordinary sight. More than troop movements, the Russians kept pestering him about the details of the nontraceable carrier wave and the theory behind it. Ziggy didn't have time to tell them about hyperspace when people were dying. Beat the fascists first and then we'll discuss theory. There's no such thing as hyperspace, Moscow Central said. It was not a materialist construct, but idealist, which was their way of saying that they didn't believe him. What he didn't understand was that they had begun to think he was a double.

Richard had been unable to stand the sitting still, the never talking, with his mother's eyes on him. He was her last, her youngest. Benjamin was saying, "And now that butcher, Khrushchev, wants to come to this country on a visit again."

"But why do you say 'butcher'?" his father asked, mildly. "Didn't he reveal the butchery of Stalin?"

"Maybe it's a trick to lull us," Morris said.

"A very dangerous trick," his father said.

"Well, maybe it will mean peace," Benjamin said. How easily they changed their opinions.

The conversation triggered something in Richard's memory. "No," he spoke up suddenly.

"Aha. Another country heard from," Morris, his mouth full of chicken, said. "What do you mean, 'no'?"

Richard remembered. Two men had been talking . . . how clear the memory was: "You remember what Herman Kahn said in *Thermonuclear War?*"

"I never read it."

"We must all read it."

60

"Really, Dean, why should I read the writings of a man who writes what we already know?"

"We will move up the nuclear scale to Insenate Spasm and Mutual Assured Destruction? I hardly think so. We've got to challenge them. We have to give them a *fait accompli.* They'll back down. The United States needs a jolt. The Allies need a jolt. NATO's in danger. The Alliance for Progress is stagnating. In the meantime, the Russians go ahead and build a massive shelter program while we diddle away . . ." This most recent conversation had been peculiar, unusual. The voices had been a little slow, deliberate, enunciating everything with an unaccustomed clarity. The reception had been better than usual. ". . . and we can remove the thorn from our side. What can the Russians do from seven or eight thousand miles away? We can send our bombers and . . ."

"They can roll over Berlin, Dean."

"Well, and is that all to the bad, Edward? It will reawaken our Allies alive to the common danger. It would be a good tradeoff. But I even doubt that move would happen. World opinion—"

"World opinion hardly counts. We would get rid of that thorn in our side, that ranting demogogue dictator with his seven-hour speeches—"

"Maybe the thorn should stay put."

"That's entirely too subtle for me, Edward."

Edward Kelley. Richard now recognized who it was. The old man who had put Laura under a spell and turned her into a whore. He hated the man. What a cynical tone. How unpatriotic.

". . . *realpolitik,* Edward. Cuba is a bridgehead in the West, a salient. Missiles ninety miles from our shore, the base from which the Russians will incite revolutions in Latin America, in Africa, and threaten our interests in the Panama Canal. All right in the teeth of the Monroe Doctrine . . ."

"Dean, that hardly has standing in international law—"

"Norbert Schlei seems to think otherwise."

"And who is Norbert Schlei?"

"An assistant attorney general."

"Dean, I'll just have to talk to some people."

"I'd really like to see you come on board with this one, Edward.

We must make the most conspicuous preparation for a military showdown, including the proclamation of a national emergency."

"You're sure of those missiles?"

"Oh, absolutely. It's only a matter of time."

"There will be no peace," Richard told the table. "It's only a matter of time before . . . war." He caught the quick looks his mother and father gave one another.

"What makes you say that?" his father asked.

"Well, the government. Important people. The Executive Committee—Excom."

"What important people, Richard? What's Excom?" his father asked.

"How do you know?" Morris asked. The incredulous, mocking look on Morris's face goaded him.

"Well, I just know. Cuba is going to be invaded," Richard insisted.

"Is that a fact or an opinion or a wish . . ." his father was saying.

"Or a dream," Benjamin laughed.

"Where did you hear that we were going to invade Cuba?" his father asked, smiling. His eyes twinkled. His father, gentle. His mother's dark eyes were focused on him. He never knew what his mother thought; sometimes she frightened him.

"We are going to war, if you can call the United States against Cuba a war," Richard said.

"Since when did you become an expert on foreign policy?" Morris said. "You don't know what you're talking about."

"I didn't see anything about it in the papers," Benjamin said.

"Well, there's a plan."

"Sure. And they told *you.*"

Well, they did, Richard thought. Invisible voices without faces or bodies. A general, Maxwell Taylor, talking to Allen Dulles, as if he were not retired . . . asking Allen Dulles's advice, over the scrambler phone.

"Hey, Richard, what's happening? The President is making you his confidant? He calls you up every day and says, Richard, I have these problems. What do I do about the economy, Richard? And what do you tell them? Go to war with Russia, and it'll give the economy a good shot in the ass . . ."

"Morris!" his wife said.

The President. Something played around the edges of Richard's consciousness, but he couldn't surface it; he was too angry. "No. There's a plan. It's called NSAM-100." He caught his mother's stare; there was something new in it.

"Why aren't you eating the stuffing, Morris?" his sister Angela asked.

"Because it's bread stuffing and I don't like bread stuffing," Morris said.

"I like bread stuffing," Morris's son said.

"How did you hear that?" his father asked Richard.

"Hear." Watch it. He should never have said anything. Every time he opened his mouth. His sleepy father . . . those inquiring eyes. "Well, it was in the papers."

"So what's this got to do with bread stuffing?"

"What paper?" his father asked.

"I don't know. The *Times.*"

"No," Benjamin said. "It was on those rock and roll records you listen to. Elvis Presley sang it to Richard personally over the radio." Everyone laughed. Richard pretended to laugh. He had almost given everything away. . . .

Ziggy had been caught. Someone betrayed him to the *Sicherheitsdienst.* He was tortured; that explained the legs. The only thing that kept him alive was his knowledge; the Germans wanted the secret of his nontraceable broadcast wave, and the name of his control, and his network. Even so, they brought him to the edge of death; the torturer's pleasure overcame practical needs. He was ready to talk, to tell them everything they might conceivably want to know. How much pain could a man stand? But the pain scrambled Ziggy's mind. He couldn't remember and they weren't going to wait for him to recover. Before he could be killed, the war ended and he was liberated by the Russians. They took him, put him in a hospital, tried to straighten his legs and made everything worse. He had been sent to Russia. He thought he would be sent to school and get a proper education in electronic intelligence.

As Richard went into the Figaro, he saw someone get up from their table and walk away. Someone new. Short, stocky man, a little older than their usual run of people . . . older than most of

63

them. Someone bumped into him and leaned over and muttered an apology, putting his hand on his arm, nodding his head. He had seen the face of the man before, but where?

"School? What did I have to go to school for? I could teach *them*. I saw the wave of the future and they said school." But there had been a purge. He had been thrown into a prison camp again, near Moscow. There he met the man who ran the Red Orchestra, Leopold Trepper. They had heard of one another.

Ziggy was given a fifteen-year sentence. It had done in his eyes. Nevertheless, he had escaped, helped by what was left of Trepper's network combined with another kind of network . . . black marketeers. Ziggy was passed along the smuggler's underground, finally making his way to the United States. Nothing—not Stalin, not the KGB—had ever stopped the smuggler's traffic, a business in jewel-studded ikons and other treasures going out; jazz records, clothes, items not available in Russia coming in.

Maybe, Ziggy would say, the partial blindness was a kind of blessing in disguise; now you could really focus (Ziggy laughed at the word) on waves invisible to ordinary sight and hearing.

The time is coming when electronics would make people like gods. "You wait and see. I'm not talking science fiction, but the extensions of man. Evolution, telecommunications, and now satellites. We'll be going to the moon soon, and then the planets and then the stars. We need new bodies. Mind commanding machine and machine commanding the universe directly, because the machine has more in common with matter than these bodies do. But the monopolies, the governments are going to keep it from us. I'm still enough of a Marxist to understand that. ATT, ITT, Siemens, Philips, the governments, all working together. That includes the Russians too, greedy bastards. They're alike all over the world. But we'll beat them. I'll get eyes and legs again, but of a kind we only dream about . . ." Ziggy's listeners were excited.

"The prophets are writing about it. *Astounding Science Fiction* . . ."

"They wrote about the atom bomb before it was invented."

". . . *Galaxy, Fantasy and Science Fiction.*"

"You know Bester's *The Demolished Man?*" Ziggy said. "They sure demolished me, but I'm coming together again. Telepaths.

64

You have to read it. Sight? Bypass the eyes and go directly into the brain. Pure signals, see through to the galaxies directly. That great cloud in the center of Andromeda is like the great cloud in the center of our own brains. Blish, Heinlein, Asimov, Clarke, they really don't know shit about science and technology, yet they managed to tap into waves from the future, coming to them from the other end of the universe."

"The universe is curved."

"A great bubble."

"Signals coming to us from the other end of the universe."

"That means that the thoughts are coming from right here. From us."

Richard heard it as he walked to the table. It alarmed him. It was the usual kind of talk, so why did it bother him? Did the conversation stop, did everyone turn and look at him peculiarly? For a fraction of a second, he felt frozen in place . . . and it felt like a long time. Then he moved to sit down as Ziggy said, "What they dream about in words, *we* will tap into and build. *We* are the scientists."

Richard sat down. They made room for him, near Ziggy. A mark of honor. Why was he feeling so depressed, so suspicious? Was he getting sick? Tarzan put his huge arm around Richard's neck. "What's the matter, Richie? Feeling down? Listen," he leaned over and whispered in Richard's ear. "I found one of the Bell parking lots. We can pick up equipment and even a truck any time we want."

"Who was the new guy?"

"What new guy?"

"The one who was sitting with you. He got up when I came in."

"There was no one new here. Maybe he was sitting behind us and it looked like he was here."

Tarzan was the big one, out of Arizona. He had been a radio operator during the Korean war and had never gone back to Arizona. He had become a wanderer until he hooked up with Ziggy in New York. A thug with a thug's face, quick to settle things with his fists, knees, or anything that was around—cutglass ashtrays, chairs, lengths of wire knotted around his waist. Big, blond, in a city of smaller, fast-moving, fast-talking types, he stood out: a cowboy. Thick fingered, it looked as if his fingers couldn't feel a thing in a world where sensitivity was required, but he was a wizard with wiring, a sorcerer with a soldering gun. Tell him what was wanted and he would scrounge, steal or build it. It was Tarzan who had found Richard a few years ago, scrounging at the surplus-equipment stalls on Canal Street. They began to talk. When Richard mentioned what it was he was looking for, Tarzan had initiated him into the art of midnight requisitioning.

The third one in the triumvirate was Marvin. Marvin claimed he was a loose mind from the Magellanic Clouds stuck in a human body. A galactic mixup. He dreamed of the time when cities would have walls made out of pure, pulsating energy, drawn from adjacent stars, camped out in space. Marvin couldn't build anything, but he had a perfect memory. He forgot nothing that he read and he read everything. He even read maps and directories for fun. He had memorized thousands of secret government radio frequencies, and what agencies *really* used them. With Marvin you didn't need to have books and papers around; ask him and he would reach into his mind and retrieve it. "Richard, what do you have for me tonight?"

It was a game they played. Richard threw out a telephone number and Marvin, remembering his line-maps, would try and trace the pathways, even when they went to blind switching centers. When he couldn't trace the pathways, they would go and connect jacks from the truck and begin their probing. "Come on, Richie, my mind needs stimulation."

"Why don't you try playing with yourself. That's where your mind is anyway," Tarzan said.

"All right, try 288-6866 . . ."

"What's the area code?"

"That's the easy way."

Marvin got up and went outside to a corner phone to see what he could find out.

Marvin remembered where every telephone line went. He talked incessantly, but also he listened . . . he had figured out how to do both at the same time. He worshipped Ziggy and Richard, but there was something about Tarzan that frightened him. "I don't know what it is," he once told Richard, "but that guy gives off weird frequencies." Marvin looked like Arnold Stang, or Woody Allen . . . a certain New York type you met in great

66

numbers at Bronx High School of Science or at Stuyvesant High School, or at City College. They were out of the mainstream, different, wild talents, chess nuts, technical geniuses—jerks, people called them. Richard had been called a jerk in school. Big glasses, thin faced, short, skinny, febrile, with high, nasal voices; a joke. Marvin had one other talent, coupled to an unending urge: sex. His penis was probably semi-erect at all times. He loved all kinds of women: old, young, fat, thin, plain, pretty, beautiful. He had developed the ability to seduce almost any woman he set his mind to sleep with. He did this by persistence. He snared them by weaving a web of talk around them. When they were worn down, or half hypnotized, he snared them with his hands. He had beautiful hands . . . hands that belonged to another person . . .

"Give me a cup of espresso," Richard said to the young waitress.

Marvin came back. "AUTOVON."

"The defense network? How did you get that one, Richard?" Ziggy asked.

"Fooling around."

"Maybe you shouldn't fool around with that one," Ziggy said.

"Well, I have a right." Richard felt annoyed.

"No one said you didn't have a right, but . . ."

The anger mounted in Richard. Ziggy wanted to monopolize everything. He had found the number himself and now Ziggy was taking it away from him.

"How did you get to it?" Ziggy asked.

The same feeling he had at his sister's returned. They were all looking peculiarly at him. "You don't own the networks, Ziggy." They were probing at him. He got up suddenly and turned and walked out.

Behind him he heard Marvin saying to Tarzan, "But what did *I* do?"

CHAPTER 5

A dinner party. The guests were assembled by the host, Mr. Camondo, an investment banker, to celebrate something or other. Perhaps Mr. Camondo made a good merger, bringing peace and amity by marrying off two warring corporate families. He was good at that. Or maybe the party was only to bring good friends in the international community together . . . although "friendship" had a different meaning in Mr. Camondo's world than it had in the ordinary world. Camondo was not his original name. That was something obscure, Polish and long forgotten. Mr. Camondo began his career buying and selling anything there was to buy and sell—fresh fruit, leather, drugs, sex, cigarettes, money—throughout Europe from his "corporate headquarters" as a prisoner in Auschwitz. "Life, it was very real, as was the dying. We weren't allowed anything, so I began to deal in promises . . . abstractions, which brought to me a kind of material existence. I became valuable. I could stay alive and keep others alive. You see that picture?" He would point to a Chagall. "Dreams. Fantasies. Legends. Myths. Floating through air. The imprisoned dream of that. What I realized was that you could sell dreams . . . if you could deliver at some point."

The house was a two-story penthouse on 94th Street near Park Avenue; spectacular. The central room was two stories high. One didn't see that kind of wood paneling anymore. It was once owned by William Randolph Hearst. The guests—bankers, news-paper, radio and television executives, statesmen, officials from the UN—were having their pre-dinner drinks, circulating, gos-siping softly. All seemed very staid. The men wore black tie. The women wore the latest gowns from Paris; and many of them had their hair done like Jackie Kennedy's. They moved under paint-ings by Manet and Rembrandt and Chagall and others. Aztec statues of the cruel gods guarded the room. "The death camp guards," Mr. Camondo always said jokingly. "I had them pre-served in stone." There were also some perfect examples from the golden age of Greece. The latter-day Greeks would have given a fortune, or murdered, to get them back . . . if they even knew these statutes existed, or where in the world they were. Here and there a number of Greek vases and amphorae were placed; they had amusing scenes on them, of men having sex with young boys.

The servants who brought the drinks and passed the canapés seemed curiously alert, almost vigilant. The men were especially big and athletic looking. But then everyone knew Mr. Camondo's tastes.

There were guests from all over the world. Englishmen, a few French diplomats, including the redoubtable Mr. Poniatowski—whom few people had ever heard of—Germans, a Swiss, two Japanese, a few Africans (Mr. Camondo was nothing if not dar-ing), a Russian, and Americans.

The conversation would have bored any ordinary person to tears. Most of it was in English, but unless you had learned the language of this world, you wouldn't even understand what was being said. Gossip, it sounded like. Who was sleeping with whom. Snatches of numbers, things like interest rates. Some talk of the art market. And yet, behind their relaxed, almost masklike faces, everyone was listening hard. It was a working party, a conference held in such a way as to avoid—as much as it was possible—observation. The party provided a kind of white noise; hard to eavesdrop. Information, true and false, straight and offensive, deceptive, was being exchanged.

The tall young man with blond hair and gray eyes, the shoul-ders just a little too strong for his dinner jacket, approached an older man. Keats. The women eyed him. He was new. He came carefully, almost deferentially to the older man, although he could, if he wanted to, physically destroy him. Mr. Kelley. Mr. Kelley was talking to a Russian and a man with a Spanish accent. Mr. Kelley spoke Russian. The Russian spoke French. The man with the Spanish accent spoke English. Keats stopped, almost casually, as though he were not walking over to address Mr. Kelley at all, but only wandering through the room. Mr. Kelley was not seated on a throne, but he might as well have been. He was the royalty; the invisible American kind, one of the world's power brokers. He knew where all the important bodies of the last forty-five years were buried—helped bury some of them himself. Mr. Kelley was a lawyer . . . or that's what he was said to be. One of America's elder statesman. Averell Harriman called him Ed. Winston Churchill called him Kelley. Giscard d'Estaing called him sir. Mr. Helphand called him my boy. Nelson Rockefeller called him fella. Mr. Kelley brought things and people and businesses together and took them apart. Presidents consulted him. Chairmen of the boards of banks and corporations, prime ministers (or those who would become prime ministers), ambassadors, rulers of Less Developed Countries listened carefully when Mr. Kelley talked. It was unwise not to. " 'The best of all rulers is but a shadowy presence to his subject,' " he quoted from the *Tao* to the young men he favored. It was one of the ways he tested them. Keats, who was awed by so little in life, was waiting for an audience. Mr. Kelley, the Russian and the man with the Spanish accent continued talking, sipping at their drinks for punctuation. Then the young man approached, as if at a signal. Although a deal was being struck none seemed to be given. The Russian and the Cuban left, as though dismissed, and the young man reported. The report was sketchy, skimming over the key points. As Keats talked, Mr. Kelley was aware of a curious thing happening to him; he had begun to feel an attraction to Keats . . . savoring the experience as if it were happening to someone else. That's why he had done something as precipitate as letting Keats preempt this conference with the Russian and the man with the Spanish accent. When Keats was finished, Mr. Kelley sighed and began to talk. "So much to do and to undo. Did they have to kill Abromowitz? What a waste. I hate fanatics. I hate crusaders. I hate patriots."

70

"He would have gone on talking, sir."

"And who would have listened? A very junior, garrulous young man. An academic, really. Who trusts a garrulous man? Students. All he would have done would be to ruin his career . . . indeed, it was already ruined."

A young woman came into the room. She was stunning. Her face was wanton, and at the same time that she appeared to be the ultimate of corruption, an innocent. She looked crude and intellectual. There was a slight shift among the people at the party, as their attention was drawn, almost unwillingly, to the girl. To show emotion publicly was a no-no, but most of the men —those who slept with women—wanted to sleep with her, to say nothing of a number of women. Her hair was jet black, but her eyes, like Keats's, were a startling light gray. She was dressed simply, but her sexuality conquered the conservativeness of her gown. She was not tall. She moved sedately, but everyone sensed the terrific power radiating from her body.

Keats barely looked at her. He had good peripheral vision and had learned to stare at something without seeming to see it at all. Mr. Kelley noted that the young man had not let himself be distracted. He approved. Even though Mr. Kelley thought of himself as being without vanity at all, he liked deference. Deference, homage . . . it hooked you before you knew you were addicted. Knowing this weakness was no guarantee that you could conquer the habit. A twinge of jealousy? He was almost in love with the young man who had the same kind of eyes he had. Mr. Kelley said, "Come, Keats. There are people who you should meet and get to know. Let's begin by my introducing you to Laura. I've learned to think of her as a daughter."

Keats knew he had passed another test. He noted the way Mr. Kelley and Laura looked at one another. An understanding. A familiarity that went beyond friendship, perhaps something beyond love.

Their hands touched. Eyes, gray eyes, met. Two sets of eyes like Mr. Kelley's eyes. They all could have come from the same family. Candid-looking eyes. Open. Relaxed muscles. No tension. No appearance of depth, subtlety, or passion. Suddenly there was an explosion in Keats's mind and body, covered up by his habit of intense inner control. Everything fell into place. Laura . . .

71

Richard Aquilino. Richard Aquilino's telephonic thread of eaves-dropping led to *this* Laura. Then the thread had branched out from her into a vast and tenuous web of connections. How had this kid come to be interested in Laura? She was like the nucleus of a nerve cell. One of the threads led from Laura to Mr. Kelley. Beware.

Something inside of Keats was being worked so fast that it was below the level of thought, almost on the level of surges of hormone . . . chemical transmitters between the nerves . . . electrical charges flashing down the intricate thread-networks. And it was as though he had fallen in love, with someone he knew. As though they had loved for many years—centuries. His *body* reviewed it all . . . *remembered it* as though what had not yet happened had already happened.

Keats was a believer in magic. He had studied it; practiced it. His magic was generated by practical things . . . there was a scientific explanation. Something, somewhere inside of him . . . at the level of the essence of things . . . on the level of chromosomes, genes, communed with the same something inside of her. As though they were brother and sister, mother and son, father and daughter, all at the same time. Some convoluted biological material in both of them, acting as transmitter/receiver and receiver/transmitter. They spoke to one another. What connected them? An intricate chain: Aquilino, Laura, Kelley . . . and now him.

Laura was Mr. Kelley's, but in what way? Were they lovers? No. Not now. No longer. He sensed that Kelley wanted *him.* He knew a few things about Mr. Kelley now. He had the beginnings of a hold over Mr. Kelley, as he did over Holcomb, but only the beginnings. Plans formed in his mind; he reviewed half-formed options. Would Laura be a rival? Could he ally with her? First he would have to separate them, because he needed to use her to capture Richard. Set up Laura as Richard's control . . . as indeed it seemed she was without knowing it . . . Could he use her at the same time to cement his relationship with Mr. Kelley?

Mr. Kelley took Keats's arm and began to stroll around the room, stopping to acknowledge greetings, gradually working Keats into another room and shutting the door behind them. "How did it happen?"

"He's a genius with telephones. He found ways of penetrating up to high levels."

"Purposefully? Who uses him?"

"On the surface he's a tinkerer, a problem solver. Pure technology is his obsession. He's not the kind that thinks through his problems. He makes astonishing leaps, but they are technological, not theoretical. Communications engineers will be fascinated. When we started to investigate Aquilino's background, we did the usual things. School records. Interviews with the neighbors on the pretext that he had applied for a government job. He did poorly in school and dropped out of high school. No college. Nothing to indicate where this wild talent comes from. There's a lot of that happening these days. Even if people can't get the right education, the world is swamped with reading matter. One journal in particular, the *Bell Telephone Journal* for 1960, helped him make a breakthrough. People are figuring out how things work on their own. Mr. Camondo, for instance. Another is this Bernie Cornfield. James Ling. They've seen something no one else has. Offshore funds, flight capital, manufacturers anguished about tariffs—these will bust open the national boundaries. And Cornfield is another man who came from nowhere."

Keats was getting very close. How much did he know, Mr. Kelley wondered. How much was just probing? They would never replace the old wisdoms, never short-circuit history. Personal connections was what it was all about. This lamentable surge of democracy . . .

"It makes you wonder why we need an MIT, or a Cal Tech or even a Harvard Business School," Keats went on. "His problem was the telephone system. He cracked it wide open and made his electronic way to the secret places, things someone in his station of life should never have heard. After a while he was detected and investigated."

"Does he know what it all means?"

"If he's what he seems to be, no. His material is too sketchy, from the point when we start to listen in to him. But a hundred or so like him, scattered around the country, even not knowing what they were doing, linked, organized, each one sampling conversations that the others didn't get to hear—supposing

73

someone was putting it all together? Then what this hypothetical hundred listened into would total up to a stunning and dangerous picture of American secret policy. I *think* he's alone—"

"But you're not sure. And you say, 'not even knowing what they were doing.' "

"It's possible. If a talent scout went looking for such wild talents, there are ham associations and science fiction associations and other kinds of groupings. It would be a matter of exciting such people. Giving them a little technical help, just enough to make such people think they've made breakthroughs, which is not to deny their very real abilities."

"When would such an approach be made?"

"If it happened, probably in high school. When Aquilino dropped out, that seems to be the logical point."

"Why did he drop out?"

"Partly because he had no future in school, partly because he had . . . a disappointing love affair. You know how adolescents suffer."

"You never went through such a period." It was a statement, not a question. Mr. Kelley had been reading Keats's file.

"I would say that most of what Aquilino heard didn't make sense to him—not consciously. On the other hand, sense could be made of what he heard, if he can be gotten to divulge it all. I've prepared a précis. Full conversations can be assembled for your reading." Keats handed a sheaf of papers to Mr. Kelley. The lead sheet had about seventy names, in descending order of importance. Mr. Kelley scanned it.

"Do *you* know what it all means?"

Another test. Danger. Tell the truth. "Sir, I have a very good idea. It points to me, to Vassili Oprichnik, to you, to Mr. Helphand in Europe, and to the whole Parvus operation. Parvus vis à vis Russia and the United States. That's why he had to be protected."

"Meaning from your superior, Holcomb?"

Keats didn't answer that.

"How reliable is all this? Now please, I'm not talking about what they fashionably call 'hard evidence,' like Bob McNamara —I see his name on your list—who won't make a move without the numbers. Tell me what you *feel.*"

74

"The Feel." Keats sighed it, making it sound as if The Feel could relate only to Kelley. "Aquilino's ears are everywhere. You have to admire the kid. He listened in to the Defense Department. High-level security advisors . . ."

"Mac Bundy, for instance?"

"Yes, sir."

"Then this Aquilino's very political."

"No sir."

"How would he think to get to Mac? Mac isn't a household word."

"Because *you* spoke to him."

"We're supposed to have secure phones, scrambled."

"He designed a descrambler."

"Why would he want to listen in to *me?* That's rather exotic knowledge."

"Laura, Mr. Kelley."

"Laura? What does she have to do with it?"

"Pure chance. They grew up in the same neighborhood. He was in love with her in high school. She seems to have been in love with him for a short while. Then she changed her mind. That's the aborted love affair I spoke of. No doubt she got tired of him. He's very good looking but not very personable. No small talk. He pined for her. He wanted to know who she talked to. He tracked her through the phones for years, on and off, always hoping, drove himself crazy with jealousy. Then he took it a step further. He began to track those to whom Laura spoke, and who, in turn, *they* talked with. Since, I take it, Laura—and yourself— are very well connected, Aquilino took a tour through the top echelons of our country."

"And John Kennedy?" Mr. Kelley said. "Because I talked to him? His conversations with his brother . . . his family . . . his kitchen cabinet? The obsession with Cuba? All those broads?"

"Yes. But nothing really systematic. A kind of sampling."

"Delicious."

"But worst of all, he listened in to . . . us."

Mr. Kelley noted the "us." But did Keats understand all the levels and intracacies of this "us"? Keats had a name, Parvus, which he was an agent of. Keats knew that Parvus was not of Russia or of America, but there were Americans and Russians, among others, in it. Did Keats understand what was at stake? Or was he a very brilliant adventurer . . . or both? He would have to make a call to Mr. Helphand. If Aquilino was too ignorant to piece it together, was Keats? Did he see the first major battle looming, leading to the destabilization of America and the USSR?

"We certainly don't want the Russians to come in on this. What have you done to contain it?"

"Taken a holding action. Holcomb wanted to bring Aquilino in. I managed to divert him. Holcomb can't believe in the accidental, or the random, wild talent. In his world, everyone who comes to his attention is an agent."

Of course Holcomb would have to be killed. It was time to fully place Parvus people inside the Coffin's covert intelligence unit. CIA, State and other agencies were already seeded.

"I played on that paranoia. I spun Holcomb folk tales of brainwashing and Russian-designed guided human missiles. I convinced Holcomb that Aquilino is controlled without his knowledge and that it's necessary to get Aquilino to lead us to his control. There is no control. I managed to get to the tapes. The transcripts are being altered. I put a cordon around the operation, which I'm running in the field using Vassili Oprichnik's people. Then I contacted a Dr. Ficino, a neurobiologist."

"Then you contacted me."

"Yes sir."

"After initiating the action?"

"Yes sir."

"You took a chance."

Keats said nothing.

"Why not simply eliminate this Richard?"

"We need to know what he knows. What those who oppose us plan. Yes, he's an innocent, he doesn't understand what he's heard. But on deeper levels, something else is at work. It is said that the deepest levels forget nothing, ever. We have to help his memory along. Something big is brewing, apparently in Cuba, as you'll see from the précis. Countermeasures. We should learn what he remembers, but keep him unaware as we mine the contents of his mind.

"I've already taken steps. The time will come when the proper machinery will be invented to be able to link people like him up, let their imaginations do the work for us. Aquilino won't run himself: *we'll* run him. First we keep Holcomb from finding out what he knows. *We* find that information out. Then we learn how he did it and whether others like himself can be welded into a potent eavesdropping force. But we can only hold Holcomb off so long. When we can't anymore, we turn to Aquilino, and fill him with our own information, what we want others to know. That's the time to let Holcomb take him and sweat out what *we* want Holcomb and the CIA to know. That information would, in all probability, reach the President. Better yet, we run Aquilino to someone higher, maybe the President himself. We are covered, protected. What we offer up is not a defecting agent, which always arouses suspicions and leads to years of debriefing, but something much more valuable and dramatic—an innocent. The ultimate in credibility. It's building deniability into the horses's mouth."

Mr. Kelley knew that ever since Keats was double-recruited in college—by the CIA and by a talent scout for Parvus working as a professor—Keats had been ambitious, power hungry, dissatisfied with being a node in a network. Now he was listening as Keats worked to convince him that what should be nothing more or less than a little side drama could be made into something of world importance. It was ridiculous to think that so much might depend on this Aquilino, a complete outsider. Still . . . there was some merit to it.

Still again, the connection between himself and Laura, between this Aquilino and Laura . . . that troubled him. How long, how many years had Aquilino been listening in to him? Aquilino knew, at least unconsciously, much more than Keats gave him credit for. Worse, he was falling in love. He didn't blame Keats for trying to puff himself up. This little operation, full of telephones, psychology, illusion and reality, it would be his gift to Keats. If Keats made a good thing of it, let him start his own little empire with an investment of Kelley's confidence . . . and some government money, of course. He suppressed a tremor. He willed his body to be still. At his age. And yet, when you got older your body betrayed you. Maybe because you thought that each passion would be the last. Come to me, Kelley willed. Hold me. There was a stillness. He shouldn't have even thought it. Keats would sense it. Keats did.

You are the wild talent, Kelley thought, not this Richard. It's *me* you are trying to run. I can't help it. Maybe I should just have you killed afterwards . . . eat your spirit. How Mr. Helphand would laugh at him if he ever knew. Did they secretly meet, this Keats and this Vassili Oprichnik, and snicker at their two masters in love with their Ganymedes? Did these Young Turks plan a coup, lulling their masters with love? When Kelley spoke, Keats had moved quite close. "Tell me. You saw Patrice Lumumba die?"

"Yes sir."

Mr. Kelley's hands moved up, gesturing, as if to take Keats's face in his hands. "Did you by some chance look into his eyes as he died?"

"I did, sir."

"Edward. Did he die well?"

"How well can you die when someone is chopping you to pieces?" Keats whispered.

"Godefroid Munongo?" Mr. Kelley moved Keats's head forward. Their lips almost met. Mr. Kelley whispered: "Did he scream?"

"He screamed."

"Remember. Remember Lumumba dying," Kelley said. "How would you like to work with Laura?"

CHAPTER 6

"I think we have company," Keats reported to Holcomb.

"He's making his move?"

"Not him, them, and it's not exactly a move yet. His contacts have appeared and are coming closer."

"How's he acting?"

"Normal. As if he doesn't know a thing. I think his contacts have spotted us."

"How do they know we're on to him? Sloppy work?"

"No. I think Morrison is doing a fine job," Keats said, letting his tone say the opposite.

"Should we increase security?"

"Not yet. That might get Aquilino killed off . . . rescued . . . or abandoned. I think abandoned. A few more days . . . a week or two. But their appearance tells us something important about the operation."

"And that is?"

"If he were a conscious agent, and *he* sensed us, he'd go to ground . . ."

Go to ground, Holcomb thought. How he hated that Limey fox-hunting talk. When he worked for the FBI in the Second World War, he and Hoover, how they hated the British.

". . . but if he's not conscious, he'll keep on listening in. If he were a conscious agent, no one would have to come out of the woodwork to see what was wrong. I think that tells us something. Aquilino doesn't deliver the take through the phones, so he must do it in person. But we haven't found the signs of any other kind of delivery. No drops. No paper, except for his notes. No microfilm. No microdots. No radio-squirt mechanisms, just a not-much-used ham outfit. No tapes. Probably he just talks it."

"Talks it?"

"He meets with someone, almost accidentally. Something is shown or said that triggers a post-hypnotic suggestion. That triggers his remembrance and he goes into a kind of trance."

"Why are the Russians doing it that way? Why not through the phone, or radio?"

"They believe in personal contact. When the meet takes place, Aquilino starts talking, he repeats everything he's heard, verbatim . . . the intelligence mixed in with the other junk. That's probably tape-recorded. Then, at another signal, he wakes up, so to speak, and has no memory of what took place."

"They can really do these things?"

That was really a good question about himself, Keats thought. Good. "They're very advanced in this field. Been doing experiments in mind control all the way back to Pavlov. I've gotten some material together for you to look over, a summary of our ongoing work. The case of the Bolshevik so-called confessions of 1936. The Cardinal Mindszenty episode. A synopsis of *The Manchurian Candidate*. A rough cut of the film, to be released soon; you'll like it. Frank Sinatra—"

"Shit."

"As soon as it's in final shape, the whole agency will get to see it—an outline of our findings about Chinese brain-washing techniques, some programs our side runs. It involves a gradual change of reality. Disorientation. Destabilization. Change the environment. Harassment. Drugs administered without the subject's knowledge. Sub- and ultra-sonics . . . which brings up the question of his probable recruitment.

"My analysis leads me to believe that it happened when he was in high school. He went through a disastrous love affair. We don't know why it broke up. There was a period of desolation and disorientation . . . a time he'd just as soon forget. I'll bet when we get to question him, he won't remember, unless he's helped along very carefully. That's when they must have made their move. For all we know, the girl may have been part of it."

"Who's she?"

"One Laura Geroyavich."

"A *Russian?*"

"No. Third generation," Keats said, but he knew he had given Holcomb something more to chew on.

"Put a trace on her. Find out where she is. Why Aquilino?"

"Radio ham, so he had the know-how. He was ripe. As for the technology, I'm having trouble getting straight answers out of Bell. They say they haven't a clue as to how it's done. I think they're holding out on us. In the meantime, we're continuing to monitor. Want to know what the Fed is going to do next week? We could make a killing."

"Jesus."

"And advance news of grain shipments to your most favored country?"

"Lemme see that stuff. I'll backchannel it and maybe something can be done to stop that shit." That meant, send it to Angleton. "It won't be the first time Bell has held out on us," Holcomb said. "Okay. Take another week."

Spring of 1962 was becoming summer. Richard had been trying to stop listening in, cold turkey. He thought that all he had to do was to stop listening, and that would be it. He didn't know how hard it would be. The blinking lights on his plastic board agitated him. The whole world was out there and he had cut himself off. He disconnected the whole signaling apparatus. The emptiness in his life increased . . . soundlessness, a world without conversation. He hadn't realized how much the world of voices without bodies had become part of his life.

He stopped going down to the Figaro cafe. Might as well make a clean break.

Of course he got phone calls from them. Ziggy wanted to know what the matter was. Had they insulted him? Richard said that he had a bad cold.

Then his mother began calling. That was strange. She hadn't done that in a long time. He told her he was feeling under the weather. Why didn't he come home and stay in bed for a few days

81

and she would take care of him. No. He didn't want to. She insisted; as imperious as ever. His father called too. Gentle, questioning, persistent. Maybe they could go out and have dinner sometime. He began to say, and repeat, "Leave me alone. I'm all right. Don't bother me." He was an adolescent again. And then the arguments began again. What was he doing with his life? When was he going to think about what he wanted to do? It hadn't happened for years. All of it depressed him. He just sat around, listening to the radio, records, reading science-fiction, daydreaming, and sleeping more and more.

He missed the voices right away. Was Marilyn Monroe just as miserable as before? Were the football Giants going to make that outrageous move to another city? Wasn't there any loyalty left . . . loyalty to fans?

He still did freelance jobs, repaired television sets and radios. Now and then he had a job with small businesses; repaired their intercoms and improved on them, rigged up switchboards when they couldn't get satisfaction from the phone company. He made enough to get by.

What about Laura? Who was she talking to now? How could anyone know so many people? But then she had always had a wide circle of friends, even when she was a little girl. In high school, she seemed to know almost everyone.

After a few days, the boredom became excruciating. He thought, it was like those articles he read about heroin addicts. Take away their habit and they went crazy. He had not been so alone since he was in high school.

He was visited by Ziggy, Tarzan and Marvin. They were angry. They had been visited by the FBI, asking questions about Richard . . . and, consequently, about them. They had tried to cover for Richard without knowing what they were covering for.

"What have you been doing?" Ziggy asked.

The tone annoyed Richard. Who did he think he was? "Same thing as always. Listening in now and then."

"Now and then? Or a lot?"

"Look, Ziggy, you're not the FBI."

"I told you not to overdo it, and never from your own phone."

"Ziggy, I'm a big boy."

"It sure don't look like it," Tarzan said.

82

"You have to tell me everything, Richard," Ziggy said, "so we'll know what to say to them if they come around again."

"Leave me alone. Let them come to me."

"They will," Ziggy said.

"Why don't you just answer Ziggy what he wants to know?" Tarzan had moved in. He was tense, but beginning to smile, getting ready to make trouble.

Richard got up. He wasn't frightened. He had enough fights in school. In fact he thought it might be just what he wanted to do to relieve the emptiness.

"Come on, fellas. Let's just talk," Marvin said.

"Let's leave," Ziggy said.

"I can get it out of him, Zig," Tarzan told them.

"No. Richard, just keep away from us till you're in a better frame of mind. We're not your enemies. It may be a lot of fun, a lot of games for all of us. Well, don't spoil it. The government and Mother Bell haven't got a sense of humor."

"Goodbye, shithead," Tarzan said to him, and they left.

Now it was worse than ever. Since Richard had made enough money to last him for a few weeks, he began to sleep most of the days and to go out at night exclusively. He began to do a lot of prowling around the city. But then, he, Ziggy, all of them had always been night people. Richard walked up to the Village a few times and almost went into the Figaro, but turned away. He tried other coffee shops. He watched couples drinking their coffee and talking. He watched girls sitting alone. He wondered how to start up a conversation with them.

It became harder to sleep during the days. The heavy traffic along Canal Street had always provided a sort of background . . . soothing if one was used to it, intolerable to those who didn't live there. But now new sounds began to get mixed up in the general sound. He didn't know where they came from, but it irritated him, and he had trouble sleeping. His stereo was always on, but seemed to have developed some trouble. New high-pitched sounds, unfamiliar sounds. He couldn't imagine sleeping without the radio going. He began to have strange, troubled dreams. Something about the sounds, whatever they were, kept reminding him of Laura. Laura talking. Laura . . . what? Doing something else. He had to do something. He had to do something with his life. He had to get into another field. Should he go back and finish high school, go on to college and get a degree in engineering? Was it too late? Maybe he was old enough now to manage it. Certainly his parents would be happy.

He took apart his stereo—everything—looking for the source of the trouble: the receiver, the amplifier, the pre-amp, the speakers. Tested each component out. It occupied his mind for a few days. He couldn't find anything wrong with it. His television began to develop the same kind of trouble. This time he thought he knew what it was . . . the raster scanning-beam, a constant hum affecting the speaker . . .

Then he began to get the feeling that someone was watching him . . . following him. Tarzan? Tarzan was crazy enough to do something like that. As he walked through the night streets, he began to turn around suddenly. Nothing. Maybe if he just went back to what he was doing, not do it as much, taper off, apologize to Ziggy . . . maybe he would be all right and he could begin to think about what to do with his life. He couldn't bear the isolation . . . he couldn't think.

CHAPTER 7

DR. Carol Rothschild was seated in front of a cathode-ray tube, scanning a subject's brain activity, when she began to feel a disturbing perturbation beginning in her body: specifically the labia, the clitoris, her behind, the back of her neck. She checked her watch: at first she thought she was checking to see if the radioactive tracer in Mr. Giminski's blood had taken effect and reached the brain. But then she realized—she blushed—that it was lunchtime.

She took her lunch with her boss, Dr. Sidney Ficino. After lunch came sex, as it did again after the day's work was done. Sidney was in love with her. He said that sex helped their creativity. He wanted to get married as soon as he could divorce his wife. No sex today, though—Sidney had a luncheon appointment. Sidney had been excited and mysterious about the lunch, only saying that it could change their lives.

Carol had once been a psychotherapist; a Freudian analyst disillusioned with the lengthy sessions in which everyone seemed to complain in the same way about the same kinds of neurosis. The money was very good, but the work was boring. That was no way to understand why humans malfunctioned. She began to feel the answer to all disturbance lay in the way the brain itself worked. She went back to medical school and specialized in central nervous system studies. The central nervous system, once terra incognita, was the last real dark continent left. It was slowly and painfully being illuminated and mapped. They were getting to know what each part did. In another few years, it would all be put together and she wanted to be the person who did it.

On the other side of the screen, a middle-aged man lay on a bed. Mr. Giminski, a volunteer. Radioactive tracers had been injected into his bloodstream. The blood, bearing the tracers, went through the brain. The flow was scanned. Electrodes were attached to the patient's head. The wires led to a box, connected to the screen. The patient's thoughts, his actions, his thoughts about action, were converted to waves and were recorded on an electroencephalograph; the tube showed picture elements of light, ranging from black all the way through the colors to pure white. White indicated hyperactivity: black was the lack of activity or thought—death.

Carol said, "All right, Mr. Giminski, now I'd like you to go through that sequence of thought again. Only this time I want you to scramble the arrangement. Imagine yourself running. At the same time I want you to recall the thing we talked about, that time when you had that wonderful experience with that woman . . . the one you met when you were on your vacation in Mexico. And here are some pictures to help you along." She blushed again. *Playboy.* "Now think about that poem we've been working on and what it *really* means. Think of it as a puzzle . . . try to do all these things together."

Memory, dreams, fantasies, real sensations. In the brain they all got confused together. Memory was a complex chemical compound with both a short and a long life. A molecule. One part comes; the other parts are summoned—even if they have little to do with one another logically—linked, associated, hard to sort out, hard to tear apart.

Mr. Giminski did what the doctor asked. She watched the changing waves, the coruscating colors going from black to blue, green, yellow, to an explosion of white, oddly enough concentrating in the speech center, and then, after a long while, dimming suddenly. The body was tense. The elements—flight, sex, analytic thinking—couldn't be brought together. After a period of intense struggle the patient was giving up in frustration. She took notes. Her ultimate aim was to correlate each moment of imagination to what she saw on the screen, to create a sort of lexicon of electrochemical impulses translated to certain unambiguous meanings. One day the whole code of human mental activity would be perfectly clear.

What would a scan of her brain have looked like as her body remembered the absent Sidney Ficino?

A Mr. Barnstable had telephoned Dr. Sidney Ficino, saying he represented the Coffin Foundation. The Coffin specialized in medical grants, emphasizing research into the workings of the central nervous system. Previously the money had gone only for hard, scientific research. Now the Coffin was shifting its stance and looking to expand its horizons, go interdisciplinary with an emphasis on Mind, following the Macy Foundation's pioneering work in cybernetics. The Coffin wanted to open new channels for research and was looking around to see what work in progress they might encourage. Some friends of the Foundation, working over at Massachusetts General Hospital, had mentioned a number of promising research projects going on around the country. The Coffin had been sent a series of papers . . . including the work of Dr. Ficino and his assistant, Dr. Rothschild. "Mr. Barnstable" knew that Dr. Ficino was very busy, but could they meet for lunch, say at the Harvard Club, and discuss the matter further?

Barnstable turned out to be a tall, willowy, somewhat effete and fussy blond young man, wearing rimless glasses. Fastidious. Probably a fag. Certainly no more than a mere bureaucrat, a funding officer of the Coffin Foundation. Mr. Barnstable seemed to have only a layman's knowledge of brain work. Ficino put himself out. He had a superb speaking voice and knew how to use it. He became overwhelmingly charming, as only he could be. He delivered a short history of brain work; the discoveries, the advances, the blind alleys, the effects of damage on various centers. He talked neurons: axons, dendrites, chemical transmitters across the synapses, exitatory and inhibitory neurons, the double signaling system (chemical and electrical), the incredibly complex interconnections, the research breakthroughs. "And yet, this chemistry, this 'wiring,' is the basis of dreams, of hate, of love, of noble and ignoble acts, of literature and art, of action in the world, and, most of all, the basis of the kind of mind that tries to see its own structure and function from within itself . . ."

Sidney Ficino could see that the young man was impressed, if not to say downright charmed. (Sidney reminded himself. Don't be too charming.) Barnstable started asking questions, some of which seemed to be science fiction. "Sort of trying to see yourself without a mirror and yet with your own eyes—from the inside?"

That was a dumb way of putting it. "That's a good way of putting it," Sidney said. He didn't know where Barnstable was headed.

"I suppose that a telephone system, with its intricate wiring circuits, is in itself analogous to the brain. For that matter, so are all sorts of interconnected communications systems—say radio— an activity of many brains. Maybe the wave of the future lies in reversing the analogy . . . understanding the complexes of connecting mechanisms of the central nervous system in terms of a radio system, or hard-wired systems." Then the conversation seemed to change. Barnstable became interested in what he called Distant Influence. "I suppose that in order for you scientists to do something with that, one must understand the connections between sender and receiver in a more *intimate* way . . . in which the experimental subject is linked, perhaps permanently, to the experimenter."

"I'm not sure I'm following you, Mr. Barnstable."

"Telepathy. I'm only spinning fantasies. Of course previously the efforts in Distant Influencing of minds have been crude—the kind of thing William Langer did with Hitler during the Second World War. Fascinating, though."

Sidney Ficino snorted. "That was mere guesswork, not even brilliant. Psychoanalytic garbage. Just what the man in the street would have said about Hitler."

"You don't seem to have any use for Freud—"

"Nor for the whole breed; Freud, Jung, Adler—they've taken psychology in the wrong direction. It's become unverifiable, metaphysical. But what does that have to do with influencing?"

"Langer's work did give us insights. As long as the insights remained in Langer's mind, we had a one-way system. But when they were utilized to have an effect on Hitler and his policy, something else happened."

"Perhaps, but Freud and his followers took what was good, solid research and mystified it, adding a few catchy names and obscuring the functions of the brain. We're just beginning to find out how memory *really* works. Sensors receiving and transmitting stimuli, neurons firing, electrical differentials, chemical transfers across the synapses, hormones, messengers . . . that's what it's all about. Biological hard-wiring.

"We're just in the infancy of this kind of research. We're charting the brain, the whole complex of connections. There are, say, maybe ten-to-the-twelfth-power nerve cells in the brain—and that's just a guess—and when we consider the way in which they interact, that yields a figure unimaginably large. The way they work is the clue to the future. We're getting to the point where we can assign specific functions, but—"

"So that we might short circuit the whole perceptual process and go directly into the brain?"

"Yes. In time."

"But given a figure such as you mentioned—and considering the way groups of people interact—to make a sort of brain of brains, one still has to consider the medium through which communication of this brain of brain goes. You're only concerned with the inside of one brain. What about those connections to the sensors—eyes, ears, skin, and memories of past events, to say nothing of dreams—all a kind of outside?"

"Well, yes, but—"

"And what is seen, or heard, can come from a very long way off. A radio program, a TV show, a telephone call. Consider the obvious connections . . . You give someone say, an electroencephalogram. The spikes in the graph, the alpha, beta, theta, delta waves, the rapid spikes and so on. Usually the patient is in front of you. That's the way you people work. Supposing the 'patient' you want to reach is far away? Such work is going on, you know. If the 'patient' knows he is being scanned, that's one thing; their knowledge interferes with natural reactions. What if the subject doesn't know they are being scanned? Or influenced?"

"Telepathy?" Ficino asked.

"Among other things. The Russians are very interested in telepathy. They call it 'Distant Influence.' Transmission through the electromagnetic spectrum . . . Do you know L. L. Vasilev's

89

La Suggestion à Distance? Or Bergier's *La Transmission de Pensée, Arme de Guerre?*"

"Thought, a weapon of war? Witchcraft."

"There have been breathtaking developments. Radar, for instance. Do you think we might ever get to the point where we might, if we had the data, be able to analyze the processes of thought, perhaps anticipate what someone far away was going to do, by recording his electrical waves?"

"If we were connected," Sidney said, "or if we had readouts, knew all about the person, had a history, we *might* come to work up a personality profile which was scientific, not mere guesswork."

Barnstable didn't seem satisfied with this reply. Ficino sensed the disappointment. There goes the grant. He stumbled. "The medium is the thing . . . the sensors . . . and the receptors . . ."

Barnstable seemed to perk up and wait for Ficino. A smile was playing on his lips.

"Radio, TV, channels . . ." Ficino trailed off.

"Thoughts broadcast through space. Powerful transmitters, carrier waves to bear them to the recipient."

"I suppose such work is going on . . . should be going on . . ." Ficino had an idea that the research Barnstable was talking about was actually happening in hospitals and universities all around the country. Fund raising had made him cagey. Barnstable wanted something. Ficino hoped that what Barnstable wanted was what he—and Carol—had. He realized how hungry he was. Ficino would try to tell Barnstable what he wanted to hear. "Maybe a shortcut is needed to find a scientific, a repeatable, demonstrable way of transmitting through an *exterior* nervous system, in which the atmosphere can carry thought. The intuitive scientist can make leaps and short-circuit over centuries of plodding, leap over the barriers put up by our colleagues. I mean we have to take chances. Big chances. We can't wait to understand the central nervous system until all the work is done."

"Distant Influence."

"If we had medical data . . . it would be crude at this stage, but, why not?" Ficino said.

Barnstable seemed to cheer up. "For instance, what if you

were brought a complete medical workup of someone you'd never seen . . .?"

Ficino said, "If it was a good record, a thorough workup . . ."

"How wonderful," Barnstable said, reached over and squeezed Ficino's hand. Ficino's skin crawled. "We'll be in touch. And by the way, I'll send you some reading matter. Do you read Russian?"

"No."

"French?"

"Badly. German."

"I'll have them translated."

And that, Sidney Ficino thought, was a good omen.

CHAPTER 8

IN the long run the loneliness was too much for Richard to bear. He couldn't struggle against his addiction. How many movies can you go to see, some of them twice and three times? How many TV shows can you watch? How many times can you go through your record collection? How long can you sleep? How many walks can you take through the deserted streets of lower Manhattan, when the small industries have shut up for the night? And, even though you know that there's no one there, between Houston and Canal Streets, you have the feeling that there's someone there in the shadows.

The traffic outside his loft was peculiar. He thought he heard voices in the noise of cars, of trucks, of the machinery in the lofts all around him. But when Richard listened hard, he heard nothing.

The junkie, or the New Year's resolver, comes to a point where' he knows, even though he has said nothing to himself about it yet, that he's going to backslide. This both agitates him and begins to relieve him. Then it becomes not so much a question of "if," but of "when." If "when" is admitted to the mind—just below the threshold of awareness—then the nature of abstinence changes. It's not forever that he has given up the habit; he can begin to play a game with himself. He can defer giving in.

Richard didn't give up so easily. He also knew that the first time he gave in, he would feel terribly depressed. So he deferred his gratification.

But then there was the other matter: what Ziggy had told him. The FBI was coming around. He had broken the law, but had he done such a bad thing? The only thing he felt guilty about was listening in to Laura. Of that he was ashamed. As for the others? Well . . . he never had any personal connection. The President? Yes. That was terrible. That wasn't right. But still. What was the worst that would happen to him? They would tell him to stop it; if he didn't, they would arrest him. Maybe, Richard thought, *that's* what he needed to make him stop once and for all: an authoritative voice from the outside.

It was day outside. The weather was beautiful, crisp and autumnal. His grimy windows made his loft seem almost twilight-like. He lay there and listened to the heavy traffic outside; the trucks rumbling along Canal Street, going to and from Brooklyn, to and from New Jersey, bringing loads, taking loads, back and forth. As usual he heard, in the traffic's rumble, the sound of voices, conversations he couldn't quite make out.

They'd come, the FBI, and they'd say, "All right, kid, we got you. What have you been doing?" And then he'd say, "Who, me? Nothing." And then they'd say . . .

No. That wasn't the conversation he heard. He heard Laura. He listened hard. He still couldn't make it out. He felt, as he hadn't felt in a long time, that somehow Laura's voice wasn't really comfortable, assured, but that she was weepy, really unhappy. Like Marilyn Monroe. Something terrible had happened to her. Should he tap in again?

The day evolved into afternoon, and then the sun began to set, and his room got darker and darker. Finally he got up and took the first step. He connected his big plastic board, with all the lights. Stars. Planets. Abode of the thousands and thousands of people, each light a sign of their life. And then he went back and lay down. Evening passed and became night, and then passed into the beginning of morning. The lights, the conversations, died down one by one as the traffic died throughout the country. A few centers were still lit up: Washington, New York, Los Angeles. He got up off the bed again and cut in the sound, and let the whole babble—subdued by this time of night—reach him. He felt happier.

He'd go . . . tomorrow he would go up to the Village, to the Figaro, and make it up with Ziggy. Maybe they could find a way to rig the whole system up in such a way as to really be undetectable. *That* was a good idea. Should he begin to listen? No. Not yet. He was easing into the habit.

He got up, turned on the light, and began to make himself some food. He hadn't eaten the whole day. Eggs. Some toast. A fresh pot of coffee. Everything tasted particularly good. By the time he was finished, it was almost four o'clock. One o'clock in the morning in Los Angeles. Was Marilyn Monroe's light on? No. He sat down at the table with the plastic screen. Where should he begin?

He felt a little peculiar. Probably because he had eaten too quickly after fasting all day long. *Something was happening to him.* He began to feel torn apart—that was the only way to describe it—his body scattered throughout the whole system. Before, all the lines reached to him, and he sat there, in the center, listening to all those voices. But now he began to feel that he was everywhere . . . that he had been drawn thin throughout the system, passed through the wires so that his ears were *in* everyone else's ears, so that his mouth was *in* everyone else's mouth, that his nerves were drawn through some aperture in his skin and passed through all the conduits, the short lines, the long lines, the cables . . . and he was hurtled through space from microwave tower to microwave tower.

And he could almost see the husk that was his body, sitting there, as if in a trance. See? No, that was the wrong word. He couldn't *see* a thing. The eyes in the husk-that-was-his-body saw the lights and the rest of him . . . the rest of his insides . . . they were everywhere around the country, in other countries . . . He *heard* his seeing self, sitting there. Get together. Get together. If he didn't, he would never survive.

That voice. Laura. He heard her voice being transmitted through his far-strung nervous system . . . Not what she said, but the *feel* of what she said. "No. No. I can't take it any more. I'm through. I'm finished. Let me alone. Let me go."

94

And another voice saying ". . . you shall pay any price, bear any burden, meet any hardship, support your friend, oppose my foe, in order to assure his survival and the success . . ."

It passed through *him.* There was something horrible about it. The voices and thoughts of others passing through him . . . like being raped. He stood up. What was wrong with him?

The act of standing up made him dizzy, but still, he felt better. It was as if the act of doing so pulled back all of his nerves. The conversations stopped. The lights continued to blink on and off. Go out. Get some air. Something was still wrong. What was it? He had pulled into himself the wrong nerve network. His head and body were stuffed with wire now. Bell's line system now consisted of his nerves, strung around the country. That's crazy. Were his eggs spoiled? He put on his jacket and coat and went out.

Walk, you'll feel better. He walked north along Greene Street. He had heard that Greene Street had been, in the 1850s, the red light district of New York. The street had been jammed with whorehouses. He imagined that he could still hear the laughter coming out . . . the music . . . the sound of cries of ecstasy . . . light and laughter pouring out of the grimy factory-loft buildings.

When he got to Greene and Spring Street, he noticed something up ahead. A man standing in the middle of the street, as if waiting for him. A mugger? He turned westward. A man, standing in the middle of the street, legs planted wide, as if waiting for him. He turned eastward. A man, standing in the middle of the street, half crouched, hands wide, as if waiting for him. Go back, south. A man, standing in the middle of the street, something glinting in one hand, as if waiting for him. He began to walk south. He had taken two steps when someone darted out of the shadows. North, west, east and south, the man standing in the middle of the street, turned, with almost the same motion, to confront the newcomer. Richard stopped. There was a short, silent fight. Knives. The waiters in the street were cut down and then dragged into the shadows at the side. What had saved him? Who had saved him? What should he do? Go on? Stop? Stand here, waiting? What? He couldn't move.

He stood there for a long, long time. The chill penetrated his clothes and began to work its way into his body. He walked in a tight circle, waved his arms, slapped them against his body. Slowly, the dawn came. He began to hear the rumble of trucks as they came back into the area. A truck came down the street, coming down from Houston Street. As it passed him, slowly because the streets were narrow, he began to walk by its side, till he passed the place where the combatants had fought. There was nothing there at all.

CHAPTER 9

MR. Kelley stood by the great window, looking out below. Everything, grass and sea, was suffused by the full moon's light. He was in the grip of a young man's passion, but like the sea, he was old, and feminine. The dark corners of the bedroom were discretely lit by moonlight. A cool wind blew in from the Atlantic. He heard the surf's roar; long waves surging from all parts of the world and the world's past, breaking on Long Island. The trees whispered, rustling. Surf, leaf-rustle, the earth's natural white noise, the planet's pulse and breath; she lived. The smell of salt was tangy, as if on wet, human flesh. Below was a long lawn, flanked on one side by a line of great oaks; on the other side by marble representations of trees: Greek pillars topped by stylized oak leaves. Colonnade of trees, stand of pillars, flanking some great theatre's floor, swept around to meet at a little stage, on which little dramas were sometimes given. The previous inhabitant had practiced ceremonial magic here. At the back of the stage—once an altar—a pitch-black entrance led into a wonderful hedge-maze. The maze led to a perfect, paradisiacal garden at the center, where the killing would take place. Knowing his predecessor's tastes, there had been real killing of real people. The shadows in the maze, the light and dark, were intricate and deceptive, though of course nowhere near as intricate and deceptive as the shadows who moved in the real world in the real

97

theatre. It was one of the best mazes in the world. Mr. Kelley had it changed from time to time.

He and Keats had spent the weekend together, working and loving. They went over the transcripts of the tapes and Aquilino's notes. They had been joined by Kelley's policy advisor. A pattern was emerging from the mass of material. Was this pattern happening, a confluence of internal fights for power, or was it being *made* to happen? Mr. Kelley felt that it was not accidental. What was the source?

A number of senior advisors and elder statesmen were clearly getting ready to implement their plan, but was the design springing out of *their* machinations? After all, everyone plotted and the plots were balanced out by one another. The pattern Kelley saw was based more on intuition than anything else, but he was used to gambling on intuition. Mr. Kelley tried to feel his way through to the source. Kennedy and his people were double-crossing Mr. Kelley and those he represented, going back on certain agreements reached when Kelley and the whole Parvus group had agreed to back him in his run for the presidency. A crisis was deliberately being mounted. The target date was most certainly in October. The plan had been initiated as far back as a year ago.

Military feints. Covert operations. Something brewing in Berlin, but with its aim toward Cuba. NATO was crumbling; an emergency to shore it up. The Organization of American States was refractory. Pompous little strutting dictators who would have to go. The Organization of African Unity was still a dream in the minds of the poets of negritude hoping to become statesmen. OPEC, a new organization, a brilliant idea, was not yet ready to be effective.

So: confrontation in order to achieve standoff in Berlin. A tactic in Angola and Mozambique, *all in order to strike, once and for all, at Cuba?* Blockade or embargo, or worse, in the works? What would be the reason given, what the cause?

The Suez closed? Not bad; a shift to the great tankers, which were being built to go around the Cape of Good Hope and bypass the Suez. More efficient and not subject to the vagaries of the situation in the Mideast. Nasser had been bribed to keep the Canal closed for a reasonable amount of time.

The Panama Canal? Cuba stands astride the Caribbean. Military buildup in Laos and Vietnam in spite of agreements for a cutback. Of those Russians who wanted peace . . . their position was being made untenable. And surely the hard-line ideologues were helping the crisis along.

He would have to contact Helphand in his observation post in West Berlin, very soon. All was part of The Way, the *Tao.* The emanations of world events would activate the actors to change their hats and put on their new masks before they appeared on both little and big stages. They came out of the maze, small or global, where the spilled blood was processed, transfigured, turned into credit and power, before it was turned into flesh again.

Laura tapped along with so many of her contacts . . . it bothered Mr. Kelley. More information was needed. Use Laura? Or was Laura playing her own game? She understood the numbers, a rare trait in a female. The fragments of information began to coalesce again into a coherent mosaic and the mosaic was the beginning of a plan. But Mr. Kelley was not so sure that so much should depend on so fragile a reed as Aquilino.

The events had cast the yarrow sticks. They had come to rest, pointing at "Breaking Apart," number twenty-three, revolution in the *I-Ching,* the *Book of Changes.* Chance had given him Keats, and through Keats, this young man who had heard too much, Aquilino. Perhaps it was important that the sticks should point to Aquilino and Laura. What convinced him was the connection, the coincidence. Fragments of a summarized conversation Aquilino had picked up stuck in his mind: Mr. Lansky talking to someone who had the speech patterns that might only belong to Mr. Nixon. Was it possible? About Cuba and their lost investments on their mind. Obsession with short-term needs. Mr. Kelley admired Mr. Lansky's mind. Had Mr. Lansky grown up in Russia instead of being brought as a child to the United States, he would have been another Lenin. He too had a superb head for the numbers and had wrought a degree of peace among the Mafia counts, dukes and barons—no mean feat.

Keats lay on the bed behind him, a slim, delicious shadow, faintly illuminated by the moonlight streaming in the window. How should he play Keats? This first time had convinced him that something deeper between them must be struck; he couldn't let sex and love get in the way. He must bind Keats to him totally, or kill him eventually. Who would carry on the great work after him? Who would be his heir?

He would raise Keats up to greatness. Kelley was the gate-keeper to power. Keats had swept him away. Yet, although Keats's body was open, his mind was closed, impenetrable. Of course he could have tortured Keats's real feelings out of him; he had it done before.

"If the material is true," Kelley said, "then there must be an agenda, a timetable, leading up to a target date. Is the President planning something he's keeping from his own CIA? And are *they* watching *him* as if he were the leader of a foreign power?" Were others planning something they were keeping from their own president, and from *him,* Mr. Kelley? Mr. Kelley's copies of National Intelligence Estimates, of the President's Daily Intelligence Report, of National Security Action Memoranda, showed little. Was Kennedy generating pressure for action against himself, so it would appear he was being forced into an untenable position? Was it an event that should be prevented from happening, helped along to happen, or just *appear* to happen? And how could the mere appearance of a crisis be used? To strengthen or weaken the President.

If Kennedy was still useful, then strengthen the President but weaken and destabilize the presidency.

"Yes." A sigh. An actor's voice projecting faintness loudly. Keats was pretending to be overcome, Kelley knew; but even knowing this, it was as though he could feel Keats's breath on his body.

"When?" he muttered. Mr. Kelley was coming to certain decisions. He would have to act half-blind. Keats would be Kelley's untrustworthy eyes. Others would be used as Keats's eyes. Vassili Oprichnik could use his own KGB subordinates; Aquilino had apparently tapped into the Russian embassy, so there would be justification. *"Without stirring abroad, one can know the whole world,"* he thought—through a linked series of eyes and ears. All liars.

Keats was an adventurer, using Mr. Kelley to advance himself rapidly in Parvus, skipping over the higher levels by making himself a favorite. Kelley had followed Keats's progress through the CIA, from afar, through reports and dossiers, just as he followed the progress of all his "children." Keats was brilliant . . . and beautiful. Keats and Oprichnik had worked brilliantly in the Congo, setting up KGB and CIA agents for one another. But they had lost the battle in the long run; the forces were too great.

Keats understood the first level: that all maneuvers were directed to your own advantage. Keats understood the second level, the national, which he had left behind when he allowed himself to be also recruited by Kelley's people in college. And thus he understood the third level, the international: the new forces which were emerging again after a long sleep. But he had shown no sign that he understood, although surely he knew of, the highest level of all, Parvus. How much did the self predominate! If too much, Keats was worse than useless, he was dangerous.

Of course there would be consultations with Mr. Kelley's principals. That would take time. The few farsighted Europeans, British, Japanese, Americans, would want advance notice. They hated surprises. It didn't allow them time to shift their investments around. Still, you couldn't call a grand council every time there was an emergency. He would ask Mr. Helphand to come, or go to him. What were the signs on the other side? What did Mr. Khrushchev think? How could they make an end-around play past Suslov and the True Believers? Mr. Helphand would have to consult with *his* own principals in Russia, Poland, Rumania, Czechoslovakia, Hungary, East Germany.

He and Mr. Helphand would get together and wander around the estate. Over there, along the shore. They would walk between the oaks and the pillars. They would talk idly at first; that was their style. Like himself, Mr. Helphand was one of the Old School, fifty years ahead of their time. Ninety-five and still vigorous. A marvel. They had both lived through vast changes—two great bloody and overt wars, revolutions, almost fifty years of covert war—all to move things into the new age. This was the most dangerous stage; the interim period, the warring-states period, when things and nations were pried apart in order to be put together again in a new way.

No rushing. Begin by gossiping of old friends, living and dead. Who had fallen by the wayside; who was moving up, or should be moved up; who was failing; who was replacing the Old Ones . . .

There was a stirring on the bed. Mr. Kelley's loins began to ache; he hadn't felt like this for a long time. Maybe Keats should be there, at his side. Get Keats connected, show him how it was done. Laura in the background to watch Keats. Her instinct was nearly perfect after so many men. But if Mr. Kelley showed up with a second, then Mr. Helphand would want one. Who? Vassili Oprichnik? He smiled. Oprichnik indeed. The Russian boy had a sense of humor in spite of his silly Brooklyn accent. And Oprichnik would be played off against Keats. You couldn't reach the highest levels by yourself.

Science? No, Mr. Kelley thought. The private meeting. The luxurious estate, the castle, the island in the Mediterranean, Bilderberg, Achnecarry, the big dacha on the Black Sea, not far from ancient Colchis where Medea practiced medicine and magic. The whispered confidence . . . the face-to-face encounter. The masks of imperturbability. The acted-out and deceptive rages. Keats was too keen on the modern age's technology. Telephony and radio could never replace the older kinds of contact. Keats would learn to unlearn all that.

Timetable? It looked like October, or November, with the elections coming up. Revolutions and elections and harvests. March and April for planting and sacrifices—the Bay of Pigs . . . what seed had been planted then?—and now in the fall Nixon might be elected governor of California. It would give him a powerful springboard for 1964. Kennedy would do anything to keep *that* from happening. How those two hated one another. Kennedy the rich boy; Nixon the poor boy. But Nixon was reasonable. He understood power, its limits, and remembered his obligations and debts. Kennedy did not.

He heard the stirring behind him. Keats had swung his feet over the bedside and was staring at his back. He was beyond vanity, he told himself. No. Don't lie to yourself. The blond hair. The gray eyes. The swell of his thighs. The flat stomach. The dust of crinkly golden hair there . . . godlike. But it was Keats's mind, no, his essence, his life force, his *Ch'i* Kelley wanted to drain and drink . . . at least that's what he told himself. The body acted only as a gateway, a vessel, a storage. The penetrable flesh was the

102

container of what lay beyond. But still, he wanted to be loved for his body too. He was getting old, but he was still strong, still vigorous. Vanity again.

Of course Keats looked lovingly at him. What else would he be doing? Keats was the kind of man who entered his roles totally. Keats had the actor's beautiful facility of deceiving *himself* for long periods of time, so he could act all the better. Did Keats also have the art of *projecting* the shield that rendered himself impenetrable? Had he learned it in those experiments at Harvard, or was it natural? How like himself . . .

Suddenly Kelley had a mad desire for real love. What a silly, pedestrian, childlike thing to want. Danger lay in that direction. *"If I cease to desire and remain still, the Empire will be at peace of its own accord,"* Kelley thought. If personal desire overcame him, chaos would follow. Great men's uncontrollable passions . . . They mistook their cocks for weaponry and the intensity of their orgasms for policy. Worse if the passions were directed exclusively at women. Heterosexual love brings on war and children . . . squandered *ching* instead of *huan ching pu nao*— making the semen return to nourish the brain. Squander *ching* and you try to make it up by a substitute . . . political power; money. Laura, though, she took the semen of innumerable men into herself and strengthened her blood. She understood it.

After the amenities were over—by that time they would have strolled past the oak and marble pillars—the business would begin; he and Mr. Helphand could begin their tour of the world's horizon, and review the flash points. The country of chrome, the principality of platinum, the *gubernia* of gold—South Africa had to go black, sooner or later: easier to deal with. Germanium . . . oil, the county of cobalt, Cuba, the Congo, Korea, copper, diamonds, the endless problems of Israel, that fool, DeGaulle, that greater fool, Mao, and the greatest fool of all, John F. Kennedy . . .

And what would the purists in the Central Committee want? Would it spell disaster for Khrushchev? He banged his shoe on the UN desk and played the fool, concealing wisdom behind clownishness . . . not a role many people would take on. Kennedy made other kinds of public display, and was the real fool. "There is no disaster greater than taking on an enemy too early, taking up arms when there are no arms." Or, when the arms were nuclear weaponry, as good as no arms at all.

Helphand would give him a sense of what was happening in those higher circles. Everything was coming together for Kelley's people as everything came apart for America and Russia.

That was the most dangerous moment. By that time they would have come to the stage leading to the maze . . . and then go into the sacred grove. They would enter alone, Kelley and Helphand. Keats and Oprichnik had not yet gone through their rites of passage. He had an impish thought. He would regale Helphand; he would line the labyrinth with modern minotaur images. The Shah. Kennedy. DeGaulle . . . would the *Organisation Armée Secrete* get that pompous, arrogant stork for Kelley's people? There, in the maze, the hard thinking, the bargaining, the statecraft, would begin. Later on technicians could hammer out the fine points.

"Balances, exchanges, trades, flows, reversals of flow, a control of liquidity, regulation of energy, personal, national, international; that's what it's all about," Kelley told Keats. *"'The highest good is like water, and settles where none would like to be, coming close to The Way.'* Harmonious balances: money, light, energy, must be allowed to flow along their natural courses; its concentrations. The worst thing is to administer total defeat, to definitively win. The best thing is to handle, regulate those who want to win definitively and so prevent the natural flow. Those who don't understand must be dealt with."

A slight creak of the bed. What was it about Keats that moved him so dangerously? He reviewed Keats's features one by one. What did they amount to that way? Yes, Keats was handsome, but not beautiful. And yet, somehow Keats could project great beauty. His buttocks didn't jut just right, and yet, somehow, they seemed heroic. Keats was a shapeshifter who made his body assume many disguises . . . anticipating Mr. Kelley's desire before he even knew what he wanted. Laura could do that. He wasn't so muscular, yet he convinced Kelley that each muscle was chiseled out of stone that melted to Mr. Kelley's touch alone. And those hands had killed. Warrior's flesh. That too excited.

Mr. Kelley regretted that he had never killed anyone directly. He knew it did something for you. Laura could do the same thing.

104

He had almost fallen in love with her. Imagine, a thirteen-year-old girl. She would have, like the legendary Chinese Yellow Queen, sucked him dry. What would they be like together, Keats and Laura? He could watch them kill one another.

Keats's words were full of sincerity and love. How like himself when he had been younger. What would it have been like to have had a son like Keats? A replica of himself? A blood son? No. As father and son they would kill one another too.

Keats introduced a slight tremor into his voice. Passion deferred was making him impatient, frustrated. He came a step closer. Coming to him. There. . . .

They would walk through the maze, he and Mr. Helphand, arm in arm, creating a script for the proper actors to follow when the time came. They would arrive in time at that perfect ending, the garden. By that time the broad strokes of what they would do would have been applied. The media campaign, the public relations people, the lobbyists, the distribution of information to the news media through the usual devious routes, and perhaps even the generation of scholarly analyses, and the think-tank studies. Maybe the time had come to finally propose a more formal merger between the two halves of Parvus? A marriage, dowry and all, and the parent companies . . . East of the Sun marries West of the Moon.

Keats, he knew, came from an old New England family. English roots, and before that roots in France, Normandy. Normans, Crusaders . . . Norsemen. A noble lineage, once rich and powerful, now impoverished. Along with their money, Keats's family had squandered their accumulation of *ch'i* and *te,* life force and magical virtue. He smiled; maybe what the Keats family had lost, he had accumulated. He had come up from the depths of poverty. Could genetics explain a Luther, a Lansky, a Stalin? Could genetics explain a Laura? It was not her body, her looks, not her ability to act, but her essence—all from parents who had neither beauty nor mind.

When Mr. Kelley was a child in McKeesport, Pennsylvania, he used to dream he was a changeling prince who had been slipped into someone else's life. Perhaps he had been stolen, planted in the womb of the person who acted as his mother to hide him from certain people who wanted to destroy him. And indeed

105

there *were* evil people who wanted to destroy him and millions like himself, by poverty and hunger.

So he started out to find who was after him. When he began to claw his way up, he entertained the fiction that thousands had copulated to produce him. Ancestry fascinated Kelley. He studied elites of many countries, how they triumphed, how they perpetuated themselves, how and why they seemed inevitably to decline. He studied secret societies and their breeding patterns . . . how some of them had maintained themselves through the centuries . . . Taoists, for instance; the Triads. The Eunuch-bureaucrats, once the real rulers of China and the Byzantine and Ottoman empires. The Roman system of adoptions and disadoptions. Octavian, on his way to becoming Augustus Caesar, managed to get himself adopted by the right people—Gaius Julius Caesar—and instantly acquired the proper lineage. But that hadn't been enough; history didn't delve much into who put up the money in Augustus's rise to power. It was then Mr. Kelley found the still more ancient Phoenician banking and religious society of the Oracle of Delphi, with its more ancient roots in China. They were the kingmakers; they were the king-deposers; they survived, under various names, through the ages. Delphi, the Cumaean Sybil, and perhaps, later on, the Gnostics, the Cabalists, the Jesuits themselves. Perhaps. Thus, people like himself decided that they had to go into the white heart of power, into the heart of modern Delphi.

It was in that time, 1918, that he had gravitated to Russia, into an upheaval that threatened the end of all dynasty, and found one of its guiding spirits, Mr. Helphand, who almost singlehand-edly had persuaded the Germans to do everything in their power to get Lenin out of Switzerland and into Russia. And Mr. Help-hand had initiated him into the true meanings of power. Empire without contiguous land, whose capital constantly shifted.

Mr. Kelley had studied the Mandarin system and how some Mandarin families decayed in time, lost their accumulated virtue, how their children became stupid, self-indulgent, unable to pass their examinations. Some families went out and adopted bright, tough street urchins who could be taught—if they had a head for numbers and a capability for learning classic poetry and literature. This restored vigor to the line. Or how the Church,

106

distrustful of family accumulation, tried to bypass biological family by its system of celibate priests.

That's why Kelley fought, almost singlehandedly, for a worldwide talent search after the Second World War. It would search out the brightest children all over the world, picking them out of the lower strata. This would assure loyalty. Revolution by penetration, by networks, by plants in high places. Revolution in the old way would no longer work. It was picking up where the British had left off, but without the elitist and racist attitudes of the past.

This case of Aquilino might not only be important, but interesting. A shame; caught earlier, an Aquilino might have been another Keats.

"Conventional psychological theory has it that you learn everything, forget nothing. That's why this Richard knows more than he thinks he does."

And what's more, Mr. Kelley thought, deep down, Richard Aquilino understood. He had to be prevented from knowing that he did.

"There are techniques—"

"I leave the details for you. I think however, that you should work with Laura. Laura should be your paymaster." There was no sound of protest from Keats.

Now the time had come. They would move to a higher plane. Kelley stood still, but his mind was filled with a summoning signal.

Mr. Kelley wanted another kind of continuity other than The Work. He wanted a child . . . a son. Their mating would lead to an issue . . . a kind of issue. Later, after they finished their affair, he would adopt Keats and teach him.

CHAPTER 10

EACH day that passed rendered Richard's experience on Greene Street more and more unreal. He decided something had been wrong with him. Sickness. Fever. When he was a kid he would approach the edge of hallucination. Whenever the fever got high. In a day or two he was all right again. Still, the feeling that he was being watched would not go away. He began to go through everything in his loft to see if anyone had broken in and searched it. At first he found nothing at all. His piles of notes were the same as always. He went through them. He had difficulty in understanding them. He scrawled notes in a hurry, and his handwriting was bad. There were papers of all shapes and sizes; scraps, full 8½ by 11 sheets, pieces of grocery bags, notes scrawled in the margins of magazines . . . It was a mess. But after all, if you're not a stenographer, and you're trying to write in a hurry, you make your shorthand up . . . and forget what convention, what set of abbreviations you've decided to use.

Some of the pages puzzled him. He didn't remember writing them. One sheet was written out in longhand, with every word clearly spelled out. "After all, he's not an intelligence officer, he's not a military analyst, trained to read and remember reams of material. So we've got to find a way of getting our story through to him . . ." Who had spoken that? And to whom about whom? Usually no names were used. After all, when people talk to one

108

another they take for granted who's talking to whom. "Hi. It's me." "How've you been?" That kind of thing. There were other sheets he had no memory of writing. He wished he had dated everything and had taken the trouble to put down the phone number.

The loneliness was getting to him. He took to dropping over to his sisters more and taking his nieces and nephews out for the day. But that didn't stop the loneliness from building up. That didn't stop the uneasiness. The sense that Laura was in some kind of trouble . . . something about that reminded him of listening in to Marilyn Monroe. Should he tap into her phone again? No. No. Keep away. He was through with that.

Whatever had been bothering him began to return. A relapse. Time seemed to become a little scrambled. He had periods when everything seemed to be very clear and he seemed to think that he could do anything he wanted to do. There were times when everything became fuzzy, and he was moving through mud. Times when he felt secure; times when everything became a cause for a pointless suspicion. When were the FBI, or the FCC (did they have their own police?) going to turn up? They didn't come. Ziggy was being too cautious. Would Ziggy inform the FBI . . . to save himself?

Finally, he gave in. He began to watch for the signal that indicated Laura's phone was in use. The next time it rang, he cut in. She was talking to some man. He sounded young. Her voice sounded impassive and cool. If she was in some kind of trouble, she wasn't indicating it.

"Look," the man said, "it's for his own good."

"Isn't it always?"

"So young and so cynical."

"I'm not cynical. I'm just a little tired."

"Let me plead with you. One more time."

"It's always just 'one more time.'"

"It's really the last time we'll ask you to do anything for us."

"What is it this time?"

"It's a question of delivering a message . . . so to speak. May I suggest that we get together, say the day after tomorrow, and I'll brief you. I'll throw in a very good lunch."

"Why can't you deliver this message yourself?"

109

"Frankly, because I'm not as beautiful and I don't mean as much to him. A little high drama is needed."

It was one of his famous quickies.

"Sounds more like bedroom farce to me."

"Perhaps. It's a question of getting the man to focus."

"Do I have a choice?"

"Of course you have a choice. But I'd be very disappointed if you didn't want to keep our relationship as fruitful as in the past. Just one more time, for old time's sake."

"For old time's sake."

"It's not as if it's dangerous," the man said.

"All right. Day after tomorrow. Where?"

"Why not the Chambord?"

They hung up. Was there something in her voice? The man she had been talking to immediately called someone else. A number in Washington. Richard added the number to his collection. This time, taking notes, he remembered to put the date on the notes, as well as the phone number. The first part of the conversation was devoted to chitchat, reminiscences about Harvard. After a few minutes, they got to the point. "I have a friend your friend might like to meet."

"You know how many phone calls a day I get? I have to watch out, you know. There are a lot of people who don't approve, including the bulldog. What's so special about your friend?"

"Well, I think you remember my tastes from school?"

"Could I forget? I used to envy you."

"Continue envying."

"Got a picture?"

"Right now there's one, dancing in my mind, exciting me, even as I talk to you."

"Well, it might just be arranged. I'm having a short interview with him tomorrow."

"Reminiscing?"

"No. Nowadays it's 'I can give you exactly two and a half minutes.' And at the end of two minutes and twenty-five seconds, someone appears at the door . . . What do you want out of it . . . I mean if it comes to pass?"

"I'm only concerned with the success of my friends and willing to do anything that will advance their careers."

"Which means you'll bill me later."

"Have I ever lied to you, have I ever shortchanged you?"

"No."

"Well then . . ."

And they hung up. The man in Washington then called up another Washington number and spoke to someone else. "I want you to run a check on someone. In about two or three hours?"

"Yes sir. Who?"

Laura's name was given. They hung up. Richard wondered; did she know about all this? He decided to wait and see if the first man in Washington called back the man in New York. After about three hours the call went through. "The first hurdle is passed," the man in Washington said.

"What's the next step? I'm new at this."

"The next step is I tell him and she calls him up. If he likes what he hears, then an interview is granted. After that it's chemistry. Does his prick go up or stay down. If I get a Public Service Medal, then I know all has gone well. If not, perhaps there will be a curt nod, or my next interview will be canceled."

"You people live precarious lives."

"Don't we all, John, don't we all?"

The young man in New York, the one called John—his voice sounded familiar by now; he had heard it before, more than once —called up someone, an older man by the sound of it, also familiar.

"Well, sir, it's all set up."

"I'm not so sure. She's on the other line."

The other line? What line? Laura's light was dark. She wasn't using her phone. Did she have another phone that he hadn't caught in his net?

"She's reluctant. I'm talking to her now."

"Surely she understands, sir . . ."

"It's not a matter of understanding or not understanding. She's more than bright, John. It's a question of nerve. One's nerve runs out from time to time. It happens to all of us. We only hope that it doesn't happen at a crucial time."

Richard recognized the voice. The older man. Kelley. The man

111

who had stolen her away from him. That's who it was. Why hadn't his rig picked up her other phone? They cut off. The lights went blank.

It was getting to be evening again. His head was swimming. He looked down at his notes again. He had been so wrapped up in the conversations, he forgot to write. What was it all about? Who were they talking about? Who was the important man in Washington to whom a message had to be gotten?

Her phone signaled. She was talking now to another woman . . . an old friend, someone she had gone to college with. She was half weeping. Her voice sounded so much like Marilyn Monroe's . . . on the edge of hysteria, miserable. "I can't do it. I told them I would do it, but I can't. I'm . . . You know . . . sometimes I wish that none of this had happened. Not the connection with father, not all the things that came out of it . . . I was once in love, a long time ago, before father . . . It comes and goes in waves, like a recurrent fever bout. I'm sick again. I'm caught between two forces . . . I was in love. I didn't know anything then, but maybe it was better that way. I thought we'd get married . . . settle down . . . have children . . ."

Who was "father"? Kelley?

"You're just having a bad moment, Laura. It'll pass. Marriage? How ticky-tacky. To *one* man?"

"No. You're right. But I'm caught. You know, sometimes I get a funny feeling . . . Like he's beside me or in me in some way. He looks at me and he shakes his head because he doesn't know what happened to us . . ."

"That old love?"

"Yes."

"Richard? Was that his name?"

"Yes."

"Laura. It's two different worlds, light years apart. You're just scared."

"I have reason to be."

"You've been scared before. When it's all over we'll have a few drinks and a good gossip. I wish I were in your shoes."

"No you don't."

"Oh yes I do. Just try me."

"You'll see," Laura said.

"Just try me. But I'll never see," the other woman said with longing.

"What do I do?"

"Laura, you'll sail between the rocks in great style. They'll find you a husband who's rich and famous and powerful and who's a divine lay and handsome. You'll see. It's nerves, honey, nerves."

"I need help."

"You've got help."

The other woman hung up. Richard heard Laura saying, "I wish he were here . . . I wish he were beside me."

I am, he thought. But I am.

CHAPTER 11

THE spring day was surprisingly chilly. The wind chased dust around the streets of Manhattan. Two men, one turning the corner of Thirty-fourth Street, the other walking down Sixth Avenue, almost ran into one another. One was dressed in a tan windbreaker, the other wore a heavy red-and-black plaid shirt-jacket; it was greasy. Workers, mechanics, on their lunch hour, Keats and Vassili Oprichnik. Being good at their jobs, they knew they had each shaken any possible tail. Still . . .

"Jesus, what are you doing here? I thought you were working over in Brooklyn," Vassili said.

The man in the tan poplin windbreaker said, "Yeah, I was repairing cars in Flatbush, but I couldn't stand it. Nothing happens in Brooklyn. I got a job fixing up sewing machines. Pays better and I'm back near the center of things. You?"

"Same story. Driving the truck. Thinking of moving out West one of these days. Maybe Los Angeles," Vassili said.

"Los Angeles? Jesus, you'll hate it. Hey, had lunch yet?"

"Just on my way. How about you?" Vassili was carrying a newspaper turned to the racing section.

"I ate but I have some time to kill."

The man in the plaid shirt-jacket said, "I'm going to get myself a pastrami sandwich and some french fried. Want to come along?"

114

"Why not? I'll have a cup of coffee."

They walked down Sixth Avenue, turned eastward, onto Thirty-third, came to a delicatessen and went in. The place was crowded. The hostess, dyed blond hair puffed up into a laquered shell told them "I can sit you at that table with those other people."

"Hey, how about a table for just the two of us?"

"It'll be about ten minutes."

"Which means about twenty."

"Lissen. I said ten." She was snappish. "I know my customers' habits."

She waved the big, plastic-covered menus. "Hey, five minutes early for the big salesmen. The models must be coming up today." Two people were getting up slowly, probing at their teeth with toothpicks, reaching for the coats draped over their chairs, leisurely, as the waitress was writing out their check.

The two men were seated a few minutes later. The noise covered their talk: a babble of talk, clinking plates, silverware, shouted orders.

"How's my principal eye doing?" Keats asked.

"My technician, Harkavy, has almost solved the problem. Do you know what I could get selling this to the British, the Germans, the French?"

"Vassili, how could you spend five or six million in a week? Which is about how long you'd live."

"Your field people have finally spotted us appearing to try and make contact with the kid. It took some doing. Had to do everything but sing 'The Volga Boatmen.'"

"I know. You have it?"

"It wasn't easy."

"When this is winding down, I'll have a proposition for you that you will find very attractive. I too am thinking of going into business," Keats said.

"I don't know if I want money. I want payment in services."

"Take it. It's good for your old age." He turned to the waitress. "I'll have a pastrami; it should be very lean. And on rye bread. The rye bread's fresh?"

"Yeah, the rye bread's fresh. We get it fresh-baked every day."

"That's good."

"Anything on the pastrami?"

"No. You got pickles?"

"Right there on the table."

"These are a little dry. Could you get me some fresh ones?"

"Yeah. And you?"

"A cup of coffee."

"Coffee? That's all?"

"All right, make it a Danish too. Cheese Danish."

The waitress went away, and Vassili looked after her, staring at the way her buttocks moved under her green uniform.

"Something is in the air, isn't it, Vassili? A big change."

"Suslov has not consulted with me. Bulganin is strangely reticent. No one tells me a thing."

"Why is Penkovsky spilling so much?"

"You heard?"

"I heard."

"Maybe it's part of peaceful coexistence. The great change from heavy industry to consumer goods. It's a way of saying, 'look, our intentions are good.' "

"The stuff he's passing is no good?"

"Khrushchev's deep thinkers figure that you people know it all anyway, but pretend you don't know. On the other hand, protection will be withdrawn soon from poor Colonel Penkovsky unless you people give us some sign acknowledging the gift."

"You're sure that's what's happening?"

"A humble analysis."

"You're a long way from the center of action."

"But I have what you want. Everything you ever wanted to know about Nikita Sergeievich Khrushchev."

"Medical information too?"

"Medical, psychological, and the way the juice runs down his chin when he eats, and who and how he likes to screw, and what he thinks of his daughter, to say nothing about modern art. You wouldn't believe how strong his heart is."

"How thorough is it?"

"As thorough as you wanted it to be. But what do you think you're going to learn from Nikita Sergeievich's dossier that you don't already know?"

"That's my worry. You always ask questions."

116

"That's what I learned in spy school. Ask questions. What do you want all this shit for? You going to practice voodoo on the Chairman?"

The waitress came back with the order. "You want your coffee now?"

"Please."

They finished their meal and talked about sports for a while. The man in the plaid jacket-shirt suddenly looked at his cheap watch and said, "Jesus, I gotta run . . ."

"Go ahead, it's on me."

"You're a real sport."

"Nothing is too good for the working man."

Vassili left, leaving his newspaper on the table. Keats picked up the paper and finished his meal slowly, drank his coffee, ordered another. He smoked a cigarette. He scanned the markings on the racing results. They told him where to pick up the dossier. He got the check and left.

CHAPTER 12

THE spring of 1962. The great plains of America begin to heave with autumn-planted life. People begin to move; the blood expands; hopes planted so long ago begin to thrive. The dance of spring begins; the baseball players unlimber their winter-chilled muscles. Others stretch and heft their guns, their grenades, and begin again to move through jungle, through desert, moving toward the great metropolitan granaries. Like sprouting wheat, little plots in the minds of men are nurtured. And others move among the precious grains, seeking to pull up what they consider noxious weeds. AID, Food for Peace, the Peace Corps, seeded with warriors, send their seed-ideas abroad to pluck the weeds.

In America the deadly battle had been joined in other ways. The heavy-weapons Big Army and Big Navy and Big Air Force boys—with their Minuteman, Nike-Zeus, Polaris, Skybolt, TFX—contend with those of a more subtle turn of mind; the counterinsurgency boys. The arm-twisting, the persuasion, the threats, the bribes, the lining up of congressional votes, the *quid pro quos* all continue. On the other hand, the attacks. You're soft on communism. Senators Dirksen and Keating and Goldwater rush to the attack. Cuba. Cuba. Cuba is the launching platform not just for revolution in South America, but for something more—battalions of Soviet troops. Missiles ninety miles from shore.

No, no, says The Fair Play for Cuba Committee, joined by the strangest people. Truman Capote and Lee Harvey Oswald . . . odd bedfellows. A strange restiveness has crept into domestic life. Civil Rights. Voter registration drives in Mississippi. Aspirations for freedom, food, democracy and dignity? Or was it something more insidious? Are we going to sit there and be nickeled-and-dimed to death by Lilliputians with submachine guns?

Even the new dances that are coming in, the Twist, the Mashed Potato . . . aren't they signs of America's loss of resolve . . . aren't they curiously tribal? Danced to insure the growth of the new grain?

Richard didn't read the papers. At best he watched television, and almost never the news. Whisperings of great events reached him via a low current, fed over wire, thrown through the air from tower to tower, and some now coming in after having gone up and down to a satellite.

Who was this "he" that had disturbed Laura so much? She needed someone. She needed *him.* She had *not* forgotten, after all these years. And maybe there was some connection between his feeling of being watched, and Laura, and this "him" to whom some awful message had been addressed.

He had lived with loneliness all his life. Still, he needed people. He began to spend even more time at his sisters' houses, playing with his nephews and nieces, returning to his lonely loft to listen. He lay on his bed and imagined little dramas. They got out of hand and became runaway fantasies. They entered his dreams. His jobs fell away. He was going to run out of money soon.

His father called him up. "I'm glad you've applied for that job."

What job?

"I think working for the government is a good idea. It's a secure job. Good hours. Good pay. Security. Of course I know that you can't tell me what it's about."

"No, pop. I can't," Richard said. What job?

"It has something to do with radio?"

"Something."

"Or telephones."

"Something like that." What job?

"The men who came to interview us said it did, but they wouldn't tell us any more. It was . . . what? A security check."

119

"Yeah. A security check."

"The questions they asked about you. About us. At first we thought you had done something bad."

"Pop, come on."

"I know, I know. But your mother . . ."

Something played around the edge of his memory. His mother. Her suspicions. Something that had happened a long, long time ago. What had he been? Five?

"You know, in Europe, where we came from, in Italy, every time they came around asking questions, it meant something bad. That's why we came to this country."

"I know, pop."

"They visited your sisters too. They even talked to the kids. I guess they have to make sure. Does it pay well?"

"Does what pay well?"

"The job."

What job? "Pretty well."

"Can I ask how much?"

How much did this supposed job pay? What was a believable figure? "Fifteen thousand to start."

"That's very good."

"Well, I know you and mom won't believe it, but I got skills, pop, and experience. I did work for the telephone company."

"Of course. I forgot."

His father never forgot a thing. Was he trying to tell Richard something? Was he scared?

"Listen, Richard, what if you came over for supper soon. It's been such a long time. Your mother would be very happy. We only see you, what, maybe three times a year? And then only at your sisters' houses."

"Well . . . maybe . . . soon . . ."

"Listen, Richard. I know we've bothered you a lot. I know how these things are. I had the same fights with my father and there came a time when I didn't want to see him or my mother again, not ever. I left, I wandered around, I got jobs. We got married, your mother and I. And she had gone through the same thing. We both understand these things. Well, we had to leave Italy and we never got to see them again. They were killed during the war.

120

I missed the chance; so did your mother.

"I promise you. No arguments. No questions. After all, you have a job now. We were wrong about you. Yes, I'll say that, and so will your mother."

"All right . . . all right. I'll come."

"When?"

"Next week."

"When next week?"

"Wednesday."

"All right. That's good. Take good care of yourself. You're all right? No colds, no flu?"

"Come on, pop."

His father laughed. "It just sounds as if your nose is stuffed, or something. I don't hear you so clear."

And his father hung up.

Richard sat there for a long time. "I don't hear you so clear . . ." his father said. His nose was not stuffed. He was fine. Except for the residual sickness, whatever it was. Who were the people who had come to interview his parents and his sisters? He had applied for no job . . . no job at all. He sensed "them" now, all around him, "them" in his wires, in his receiver and his earpiece, inhabiting all of this equipment.

His parents weren't dummies. They had spoken to him many times what Europe had been like . . . why they had come here in '34, '35 or whatever . . . around that time, running away from the stifling air in Italy to a freer climate. His father had been trying to tell him something in his gossipy way. His parents were worried, and now he had drawn the attention of "them" to his parents and his sisters . . . What was he going to do? Just stop? How could he stop when Laura was in such trouble? Maybe if he went to visit her. . . .

He walked into the Figaro cafe, as if there had been no argument with Ziggy. As always, Ziggy was there, Marvin, some of the others. Tarzan made room next to Ziggy.

"It's been a long time," Ziggy said.

"I'm sorry . . ."

"Don't worry about it, Richie. You're in trouble?"

"I don't know."

"You're in trouble, believe me. And don't worry. We checked the table for a bug."

Checked the table for a bug? He wouldn't have thought of such a thing.

"And if they are pointing a directional mike at us, we're making enough noise to cover what we have to say. What happened? Tell me all."

And Richard began to tell Ziggy the whole story—what he'd done, how he'd violated every precept Ziggy had given him. He downplayed Laura. He couldn't help himself. He didn't want to look like a snoop.

"You did all that? You got *that* high up the ladder? No wonder they came around. We got to talk the know-how sometimes but the question now is what to do. The first thing is to lay off."

But Laura was in trouble.

"You don't like that idea?"

"Someone I know is in trouble."

"But not as much trouble as you're in—or maybe us. We had visitors too. We just laid off for a while, gave them a story that we wanted to sell what we had to the phone company, but we'll never do it again. But we never got anywhere near the places you did. Jesus, I can barely wait to hear—"

"So what do I do?"

"What do *we* do. The fucks. The fucks. All over the world, they're the same. They sit on your talents. They only let you do things if you work for them."

"Who's them?"

"Mother Bell, who else? The phone company's worse than the CIA. They have their *own* CIA. Aside from your friend who's in trouble, what did you hear that was so special?"

"I don't know. Nothing."

"All right. Listen. You begin to taper off. You can't tell me what kind of trouble your friend is in? No. You don't want to? You don't trust us? Never mind. It's going to take a little time to set up, but we'll do it. I want to fight those bastards . . . I want to have some fun with them."

"Ziggy, that's crazy—"

"No it's not. I'm going to give you a number. If you're in real

122

trouble, you call up this number. If I can't be reached, then you'll get instructions on what to do next. I'm going to give you a simple set of codes and the real story of what to do will be buried inside of the information you get over the phone. When we're ready to establish contact, you'll be told that too, but not in so many words. I'm going to write this down. You have to look at it and memorize it. Then burn it. Who's got some paper? Marvin, listen to this. What am I going to do with the paper without a pencil?"

Ziggy was bent over, peering through his thick lenses, close enough to see it with his almost-blind eyes.

"All right, read this, Richard," he whispered. "Got it memorized? You see how the system works? What are you doing?"

"Putting it in my pocket."

"Put it in your mind. Burn the paper. This will take a few weeks to set up right, but by tomorrow night we'll have the beginnings of a network going, looking out for you. Then by summer, it will mostly be in place. For fall, I'm going to have a Science Fiction convention. Maybe we'll do it in Boston. And that's when we'll really be ready to go. September."

"September?"

"Sure. We'll get all the space freaks together. The people with the tinfoil suits, and the glass-globe space helmets, the ones who have already been to the moon, never mind what Kennedy says. And in the middle of it, there we'll be. Listen, this isn't the time or the place. You should be going soon, but I have to hear what you heard that got those people after you . . ."

But Richard couldn't stop listening. When he got home, he was determined not to do it again. But then the trouble started. He turned off the lights on his great plastic board, but they remained burning. He even pulled the plug. They continued to burn. There was something wrong with it. Was it melting? It wavered. He went over and felt it. It still felt solid. But his hands felt sticky, as if parts of it had stuck to his fingers and palm. He tried to back off from it. It stuck and attenuated, finer and finer, till it was a set of thin, glistening, transparent threads along which the little lights had become imbedded, and were drawn thin, finer and finer. "Jesus." He shook his hands. They wouldn't come off. He felt the pulsations, words, messages, conversations, going

123

through his body. His words, thrown into the wires, so many times, were now flowing back to him. He heard himself saying, "Look, sir, there's danger."

And heard the President answering. Laura's voice coursed through him. They had a three-way conversation. But he knew it was impossible. And other voices, beginning to chime in, all growing in intensity and strength, until his whole body was animated by conversations.

After a long while it passed, leaving him shaking. He was going mad. "They" were trying to put madness into him. He was sweating, but everything was still there, in place, normal. The board was dark. He was weak. He lay down again. And that was, he was to think later, the first of his spells. He tried to remember what it was that he had heard . . . but he couldn't . . . not clearly. Something very dangerous. There was a little relapse toward morning. A voice said, "Surgical strike . . ." And he felt a knife-point jab of pain in his groin.

CHAPTER 13

A few weeks passed. Mr. Barnstable didn't seem interested. Ficino was worried. Should he telephone Barnstable? No. Wait. Had anything gone wrong? Was Barnstable tormenting him, playing with him? Carol noted his preoccupation and wondered what was wrong. She wondered if she had anything to do with it.

Finally, Barnstable called. "I was very impressed with our lunch, Dr. Ficino, and I've tried to convey that impression to my superiors."

His voice was definitely fruity, Sidney thought.

"You know we're under constant pressure, bombarded by grant proposals. We have great difficulty in deciding what to fund and what to reject. Coffin doesn't want to throw its money around . . . and yet, our mandate is to spend. I've talked about your work with our president. He's impressed, as I am, but there's a 'but' . . . ."

"What's the 'but'?"

"I wonder if we might meet again; I have a proposal. The Harvard Club, shall we say this Thursday?"

"I'd be delighted. . . ."

They met. During lunch, Barnstable seemed reluctant to discuss grants. They talked about many things. Barnstable went through what seemed to be his whole life: childhood, family,

125

education. He name-dropped, using first names and even nick-
names. Ficino thought he would go mad. Twelve-thirty passed on
to one o'clock and became two-thirty. The dining room thinned
out. They had dessert; they had a few cups of coffee; they had
brandy. Then Barnstable suggested they go down to one of the
lounges and talk a little longer.

They sat side by side on a couch. Barnstable put his attaché
case on his knees, opened it, and took out a large, thick envelope.
"In a sense—and you will understand our caution—we want to
make very sure. After all, the disbursing of money, even for
worthy research, is not merely up to me. We could get hung up
for a year."

Ficino couldn't help saying, out loud, "A year!"

Barnstable put his hand on Ficino's thigh and squeezed, com-
fortingly. "I want to move ahead on this just as much as you do."

Ficino wondered what "this" was.

"If I come up with good projects, I move up. Now I'm going
to propose something. It's . . . well, in the nature of an experiment." Barnstable kept his hand next to Ficino's thigh. "To be
frank, we're asking you to do some speculative work for us and
then, why then we'll see. I don't want to deliver any hard promises. This is a humiliating position for a person of your reputation and I will understand perfectly if you just reject us. But it's
not up to me alone."

"What is it?"

"Some of your remarks about the future of Distant Analysis—
personality diagnosis at a distance—really fascinated me and, for
that matter, fascinated my superiors. I didn't do such a great job
in transmitting your thought—but then, I'm only a layman talking to laymen."

Ficino started to protest that he hadn't said any such thing,
but stopped himself. "I'd certainly be glad to make a presentation—"

"Their procedure is not to talk to anyone directly, unless they
know them very well indeed. I am the sole intermediary. This
envelope contains a compilation of raw data about some nine
individuals. What would be useful would be to have an evaluation
of these people. How they are likely to react in certain stress or
crisis situations. The material, alas, is spotty. Some of it is soft and

speculative. Other parts contain some useful, hard medical and diagnostic data, in both stress situations and in times of normality.

"I must admit, Dr. Ficino, that of all the grant prospects I have interviewed I tend to favor you and the approach of your little research group. It should be bigger. Much bigger." Barnstable smiled charmingly. It made Ficino nervous. He hoped he concealed his feelings.

"What I'd like you to do is to make an evaluation of these people and get it back to me as soon as possible. Dr. Ficino, let me be honest. I'm taking a big risk, giving you this material. It's highly sensitive, and so I don't have to tell you—"

"Confidential, of course."

"There are no clues to the subjects' identities. But . . ."

What he's telling me is that if I do this right, Sidney thought, I should know who these people are.

"After I've seen your evaluations, you might work up a draft proposal for a grant. I would look it over, float it around to certain Coffin members, get their reaction, do a little politicking. Then, together, we might work over the final draft. Most people don't know it, but we at the Foundation tend to favor a certain proposal style. You'd be surprised how many worthy proposals are shot down because of style and style alone. I could be very helpful in this regard. Then . . ." Barnstable smiled. His smile was brilliant, engaging, seductive. His gray eyes seemed to emerge suddenly from behind his glasses . . . commanding. Sidney had to admit he looked quite beautiful.

Barnstable leaned back, curved back, almost spineless. He sipped his coffee. Dabbed at his lips delicately. "What might follow is . . . No, let's take the positive approach and make the best case. A six month's grant for starters. The go-ahead to hire more research assistants. More equipment, or hook-ins to equipment in other centers—telephone links. Some wonderful technology coming down the line. Expanded facilities. Help for the Hospital, and the University, of course. Then, a breakthrough. And perhaps, after that, a conference. Why not Jamaica? The Bermudas? Addis. Everyone likes to conference at Addis.

"Yourself convening the conference. The most important names in neurobiology. A few stars to bring the others along; after all, don't want to miss an important event. Travel expenses.

Honoraria. Press coverage. People would be scrambling to come aboard. When you present your paper—and your assistant; I note that your names frequently appear as co-authors—it will command attention. The first conference on . . . 'Remote Assessment Profiles.' Can't call it Distant Influence—the Russians have the corner on that title-market—so it's R.A.P."

Ficino had always had a suspicion about the way things got done. Now he knew. Did he dare ask, *why me;* would it spoil his chance?

"You're thinking, why me?" Barnstable said. "Aren't you?"

"It crossed my mind."

"Delightfully understated. In the first place, you are not the only 'me.' You're the best of the 'me's.' Look, what I said about you being one of the best is not rhetoric. I conned you not. I've really read your work—yours and Dr. Rothschild's—although I admit it was hard sledding, and I've had a Harvard education, postgraduate work at Oxford. But I also verified it with some experts. You've got something extra. Personal presence. You can sell it. Scholarship, sad to say, is not enough. You're credible in the community; you'd be surprised at those who are jealous of you and have held you down. But is all this enough? No. Prestigious figures who have arrived tend to be obdurate, hardened and hidebound, very jealous of their domains. People who are relatively unknown are flexible and open. I also admit to you that I have a hidden agenda, which you've already suspected.

"I do some public relations consultation for a number of electronic firms on the side. Radio, radar, medical telemetry—Distant Influence—telephony, that kind of thing. That's where the wave of the future lies. That's where real Distant Influence is going to go. Think of two miniaturized devices in a telephone. They would record your blood pressure, your heartbeat, your brain waves, monitor stress, do chemical analysis of your breath, all through your voice and your breath. Well, that's a one-way system. Supposing that there could also be feedback. The opposite of diagnosis is treatment. Of course that's crudely put, but you see where we are heading . . ."

"Are there such things?"

"Not yet. But it's the wave of the future. The medical and biological establishment, the old guard, exercises control over the flow of funds; foundation, university and government funding for research. These are obdurate people committed to their pet theories.

"I'm going to send you some more material—and again, I don't have to tell you it's sensitive—about ongoing experimentation. You should get thoroughly acquainted with it. Unfortunately, most of it's been carried out by electronic technicians, not real medical people. What we need is an interdisciplinary mix. A team. We need people who can work in concert, as you and Dr. Rothschild do. Let me make an educated guess. She has the intuitive sense and you provide the analytical power. Am I right?"

"Well, yes—"

"Perhaps it's better that, well . . . you don't have to talk to her about this yet."

"Why not?"

"Well, yes, you do have a . . . relationship."

How did he know that?

"You'll ask her to help you with these . . . R.A.P.'s." Barnstable laughed. "I'd do the same thing. But the less she knows, the more her intuitive processes and powers will be sharpened, don't you think?"

CHAPTER 14

HOLCOMB was becoming more edgy every day. The Russians had finally shown up and tried to establish contact with Aquilino. But something had scared them, or Aquilino, off. Something smelled wrong. Holcomb couldn't put his finger on it. He had questioned Morrison again and again, walked him through it. What was it? The contact was too clumsy . . . too obvious.

The effects of Keats's spell were wearing off. If he dared, he would have asked someone to privately check his CIA files about his short imprisonment in Moscow, but to do so would raise awkward questions, unwanted attention. He didn't like the tenor of Morrison's secret reports to him; Morrison felt that something was wrong and he didn't know what. The drugs Keats was using on Aquilino—where had he gotten them from? What were they, exactly? Aquilino was becoming unstable, panicky. Would his mind be wrecked in the process? Keats, that pretty Harvard boy, was fumbling the ball. Or was he covering up the real operation? Was Keats *protecting* Aquilino? Oversubtle. He should never have let Keats play a mind-game with him and talk him into anything this elaborate. He had been faked out, outmaneuvered, outflanked, and he would have to ride it through to the end.

Was Keats a double? Holcomb smoked cigarettes. The air was full of smoke shadows. His hands were spread flat on Keats's file, as if the palms could absorb knowledge. The cigarette stuck up delicately between his thick first and second fingers. A small glow in the darkness. Put the cigarette coal to Aquilino's balls and . . . really, it should be so simple. Hot ashes fell on the back of his hand. He held it still. Self-punishment. Next to it was the complete Aquilino file. Holcomb sensed gaps. He'd gone over it four times: memos, transcripts, copies of all of Aquilino's scribbled notes to himself—codes or cryptograms?—lists of telephone numbers, names, schematics, circuits. The government was in for a real shocker. Security was a sieve. The government should have built a self-enclosed and totally secure communications system during the Second World War, when it had the chance.

He could have sent the information of what was happening through a back channel, bypassing the usual chain, right on up to Langley, but they'd have questions and move in on his operation. They'd also question why he was running the operation this way. He had to route his reports right on up to the legal counsel of the Coffin, this Mr. Kelley. Kelley was supposed to send them on to Langley. No direct contact. Langley would send down instructions.

The worst part was, he was beginning to doubt his own operation. Holcomb had been offered the job when he came home from Europe. He was looking for an assignment at home. It was agreed he would "retire" to this job. He had caused enough waves. Did the chain of command really to go Langley, or branch off somewhere else from this Mr. Kelley? He had assumed the operation was a Company one, but now he didn't know anymore. Something smelled wrong. How long did Keats have the Aquilino files in his possession? Time enough to have them edited and retyped? Just might have. Holcomb sensed gaps and insertions. The tapes had gaps in them too, but there might be an explanation for that. Aquilino wasn't at his listening post all the time.

Holcomb backtracked along Keats's history, looking for some point in time when Keats could have been turned around, or double-recruited. After he had joined the agency? Doubtful. Before joining the agency? Maybe it had happened in college. Was he a sleeper? College was when they got Burgess and Maclean. Harvard or Yale, that was like Cambridge or Oxford. Makes them snotty; think they're gods. Keats had participated in some high-level, experimental intelligence-related psych

131

programs at Harvard. Mind control, mind liberation. What was *that* all about? There was a gap in Keats's file. Also a higher classification; neither Holcomb nor anyone at his level had a need to know. Refer to . . .

No, Holcomb couldn't send for those other files without causing more trouble than he could handle. After all, it figured that Keats had friends in high places. What the hell had gone on at Harvard? Or maybe it happened in graduate school, the London School of Economics.

Someone comes to recruit you. Join the CIA, or whatever. Or maybe it's your professor. Lots of fun. Adventure. The Great Game. Christopher Marlowe was an agent. Sir Philip Sidney. John Donne. Sir John Dee, Beaumarchais, Byron, Daniel Defoe, Roger Bacon, T. S. Eliot . . . And hadn't Dante himself done propaganda work for the great banking house of Bardi? Good company, right up there with the greats. You say, sounds interesting. The recruiter says, we'll be in touch. But there's a watcher . . . maybe another student . . . maybe another professor, waiting to move in. The second recruiter says, *he's* the next step up the ladder . . . or there is a parallel ladder. He's friendly, warm, and takes the trouble to speak your language. You like him. He likes you. He says, for you we have special plans. Why waste your talents in mere spooking? Deeper cover inside of a cover. Chinese boxes. Maybe the second recruiter even gives you an assignment. A small thing. Who says it has to be from *our* side? Why not *theirs? They* have their talent spotters who follow *our* talent spotters. Before you know it, you're working for the competition . . . no, *a* competition, one among many, Russian, British, French. American society was porous like that.

The Russians? For once in his life he wanted to have a heart-to-heart talk with some Russians . . . certain Russians. His great enemy, El Supremo, for instance. There were times when you traded, even with your personal enemy, the man who has tortured you.

If he were to do it right he would have to spend days, weeks, going over the files, checking, cross-checking, building up a real story. He didn't have the personnel to assign. He had to keep running things from day to day. He was no longer in the field, didn't control his assets directly anymore. Logically, the only

132

kind of action he should take was to get help. Where? That presented problems. And he *did* have a wife . . . true, they had little to do with one another anymore. He had two kids, one in college. He was building up a good pension. He had to be careful and wait for somebody else to make a big mistake.

The fact of the matter was that he no longer trusted his own government. Rumors circulated; the agency itself was honeycombed by tunneling moles. Internecine warfare raged quietly, bureaucratic combat just as deadly as the real kind. The FBI fought with the CIA; Naval, Army and Defense Intelligence were at everyone's and one another's throats. The National Security Agency was saying that future intelligence gathering would be exclusively electronic; get rid of the field assets. Rumor was, Mafia hit men were being used instead of their own people. The intellectuals said that intelligence should be *all* analysis. Read the trends. Do it from a desk. Reading! Jesus! The Old Guard, the Ivy Leaguers, wanted to be just like the British; they had a foolish love for disguises, trickery, and crazy weaponry . . . plastic guns you could conceal up your asshole. Even Business was beginning to complain about the Company, calling *it* Big Brother. The Company had become so big that it was dividing into a thousand autonomous duchies—intelligence feudalism. Dukes and counts and knights were out to get one another. Data, information, intelligence became sacred treasure.

But the worst of all, really, was that there were moles, agents of influence, among the President's close advisors. Intellectuals. Closet socialists. So *many* Ivy League types. The place was riddled. The best agent is the agent who doesn't know he's an agent. Kennedy didn't trust his own CIA, not after the Bay of Pigs. Rumors of his setting up rival operations. So naturally the Company didn't trust Kennedy and his advisors.

You develop an instinct. He made a quick survey of the operational failures. What faction in the Company had initially backed Castro's revolution? Why had that crazy Bay of Pigs operation been mounted in the first place? Who lost Egypt to the Russians? What had led to that fancy fiasco in Eastern Europe? Abortive uprisings in Poland and East Germany. The Hungarian Revolution. Total defeat. Holcomb had lost a string of assets stretching all the way from Berlin to Warsaw and Budapest. Incompetency?

Yes. Stupidity? That too. But what else?

He lit another cigarette. The flare of the match illuminated his office. He scanned it fast. An exercise. He reviewed what he had seen. Always good to keep your hand in. He had a little difficulty in remembering everything he had seen in the short flash of light. He was getting older; losing the touch. If his life depended on remembering, he would be dead. He got up and walked around the room in the dark. He touched things and identified them by feel. He felt better.

He needed help. He was isolated. Should he just have Keats killed, do it *his* way? Yes, but not yet. Without Keats he would not get at Aquilino and his control. Who could he get to do it? People all over the world owed him favors. Keats was covering himself nicely. He and Keats were inextricably intertwined. Was Keats going to kill *him?* Perhaps. Sooner or later, yes. Did the thought scare him? Well, he had time. Keats had him frozen in place, but Keats *needed* him, too. What scared him worst, he decided, was the chaos.

In times like these, what do you do? You don't know who to trust. You create a shadow network . . . a one-time intelligence operation. An informal network built on favors owed. You pretend you still have the power and you place yourself at the center of an operational universe. Your helpers have no need to know: they owe you. He had done it before.

He reached for the phone; what time was it in Berlin?

He remembered; no. They would be listening. Aquilino might be watched, but the listening post had new listeners . . . his own subordinates, patched into Aquilino's system.

The old procedures. When modern equipment is unreliable, you do it by hand. The thought made him feel good. It was what he was best at. It was what he had done for so many years.

Holcomb would force the issue. He would stage an explosion of impatience and temper and insist Keats shit or get off the pot. Begin putting on the pressure faster. Two weeks . . . it was all he would give Keats.

134

CHAPTER 15

WHEN they appeared again, the men had been very nice about it. They were sympathetic, almost apologetic. They had come into the Aquilinos' little office and sat down. They were offered coffee. No? Tea. No? Richard's mother had come around from her desk, pulling her chair after her. One of the men noted that she was a big woman. She was wearing a smock and her hands were in her pockets. The father had come from his desk, on which were spread the account books, and had brought his chair with him. They sat there, almost knee to knee, in a tight little circle. One of the men reached into his pocket and pulled out a small notebook and turned to the middle.

"You have more questions?" Richard's father asked.

Outside, in the other room, some men came and went. Out in the yard, back of the apartment house, the lot, the heaps of junk dappled by sunlight and passing clouds.

"I don't know how to say this, Mr. and Mrs. Aquilino, but we think that your son's in some kind of trouble." He sensed the mother's sudden tension.

"Could I ask again who you are from?" the father asked.

"Sure could." They both pulled out identification. "We're from the FCC."

"FCC?"

"Federal Communications Commission."

"So what's Richard done?"

"To begin with, he's listened in, through the telephone, to a lot of people. He's overheard a lot of private conversations; that's against the law."

"That's not a nice thing. My son did that?"

"Your son, sir."

"He shouldn't do such things, should he, dear?" The mother didn't move. She was the kind, one of the men noted, to whom her children were always right, no matter what they did. He had met the type before. He wondered if they could understand the nature of what Richard Aquilino had done. How could such simple Europeans understand high technology, or, for that matter, spying? He looked at the other one; Corson. Corson was impassive. He was ready, if he had to, to play the heavy.

"How did he do it?"

"How is a very complicated question, Mr. Aquilino. Let's leave it at this. He found a way to bug . . ."

"Bug?"

"Tap."

"Tap. What is to tap?"

Morrison noted something peculiar. They were Italian but they didn't speak with Italian accents. He would ask about that later. "Listen in to."

"He could do that?"

"He found a way."

"All right, so tell him not to do it."

"It's not as easy as that."

"There's a fine?"

"Usually."

"So fine him; I suppose you have to."

"It's not as easy as that."

"He has to go to court? Jail?"

"It's not as easy as that. True, he's violated more laws than we can count . . ."

"By just listening in to someone—"

"A few hundred people."

"My goodness. You hear that, mama." He never called her that; it was a signal. She shook her head. "Okay. So we'll tell him and that will be the end. He's really a good boy."

136

Morrison sighed. There was still no use for Corson. "He's listened in to some very high government people, VIP's."

"VIP's?"

"Stands for Very Important People. The point is, Mr. Aquilino, that he's overheard matters of importance, perhaps involving matters of national security."

"You're saying he's a spy? Is that what you're saying, he's a spy? Richard? Excuse me, Mr. . . . please, let me see that card again."

"Morrison."

"Mr. Morrison. A spy?"

"Might be."

"Excuse me again, Mr. Morrison. A spy has to be smart. Am I right? It has been the burden of our life that Richard has not been . . . well, too bright."

"He's been bright enough," Corson growled.

"It's just that . . . well, he may have fallen into bad company," Morrison said.

"Who?"

"We don't know. We do know that there is contact."

"Who, the Russians?" Richard Aquilino's father asked.

"Maybe."

"Oh my God. You hear that, mama? The Russians? No. Not him. He's a good boy. He's patriotic, very patriotic. He couldn't have done that of his own free will. I'll tell you the truth about something. He was always a little ashamed of us because we weren't really American. We weren't born here, but I mean we're citizens."

"We know."

"We came here. We had a few cents. We built a small business. It does pretty well. Richard could have gone to college, like his sisters—"

"Yes, we know." Morrison had always been uncomfortable putting pressure on innocent relatives.

"In Europe, I was something of a scholar, sure, self-educated. I have respect for learning, wherever it comes from."

"Look, Mr. Aquilino. We know this. But that's beside the point."

"He played around with the radio, even when he was a little kid. That's fine for a hobby, Richard, I said, but what are you

137

going to do when you grow up?"

"Well, Mr. Aquilino, we see what he's done when he grew up," Corson said.

"The arguments we had about it—"

"Sure. Look—"

"What kind of Very Important People?"

"Some senators. Some business people. A few military people. The point isn't so much what he heard, but who his contacts are and what he told them about what he heard."

"And you think Russians?" The father shook his head.

Morrison and Corson were getting nervous about the mother. She said nothing at all. They knew she understood English, that she ran the business.

"Look," Morrison said, "if the Russians feel that we are moving in, they might do something. Or if Richard decides he doesn't want to continue doing what he's doing, they might apply pressure in other ways."

"What kind of ways?"

"On you."

"On *us.*"

"Yes, sure, hostages. Look, I'll be straight with you. They might want to get at you to put pressure on him. Maybe we should protect you."

"Protect us? How? Police? We run a business, we can't have police around here. It would scare off the customers."

"Well, it might happen that you might want to take a vacation."

"Where?"

"All expenses paid, until this is over. We want you to think about it and we'll be back in a few days, a few weeks . . ."

"But our son."

"Don't mention anything to him. It'll only be worse. We're pretty sure that he doesn't know what he's doing and we want to find out how it all works. Be patient. Have a little faith in us. And start winding down the business for a while. You need a small vacation."

"This is so sudden, so shocking. Give us a little time to think . . ."

"Sure, but if anything should . . . well, bother you, here's my card. Call up this number any time, night or day."

The men got up and left. Richard's parents sat there for a while. Richard's mother took her hand off the gun and out of her pocket. Her fists were clenched. She opened her mouth. Her husband turned his eyes toward the door: a warning. They got up and went outside, into the junkyard. They walked in the bright sunlight, a big woman and the little man.

"So that's what his talk was all about. NSAM–100, eh? Why weren't we warned?" the father said.

"Samael, who are they? Americans or the Russians? You think it's him?"

"Does it matter, Lilly?"

"I told you to leave him alone, Sam," she burst out. "I told you to stop with those stories . . ."

"Lilly . . ."

"I should have killed them . . ."

"Better you didn't. Well, there's no help for it, we have to act."

"Leave him?"

"No, we'll be watching him. Come, there's a lot to do."

CHAPTER 16

SIDNEY Ficino went back to his office with the case histories in a state of high excitement. He left instructions that he was not to be disturbed by anything. He sent a note to Carol Rothschild, putting off their evening sex. It would leave her puzzled and disturbed, but that was good; it would make him more desired afterward. He called his wife and said he would be staying very late, maybe sleep over. They had a short and bitter argument until he slammed the phone down on her. He had never gone this far with his wife. Good. If this worked out, he would leave her. The children? He would deal with them later. They were almost old enough to be on their own. He took the nine stapled sheaves of paper out of the thick envelope and began to skim them. He wanted an overview of the territory; he would go back and read them more carefully afterward.

Seven men; two women. In most cases, the material was sparse, abstracted. Each case history ended with a hypothetical crisis situation and the question: how would the subject probably react?

Two of the case histories included complete medical workups and history . . . electrocardiograms . . . EEGs . . . injuries . . . diseases reaching back to infancy . . . chemical analyses . . . psychological and social material . . . work records . . . a series of past stress situations, times of crisis, general observations about

140

how the person had reacted to each situation . . . sexual habits. There was nothing specific to identify the subject.

The first two were political figures. Statesmen. Leading national figures. Something familiar about them. The third was an important figure in medicine. Something familiar about him too . . . a medical czar. Physical characteristics. Speech patterns . . . control of a large medical facility . . . a general hospital . . . public service in Washington . . . international conferences . . . National Institutes of Health . . . presidential commissions . . .

Philemon Baird! The consummate health politician! That's who it was. Philemon Baird held a stranglehold on grants and mental health in America. And it must have been Baird who stood in his way in the past. There were clues in the case history; clues that would help Ficino in the future. He now knew of some of Philemon Baird's desires . . . some weird peccadillos . . . This discovery made the first two cases seem more familiar and the fifth and sixth almost recognizable. Were they all *linked?*

Ficino put the case history down and tried to control his excitement. It would get in the way of his analysis of the other cases. He picked up the fifth case, the first woman. Familiar. Familiar. He knew her. He stopped himself from naming the name to himself, the way he deferred an orgasm. He went back to the first case, the first statesman. And then, suddenly, it was easy. Why hadn't he seen it the first time around? It had to be President Kennedy. No, it couldn't be. He shouldn't even be looking at something like this. He was shocked.

He went back to Philemon Baird. Baird's crisis situation was this: this "hypothetical" and prestigious figure was asked to fund research with living subjects—delicate experiments that might cost them their health, their sanity, even their lives. What moral struggle would take place in his mind and how would it be resolved? Philemon Baird? The strong electroshock and lobotomy advocate, the advocate of drugs, tranquilizers, stimulants, and just about anything else? Half his cases, it was rumored, were experiments on healthy people. Wouldn't hesitate for a second.

He went back to the first "statesman." A confrontation with another world statesman which threatened his position, if not his whole thinly disguised constituency. Which would he choose;

141

keep his position or endanger his constituency? The first statesman's opponent in the crisis was—of course, the second case history. Clearly the man would defend his position and take on the highest risks to do so.

Thus, the second case belonged to . . . Clearly, in spite of the masking, it could only be Khrushchev. The experimental and hypothetical crisis situation was not the Bay of Pigs, but an event Ficino had never heard of . . . perhaps it was still an experiment, a simulated global crisis. That shoebanger? Short, pudgy, pugnacious, communist . . . He wouldn't hesitate.

Ficino put the folders down. Why was he entrusted with such cases? Why had he been given the medical histories, which looked perfectly accurate? Where did they come from? Move on. Come back to the others. Calm down, Sidney Ficino told himself.

The fourth case was that of an older man, about sixty-five, a figure of command . . . perhaps a banker, rich, powerful, a maker and shaker, moving in a world up there above his imagination . . . No medical data. All the documentation was the most fuzzy, merely speculative. Much more in Carol's line . . . *Carol! The fifth case history was Carol's! And the sixth was himself!* He took deep, calming breaths. He didn't know whether to be frightened or proud. He was being entrusted with heavy sensitive material. He went back to the fourth case. Bisexual. Rich. Poor origins, risen to the top. Not a well-known figure, but a broker of power. What was it that a broker did? Ficino had no experience with such people. The crisis situation involved a conflict of interest. The "banker" had investments in certain foreign countries. And yet, at the same time, his own country, the United States, had bad relations with a number of those countries. In the case of a threat of war, who would the "banker" back? Off the top of his head, Ficino thought that such a man would have no morals, no allegiance to anything except himself and his investments . . . But no . . . leave that part to Carol.

The fifth case, Carol's. Professional attainments in social work. She comes to a crisis in her life. She changes her profession and her life. She goes back to school and becomes a lawyer. She goes to work for a prestigious law firm. There, she exhibits superb abilities. She will rise to the top . . . in time. She has an affair with one of the senior partners, her immediate superior. In the long

142

run, she is smarter and perhaps tougher than her boss. Aspects of her life Ficino had never known about . . . were disturbing . . . Some gleanings from the psychoanalysis she had gone through. Some insight into her latest sexual partner . . . She manipulated her partner without knowing she did. No. Absolutely startling. The lawyer had actually been a virgin until she slept with her boss. Her situation, like the one before, was a conflict-of-interest situation. She was offered a case that belonged to her boss. Her boss was about to make a terrible blunder. She sees he cannot handle it. What does she do? Warn the client? Perhaps take the case away from him? The warning message Barnstable had given him was clear. Tell her nothing . . . yet. He leaned back and closed his eyes. He was a little hurt by what the case speculated, what she thought of him. He thought of the Carol he made love to, twice a day, and *this* Carol . . . He grew excited. No. It was a matter of controlling her. They were wrong. Why should he assume they were right?

He read the sixth case—himself—eagerly, as if reading about someone who was very familiar, and yet a stranger. Who had been spying on him and Carol? What else could Barnstable be but CIA? Where else could such material have come from? He blushed. He was spared nothing. His pretensions were exploded. But his brilliance and drive were noted. His morality . . . "His ethics are such that he would be completely cooperative in any phase of our program, regardless of how revolutionary it may be." His marriage was described. His impossible situation at home. His children. His wife's vindictiveness. Some notes on how he and Carol . . . Carol's restiveness . . . her guilt . . . her impatience with him; when was he going to get the divorce? Her weaknesses, longings, needs he had never seen. Their two histories did something peculiar to him . . . they excited him. There was something sexual about them. He wished Carol was here. He would deal with her in another way . . . The crisis situation was very much what was happening to him now. And instead of being unresolved, for him to figure out, there *was* a resolution to the case. Just what he was going to do. A brief vision of the future. What successes flowed from his decision. Exciting. *Get on with it. Get on with it.*

He sent out for sandwiches and coffee. It was getting very late.

143

The rest of his office, beyond the pool of light, was in darkness. What did they have there? Microphones? A camera? My God. It depressed him and cooled off his excitement. And then, he closed his eyes and visualized himself, Carol, as they must look . . . and the excitement returned.

The seventh case was that of a much younger man, obviously not in any position of command. Obscure. Yet the case must be in some way as important as that of Kennedy's and Khrushchev's, since it was included with the other cases. Technological obsessions. Pathological shyness. Parents? Quite rich. Very important. Father sits as a director on many boards. Mother in charities. Many committees. No time for their son. Brought up by nurses and tutors. Tall, good looking, but thinks of himself as ugly. The parents can't get their child to live a life appropriate to his class. Won't go to college. Hangs out with lower class elements. Motorcycle types. Obsessive interest in radios and cars. In high school, he has a disasterous relationship. He's serious. She's not. Then the young man begins to have a series of breakdowns. A few psychotic episodes. He begins to imagine he hears voices. In and out of asylums for short periods of time. But the voices he hears are really memories, replays of conversations he has overheard in his own house: his father talking.

The information is valuable. Business rivals of the father can make use of the son's knowledge. Someone appears. He's sympathetic to the boy. A spy sent by the business rival. Gets close to the son. Nurtures the son's hatred. Plants the notion of revenge in the boy's mind. Turns him into a spy against his father. The ethical crisis-dilemma is not really the son's, but the parents'. What can be done, if anything, to help the young man to health . . . and perhaps help him to forget what it is he has heard? Or is institutionalization the only answer? The father's dilemma is that he loves his son, but his affairs involve a great deal of money and power. What if his son cannot be "cured"? Psychoanalysts and psychiatrists have been tried. No help. What recourse? Chemotherapy? Or some still untried course of treatment? But what would that be? The hypothesis: a bold and dangerous experiment is indicated to the father which may succeed or cripple the son. What to do?

The eighth case was the other woman's. Ficino wondered, why

144

two women only? She's young, beautiful, determined, and comes out of relatively poor origins. Her parents are both teachers and they are ferociously ambitious for their child. They want their child to be a professional. There was no medical information, but a thorough physical, an almost pornographic description of her. A young man falls in love with her. He comes from a wealthy and important family, but he is a wastrel and irresponsible. Of course! The young man! And is the father the "banker"? The girl's parents help to break up the relationship. In reaction, perhaps to spite her family, she then runs off and has an affair with a much older man. She's only fifteen. The older man takes her under his wing, educates her, but in the process seems to make a whore out of her. A very successful whore, moving only in the highest realms.

The ninth case was the most puzzling of all. A man who came from Europe when he was quite young. Spoke foreign languages. Runs an export-import business. Establishes ties with European businessmen, some of them of a shady character, dealing in varieties of contraband. There was no crisis situation to solve; only the request for a personality assessment. There was something sinister and disturbing about the case . . .

Now he was ready for a third reading.

Ficino took some Dexedrine to keep himself going. He hadn't done this much intensive work since he was in college. He felt more alive than he had in years. The case histories, with their attendant requests for personality assessments, the crisis situations, were clearly—as Barnstable had said—an important test of his abilities. Were they all interconnected? Were any of them merely diversions, control cases? Were they important in their own right? What was the meaning of showing Ficino his own case, and Carol's? If he got Carol to help him, then would she supersede him? He *did* need help. He decided that the histories of Kennedy and Khrushchev, or himself and Carol, were the diversions. It was the other people who were in some way important. Those were the ones he would show to Carol.

Don't cut corners. Stop thinking for a while. His mind was becoming fatigued. No, wait. That couldn't be right.

Why would he be passed material that was obviously so secret about the American President and the Russian premier? Think.

Everything was important. Leave it alone. Return to it when you're fresh. Go home? No. He couldn't contend with his wife. He stretched out on the couch. Sleep here. He couldn't sleep. The stimulant was working inside of him. He had to sleep. The couch smelled faintly; leather mingled with something subtler and lingering. Carol. He half dozed and had fantasies. He envisioned, in the dark office, himself, standing in front of a distinguished audience, delivering a speech. Faces formed in the darkness. The smell of the leather faded; Carol's smell emerged, turned loose by the leather each time he moved, and the creak of the couch excited him. Here, where his head was, her head had lain. There, where his hips were, her bare behind had been.

Ficino got up and walked around in the dark. He was too excited; he had to drain off energy. He wouldn't be able to sleep otherwise. And it was hot. He took off his clothes and lay naked on the couch. He imagined her above him, her hanging breasts brushing him . . . she would never do it that way . . . Barnstable's sardonic smile . . . He lay down again. The chill of the leather shocked his skin. He had an erection. He shut his eyes, and began to masturbate. He had new insights into her now and it affected his fantasy. As he began to approach climax, little memories, flashes from what he had read entered his fantasy more and more. Carol. His penis began to become limp, and the fantasy started to slip out of his control, take on a life of its own. Something emerged from Carol. Instead of being totally responsive, she began to become agitated, inventive, lascivious, demanding, beginning for the first time to become like . . . like that other woman in the case history . . . and it scared him. But Ficino remembered her fears, her qualms, her secret, timid life, her guilt, a guilt that a knowledge of psychoanalysis and therapy had never wiped out . . . and somehow, without talking, he used his new knowledge of her to reestablish his dominance. His penis grew rigid again, aching, bigger, it seemed, than it had ever been before. But then, he remembered. If "they" were watching . . . Masturbation, he told himself, it was a natural act. Normal. Went on even when you were quite old and no matter how much sex you had. Normal. Normal. His penis remained defiantly rigid, but he couldn't bring himself to come.

146

After a week, Ficino sent the cases back to the Coffin Foundation, to Mr. Barnstable. He received a phone call from Mr. Barnstable. "You've done a brilliant job, Dr. Ficino. Such sensitivity. I think it's almost perfect. However, the Coffin is simply not interested. I'm not only sorry, I'm devastated."

"I guess it's all over now."

"Well, not really. Others are interested, but from a slightly different angle. Metatronics, a lively and small electronics firm I have an interest in, is very involved in a new field, psychological telemetry and telemedicine . . . the kind of thing we talked about. I took the liberty of sending them your reports and added some material to it . . . a word or two, anticipating the future. Metatronics—the president of the firm and I went to school together—is going to send you a consultant's fee, some of which is for yourself, for the work you've already done, and some of which is for the work they would like to see done. They are willing to provide instrumentation and some telephone linkups to experimental machines being tested around the country. You'll be quite excited by what's on line: you'll get a quantum head-start over the others in your present work, to say nothing of being in on the ground floor of what's coming down the pike."

"What kind of instrumentation?"

Barnstable laughed. "There's the true scientist for you. I knew I made the right choice. Aren't you going to ask how much?"

"Well, I . . ."

"You mustn't be ashamed to ask such questions."

"Well . . . yes . . . you're right. How much?"

"Fifty thousand. Ten for yourself. The other forty for your work. You're going to have to hire some technicians, an accountant . . ."

Ficino was shocked at the size of the—what? Grant?

"Well, there's something called axial tomography. It's a device for scanning the body, or the brain, microslice by microslice. Costs a fortune, but in due time there'll be one in every major hospital. Right now there are only two machines like them in the world, shared by a number of researchers via telephone linkups, and through a coaxial cable . . . very much like television."

"I don't know what to say."

"What is there to say? As they say, take the money and run with

147

it. Or am I mixing metaphors? Incidentally, a cautionary word. I did suggest that the material was quite sensitive . . ."

"I haven't shown it to anyone, except . . ."

"Of course. But you did mail it to me. You should be more cautious. After all, you don't want some misguided and overenthusiastic person to accuse you of espionage, do you?"

CHAPTER 17

"THEY'RE gone, Mr. Keats, "Morrison said over the phone.

"Who's gone?"

"The family. Aquilino's family."

"What do you mean, 'gone'?"

"Just that. Disappeared."

"Gone where? Didn't you have the place staked out?"

"We decided to take them into custody according to plan, and they weren't there. We found a whole network of tunnels underneath their junkyard."

"What about the sisters?"

"Gone too. Husbands, children, all of them."

"Look, a family doesn't just disappear into thin air."

"They split, Mr. Keats. It was an operation. We got close and they vanished."

Keats whistled. His mind was working fast. Completely unexpected.

"Should we bring Aquilino in?"

"Are the Russians still hanging around Aquilino?"

"Yes."

"Let me consult with Mr. Holcomb. My instinct is against it. This will be an additional shock. He'll be destabilized soon. He'll have to start running to his primary or backup contact. I'll get back to you. Just don't let Aquilino disappear too, you hear?"

"Vassili, your people have double-crossed you." Keats spoke into the transmitter. It switched frequencies automatically every three seconds—a simple but effective scrambler.

"Who?"

"Your bosses in Moscow."

"What the fuck are you talking about?"

"The family, the Aquilino family. They've been vanished into thin air. Probably on the way to—"

"John, we have no operation of any kind running these people. What do you mean, vanished?"

"They had a visit from Morrison and Corson."

"I know."

"They went home, up to their apartment. They didn't come out. They're gone. And so are their daughters and their families."

Vassili began to laugh.

"It's not funny."

"Well, if we don't run them, and I assure you we don't, and you don't run them, who does?"

"We're going to find out, but that will take time. Holcomb will have a shit-fit. Skip all the steps up to the last one and start the kid running. Maximum panic. You know what to do. You have the lady?"

"Mokroye Delo? I have the lady."

"All right. Get going. I have to report to Holcomb."

"It's going to take a few hours."

"How many?"

"About three, four."

"I'll delay the report to Holcomb as much as I can," Keats said.

The next thing Keats did was to call for a complete investigation of the Aquilino family. Everything, from their arrival in the United States up to the present. He cabled a contact in Rome asking for any possible records on the Aquilino family.

He then called up Ficino.

"Mr. Barnstable. How nice to hear from you. I'll have some reports for you soon. Things are going very well, very well indeed. Your people aren't going to have any regrets."

"I'm sure not. In the meantime, there's a favor I want from you."

150

"Anything, Mr. Barnstable, anything at all."

"You will prepare yourself for a guest, a so-to-speak experimental model. I'll give you complete instructions. I want you to house him somewhere in the hospital till you're ready to work with him. Isolated. Arrange it."

"I'm not set up to do work like that. We've always worked with volunteers."

"He is a volunteer. Thing is, he's in a disturbed frame of mind, but he is a volunteer . . ."

"Will he sign a release, Mr. Barnstable?"

"You're a big boy now, Sidney. You became a big boy when you took the money. You became a big boy when you looked over those case histories. Don't fuck around with me, Sidney. I want you to get Carol Rothschild ready to work on this person."

"What am I going to tell Carol?" Ficino was shocked at the change in Barnstable's tone: it was hard, brutal and took him off guard.

"Use your imagination, Sidney. Do your job right and you're going to move right to the top. International reputation. Foul it up and you can retire and go into general practice."

"But Carol?"

"Right now, she has no need to know anything. Listen, Sidney, you have a golden tongue. Why don't you use it. You can delude your wife, surely a few little lies to Dr. Rothschild shouldn't cause difficulty. *She* at least loves you. Just get a room ready for this kid . . . and remember, he's had a psychotic episode."

"I . . . we don't know how to handle—"

"Sidney, this is on-the-job training. Get ready. A few days, at most. Goodbye."

Keats took the elevator up to the next to the top floor of the Coffin Foundation. He announced himself to Mr. Kelley's secretary. After a few minutes he was ushered in.

A simple desk and clear. Antique wood with a deep sheen, and golden lights dancing, imprisoned in the wood. Behind, a picture window, looking eastward, over the East River, toward Queens and beyond that, toward the Atlantic.

Keats said:

"Shock goes here and there.
Danger.
However, nothing at all is lost.
Yet there are things to be done."

Kelley smiled. The *I-Ching.* Keats was learning. And waited.

"The parents, Aquilino's family. We did the usual thing, approach them, begin to tell them stories about their son. Scare them a little. Question them. Increase his isolation. We had preliminary interviews. As soon as we got closer, they disappeared. They were prepared. That speed of reaction is not accidental. It was a practiced reaction. I don't think Holcomb is finessing me and took them. He *is* getting suspicious and beginning to play his own game, but that is not the one. Then I thought, Vassili . . ." It might be useful to plant hints of suspicion in Mr. Kelley's mind, Keats thought. After all, Vassili was a possible rival.

"I can vouch for Vassili."

"I'm having the family backtracked before they came to this country, and in greater depth than before. They're gone. A simple immigrant family cannot disappear like that without preparation and the right connection."

"And?"

"We'll get a history, but it might be a legend—"

"You mean you concocted a fiction for Holcomb, and now the fiction might turn out to have something to it?"

"I'm not sure. They came from Europe in 1936. Their passport's Italian. Their name's Italian. They're Jews . . ."

"Sephardic Jews?"

"Possibly. But they are not Italian. Perhaps German, possibly coming from further east. Everything has checked out, but now something feels very wrong. Gaps. The documentation might be false. We'll see."

"And in the meantime?"

"We'll cover and jump a few steps ahead. I will need Laura, however."

"That is up to her, John." Kelley sat there as Keats nodded and then left.

Keats let Holcomb say it for him. "They're Russians."

"Now we'll step up the tempo," Keats told Holcomb.

"The whole family are agents. A family operation. That's hard to believe."

"Why? Been in a place a long time. They trained the son . . . years of suggestion and conditioning. He didn't even know what he was. That's why we had so much trouble. I think we're close."

"The Russians have no respect for families. Okay, he's all alone now. What if he chooses to do nothing at all?"

"Their operation is being folded up. He'll move, Mr. Holcomb. He's got to move. We're putting interesting drugs inside of him. The drugs are breaking up his conditioning. He's disoriented. He's going to be terrified."

"What are you using, truth drugs?"

"Something better and more effective. LSD. Lysergic acid diethylamide. He's already paranoid, terror stricken. He's going to think he's going mad and he's going to want someone to help him. He'll start moving. And when we've been led to his control, that's the first step. They must have set up a series of fallback options. That's their standard way of operating. Then comes the next step, when we take him apart. A few more days."

Holcomb wondered. Were these the experiments Keats had participated in? "I'm giving you another two weeks. No more. And this time no one better escape."

CHAPTER 18

RICHARD came home from his parents' house. It was funny. No one had been home. He could never remember a time when his parents hadn't been home. He was supposed to eat with them. They had been looking forward to it. He had tried to call his sisters; first one, then the other. They hadn't been home either. He tried calling them a few times, wondering if he had made a mistake in dialing. The phones were working, but no one answered. Had he gotten the day he was supposed to eat with his parents all wrong?

As soon as he stepped into the long stair-hallway leading up to the various floors, all the way to his loft on the top floor, he felt that something was wrong. He went up cautiously. It was quiet. The small businesses that owned the lofts under him were shut down for the night.

He opened the door to his loft slowly. It was completely dark there. He switched on the light. And switched it off again. He stood there, trembling. Get out of here! He couldn't move. She was there . . . The equipment had attacked her . . . One flash; that was enough. She was there. She was dead. The equipment had attacked her . . . He stood and listened. He heard nothing. No sound, not a moan, nothing shifting. Nothing at all. No breathing. Only his own, which was very very fast. Don't turn it on. You know what you'll see. He turned it on. She was there. Dead.

154

Naked. Strangled. Gray eyes staring straight at him. Black hair entwined with delicate and colored strands of telephone wire. He closed the light again. The smell reached him. Heavy, sticky, sweet and putrid. Get out of here, call the police. He heard a sound? A flat clack of black plastic, telephone on telephone, wire rubbing on wire. He turned on another light. Someone had killed Laura and broken every piece of equipment he had. Someone had killed Laura *with* every piece of equipment he had. Shards of plastic had entered her flesh. Her dress, on the floor, was drenched with blood. Blood in rivers. Only her eyes, alive, reproachful, not alive, dead, just looked at him . . . looked at the door through which he must enter. Were they somewhere in the room? He felt around. He picked up a wooden chair. He would kill whoever had done it.

His life was over. He was through. All these years he had kept hoping he and Laura could get together again and start where they had left off . . . those years ago when she had been taken away by that older man. And she still thought of him . . . wanted to come back to him. What was the point of anything anymore? The older man. Mr. Kelley. He did it.

A whisper of sound. The building creaking. A faint noise. Wind rattling the escape hatch on the roof. Sounds. Whoosh . . . Whoooo . . . You . . . And a blast of sound. Youuu. Where did the sound come from? He got up. He couldn't stand it any more.

He turned off the light again. He began to weep. He stood up and turned and backed out through the door. He looked down the long long flight of stairs. Five stories. Throw himself off. He began to walk downstairs, slowly at first, then two and three steps at a time, until he was running down like an athlete, taking the steps four, five and six at a time, and shot open the bolt at the bottom and was out in the street, running fast, getting away from Dead Laura in his loft.

"There he goes," said Morrison. "Get moving."
"There they go," Dudintsev said into a microphone.
"Call up Keats," Morrison told Corson.
"Just keep up with the Americans," Vassili told Dudintsev.
And watching the two sets of followers, Russian and American, following Richard, was a third set of followers.

155

CHAPTER 19

STICK to where the ordinary people go. Keep your feet, your hands, your body moving. Run away from everything. The train, a local, made its way, stop by stop, toward Manhattan . . . Junction Boulevard . . . Jackson Heights . . . Woodside . . . Queensboro Plaza . . . Court House Square . . . Time played funny tricks on him. The train crawled between stations. The doors seemed to stay open too long at each station. A dangerous place to be.

Laura was dead. What had happened to his parents and sisters? He realized that if one of them, whoever "they" were, would just come up to him and say something like, "We just want to talk to you," he would talk. Oh, how he would talk. I didn't do anything. I'll tell you anything you want to know. I eavesdropped on the President. Sure. I didn't understand what he was talking about. Why? Because it was fun. What secrets?

He looked up. People were staring at him. He giggled. The hunted knows who the hunters are. They edged away from him. Shut up. Look ordinary. Richard got up and walked into another subway car. Lots of people there. Get lost in the crowd. Lots of weird people there. Weird city. Nobody would notice another ordinary nut. Go into a bar. Have a brew. Hang around for a while. Call Ziggy up again. Go through Ziggy's security procedure.

156

"You never know who's listening in," Ziggy's voice said in his ear.

Whatever was in him acted up. There was a rush and he felt as if he was fused to the rattling subway car and its vibrations were his vibrations. What was it they had slipped him? Would it kill him? Was he dying?

Sit still. Control yourself. No, it's not a poison; it must be some kind of drug. His nerve ends began to stick their way through his skin and pierce through his clothing. They began to fill the subway car, entangling everyone, reaching in to them, through their skins. He began to feel what everyone was feeling.

It'll pass. It'll pass. You'll get off soon and feel better. Get to Ziggy, he'll get me out of this. But how would he be able to leave the subway car if his nerves were intertwined with everyone else's?

Holcomb said, "Keats, when this is through, I'm going to have your ass. Why didn't you take him in Queens when you had the chance? You let him get away."

Keats held the phone away from his ear. "Not so, sir. I think he went to Queens to throw us off the track. He's acting confident. Now he's moving toward his control. I've got people on him. He's on the subway headed back into Manhattan." Keats was in a command post, an office in the Paramount Building, high over Times Square, looking down. There were radios and telephones in the room.

"Keats, I don't have to spell out what I'll do to you if you let him slip away."

"Mr. Holcomb, I'm with him all the way. He's made phone calls. I've got a car paralleling the subway. I've got people *on* the subway. Don't worry. I figure he's going to surface around Times Square. We'll take him there, as soon as he makes his contact. He's almost out of his mind. He's panicking. He's finally leading us to his control."

"I'll be here. I want you to report every half hour. Now run through all the procedures again, and all the optional moves."

Keats went through it again, bored. Tradecraft bored him. When he hung up with Holcomb, he picked up one of the radios,

157

the Russian one. Use the wrong channel and the thing would explode. To be used for a short time only. One time. "Well, Vassili?"

"The schmuck is on the way."

Richard stood at the side of the bar; it was on the west side of Times Square between Forty-second and Forty-third Streets . . . Pimps, hustlers, male and female prostitutes, his body was half in and half out of a telephone booth, ready to run. He heard the phone ring again and again. He muttered, "Come on, Ziggy, answer it." No one at the bar seemed to notice him. They drank. They talked. They watched television. After the fifteenth ring, the phone connected. This time it wasn't Ziggy's soft, German accent, but a number of alternating voices, each saying two or three words at a time, combined to give Richard a message. He could sense the interruptions because he knew what to listen for: the punctuations, switchings, pauses where there should be no pauses if spoken by one person . . . relay clicks . . . each voice pitched differently, with slightly different accents. Ziggy had put together the combine all around the country; he had done what he said he would. Richard began to feel better. The string of numbers included the hour to call back, the number to dial, the number of phones or phone booths and their locations to call from. A real Ziggy operation coming to him from all over the country. The backup times if the initial contact failed. Several phones were in buildings on different floors (were there phones in the corridors?). Only a half hour to recontact. If he had to wait a long time he would go off the deep end once and for all. He hung up the phone, went back to the bar and ordered another drink.

He watched the baseball game on television. A commercial filled the dead spaces between innings. A girl came on. Selling something. Laura! But Laura was dead. Dead in his loft, two weeks ago. No. It was someone who only looked like Laura. Hallucinations. Maybe Laura wasn't dead. Then what was the blood on your hands?

He looked up at the screen. Yes, it was Laura. No, this time it wasn't an illusion . . . painful. He could see the baseball game

158

right through her. The pitcher looked toward the mound. He shook off the call. Closeup: the pitcher's face frowned, just the way Laura used to frown. Laura, how much he had loved her. Now he was free.

"Richard. Look my way," his beer told him.

"I won't. Go away. You're dead. Laura, I loved you."

"I know. I loved you too, Richard. Please, Richard."

"All right, what's the difference?" He looked up. The scene cut away. The baseball game began to fade. The President of the United States appeared. The baseball crowd roared, cheered, whistled. Some boos, but there are yahoos who boo anything and anybody. Laura waved John F. Kennedy to his seat, behind a desk. "Take it away, Mr. President." Kennedy nodded to her and began to pass her. He stopped. He gave Laura a quick kiss and patted' her behind, and winked, right at Richard. "You son of a bitch," Richard muttered. But it was only his mind playing tricks on him.

In his vantage point, Keats received a call. "Should we go in and take him?"

Not yet, Keats thought. It was still too soon. "Is the back secure?"

"We've got our people there. One man inside the bar."

"Wait until he comes out. Then make your move."

Keats reported back to Holcomb, telling him where Richard was. "He'll be coming out soon. He's just made another phone call. He'll be establishing contact."

"No. Take him now."

"But—"

"You heard me, Keats. I don't think anyone's going to turn up for him. They know we're after him. That's why his "family" left. They're just throwing him to us. I've seen it a thousand times. I've had experience with this kind of thing."

"But—"

"That's a direct order, Keats. No more games. Bring him in as soon as you take him and we can begin."

"Yes, sir."

Keats's team reported. "Trouble. We got company."

159

Keats looked out the window. Now two sets of cars and two teams flanked the bar entrance. Vassili's people had gotten there just in time. It wasn't going to be easy.

President Kennedy was back. He began his address to the nation. Ghostly baseball players flickered through his face. Richard suddenly knew everything he was going to say. Richard *remembered* what the President *was about to say.* But how did he remember? Richard suddenly felt that the President had to be prevented from saying those words. Not saying them would stop what could happen from happening. But the President went on. As he talked, the screen seemed to fill up with a final and holo-caustical fire, to go almost completely white, to blaze and pulse in time to the solemn cadences of a voice announcing a national emergency. No one else in the bar seemed to notice. The President spoke to Richard of the crisis that had been brewing now for months and had now come to a head. Nuclear missile sites in Cuba had been built . . . the danger of America . . . ninety miles away . . . most of America within reach of nuclear warheads. There was a cut to Russian ships, plowing through the Atlantic, bearing atomic missiles to Cuba. America could not countenance such a violation of the Monroe Doctrine. An embargo. National security. The Russian ships must turn back. Nuclear confrontation.

And Richard was full of hatred for this man who had made it happen just by speaking about it. For one clear second Richard almost put the reasons for his persecution together. Something was missing. Those words must *not* be said. It was a moment of clear, cool reasoning . . . and then he lost it. Richard was saying, "No. No. *No . . .*" His voice was raising in intensity and anger to a higher pitch. "Don't say it. You mustn't say it. I won't let you say it." People were turning around, looking at him, edging away from him. The bartender was on the phone, calling for the police. He began to run.

From his perch in the Paramount Building, Keats could see most of Times Square laid out like some enormous stage set. Both teams of actors were in place. What was happening on the street, *that* was going to be the real drama, not what was playing in the

160

movie houses and Broadway theatres. The bar was flanked. Only in this case, Keats thought, the shootout is not the denouement; it's the beginning.

Four cars had drawn up, occupied by drivers only, keeping their motors running, manning communications, standing in spite of any number of No-Parking-or-Standing-At-Any-Time injunctions. The great random factor was all the passersby in the Square. They too were actors, part of the scenery, but they didn't know it . . . the crowd necessary to mask the operation . . . all recruited as temporary agents. The crowd was the maze through which the experimental animal was going to be driven. There would come a time, Keats thought, when television cameras would be placed all over and the operations would be in real-time.

Richard shoots through before anyone can react with the proper speed to grab him. He's running across the street, not even bothering to dodge cars that screech to a halt to keep from killing him. He's in the Square and sprinting; the only thing on his mind is to get to shelter from the coming nuclear storm. Across Seventh Avenue someone jumps into his path. Richard knocks him down, runs right over him, just the way Frank Gifford used to do it, veers, running northeast up the middle of the street. That's the point where Richard becomes aware he's being chased. Behind him there's a shout in Russian.

One of Keats's people's radios: "He's theirs! It's them, all right. The fuckin' Russkies. Why don't we get them? We need help."

"You have your orders," Keats radios back. "Don't take any independent action. You hear?"

There's no answer from the car.

"Did you read me, Morrison? Answer me."

Reluctantly: "Yes, sir. I read you. What if they start shooting?"

"Then, and only then, respond appropriately, but with great care. You're in a crowded area. Keep that in mind."

"Will those bastards keep that in mind? They don't have much use for life."

"Get moving. I don't think they want an international incident."

161

All begin to run after Richard. People who have been run into by Richard are smashed into again. A wake of jostled, pushed, bowled-over people marks Richard's run. Many turn around to watch. They can't see much. It's too crowded. Times Square. A crook being chased by cops. The team cars begin to drive. One pair sideswipe each other. A clashing of metal, tinkling of breaking glass, chrome runners peeling off. Men pile out, face one another, hands reaching under their jackets, shirts, nylon windbreakers. They face one another until someone yells, "Get moving. Get moving. He's getting away."

Up above, in his command post, Keats began to laugh. He saw runners tripping one another. Keats loved complications, knots, incredible tangles. He loved solving puzzles, the harder the better. The whole operation had become clumsy, intriguing. In order to solve it, Keats's mind worked faster.

He saw Richard suddenly, east, on the corner of Forty-fourth Street, knocking over some innocent couple from out of town. Richard stopped for a second. He said something to the two people. Instead of seeming to yell at him for his rude act, they shrunk away. Richard turned and continued to run.

Keats's American radio signaled. He switched on. Someone, not Morrison, reported. "We're stuck here. Morrison is trying to show the cop his identification. The cop thinks he's trying to reach for his gun."

"Go help him. Talk to the cop slowly, clearly, loudly. Smile. Think of him as a very skittish and dangerous dog. Use simple words. Got that?" Morrison had to be moving to get to his appointed place.

In the middle of the crowd around the crashed cars, in the middle of the cops, in the middle of the stink of car exhaust and the din of horns, a man wearing a yellow shirt, brown tie, sank slowly to the street, held by the press of the crowd which prevented him from being slammed forward by the silenced bullet. The pens in his pocket disappeared, replaced by a huge, spreading red stain. At first no one noticed that he had slipped to his knees. They were all watching Morrison trying to explain who he was without anyone else knowing. They were enjoying the other

162

driver's rage. The New York cops had already gotten the idea that Morrison was a Fed, FBI, and were making trouble.

Then someone noticed the fallen body, the blood on the shirt, the dead eyes, the face set in an astonishing calmness. A woman screamed. Others backed away. A little circle was made. "He's shot. He's shot. He's shot. There's some nut with a gun here."

"I didn't hear a thing."

"Jesus, let's get the hell out of here." People were beginning to scatter in panic. The cops and Morrison, who was still trying to show his government identification, were almost swept away by the stampeding crowd.

"It must be that nut . . ." one of the cops said and turned to go and radio for more help. Morrison slipped away.

Richard emerged into Times Square, pausing at the corner of Forty-fifth and Broadway. He couldn't see much, except a big crowd further down on the Square. Traffic tied up. Horns blaring. The sun was beginning to set. Some of the Broadway movie house lights were beginning to blink. *Phantom of the Opera* at the Palace. *Guns of Darkness* further on. Behind him, toward the east, the sky was deep blue as night came on. To the west, everything was golden. The shore of New Jersey was incised beautifully against the eye-catching gold. Sunfire, the ultimate atomic fire.

There were the three phones he could use. One was in the basement of the Times Building at Forty-second Street, one of the public phones. One was in a street booth at the north end of Times Square. The third was in the building on Seventh Avenue, right around the corner . . . on the fourteenth floor in an office. He decided to use that one.

There, coming down on him from the north. There converging from across the Square. He turned. Yes. Coming from the south. Men. They hadn't spotted him yet, but Richard sensed that they knew where to go to get him, triangulating on him as if he were a radio beacon. He moved fast, into the office building.

Deserted, dirty lobby. In the back an old elevator operator dozed on a stool. He sneaked past. The old man continued to sleep as Richard began to walk up the stairs.

The fourteenth floor was empty. Deserted hallway. Dim bulbs.

163

Frosted-glass windows set in old-fashioned wooden doors, painted over with dark stain, laid over and overlaid until they are all almost black. Flaking signs on the glass, small businesses. Hexagonal tile floor. Clorox cleaner. Rubbed-in dirt swirls. Did anyone use this floor at all? Should he stay or go down? He walked along the corridor and stopped to listen at each door. No lights inside the doors, but the offices obviously faced toward the outside because the hot and golden glow of sunset filtered through the frosted glass. He found the office he was looking for. He tried the door. It opened.

He was in an anteroom that hadn't been used for a long time. Only one desk there, covered with a green blotter, turned gray by dust. It was quiet. Find the phone. Maybe in the inner office. One that was never disconnected. New York was full of such phones, abandoned but still usable. The inner office was deserted, except for a desk. No phone. How was he going to make his phone call to Ziggy if there was no phone?

Maybe it was in one of the desk drawers. He went around. The desk was close to a window. A chair was backed up against the window. The squeak of its unoiled wheels made him jump.

He looked under the desk. A telephone wire, but it was cut. Richard examined it. It was an old cut, dusted over. Relax. He opened the drawers one by one. Nothing. Yellowed memo papers, used and flimsy stencils, dustballs. Clips. Pencil shavings. His nose was beginning to itch. He felt watched. He straightened up and began to look around the room for a camera eye.

He walked around the room. Not even a filing cabinet. Two closets. He opened them. The first one held nothing at all. The second was full of telephones . . . a graveyard of telephones, piled as high as his shoulder. Old telephones, some of them he had only seen in museums. New telephones. Some dulled, others gleaming. A tangle of cut-off wires, bristling like spines sticking out the plastic and wood mass. A closet full of corpses, a whole history of telephony. Richard's curiosity almost took over. He wanted to sit down right there and begin to take them apart, see how the old ones worked. The whole pile shifted slightly, settling into a more stable position.

No working phone. Or was the working phone in the pile? No, everything was uniformly dusty. No sign that anyone'd been there in a long time. He looked at his watch. It was almost too late for the contact. He'd have to go downstairs and try to reach the next nearest phone on the list. But by that time, even if he ran all the way down the stairs, it would be too late.

Richard worked his way around the two rooms again to see if he'd missed something. Maybe the phone didn't look like a phone; a Ziggy trick. There was nothing at all that indicated a telephone or any kind of sensing device monitoring him. He looked up at the ceiling lights. It might be there, but it didn't feel like the watching was coming from there.

He walked over to the window and raised it. It came up easily. That was strange. The roar of traffic came in as the sun dipped behind the rocky cliffs of New Jersey. The window let in the pulsing Broadway lights. *Judgement at Nuremburg. A Shot In the Dark.* Getting brighter as the night came on.

A sudden memory. When was it? 1959? John F. Kennedy campaigning for president. Richard was standing down there, among the crowd cheering, when Kennedy's motorcade had come through. He had seen Kennedy, sitting on the back of the convertible, waving to the crowds, left and right. Richard was lucky, tall enough to see over others. Kennedy's head and waving hand. Kennedy looked his way and, Richard was sure of it, their eyes met. And then the man who would—and did—become President, was gone. He felt a glow then . . . a feeling of awe and worship . . . then . . . almost as if there had been some bond struck in the meeting of the eyes. He didn't feel that way now. He wished then, as he wished now, that he could get a good, long look at Kennedy. If he had been in a place like this, he might have seen the whole procession clearly. An unobstructed view.

Across the Square, through the air, in another building across the way, Richard saw a man sitting behind a desk at another window, looking directly at him. Richard could see every feature. The man smiled. Blond hair. Neat dark suit, in spite of summer. His mouth moved. He seemed to be talking to someone, but looking right at him. Their eyes met. The marquee lights came on. The face across the way turned orange and green, the teeth red. Off. On. Was the man talking to him? Richard pointed at himself and raised his eyebrows as if to ask, "Who, me?" The man picked up a phone and dialed, looking at Richard all the time.

When the man finished dialing, one of the phones in the closet rang. Richard jumped. He turned and ran to the closet. Which one? One of those phones was still connected. Richard began to scramble wildly through the phones, lifting one after another, trying to find the one with the live wire. But they were entangled. Wires cut at him as if the mass were alive.

Then, one by one, all the phones began to ring. At first they rang singly, their sounds overlapping. All kinds of sounds . . . flat, like a clapper on wood, deep, almost soprano, shrill and commanding, shallow, like a buzz. Gradually they began to become synchronized, falling into a single phase till the totality of it became deafening.

He raised his hands, as if to plead with the other man, only a hundred or so feet away, but the man was gone.

Richard turned and began to run across the office. He had to get out of there. Don't use the elevator. Get down the stairs. He opened the door.

A fist, smashing into his face, hurled him backward.

CHAPTER 20

THE blow was calculated to stun, not to debilitate. The two men moved in. At last he was face to face with them.

Morrison followed up his fist to Richard's face. Richard, backing away, yelled, "Take it easy. Wait a minute. You didn't have to do that. Let's talk. I give up. What do you want?"

The men didn't answer. They moved after him, silent. Morrison first, Corson behind. Corson moved around to flank Richard.

"All right. All right. I give up, I tell you."

Neither Morrison nor Corson said a thing. They didn't even seem to hear Richard. They just kept coming. Richard backed away. He was in the inner office. Corson was trying to get behind Richard. "Who are you? Are you the guys who have been following . . . what did you do to me?"

Morrison was cold about it, almost scientific. The thing was to work Richard over quickly. To break his will to resist. No questions. No answers. No talking. Just blows in total silence. Terrorize him. Make him think he's dealing with madmen, so he'll be ready for Holcomb's interrogation: make him grateful to see Holcomb.

A short jab, fingers extended, caught Richard low, made him gasp and double over. Corson, half behind him, grabbed his hair and jerked him upright while Morrison gave Richard's face two hard slaps. Punches and slaps all over the head and body. Fast.

167

Get him backward. Spread him over the desk.

Morrison had his training in interrogation at the International Police Services, a CIA proprietary. Morrison had learned all about the body, its nervous system, its musculature, its weak and tender spots, all its pain nodes. How to hurt without damaging, or how to cripple. It was not physiology from a doctor's or artist's point of view, just what the body can take without going mad— or worse, dying.

"What do you want? Wait. Listen. Just let me talk—"

Edge of the hand to the neck: pulled punch. Jerk the head backward. Silence. Silence. Neither one of them said a word.

Time slowed up even more as the drug inside of him reacted in strange ways.

Richard was pulled down across the desk. Corson readied with one hand (while the other held its grip on Richard's hair) to grab first one arm and then the other, to spreadeagle Richard across the desk.

Richard kept his head up . . . slowly being pulled back. Once his head was pressed back on the desk top, he was through. And yet he worried . . . what if my hair is torn out . . . I'll look funny. His head was still raised.

Corson was surprised at the strength of Richard's neck.

Richard could see those slow and floating fists, hear those thuds and slaps coming. Morrison's hand was reaching between his legs, for his balls. Richard bellowed. Time speeded up again.

Richard was stronger than they expected. His foot lashed out, aiming for Morrison's face, but hit his fist. The other foot kicked and this time Morrison, before he could turn his head, was hit grazingly across the face. His eyes teared. Blood began to trickle from Morrison's nose. He was infuriated. Keep cool. Ideally, this should have been done in a prison or a safe house.

Richard's body was going crazy. The drug-rush flooded his spirit. Time slowed up in his mind. Time speeded up for his body. Visions. Keep your mind on here and what's happening. He was beyond his body; he could almost view it with detachment. He stood at the side; he hovered above. He watched the three of them. He could think of other things. He gave that thing that was Richard's body instructions. Twist. Writhe. Kick. Bite. Scratch. Keep those feet moving. No. Not too fast or you'll have your hair torn out. Punch coming. Anticipate the pain. Not so bad. Morrison was on top of him, pinning him, almost smothering him. Morrison's hands were groping along his body, reaching, reaching again to grab and twist his testicles.

Plenty of time. Hours of time. Years in which to plan each and every move. He heard a voice, a high-speed monotone, questioning them: "Who are you? What do you want? Why don't you stop? I'll tell you anything you want to know. Why are you chasing me? What did you do to me? What did you do to my mind? Why did you kill Laura? Where are my mother and father?" At the same time he remembered the little spell his father had taught him. He invoked the Angel. "Oh most holy God. Blessed be He. I need helpers . . ."

Morrison and Corson only heard a wordless cry . . . a rising and falling sound, almost chantlike. Terror. They thought they almost had him.

But the body was wise, terrified in its own way, and continued to struggle. Lots of time. Time enough for Richard to reach out and grasp the man's fingers and jerk backward, backward, and see the expression on his torturer's face, his body, reacting, his face contorting. The Angel had responded and was beside him.

Morrison swung to shove an elbow into Richard's neck. The pain slowly reached Richard, jumping the gap from where he was being beaten to where he was watching. Richard's body's foot shot out again, catching Morrison in the chest and throwing him backwards; and, uncontrolled, unstopping, Richard's body curled into a ball and his feet shot backwards, behind him, over his face, crashing into Corson's face. Richard followed his feet, his legs, over the desk, landing on his feet between the chair and the desk, his back smashing into Corson, almost knocking him out the window. Get out. Get out. Get out.

They converged on him again. Morrison, in spite of his training, was getting angry. He hadn't expected this. They had told him Richard was softened up.

Four men had come into the office behind the struggling group. They moved in fast, silently before they were seen.

A swift milling. Fists moving. Hands chopping. Knees, elbows, legs and feet kicking out. Blackjacks. Richard was in the middle of a storm of fighting, trying to work his way out. No one was

169

hitting him now. Guns were drawn, Morrison and Corson. No one was making any noise at all. None other than breathing, panting, gasping. He could hardly see his body. All of them . . . they had become as one beast with many limbs, fighting itself . . . There. He burst free. A gun was in his hand. Had he grabbed it from someone? A pistol with a long clip. Morrison raised a gun to fire. Richard jerked up his hand, screaming (the only voice) "Leave me alone. Leave me alone. Leave me alone." And heard another voice . . . a memory from the past, the voice of a woman saying, "Leave him alone." And, towering over his head, his mother, like some great and radiant angel, shooting . . . something or someone outside the apartment door . . . or was it a closet door? He had forgotten all about that. Was she shooting at some demon that had come after him? The sound of the gun, fired so long ago, in his ear, didn't so much deafen him as blind him, so he could never remember who or what his mother shot . . . or that she shot at all. Him, almost like his mother . . . he stood there and began shooting . . . spraying the whole room, all of them. For Laura. For his mother and father. For his sisters. For their families. For his own wrecked and persecuted life. It was strange: he heard nothing. The gun jerked in Richard's hand. Shell casings dropped onto the floor, making odd, tinny sounds. He began to run.

Down the stairs. Get out.

The only family he had left was Ziggy.

Fourteen flights. Somewhere, he threw the gun away. His legs were weak and trembling when he reached the lobby. The old man wasn't there anymore.

And he was out into the street, trying to run, staggering. His face and body were beginning to hurt.

And he ran into the arms of the police, who had been warned to keep their eyes open for someone who had gone crazy. Richard was subdued. He was handcuffed and thrown into a patrol car. Two cops flanked him; two more cops sat in front. The cops on either side held him; he couldn't move. They were trying to calm him down.

"Where are you taking me?"

"You need help . . ."

"I'm not crazy."

"Who said you were, kid?"

170

"They tried to kill me."

"Who's 'they'?"

"They're up there . . . all dead . . ."

"Sure, kid, sure . . ."

"I shot them . . ."

"Sure, kid."

"You don't believe me. Aren't you going to look?"

"Don't worry about it."

"You're not cops . . . Where are you taking me?"

"It's for your own good."

"I killed six people."

"Hey, you're right up there in the big time."

"You're taking me to the looney bin."

"No. We're just taking you to some people who can help you. Take it easy."

They were more afraid of him than he was of them. He heard them radio in to their headquarters. They were going to Bellevue. Then a different operator at headquarters radioed back: Bellevue was full and they were instructed to take Richard up to Columbia Presbyterian.

Behind a patrol car, a panel truck started up and began to follow.

Keats made his phone call. "Mr. Holcomb. They got him away. We almost had him and part of his network, but they got him away and . . ."

In the room where Richard had fought, four of the bodies stirred and rose after a few minutes. Morrison and Corson continued to lie there. The four brushed themselves off and straightened their clothes. They didn't look at Morrison or Corson; they had seen enough dead bodies in their time. Corson's head had been blown open; the features were gone. Morrison had been hit across the chest, with real bullets. They left.

Keats made another phone call. On impulse, he tried something. " 'What was to be laid aside has been set up. The fish has not been allowed to leave the deep.' "

There was a pause. A chuckle. Was Mr. Kelley pleased?

171

" 'Block the openings . . . shut the doors . . . and without stirring abroad, the whole world will be known . . .' "

Keats was beginning to understand Mr. Kelley. In Mr. Kelley's favorite book of writings—which Keats had taken the trouble to read a few times—it was said that the hub had thirty spokes. Keats, who had been on the wheel, was now moving down one of the spokes to the center. Mr. Kelley's spokes reached out everywhere. "Without stirring abroad . . . one can know the whole world." But this Richard, he was a hub too. A hub on a runaway wheel, not attached to any cart. Without stirring, this Richard had come to know the whole world too. He really had. Keats, who had access to Richard, was even beginning to feel a slight advantage . . . and a loss of awe for Mr. Kelley. He would find out all that Richard knew and control the flow of intelligence to Kelley.

The patrol car drove across Manhattan and turned north onto the West Side Drive. Behind it, going onto the parkway, even though trucks were forbidden on the Drive, Ziggy's panel truck followed. It kept back out of sight, behind the traffic. As soon as the driver and the passengers in the panel truck knew, from tracking the patrol car's radio transmission, where it was headed, the truck turned off at Seventy-second Street. The patrol car continued up the Drive.

The lights of New Jersey made dancing light tracks on the water. The Palisades Amusement Park glittered and the many spokes of the great Ferris wheel turned.

172

PART II

CHAPTER 21

WHEN Dr. Carol Rothschild came into Dr. Sidney Ficino's office, she walked right by his secretary and into his office. She had never done anything as bold. Ficino realized that he had made several big mistakes. Now he was going to have to pay. How much could he tell her?

She was pale, almost white. Ficino said, into the phone, "Excuse me. An emergency has come up. I'll call you back." He hung up the phone and said, "What's the matter, Carol?"

"Sidney, just what is going on?"

"Just a minute." He switched on his intercom. "Clara, Dr. Rothschild and I are having a conference. We don't want any interruptions."

"First, I—"

"Why don't we sit down, Carol." Sidney stood up. Play for time. Keep your voice calm. Sidney was a short man, running to fat. His hair was thinning. But nature had compensated Sidney by giving him a deep, resonant voice, a quick mind.

"First I get a call—"

"Carol, please. Do you want a drink? You need a drink . . ."

"Just some coffee."

Too stimulating. Liquor. A stiff shot. He got up and walked around the desk to the cabinet. He was thinking fast, monitoring every move Carol made. Slight shock. Shallow breathing. Pulse

175

racing, no doubt. Anxiety. Outrage. Deep breaths, trying to get control of herself. "Sit down, Carol. Please. Darling . . ." He gestured toward the deep leather couch; those associations were strong . . . use every advantage you can.

"I don't want . . ."

He passed her. He touched her hand, took it, squeezed; very nonsexual. "Please. Carol. It's about that young man? Come on, sit down." He was almost a half-head shorter than she was. "You saw him?"

"Sidney, what is this all about? We don't do this kind of thing."

"And maybe that's our trouble," he said. "We're overspecialized." He mixed the drink. Made it stiff. Little ice. Mixed one for himself. "Come on, Carol. Sit down." He handed her the drink. His other hand rubbed her back slowly, soothingly, going up and down to her neck, almost down to the jut of her behind, but not quite.

She moved away from his hand, almost as though repulsed, but she took the drink and she did sit down.

"All right, Carol. Maybe I've been playing games with you. And maybe I'm even a little afraid of you. Dr. Ficino loves games. You got this 'urgent' communication from me. Go down, take a case history, begin giving therapy to this young man. He's disturbed."

"Who is he?"

"He's going through a psychotic episode . . . You try to call me up; what's this all about. Suddenly Dr. Ficino is unavailable. Dr. Ficino is unresponsive. Why did he do it this way? Carol, I have this terrible thing in me. We've talked about it before. We've talked about it at lunches and over cocktails. We've talked about it right there, right there on that couch, the two of us, naked—"

"Sidney, stop it."

"Ficino likes to play games. But it's not merely a game. It's important. You don't know how important this can be to us."

"Who is he?"

"You want to know who this kid is? Frankly, I don't really know . . . A 'someone's' kid. A 'someone' who's very important. For a variety of reasons—reasons that may become quite important to us; reasons that can lead to the realization of all our professional

176

dreams—we should take care of him. For God's sake, Carol. You had experience in psychiatry before you switched to neurobiology. You had patients. You've dealt with psychotics—"

"Not since my residency."

"You've done therapy—"

"Not for five years."

"It's not a skill that goes away. Anyway, you have that god-given gift, the *feel*. You're the only person I know—*and trust*—who combines two important skills." Time to begin switching to the attack. "All right, what is it you saw that disturbed you? What disgusted you?"

"I wasn't disgusted."

"What frightened you?"

"I was *not* frightened."

She took a sip of her drink. She breathed deeply. Because of the depth and softness of the couch, she had to work to sit straighter. The leather creaked. He hoped the creaking of the leather would remind her. She drank off a quarter of the drink. Good. He moved toward the couch. . . .

Not being able to reach Sidney Ficino, Carol had gone down to the section where the young man was being kept. It was in a part of the hospital she had hardly ever been, in the psychiatric section. She was greeted by an attendant and led to a little alcove. She moved in quietly and sat down in front of a one-way window. She saw a room. A bed. A little table. No windows. An overhead light. A young man was sitting on the bed naked. His body seemed to be almost in repose. It was beautiful. She almost blushed and looked away. The young man's head turned into the light, toward her. The face was twisted, tortured. Such anguish. The face was different from the body . . . tense. The head and body might belong to two different human beings. The eyes stared in horror at something between the wall and himself. Whatever it was he saw, his eyes followed it. Hallucination? The message reached the body. Why so slow? The body tensed now. Muscles stood out. There were discolorations on his body and face. Bruises. Had he done this to himself? The penis was erect. Suddenly, the eyes focussed and looked at her. She felt . . . what was the matter with her? He opened his mouth. He emitted a

177

sound . . . high, ringing, a beep tone. The speaker above the one-way window transmitted the sound to her. A little static. The sound made her even itchier. The flow was stronger. She felt uncomfortable.

"How long has he been here?"

"Three days."

"What's wrong with him?"

"A nut."

"Why is he like *that*, naked?"

The attendant shrugged. "Those are my orders."

"Who gave you those orders?"

The attendant looked puzzled. "Why, Dr. Ficino. Should I let you in?"

She looked at the body again. Pectorals. The ridge that the external oblique muscles made as they shaded into the behind. The enormous tension . . . The thighs, rigid, swelling. All the signs of terror. The triceps ridged as if pushing something away . . . The penis . . .

"No. I'll be back," she told the attendant. She left.

Sidney was sitting beside her. He had moved there while she was telling what she had seen . . . omitting certain details. Sidney's hand was on her thigh, just above her knee. "Why was he brought *here?* We don't have the facilities. Why is he being kept like that?"

"Like what?"

"Without clothes. Isolated."

"We're keeping him like that . . ." Sidney's hand squeezed her thigh. His voice deepened. He sighed and looked ahead, as if remembering. We're keeping him like that because that's the way Barnstable recommended he be kept. And with Barnstable, a recommendation now had the force of a command. "It's a kind of shock. Bring him out of his state."

"Well, it certainly hasn't worked. That's barbaric, primitive, Sidney. They haven't done that kind of thing in years."

"It was recommended—"

"We have a case record? You sent me down without the case record."

"You remember the cases we worked over, Carol, the remote

assessment? Remember number seven, the young man who was so disturbed? The rich father? The business secrets? That's him."

"Sidney, we don't have the facilities for this kind of work."

Sidney's hand stroked further and higher. She drank a little more. She was upset; was she relaxing? He turned toward her and leaned over; he kissed her neck. His hand worked its way along her thighs, and began to slip inward, between her legs. Her legs parted slightly, but her back became more rigid; she refused to lean back. Now he leaned down and kissed the white cloth of the laboratory coat, where it covered her breasts. "Sidney . . ."

"Carol, we've been together now for a few years. My love for you still grows stronger." Be careful, he thought. It was only eight months since they had begun having sex. It had been a long project of seduction. Now he knew why. They hadn't even spent a night together in a proper bedroom . . . only in the office. The first months were spent getting to know her body thoroughly, to know exactly what gave her pleasure, what opened her up, what made her trust him. He adopted a set sexual approach, because she seemed to find security in the predictable. It allowed her to lose control in a safe and charted pattern.

"That young man . . ."

"Carol, that young man is not the issue. I have to say it." His hand, almost absentmindedly, had reached above her stocking tops. There, he let it rest, moving his fingers slightly to feel the flesh. They had sat there in the past, in just this position, talking professionally, letting the arid words of their discipline defer their excitement, become part of their foreplay. "You've had it easy. *We've* had it easy. We go along with our machines and we map the way the central nervous system works almost neuron by neuron." He squeezed hard. As if becoming aware of his hand, she reached and put her hand around his wrist and tried to remove it. "There! Shall we tell one another the pathways the signal of that squeeze went? We know, but there's a something else that we don't know. We accrete knowledge at a snail's pace. The people who come to us are volunteers and they work under restricted conditions. Or we get those who have suffered some injury to the brain. We make small, incremental gains. And from time to time we write papers, which . . ."

I write the papers, Carol thought; you just put your name on

179

them because you're the boss. Sidney had become more and more of an administrator and less of a scientist, especially in the last year, since they had gotten grants.

He put down the glass. ". . . papers which get properly printed in the proper journals, but only after months pass. You've been complaining that you didn't really have much real material to work with. The fact of the matter is that you're really comfortable with this approach, this neuron-by-neuron approach. But what we need is a real-life, real-time situation. Someone in the midst of some kind of breakdown."

"Are you saying that this man is our experimental animal?"

"No. No. He's just one of the keys to experimental . . . subjects." He upset the soothing pattern; he moved quickly and squeezed the inner bulge of her thigh again, reached his other hand and shoved it under her lab coat and blouse, cupped, almost grabbed, her breast, turned his body and head and was now kissing her face, all over. She struggled slightly. She moaned. His hand moved up now and was under her pants, reaching fast to touch each area that would excite her . . . but harshly.

She gasped: "Sidney . . . stop . . . we have to talk."

"Carol, there are lots of ways of talking. This is one of them. Body to body. That's what's made our work so good . . . love and intellect."

She resisted, but he could feel her beginning to writhe. She was surprisingly moist. Usually it took a long time. He unbuttoned her coat, her blouse. He teased her nipples with his teeth. He made his voice go deeper and deeper, until the resonance was affecting her. He was speaking to her breasts, to her belly, as though her body were some kind of delicious ear. His finger played furiously on her clitoris. "Carol. We have an opportunity. Why don't you just let go? I mean really let go for once."

"Sidney, I've let go . . . But Clara's still out there. Clara."

"Fuck Clara." Sidney got down on his knees in front of Carol. He yanked her pants, garterbelt, stockings down below her knees and was kissing, biting her thighs. Her hands were on his head; she was both pushing and pulling. He moved his head up closer and closer.

It was more than a matter of pressing Carol's right buttons. He

180

needed her. Barnstable had made it clear: he couldn't alienate her. Sidney was calm; Sidney was excited. He unbuckled his belt and unzipped his pants. With one hand he pulled away at his pants and underpants. He hoped he was doing it gracefully.

The situation was unexpected. It was confusing her. He counted on the unexpected. Her body was excited while her mind drew back. She could almost watch both of their reactions as if . . . as if she were tracing neural activity. He was agitated; urgent; he was taking chances. His need came close to turning her away . . . there was something pleading, begging about his manipulation. She had never seen him like this before. He kept whispering, "Carol. I love you. Carol, I want to marry you." His head moved from side to side, kissing the insides of her thighs, licking, moving his head forward. A kissing and licking frenzy; he was a man attached to a mouth with its own volition. She resisted, trying to keep her legs together. He pushed inward, the motion of his head forcing her legs apart, and plunged his face into her vagina, his tongue moving furiously, not giving her a chance to recover. She was getting more and more excited, losing control of herself. Her clitoris was against his teeth. She was terrified. What if he bit her? Soon she would begin to orgasm . . .

Suddenly he stopped and drew back. He stood up. His penis was erect; it was blood-filled as never before with Carol . . . it ached. He said, panting, "No. I'm not going to do it this way. Ficino is through playing games. There are things I have to say to you."

He looked ridiculous standing there like this. So did she. She moved her legs together. She started to straighten her clothes.

"No. Leave it alone. It's time for some home truths. Carol, underneath, you're a winning, warm person, but it's buried deep. You're exciting. No, *potentially* exciting, but you don't want to recognize what you are. I think the longer you work on our projects, the more detached and icy you become, the more detached from living, human concerns. Carol, we can never let ourselves forget that the ultimate object of our studies is the liberation, the transcendence of the human being . . . and we can never let ourselves forget that the human is *more* than an aggregation of biochemical wires shooting messages . . . We dissect everything, Carol. We play God, not in order to control the lesser beings, but to liberate ourselves . . . to become God . . . for *everyone* to become God . . ."

"Sidney . . ."

"Carol, you remember the first time you had an orgasm? You remember how long it took us to reach that plateau? Carol, you're thirty-six now. Until a few months ago you never had an orgasm. There's more than one reason you left psychotherapy. You were afraid of human contact. It takes two to make contact. You are afraid of *yourself.*"

"Sidney, I . . ." She pulled at her clothes.

"Leave those fucking things alone and listen to me. Nothing humans do is anything to be ashamed of. Do you think Clara is going to burst in here? And if she did, so what?"

"No, but—"

"Are you ashamed of the way we look? When you left therapy, went back to school, and got into this area of research, you made the right decision, but for the wrong reasons. I looked up your history, Carol. You were good. Really good. You had a certain something . . . a winning quality that engendered response from your patients. *And that was what frightened you.* You were afraid of what was inside you.

"Carol, do you think I hired you only because you were a top student? The first time I saw you, I saw a deep and latent fire that marks the great scientist. We work well together, and not because of our minds alone, Carol, but because of our bodies, too. You can't sit on your intuitions. We do our research with our brains, our cocks and our cunts. Well, now we stand on the verge of . . . the big time. All I can tell you is that certain people are interested in our work. Certain people are ready to fund a more expanded research. Carol, I don't only need you because of my love for you . . . but because you can have the feel."

"Who . . ."

She has no need to know, Ficino thought. Still, he had to tell her something.

"I've never had an unwilling patient before. I can't do objective tests on someone who doesn't cooperate, who's psychotic."

"Calm him down. Talk to him. Be patient. He'll respond to you. Carol, this isn't a neat world. We want to do good research, but

182

we don't control the money to do it. All kinds of things that have nothing to do with one another get mixed up together.

"The Coffin Foundation is interested in us." That's the story he would stick to. "We've gotten money. We can get more. So they come to us one day and say, look, we'd like you to do us a favor. A *personal* favor. What's the favor? There's this kid. They don't tell me who he is. This kid thinks he's in a public psychiatric center. I suspect that he's the wayward and psychotic son of someone important, someone tied up with the Foundation. Maybe one of the trustees. Whoever it is, they're ashamed. You know how relatives can be . . . the stigma of insanity. They want confidentiality. A little favor. What's the big deal? You've had the experience. They don't say to you, 'if you don't do this, there'll be no grant.' But we're grown up, we live in the real world, we know how it works, don't we, darling? Look. There's no telling how far we can go."

He came to her then, embraced her, and started to make love. It was exhilarating for him. For her, it was something less. He wasn't telling her everything. There were a lot of questions she didn't dare ask. She wondered, as she pretended to get excited, if she was really frigid. The more she worried about these questions, the more she had to pretend to be excited.

It went on for a long time. She felt no response in herself. She felt despair. She would have to think . . . think. Then, when it was finished, they lay there for a while and talked. Sidney was full of the future and what could lay in store for them. Afterward, they got dressed. It was already four o'clock in the afternoon.

Carol went downstairs again to the room where Richard was being kept. She watched him again through the one-way mirror-screen.

He was sitting there, legs crossed, just staring ahead. He was silent. Still naked. How pitiful he looked. She sat there, looking at him for a long time. Then something began to happen; an uncontrollable urge, and she began to have the orgasm she didn't have with Sidney Ficino. After a long while she got up and walked out of the viewing alcove. She told the attendant, "Let him get dressed. I have to talk to him."

When she walked into the room Richard was being kept, old

habits asserted themselves. She smiled. "Hello," she said, "I'm sorry I kept you waiting. So many people are in trouble, aren't they? We're so understaffed."

Richard's head turned toward her. Slowly. He seemed to have difficulty in focusing. A minute passed. Two. Five. "We should talk, shouldn't we?" she asked.

He said nothing.

"My name is Carol. What's yours?"

He waited. Then he said, "You know."

She smiled. "If I know, then why am I asking?"

He said, "You know."

"No I don't. Look, why don't you just give me your name? Your first name only. Or make up a name. So I can say something other than, hey, you. All right?"

Richard raised his hand and waved her closer. She moved and smiled. Nothing to be afraid of, she told herself. Anyway, the attendant was watching through the window. Richard looked around, and then held up one hand as though it were a pad, and made writing motions. Carol reached into the pocket of her lab coat, took out a pad and a pencil and gave it to him. He wrote on it: "The people who brought me here are not cops." He passed the pad and pencil to her.

She was about to say something but had another thought. She wrote on the pad, "Who are they?"

Richard wrote, "They're Feds."

She read the message and raised her eyebrows. She shook her head. He nodded up and down vigorously. She tore out the first leaf and gave it to him. He looked around as if wondering where to throw it. He crumpled the leaf and put it in his mouth. Carol began to laugh. She reached into her pocket and took out a pack of matches and gave it to him. He understood. He lit a match and burned the leaf. She wrote on the pad, "It's not true. This is a public institution. I want to help you. I'm a doctor. My name is Carol Rothschild."

He read the message and shook his head, but he had the beginnings of a smile.

"Why are you here?" she wrote.

He didn't answer.

"Do we have to keep doing it this way?" she asked out loud.

184

He looked suspicious again.

She said, "All right," and wrote, "why are you here?"

He took the pad and wrote, "I think because I heard something terrible about the President." He didn't give her the pad, but held it up for her to see. Then he pulled it back, tore off the leaf, and burned it.

They had begun.

CHAPTER 22

HOLCOMB sat in the dark and surveyed his losses. He was not a philosophical man by nature. His whole body craved action, revenge. Maybe body determined everything. These days he had to wear glasses; a sign of deterioration. His hairline was receding. His body was jumpy, but action at this time was just the wrong thing.

Blown, bungled or torpedoed?

Maybe he had been looking in the wrong direction. So hard to tell these days. Everything was coming apart. Holcomb's years of training and combat in the European shadows, facing always eastward, habituated him to think it was the Russians. It had become part of his body, part of his nervous system. They had reinforced that feeling when they captured and tortured him. But what if that was what Keats—and those behind him—wanted him to think? His new instinct was beginning to tell him something else. Morrison and Corson were dead. That girl, the secretary, was dead too. He was in trouble. He would be blamed.

Not only was Aquilino being run, but his whole family. They disappeared as soon as the first pressure was applied. The sisters and their husbands. Gone. Into thin air. God, how many years had they been in place, with their small-business cover?

He had to think up a story for his superiors, one that would fit the report he and Keats had filed. How long did he have? A few

186

days? In the meantime, he continued backtracking through the files. He could see that he was going to get nowhere. He would write his reports in such a way as to cover himself and give them Keats's head on a platter. But, in the meantime, there was other action to take.

Revenge. Corson and Morrison had been more than his subordinates and co-workers; they had been friends.

The three of them sat there, around the little table in Ziggy's truck, drinking Rheingold beer out of cans, thinking.

"What are we going to do?" Marvin asked.

"He's in there, somewhere," Tarzan said. "We have to find some way to let him know we're out here. I say we go in and claim we're his relatives. It's easier than you think."

"No," Ziggy said. "We run this like an intelligence operation. He's not in some ordinary looney bin. That was no cop channel we were listening in to. Who knows what they're doing to him? If he knows we're out here, then they can sweat it out of him. First, we find out where he is, precisely. We penetrate. We probe. We go from telephone to telephone, we try radio, if they're using that, until we find out. Logically, he should be in the psychiatric ward, so we can start there. But I'll bet you it isn't an ordinary psychiatric section."

"Then?"

"Then maybe we think about it . . . and then after we've thought things out, we go and get some professional help."

"From who? The police? The CIA? The FBI?" Marvin asked.

"No, stupid. That's who has him."

"Which one, the CIA, the . . ."

"Same thing. Doesn't matter. Maybe we go to the government's natural enemy."

"Who?"

"The Mafia."

"Sure, we go to some hoods and say, listen, here's a thousand dollars to put the snatch on Richard."

"But we don't have a thousand dollars," Marvin said.

"We have something to sell them."

"What? A radio? A telephone?" Tarzan asked.

"Tarzan, you surprise me. We're going into competition with

187

ITT, and with Mother Bell. The Mafia already got the wire service but we're going to sell them a whole secret telephone network, equipment, lines, the whole shmear . . . A system which cannot be penetrated by the police, by the FBI, by the Internal Revenue Service . . . And we're going to manufacture it ourselves."

"With what? Scrounging or stealing equipment is one thing. You're talking—"

"Most of the lines are already in place. We're going to design the piggyback and patch equipment so that when Bell, or the government, have their new toys up there in the sky—the satellites and the rest of it, and all the other stuff that's coming down the line—we'll already be there, in place. The Mafia should invest in a little R&D, a small factory, and the continental network. The first payment is going to be Richard. After all, we can't do anything without our top engineer, can we?"

Keats reported to Kelley. "The family came from Europe in 1936. Their passport's Italian. Their name is Italian. They *are* Jews. But I don't think they're Italian. They come from further east. Our sources in Rome indicate that there's more to the story. Their documentation will be highly professional. They were political in Italy. Communists. Probably part of the whole European network of the Communist International, being run out of the Soviet Union. However, the speed of their departure seems to indicate that they ran into some kind of trouble in 1936."

"Small-business people?"

"That's the cover. The parents run a small international empire . . ."

"Dealing in what?"

"Whatever's hard to get. Arms. Drugs. Clothes smuggled into Eastern countries. Some of the new computer technology is going there too. Music. Bootleg records. Investment in risky propositions. Loan-sharking to loan sharks who bank for usurers. Ventures in flight capital. Possible retailing of information gathered by their network. They're very special. You come to them by appointment. Contact is hard to establish; you go through a series of dummy facades and cutouts. You have some exotic need? They fill it, if they can.

188

"The woman runs the operation. A very tough lady. I'm having one of our contacts in Moscow Central see what he can find out about her. The husband, we are told, handles the numbers and the percentages. On the side, he's a language scholar, and a Cabalist . . ."

Mr. Kelley was suddenly alert. Alarms went off. Keats sensed it and waited. Kelley calmed himself. It would take some thinking through. "Do any of our 'friends' in the same line of business know about them?" By "friends" he meant contacts in the Sicilian Mafia, the Corsicans, the Calabrese *n'drangheta,* the North Africans, Odessans and Georgians . . .

"I don't think so."

"Can you imagine the only son knowing absolutely nothing about what his parents do for a living. Did he have some strong and emotional need not to know?"

Keats shrugged; what was Kelley getting excited about?

"And what about the parents? Did they in turn know what their son did?"

"Until we approached them with our prepared story, they claimed not to. However, this report throws everything into doubt, doesn't it?"

"The fiction you invented may have turned out to be the truth. Maybe he's a lot of everything you invented for Holcomb, only not Russian. Do you know the legend of the *golem?*"

"The creature made out of clay, whom you activate by putting some message into its forehead, or something like that?"

"That's the crude version of it. You put the letters spelling 'truth,' *Emeth,* into its forehead and it becomes activated. The *golem* makers of earlier days were involved with the act of creation, duplicating the work of God. In Cabalistic lore, there's another version of activation: it comes out of the assemblage of all the sacred letters in all of their possible combinations . . . the Hebrew alphabet. The sacred letters originally are a scrambled heap. The learned adept makes a creature out of earth, or clay, and then begins—there are several versions—to circle the object, saying all the letters, or their numerical equivalent, in certain combinations. One goes in one direction—say clockwise—to give the creature life. One goes in the other direction, say counterclockwise, saying the combinations in reverse, in order to restore

189

the creature to its original condition."

"A kind of holy cryptography?"

"Around the time of Jesus, the Cabalists split: Hebrew Cabalists and Christian Cabalists. They were traders, spies, mystics. The Gospel according to Saint John contains Gnostic Cabalism. It led to an underground war that went on for two thousand years. And so did Aquilino receive teaching, the lore of combinations and the lore of numerical permutations, which enabled him to go higher and higher, reaching up to the secret places, not of heaven, but of policy. Through telephones."

"But this involvement with the material, in this case telephony and radio, is done by someone who doesn't know what his task is, or that he even has a task? And finally, at some point, with the right combination of words, with the right combination of impulses, the *golem*, the sleeping spy, awakes, is activated?" Keats said.

"That is what you must make sure of, my dear boy. These Cabalists half activated him. He was to bring his stolen knowledge back to them. *You* have, as it were, half-activated this *golem*. The halves don't match. He must not awaken into the reality someone else has chosen, but ours. He delivers the stolen truths to *us*. Then we will have one more task for him. To deliver it back, but changed."

After a week, signs appeared to Holcomb's now-cleared vision that the Coffin was definitely not what he had thought it was. It was, in fact, an operation of the competition. The Coffin's true mission was not so much to keep any foreign intelligence agency from penetrating business, but to keep American, maybe Allied intelligence out. An admission to himself that his obsession with the Russians had blinded him. As he admitted to himself that *he*, and the CIA, was the cover story, a memo came down the line: due to budgetary considerations, there would be a cutback in certain services deemed not to be essential. It was as though somebody up there was reading his mind. There would be strong accounting guidelines set up. Cost effectiveness would be *the* watchword, as it was in the Defense Department under McNamara. The entire Aquilino operation, for instance, was showing no results. Holcomb would have to give up one of his

190

secretaries and a receptionist. Of course his remaining secretary, having to do double work, put up a stink; he had trouble persuading her not to quit. Holcomb was also enjoined to cut down his use of the phone and the telex; he was to keep a strict log. That effectively cut out a couple of back channels Holcomb kept for himself. How do you fight a war without phones and telexes, unless you pay for them yourself?

Each operation required an in-depth memo explaining its usefulness. How, then, could Holcomb justify sending a man to Italy to follow up on the Aquilino family? He would have to have the work done through normal channels. Not only would that take more time, but it would be easy to read by prying eyes. They were watching him.

Holcomb had to move faster than he wanted to. He sent for help to three places: to Germany, to Italy, and to an old friend in the New York FBI office involved in surveilling certain American personnel at the UN and running a Russian double there, code-named Fedora. He was calling in his chips.

Holcomb asked Braunstein for help. He set up a private channel through the Germans at the UN. In order to absolutely insure Braunstein's help, Holcomb transmitted a message, using the words, "The Parvus Game." Holcomb played on Braunstein's obsession. Secret intelligence and magician societies within intelligence agencies. That was enough. And anyway, Braunstein owed him. Braunstein replied almost instantly: he was coming in, personally. Braunstein would fly directly from Berlin. Holcomb had pushed the right button. They would take the meet at Idlewild Airport.

Braunstein had worked for the *Sicherheitsdienst* in the old days. His name was not Braunstein then. He was reputed to have uncovered Canaris's links to the British as well as connections to the Third Rome Underground in Moscow. He, Braunstein, had personally looped the piano wire around Canaris' neck on that gray, chilly day in 1944. Very early in the war, Braunstein had seen that the Germans were going to lose. In 1942, he offered to cut a deal with the Americans: his services and his files—or at least part of his files—and his own personal network in exchange for freedom—and a chance to serve. Holcomb was the OSS officer who saved Braunstein from prison. He met Braunstein

191

and took back real treasure: files on Russian networks throughout Europe, links to the German agents who had been caught and left washed up in Russia.

The hot war against Soviet communism never materialized with the vigor Braunstein had hoped for. He saw in it the restraining hand of Parvus. To Braunstein, communism, business and Christianity were the three faces of Judaic thinking: a monstrous plot to subvert the world, to destroy the old Germanic cultures of the Angles, Saxons, Goths, Teutons, Allemands. Braunstein was convinced that the Bolshevik Revolution inside of the more liberal April Revolution had been funded by certain large, international corporations. He had whispered knowingly about Morgan, Du Pont, Nestle, Sandoz, Imperial Chemical, I. G. Farben, Vickers, Schneider-Creusot, factions in the Vatican, the Rothschilds, the Warburgs, the Wallenbergs, the Harriman interests in old Russia . . . while appearing to fight Russia, he fought Parvus. He had constantly talked about Parvus in the days when they had worked the Berlin Tunnel operation together. And now the words "the Parvus Game" were bringing him in.

Ziggy, Tarzan and Marvin made Ziggy's van their headquarters. They moved around. When they had to, they connected to street phones in quiet, out-of-the-way booths, or sometimes to still-working phones in empty offices in a number of buildings. Ziggy also made use of safe houses of intelligence agencies, police, foreign governments and corporations when they were empty. Never stay still.

Probing through any communications system without a schematic is truly a blind man's art. For this Ziggy was eminently qualified. Columbia Presbyterian's telephone system was a piece of cake. At least this time he knew what, or whom, he was looking for, and where it was more or less. It took three days. He located Richard because he heard people talking about him. Several men and a woman. One Barnstable, a Dr. Ficino, a Vassili Oprichnik, a Keats, a Dr. Carol Rothschild, a technician called Harkavy and another called Ziegler. The technicians talked only to Barnstable, whom they were linking up to Richard in some way. After a while he realized that Keats and Barnstable were the same person.

Ziggy encountered a set of signals that were new and puzzling

192

to him. Not voice, but something else. Wave pulsation: medical telemetry. Ziggy listened carefully . . . using the blind man's sense. He felt something . . . something . . . no, *someone* . . . Richard. Richard was at the center of this web of pulse and wave patterns. The totality *was* Richard. A fierce excitement began to grip Ziggy.

The setup was peculiar. Before the lines went through the regular hospital switchboard they were routed through a special switchboard set up in some part of the hospital. But they joined the regular Bell telephone lines, as even the most secret of military lines had to. At the switching center, the lines branched apart, were routed all over the country, and came together in Washington where this Ziegler was. The end-user, if there was such a thing in this business, was Barnstable, also known as Keats, who worked out of the offices of a foundation called The Coffin Foundation. There were other links; it would take a long time to find out what they were.

Ziggy telephoned Moe Allerdyce in Washington. Moe Allerdyce was a military traffic nut; he loved to listen in and play general. He had caused five red alerts in the DEW Line—and corrected the condition just in time to avoid general war. Ziggy asked Moe to check the Washington number out.

Then Ziggy read the Coffin Foundation number to Marvin. "Ever hear it before?"

"Yes. That's one of the numbers Richie was listening in to."

By now, Ziggy began to intercept voices. Richie's voice, talking to this Carol Rothschild. A tap. The voice signals paralleled the other pulse and wave signals. And then he understood what they were; life and body signs of all sorts. The excitement grew, for he saw that they were on the verge of the great breakthrough, delivery of diagnostic signals—medical telemetry. It would only be a question of time when they could deliver in the other direction. And that would be the beginning of the linkups, the extensions of man. He would be able to "see" again. He would be able to "move" again. In the meantime, he listened.

There comes a time in the Game when the only thing to do is to watch, wait, gather information. When you have set the trap and baited it. You inch forward, backward, sideways, making infinitesmal moves, getting as much positional advantage as you can. And it is at times like these when the very rules of the Game may be changing entirely, and you find yourself working with your enemy.

A great deal rode on Richard. Kelley had thrown resources to Keats. He had opened doors. He had established connections for Keats, which were more valuable than money itself. Certainly, the money flowed . . . from the Department of Justice and from the CIA into the National Institutes of Mental Health, where it went upstream, disbursing into a series of tributaries, to flow out again after short sojourns underground to hospitals, to universities which contracted out work to a new firm, Metatronics. Metatronics then subcontracted work to Dr. Ficino. The money traveled along complex and devious routes, losing its identity of origin in passage, becoming money to which no history was attached.

Keats, as Barnstable, was now the president of Metatronics. He was building an empire, scattered in pieces all over the country, connected by lines and equipment leased from Bell, from RCA, from General Electric. Mind-probing medical equipment was used on a sort of rented and time-shared basis. And almost immediately, the consulting work began to pour in, providing the much-needed capital for Keats's work. The money was handled by Laura Geroyavich. Dr. Ficino was the chief executive officer. The team was joined by Vassili Oprichnik, who worked under the name of John Prysemsyl.

Metatronics could call on the resources of the psychological warfare sections of the CIA, the DOD, as well as the use of some sophisticated electronics of the NSA. It was a growing concern.

The next step Holcomb took was to appeal, respectfully, to Don Calogero in Catania for information about certain people. Holcomb had worked with Calogero during the Second World War. Calogero was a kind of royalty, too old to come from Sicily in person, but he owed Holcomb.

The people Holcomb wanted information about, Aquilino, set off alarm bells in Don Calogero's mind. An ancient name in Sicily. Powerful people. Of them, the less said—or even thought—the better. They had left these parts a long time ago, but they had left certain guardians; their own little circle of Men of Respect. Controllers of certain chasms, caves, passes, tunnels. Founders of the Mafia.

Don Calogero got another message at the same time. A box. He had not lived this long by being stupid. Caution was what you learned on your father's knee. He had someone unwrap his gift for him. Far away. The unwrapper came back with the contents, smiling a little because he was glad to still be alive. Inside the larger box, there were a number of smaller boxes wrapped in a newspaper. The newspaper's headline said, "Suspected Mafioso Vanishes." His oldest rival. The first box contained a pair of human eyeballs with strips of tape over the pupils. The second contained two blood-crusted ears stoppered with lead plugs: no doubt the lead was molten and poured into the ears when they were still attached to the living man. The third contained lips and a tongue skewered together. The fourth box contained a tape recording; no doubt a recording of the screams to delight Don Calogero. There were also some instructions about how to use the documents. Don Calogero sighed and muttered. This testified to the power of the Aquilinos and their network. Were they everywhere? Indeed, they might be living next door and watching Don Calogero at that very minute. Taking no chances, he had the tape played very loud, so that the Aquilinos in the shadows would hear he had gotten the message and was responding to the gift of his rival.

At the same time, following the instructions in the gift, Don Calogero sent a mission to Rome which appeared to make the inquiries Holcomb requested. Holcomb would be sure to have someone watch his moves. One set of documents were secretly planted in the Archives, and then much less secretly retrieved, as if the object of a search, and then duplicates prepared to be sent back to Holcomb. Poor Holcomb. A stupid man. An impulsive man. Did he imagine that the favors done seventeen years ago retained their value? True, some favors matured like wine, gathering interest and flavor, building up for hundreds of years. Others had to be collected right away or they spoiled, like meat left in the sun. The game had changed a dozen times since they had last seen one another.

Back in America, one Candelli, an American, showed up bringing copies to Holcomb, of certain files about a certain Aquilino family, originally from L'Aquilla, and then from Milan . . .

Step by step their network grew. First the big centers. New York, Boston, Washington, Miami, Atlanta, Chicago, Detroit, Denver, Houston, New Orleans, Seattle, San Francisco, Los Angeles, and then smaller centers in between. Ziggy, Tarzan and Marvin plugged people in, the technology fanatics, the dreamers, the outcasts. Great fun. A hoax. Outwit the invaders from space, who had landed in Washington, who had taken over Mother Bell, who sat astride and monopolized the radio and television networks. Low on money? Little technology, other than what could be scrounged or stolen? Not to worry. There was the somnolent world of communications, like some fat and senile empire, ready to have its equipment turned to use.

A convention in September? Great. The dreamers would assemble in Boston, or New York, to exchange their dreams. Science fictioneers would meet the astrology and alchemy nuts.

Getting in touch with the Mafia, however, presented more problems than they had anticipated. Ask the wrong question and you end up with broken legs at best; at worst, dead. What *was* the Mafia? Which one of the principalities could understand what they had to offer? Which one had the ability to rescue Richard? Of the incredible list of phones Richard had tapped in to—stored away now in Marvin's remarkable memory—which ones led to the Mafia? The only way to find out was to tap into all of the numbers Richard had listened to, but there was no time. They had to take a chance. After much discussion, they decided on one particular coffee house on Mulberry Street: the Queen of Heaven Coffeehouse.

They made a night visit to the major Bell trunkline center in Chinatown, under the Temple of the Four Corners. They tapped into the Queen of Heaven and got ready to install devices that would cause trouble on that circuit.

Tarzan stole a telephone truck. That was easy enough. Wearing the tools and insignia of the telephone repairman's trade, Tarzan began to check out certain phones of coffeehouses, the Queen of Heaven among the others. When Tarzan was finished there were funny sounds; clickings, whirrings, static, crossed lines, many voices, some police traffic, and now and then one of the conversations was repeated.

Then Marvin was sent as emissary to sell their services. He was told to say that it had come to the attention of certain parties that their phones were bugged. What was this? Was America becoming a police state? These certain parties would offer to sell a sure safeguard to protect people from unwanted attention. If the Mafia was interested, they would move on to bigger and better things.

Marvin didn't come back for hours. Ziggy was calm. Tarzan was worried. Marvin was captured. Marvin was mistaken for a cop. Marvin was tortured. And Marvin wouldn't be able to hold out. Tarzan and Ziggy had moved the van. Marvin wouldn't be able to tell his tormentors where they were.

Marvin contacted them late at night. They picked him up, a little frightened but elated.

"What happened?"

"It was weird."

"What *happened?* Tarzan said.

"I started out for the Queen of Heaven Coffeehouse. I took the bus crosstown. I was going to get off a few blocks away, like we said. I walked past a few times. I was ready to go in when someone comes up to me . . . you know, he moves sideways and talks out of the side of his mouth, and looks around all the time."

"You must have acted suspicious," Tarzan said.

"No. No. I acted very normal."

"What happened then?" Ziggy asked.

"He said, 'We been watching you. Whaddaya after?' I started to explain, but he says, 'Not here, stupid. Let's take a walk.' I thought we were going to go in the coffeehouse, but he steered me in another direction. That's when I got scared. We ended up in this really ratty restaurant. I always thought the Mafia ate good. Terrible food. Dishwater coffee. The place was full of whores."

"You must have liked that part," Tarzan said.

"You know what? This guy was *them.* It came out slowly. In the conversations. We felt each other out, for about an hour. I mean, though, he spotted me and that meant something. Then I did what we said; I said that I was a salesman and we were in compe-

197

tition with the telephone company. And if people were having trouble . . . He gave me a look. I said, we can sell you the latest, most sophisticated equipment, top secret, just like the FBI uses —secure lines, scramblers, descramblers."

"Did you talk about Richie?"

"No. You said not to the first time. But they're definitely interested."

"How long did all this take?" Tarzan said.

"About three hours."

"So what kept you so long?" Ziggy asked.

"What do you think took him so long? He had to get laid," Tarzan said. "Didn't you, creep?"

The old fascist files, delivered by a Mr. Candelli, from Rome, confirmed what Holcomb suspected. Communists. KGB. Long-time agents in place.

The Aquilino family were originally from a town called L'Aquilla. They had gone to Milan to work in the factories in 1928. By 1932 it began to be suspected by Mussolini's secret police that there had been a substitution. The Aquilinos who left L'Aquilla were different from the Aquilinos who arrived in Milan. The new Aquilinos had become agitators and organizers in Milan. The secret police watched them, but for some reason they had never had the husband and wife arrested. Were they under some kind of protection?

In 1936 the Aquilinos disappeared, quite suddenly. The files speculated that they had been recalled to Russia. The Moscow trials were going on. Agents all over the world were being recalled, being executed. The old Bolsheviks were being purged. But Holcomb suspected that those trials were only an elaborate piece of cover theater. Stalin had eliminated his rivals, but had probably kept his lower echelons in place. They had gone back into the world, all over the world, under the best cover of all: they were supposed to be dead. The Aquilinos had been sent to America.

After taking appropriate evasive action, Holcomb met Braunstein at Idlewild Airport. They retired to one of the airport hotels where Holcomb had rented a room for Braunstein. On the way to the hotel, Holcomb noted that there were men all around, keeping their distance. Holcomb was afraid he had been blown, but they were Braunstein's people. After the hotel rooms had been swept for bugs, Holcomb began to brief Braunstein. Braunstein listened, getting more and more excited. He agreed with everything Holcomb felt about the Allies being honeycombed with moles, except the moles were not Russians, he said. The game was more complicated than that. "I have learned much of the Parvus Game since we talked last. You remember, you thought I was a little crazy."

Holcomb started to deny it.

"Yes. I could see the way you looked at me. No matter. I was on the verge of some great discovery. The past few years have more and more confirmed it. First and foremost, instead of being dead, the great and mysterious Parvus is still alive. Ninety-five years old but alive. Amazing."

Braunstein plunged into conversation as if they had never parted. Time slipped backwards. As Braunstein warmed to his topic, his face became animated; he began to look younger. They were back running the Berlin Tunnel operation. "It was Khrushchev's speech at the Twentieth Party Congress that started the next stage of Parvus. The putting of the stake through Stalin's dead corpse. What a shock that speech was. What the Moscow Trials had failed to do, what the pact with Hitler failed to do, the speech did. Party members deserted in droves. No more communism. It wasn't needed. One can really trace the beginning of the split with the Chinese from that point in time."

"What split? They're still together."

"I know what your leaders think and say. But they are wrong. The split is surfacing. There's been universal unrest, domestic conflict in capitalist and communist countries alike. Even the Russians began to experience trouble. Strikes. The rising of national minorities demanding their freedom from the Great Russian Overlord."

What did it mean? The Parvus Game was emerging, enlarging, gathering force and momentum, a state within many states. Civil war on a world scale. Takeover of the vital places. Having been hunted by the secret services, Parvus had changed colors and become part and parcel of the opposition. No longer was the struggle between good and evil, between the day and the night,

199

between the god and the satan possible. That was becoming a piece of theater, the grand and diabolical dialectic in which they, Parvus, would play both sides of the war, and so win.

It was a man named Alexander Israelovich Helphand, who wrote under the name Parvus, a Russian revolutionary of the late nineteenth century, who gave up his revolutionary ways, came to live in Germany, and found ways of giving material support to the vision. This Helphand dreamed of an end to nations, of an end to the divisive customs and languages of people, to the end of their traditions. He talked to the internationally minded leaders of the international corporations. Some bought it.

All one had to do was to read Helphand's writings. When the Russian Revolution broke out, Helphand-Parvus persuaded them to send Lenin to Petrograd from Switzerland in the sealed car, to keep the British and the French from executing him.

Why, Braunstein asked rhetorically, had such disastrous settlements been made after the Second World War, in such a way as to create maximum difficulties in the years to come? Was it a drunken Churchill, a sick Roosevelt, a stupid and murderous Stalin who had delineated the spheres of interest, determined where the small and deadly struggles were later to be carried out? Or was it the advisors, the viziers with the facts, figures and particulars, who stood behind the leaders and whispered into their ears, saying, give this up, but keep that? Split Germany. Split Korea. Split Vietnam. Divide Berlin.

After Braunstein finished talking, the seed he had planted so long ago began to germinate. Holcomb's faith in the predictability of the KGB began to waver. Holcomb briefed Braunstein on Richard's operation, and the disappearing Aquilinos. His suspicions of Keats, of the cover operation for which he worked. Braunstein got excited. There was something about Richard Aquilino's operation that reminded him of something, someone . . . an operation run out of Berlin in the Second World War. A deep penetration . . . a genius with radio. A supreme musician in the grand spy orchestra—a soloist. He would check into all of it from his end, and promised support at this end. There would be people to help Holcomb. "And perhaps you are in a good position, just where you are. Inadvertently, you have done what Parvus did. You penetrated them."

200

Holcomb noted further signs that he was being undercut and plotted against. Some of his staff were no longer eating in the Foundation cafeteria. Did that mean they were using lunches for meetings elsewhere? A palace revolt? He decided to check. He began to take his lunches in restaurants surrounding the area. After the third try, he found some of his personnel. It was clear, from their reaction, that they were conspiring against him. He had to act before his power base was gone.

CHAPTER 23

THE room Richard was being kept in had been turned into a monitoring box, a kind of gigantic stress-analyzer and lie detector. Its walls were embedded with instruments that could receive —and broadcast—signals. The broadcast signals could stimulate or disorient Richard . . . possibly even plant or reinforce notions in Richard's mind. Keats had already staged a number of conversations for Richard to hear.

Keats worked out of a safe house, running the operation and his new firm, Metatronics, some blocks away from the Coffin Foundation. There, he reviewed video and audio tapes. Keats controlled Ficino. Ficino controlled Carol. Carol had to control Richard. The thought began to occur to Keats: could he use Richard to play his own game with Kennedy?

Two voices spoke quietly; Richard and Carol, secure in the illusion that they were alone on the planet. She had taken to doing her interviews at night. Was it a way of eluding Ficino? Their relationship was deteriorating. On one screen, ghostly colors, ranging from blue-green for cool, to yellow-white for hot: a thermogram keyed to emotional activity. Still crude. Precision would come later. Ideally, Carol and Richard should be naked, to be able to pinpoint what parts of their bodies glowed hot or cold.

Carol probed. Richard resisted. After the first frightened babblings, he tried to fight back with silence. He had raved of a world bathed in atomic fire, visions, demonic voices (out of his primal past, she thought), speaking as public figures. Household names. Carol decided: it was a paranoid schizophrenic delusional system of enormous proportions. The highest forces of government were out to get him. He claimed to have had a prevision of some great catastrophe. He claimed he had been drugged, chased, beaten, driven crazy. There were bruises on his body; self-inflicted?

A whole battery of tests was administered, including EEGs. No brain damage. The bodily fluids showed minute amounts of unexplained substances. What were they? Drugs, or auto-produced? But then she didn't have a long medical history so she didn't know what was normal or abnormal. The lab couldn't tell her what the trace chemicals were.

Richard didn't trust her at all. He had to keep his mouth shut as long as he could.

"You can talk to me. There's just us," she said.

He knew better. He had glimpsed a world in which everyone listened in to everyone else. Keep your mouth shut. "They" had to be listening. Keep quiet, at least until Ziggy found him. He had to get to a phone.

The old methodology was too slow, Carol thought. It took years. She couldn't afford the luxurious hours, the years of waiting. It was a tenet of that kind of therapy that the patient had to *want* help. Richard didn't want help. She had to take the lead. Sidney was pushing her. That bothered her. Something was on Sidney's mind; he was almost hysterical these days.

"If you don't help me, I can't help you. Why don't you tell me your full name, where you live. At least I can get in touch with your parents. They must be terribly worried about you."

"You think I'm crazy."

Yes, she thought. She took a chance. She laughed. "What would you think if you were in my position?"

A bitter, almost ironic smile twisted his lips. A signal. What did it mean? Probably the parents were the last people he wanted to see. The parents were always responsible. But she had to know. "You have to trust someone. Really, I'm not with the . . . Feds.

Do you mean the FBI? You should trust me."

She delivered each statement gently, patiently. He sat there, stony-faced. Really, she thought; he was quite handsome. Was she wearing him down with kindness and patience? She chafed; she was being kept from her real work.

He wondered why he was being kept in isolation. He felt crippled without his network of people and equipment. He had never realized how much a part of his life, his nervous system, the telephones, the radios, the distant voices, had become.

Were they still putting things in his food and drink? No, probably not. The fits, the seizures, they were going away.

Another doctor came. A Dr. Sidney Ficino. He was short and plump. He smiled heartily. He had a deep voice. He exuded confidence. When Richard told him that he was really a government shrink, Dr. Ficino laughed long and loudly. But there was a certain note in his voice: the man was acting.

Three men were attendants. They were thuggish, but dressed in white. They brought him the food and drink, and the science fiction books he had asked for, and changed the linen on his bed, and made small talk with him. He got into an argument with the one named Will, who was a rabid Giant football fan. Richard told Will, before he thought about it, that he could kiss the Giants goodbye in a few years. They were going to be moved out of New York.

"How could they do a thing like that? I don't believe it," Will said.

"They can do anything they want. They don't give a shit about people like us." And that wasn't the half of it. If Will only knew. Should he tell Will what he heard the gamblers saying? The line . . . the point spread . . . "You better believe it. I know."

"Bullshit. What's *your* pipeline? The Maras call you up and say, Richie, kid, we're thinking of moving our operation out of New York, whaddaya think?"

"I heard."

"Heard who?"

Richard shut his mouth. The conversation petered out. Clearly, Will thought Richard was crazy and that meant that Will wasn't a guard, but an attendant.

She was patient. She was warm. She had never done things

204

quite this way before. Sidney was on her back, getting more and more restless, demanding results. When was she going to get Richard hooked up? New equipment was being brought in. She was instructed in the use of the equipment. There was wiring all over the place. Telephone hookups were being connected to the equipment. "Telemetry," the installing technicans explained.

"Where do they lead?"

"You'll have to ask the telephone people."

She asked Sidney about this new setup. "Well, some of the equipment is new, experimental, in R&D. There's only one of a kind . . . shared by researchers in many places."

"Where is the equipment?"

"I'm not sure, but what's the difference?"

He didn't want her to know. She would find out. Where did all the money come from? The Coffin Foundation? Their library was being expanded.

Their loving became more perfunctory. There was more personnel around. Sidney had more to administrate. He seemed to be spending a lot of time in conference. There was more paperwork. Instead of being hurt, she was glad. The spell Sidney held over her was breaking. But she still needed him and resented needing him. He was the gatekeeper to success. "There's terrific pressure on me," he told her. "The rich, Carol, they're not scientists. They think that all you have to do is to wave that magic wand. They're used to getting just what they want. Are you getting anywhere? Are you keeping your notes up to date? Get them typed out. Has he started to loosen up?"

"I'll have the notes typed up soon. Everything's so incomplete." She realized that she was reluctant to do it.

"We don't have much time."

"What does that mean?"

"Well, you should have established trust."

"Why don't *you* do it?"

"Carol . . ."

"You're asking me to do something in a short period of time that should take years. You would think that his parents would be more concerned for his mental health. Sidney, why can't we bring in someone else to do this? I want to get back to my work."

"You will. With him."

205

"Richard?"

"You've got a classic psychotic there. When you gain his confidence, we can begin to make breakthroughs. We can build up the first definitive lexicon, *the* map of his disturbances. You'll write up a paper . . . our paper . . . and *you* will deliver it at the conference . . ."

"What conference?"

"It's a surprise. Kiss me again that way."

She felt protective of Richard. There was something wrong with what Sidney wanted. He had lost his sense of proportion and morality. "Sidney, that will take years."

"Not as long as you think. These telephone lines go all over the country. Knowledge banks are being built up. There's a Manhattan Project of the mind going on."

"Every person is different, Sidney."

"Yet alike. We're all biojelly . . . everyone in the world has the same jellyware. We're breaking down the mysteries of the ultimate black box."

"Black box? Jellyware?" What kind of talk was that?"

"The brain. Cybernetics."

"Carol. I'm raving. I'm going half-crazy. I don't want to blow this. We know he's scared. He thinks the whole government's after him. It's classic. He's heard voices. He thinks he's heard the President talking to him. Maybe he really heard the President. Maybe they weren't hallucinations of an auditory nature. Not all 'voices' are psychoactive."

"Sidney, psychotics are not amenable to the classic disciplines. Paranoid schizophrenics are incredibly cunning. They construct whole world-systems tied together by impeccable logic. They can take the slightest cues . . ."

"But where do those cues from from?"

"Anywhere. The newspapers. Television. A conversation overheard in the street. A conversation you heard your father having. They can take these minimal hints and fit them into their delusional system. Sometimes their constructs make sense, anticipate the real world. Everything is grist for the mill."

"Maybe there are traces, memory traces, lurking in his auditory centers. Can you imagine what a stir we'd make if—"

"Sidney, we're years away from that. It's science fiction, magic you're playing with."

"We might be closer than you think . . . I think you should start catching up on the new material that's coming into our library."

What was he hinting at? He was trying to tell her something without telling her directly.

"Push a little, Carol."

What was Sidney concealing from her? She was upset. She didn't want to go home. She was sexually excited and Sidney could do nothing for her anymore. She sat in her office and reread her notes, went over the test records, glanced through new journals. But she was restless. Lonely. She hadn't been lonely for a long time. Where was there to go? She wandered the corridors, but she knew she wasn't wandering. It got late. She could hear the hospital becoming quieter. She sent out for food and ate a sandwich. She got up and went to look at the new machinery, looked at the wire entrails which disappeared into boxes, to go . . . where? Another attendant, Martin, was on duty outside of Richard's door. Was he an attendant, or a guard? What was she doing here? She nodded. He opened the door. It was dark inside.

Richard heard. Someone had come in. There was a flash of light. He lay very still in bed, his body tense. Now it would start, he thought. Thinking he was asleep, they would come to the edge of the bed, stand over him, watching, and then, suddenly, they would strike. That was the way he imagined it to be; that was one of the ways Ziggy told him they did it. He was prepared to move quickly. Richard kept his eyes closed. He waited. He heard breathing. He smelled perfume. The doctor's smell. Heard her breathing. He listened and sensed something else . . . something new . . . a loneliness. He relaxed. The bloodbeat in his ears went away. He heard better when he was calm.

Scanning the monitored records, Keats was beginning to strip them down to their *real* nakedness. Physical nakedness was amusing, but not the kind that counted. He wanted to get down to their inner being. He was beginning to see their real erotic sensuousness. They wanted to fuck one another. Keats grinned.

207

Sidney wasn't going to like that. In Keats's world there was no such thing as one person belonging to another. And, if Mr. Kelley was to be believed, all belonged to The Way. Sidney would just have to get used to the idea.

Richard had a good body; very good. He would have made a good agent . . . if he had had the right beginnings. Too late. You got the taste young. Carol's body left something to be desired. Her breasts were too big for his tastes. They should get used to fucking under observation. Keats had learned; in his world there was no privacy. If you wanted privacy, you had to do it another way . . .

CHAPTER 24

ON another screen, sets of dancing lines: stress monitoring of the voices. Every now and then superimposed red arrows appeared, indicating excitement. When the voices said something that interested Keats, he pressed a button and a yellow arrow appeared on the tape, marking the place. It meant "follow that up." Richard was on the bed, lying down, sitting up, crossing and uncrossing his legs, drawing his knees up like some restless schoolboy. Sensors monitored the activity of the bed, Carol's chair, all the furniture in the room. She seemed to draw closer and closer, subtly edging her chair near, unaware of what it was she was doing. The bed jiggled and creaked. A lot of activity. A kind of ritual foreplay.

The speaker at Keats's elbow crackled. The voice of the Metatronics technician, Ziegler, said, "We're nowhere near a sensitivity capability to get a complete mapping. It's still very primitive . . ."

Stupid man, the intuition bred out of him. The technician believed in nothing unless his instruments told him it was so.

"Can we begin a little feedback?"

"Soon . . ."

As a child, Richard used to read in bed late at night, listening for the slightest sound. He was afraid of the dark. His parents nagged him to get some sleep, not to ruin his eyes. He was prepared to turn off the light and thrust the books under the covers if they came into his room. He read: worlds in which strange creatures battled; crystalline universes alongside the disorderly one he knew.

A door-creak. He used to pretend to be asleep when his father or mother came into his room and stood over him. They would look down at him, listen to his breathing and know if he was asleep or awake. His mother would touch him. Her big hand would tell her if he was really asleep or not. She knew everything through her hand; and her sharp gaze penetrated everywhere. It was as though she were perpetually alert for something . . . even for the creatures of his imagination. She would say, "Richard, go to sleep." She was a guardian.

Sometimes, between sleeping and waking, evil and mysterious creatures were in the perpetual act of coming from a long way off to get him. They had a way of getting to you. They short-circuited space and time. They could come through your closet, lurk in the shelves of the chest of drawers, because they had ways of altering their shapes. His mother could protect him. She had great strength. If he only knew how or when they would come for him. They had come for him and they had captured him. Sometimes he would set up strings with cans or bells, tie them to the closet, or the chest of drawers. The clacking rattle would warn him.

When his father came, it was because he wanted to talk. His father was more like him, a dreamer. When he wasn't working on the account books, he would read his scholarly material; many languages, especially Hebrew. They were both great readers; his mother read the real world. "We read the same thing," his father once said. This puzzled Richard. His reading in radio and communications had nothing to do with his father's.

His father would tell him stories until his mother would come and chase her husband out. Once, he heard them whispering: "Why are you filling his head with these tales? Aren't there enough real *gilguls, dybbuks, shaitans, shedin* in the real world?"

"That's my way of telling him . . . gently . . . preparing him . . ."

"He doesn't need to know these things. He's like you, a dreamer. Sometimes I wonder how you ever got into the business."

"It's in the blood, handed down through the generations from father to son. They needed me."

"They needed your talents. You were a great codebreaker. You came with the deal."

"If you have learned to decipher the act of creation, the place of precryptation, what petty mysteries of mere humans could withstand me? I saw you making a speech. Your hair blew. Your face glowed. I fell in love. Could you withstand me?"

"Am I a code?"

"To this day you are an ever-recurring mystery, coded in such a way as to make me desire to break it, because the message is different every time."

"You are a crazy Jew."

"And you are a crazy Tartar, Lilly."

"I had such contempt for you when we were assigned to work together."

"That's because you were the flesh, the doer. I was intellect. You understood that you needed me to read the signs."

"You weren't such a pure intellect. For a dreamer you were always after me to go to bed."

"It's a weakness, I admit it. But that too is in our tradition. I turned aside your contempt by weaving spells. The first time I looked at you, looked at your body, I thought I would fall down in a faint."

"Say some spells."

There would be a silence, but a noise of movement. Doors would close. . . .

Did Richard feel locked out, Carol wondered? "Why did you think they were evil, Richard?" she asked.

Her voice sounded sad, lonely, preoccupied. Had he been talking out loud? Could he trust her? He didn't answer.

"What kind of stories did your father tell?"

He didn't answer. He felt a stirring and prepared himself to leap out of bed, but it was her hand on his forehead. "Don't be afraid. I won't hurt you."

"Different kinds. He told me adventure stories, stories of our

211

families. Stories of magicians . . . I think they were magicians."

"Magicians?" Had Richard's disturbances started then, with tales of terror told to an impressionable boy?

"One he liked to tell over and over. It was always about knights, battles, merchants, wise men, evil ones. Magicians who could become invisible and summon strange forces to help them. There were sword fights. In this one story, it took place once upon a time, a long time ago. Sometimes it takes place on a hill, or in some kind of open space. A city square. Sometimes it will take place in the kingdom of Sicily . . ."

"Sicily?"

"My father's family originally came from Sicily. My mother's family is Russian, Tartar, going back to the Mongol invasions."

"How do you know that?"

"We had records."

"You're Italian then?"

"Not exactly. Jewish. In those days, in Sicily there were Christians, Jews and Mohammedans. It was a golden age; everyone lived in harmony. Saracens wearing long, flowing robes; fierce fighters. There were knights. Armor. The knights were always Christians . . ."

What was the significance in the way Richard said the word "Christians," with contempt?

". . . Normans . . . Greeks . . . Jews . . . Dalmatians . . . smugglers . . . Teutons . . . scholars . . . doctors . . . merchants. There's a great good king. Fredrick II. *Stupor mundi.* He was a great, good and wise man. But he gets sick and dies . . . or maybe he's poisoned. Then anarchy begins to rule the land. Oppression. Misery. Injustice. The oranges rot. The merchants are squeezed by taxes. Priests come and torture the Mohammedans and the Jews, wanting them to convert. Knights from the north, from beside a misty and cold sea. They wear black armor and red crosses dipped in blood. Things get very bad. They rule. Great battles are fought. The knights are all big and blond. The people are small, dark."

Had Richard's father reversed the folk tale in which the blond knight is always the hero? "Why blond?"

"I don't know. That's the way my father used to tell it. He hated blond people. Say, that's funny; when she was younger, my mother had blond hair."

212

"Did they hate one another?"

"No, they loved one another very much."

"They're dead?"

He didn't answer. What was she going to say now, talk to us or your parents and your sisters are going to die? "There's a battle. Maybe it takes place in Palermo. I can't remember. Because sometimes the story takes place in Seville, Venice, Frankfurt, Moscow, Odessa . . . The places change but the story stays more or less the same. It always seems to be happening to the same people . . . or the children, or grandchildren of the same people.

"There are two men. One's the knight. He wears the black armor. The other is small and dark; not a knight. He's quick and tricky. His eyes move quick and his mind works fast all the time. He can change shape. But the trickery doesn't help, not at first. He loses. The knight beats up the small man. Sometimes he's killed, but he's not really killed. I mean sometimes he's cut into little pieces but he always comes together again. Or sometimes he just disappears into thin air. He has a thousand ways. He wins the fight, but not right then. Later, and maybe in another country. You see, he has mysterious helpers. There are thirty-two of them . . ."

"What do the thirty-two helpers mean to you?"

"Twenty-two mystic letters, and ten numbers. You say some of them in certain ways, and they become what you want them to become. The magician—"

"He was a magician?" Letters? Numbers? She didn't want to interrupt the flow.

"Yeah. He loses in 1251. He gets revenge in 1282. And then it starts all over again."

"Why those dates?"

"Those dates start the story." Richard stopped, remembering. He hadn't thought of those stories for a long time. "The magician wakes the magical helpers who, in turn, wake up some kind of force. Sometimes it's a giant, sometimes it's something else."

"Why are they fighting?"

"It's a blood feud. It's about some kind of treasure. But also it's about an imprisoned princess who's guarded by something terrible. Maybe it's a dragon. If you learn the spell and can say it, then you can get past the dragon."

213

The king, the father, the President . . . Keats thought. Not much emotional reaction. Something was coming together for him.

"And the princess?"

"She was taken away and imprisoned somewhere, in a cave, or a castle, guarded by evil spirits. In the story you had to first beat the creature that disguised itself like a knight. Then you had to have magic to release the princess."

"How did the magician find her?"

"The master of the names said them, in a certain order. The names became things, places to stand, pathways between things. The naming of each name brought you closer. Then you finally can figure it out: you can *say* where the castle, or the cave was . . . and you could *see* where she was. Then, when you found where she was, you need spells to reach her, and spells to waken her, and spells to release her, turn her back from being a putrid hag into a beautiful girl." But maybe she didn't want to be liberated. It didn't matter. His princess was dead.

Carol wondered: what did the princess mean to Richard? Was the folktale a vision of trying to unblock his own stifled sexuality? His mother? And what was the creature who guarded the princess, the "dragon"—was that the father, the father who would have to be slain? She remembered the "case history" she had worked on with Sidney. The powerful father. The secrets. Sidney had been setting her up for this boy. Why didn't he trust her?

Richard wondered: was he saying too much?

"Your father sounds like he's a nice man."

Sounds? Or sounded? Why was she asking him these questions? Why didn't the rest of them come to trade? For your parents . . . tell us . . . what for what? They wanted something from him. Hey, fellows, anything you want to know. Well, he knew something. He had *something* that someone wanted badly . . .

The bed was agitated. Keats heard the squeaks. Something was exciting Richard Aquilino. Listen. Scan. Wait. Numbers. Fairy stories. Waves. Folktales. Letters. Myths. Codes. A world of magic and Cabalistic wisdom and cryptography. He loved it. Yellow arrow markers. Go back over. Call up a few friends in

214

Bloomington and talk to the folklorists, the myth-and-intelligence collectors and tell them the story.

As for the princess, Keats was going to see her tomorrow, or the day after.

Richard was excited. Suddenly, he felt a power. It was something that he didn't know, but he had it, whatever it was. Did his body tense? Relax. Forget. Forget you figured it out. Wait until she's gone. "We can arrange it so that we trade off the Jupiter missiles in Italy and Turkey . . . they're out of date." Was that it?

He was sitting up in the bed now. She was sitting on a chair next to the bed. They sat in darkness for a while. Only the sound of their breathing. It was still. They felt close.

"What do your parents do?"

Do? Did? "They ran junkyards. Owned some real estate."

"Ran? Are they dead?"

He listened for the tone. Innocence or a sarcastic wisdom. Cunning? He didn't answer.

"What's wrong?" Junkyards? The son of a powerful trustee of the Coffin Foundation? Junkyards? Was Sidney's case history wrong, or was Sidney lying? Or being lied to? "Would it bother you if I smoke?" she asked.

"No. There's an ashtray on the table."

The flare of the match showed her face. The match's distorting light made her look as if she were frowning. "And what about the princess? What was she like?"

"My father never really described her. You know how those stories go. No one has faces. She was beautiful." She had black hair and gray eyes in a very white face. She disappeared, or she was stolen away one day. Thirteen years old. Laura. Someday he would get her back. She was dead, but he had seen her after her death. She had to be rescued . . . or revenged . . .

When he was little, he used to watch his princess playing in the street, skipping rope. He was ten. She was eight. He fell in love. But he could never tell her about it. She would laugh at him. Little boys didn't fall in love with little girls. Boys played games. Boys played at being soldiers, cops, robbers. Boys fought. In his neighborhood, no one wanted to be the cop.

He began to read *Popular Mechanics* and *Popular Science*.

215

Popular Radio and *Popular Electronics. Scientific American. Science.* Books of math. He took apart clocks and put them together again. He took apart the family's radio and put that together. It worked better than ever. He began to build his own radios, crystal sets, and then operated a ham station. When he looked at wiring, it all made sense to him instantly. He read college physics texts and began on advanced material before he was even in high school. He considered the implications of relativity. School bored him. His teachers began to think he was stupid. He would have stopped going to school, but there was Laura.

He watched Laura grow up and become a woman quite early. She always had boys around her. Older boys began to elbow the kids of her own age aside. Her eyes sparkled. Her voice commanded. He loved her. It became harder to come close to her. Had he waited too long?

Carol lit another cigarette. It was a breakthrough. He was talking. Should she interrupt? No. Keep quiet.

The shyness grew like a sickness. Talking to people gave him trouble. His father and mother were distrubed by his bad marks in school. After all, his father was a scholar of sorts. And wasn't it time to give up this childish hobby and pay attention to his schoolwork? Boys went with girls. Things happened in the hidden corners of school. There were dates. Movies. Proms. He wasn't involved in any of it.

Laura became more and more beautiful every day. Even though she was twelve, thirteen, she was a woman. Grown men began to hang around her now. There was a terrible and dirty hunger in their eyes. He raged but he didn't know what to do. And yet, he thought, she was aware of him, laughed at him from behind her mask. Her face was beautiful, impenetrable, the center of all things. Inside, he wanted to believe that Laura was the same as him. Gray, luminous eyes. How could she listen to all that boring talk? He listened to pop music. When he was alone, he played his records; songs of thwarted love. Elvis wept his tears for him.

The buildup of the initial set of traumas, expressing itself as a pathological shyness? Carol lit another cigarette. Her mind drifted. She remembered her own childhood. Also lonely. Also feeling strange, different. Plain face. Glasses. Braces. Skinny. If

216

boys ever talked to her she overwhelmed them with talk. It burst out of her like a flood. They were disgusted. Booktalk. She changed suddenly. Her breasts grew large . . . her behind became too big. She was clumsy. She felt gross. Now that she had a body, boys came. She repelled them. She always said the wrong thing. Her clothes didn't fit right. But underneath, she was beautiful. She had a beautiful mind. She had such intense longings. Refuge in books. Psychology. What made people tick? What made *her* tick?

How alike she and Richard had been, but they had made such different things of their lives. What if they had met . . . then? Two shy people. How ridiculous. She was at least ten years older than he was. Worlds apart intellectually. What was happening to her?

They were talking, Keats thought, exchanging confidences so that they could trust one another. Intelligence services were like nervous systems seeking to evolve into brains . . . longing to be centralized. It couldn't happen. Not when your various nerves could introduce their own peculiar messages anywhere along the line of transmission. Then too, the center did not want to hear certain things that were unpleasant. Or a cluster of agents and their lines of transmission could go rogue, become autonomous, feed in false messages. When you realized that, you understood why you were no longer bound to the chain of command. That's what he had done and that's what Holcomb was trying to do. Amusing to watch him struggling to put together his own network. Fine. That was the network he was going to hang Holcomb with.

Finally, one day, Laura seemed to take notice of Richard. He never figured out why. What happened between them was too short. She just came to him one day, and everything he had dared to dream of happened, and even more. He had won the princess for a few days. Then . . .

"Then?"

He stopped. He sat there, remembering. There had been one golden moment and he had fallen under her spell forever.

They had gone to the roof of his building. It was autumn. The sun was warm. What was ordinary was transfigured. He was on another planet. Light and autumn warmth was spread evenly everywhere. Even the roof tarpaper was transfigured. A million little particles embedded in the tarpaper shimmered and became stars. Benevolent heat, soaked up by the roof, radiated upward onto their bodies. Each building around them, all the way up to the distant towers at the center of Manhattan, sparkled. Laura looked at him for a long time. Then she nodded, as if to herself, as if making up her mind about something.

He was paralyzed. Say something. What do people talk about? He didn't want to talk about radios, or telephones, or his jerky friends, or his distant ham-radio contacts. He was scared. She moved closer. Her eyes gleamed. The pupils seemed to widen till they almost seemed to fill her eyeballs. Gray became mysterious black. She put her hands on the sides of his face and pulled him close. He closed his eyes; she didn't. She kissed him. His body began to shake. His penis rose. He was afraid she would notice. He tried to draw back, and she moved her body against his. Then she began to undress him.

He couldn't talk. She took off her clothes and moved his hands along her body, to her breasts. A small wind chilled parts of his body that had never been exposed to the outside air before. Her eyes kept looking at him looking at her, as if his gaze could excite her. They were penetrating, penetrating. He fumbled. He didn't know what to do. She was gentle. She helped him. They were on top of their clothes. He was on top of her. His eyes were shut tight; he didn't dare to look. She put his penis inside her. High above, circling seagulls shrieked. Pigeons cooed. The traffic hummed, warming up the air. He *heard* the vibrations of the sun's light. He was connected to everything. He was sure he *felt* all the city's electrical-wave traffic passing through him . . . Everything . . . images, conversations . . . It was all so simple and beautiful. He plunged again and again, his arms around her now. The more he jerked, the more sensitive to the city's electricity he became. Finally she began to shriek. He stopped. "What's wrong?" he asked. She didn't answer. Her face had contorted. Her eyes stared up. He saw bits of blue sky and cloud floating there. A stillness surrounded them. They lay there in the sunlight, still and waiting. Bit by bit the world reconstituted itself and she smiled at him. White teeth in a slightly tan face. Black hair that swallowed all light. White body on that black tarpaper. Small and perfectly formed breasts; nipples like the tips of delicate fingers. The hips not quite formed into true womanhood. A small public smudge. The moment seemed to last forever.

Richard was silent. Had it really happened, or hadn't it? Carol lit another cigarette. She wished she had had such a moment, even one, of love. They sat there, perhaps for another ten minutes, neither of them saying a word. What was the time? Three o'clock in the morning? Carol didn't feel tired. Gently, she said, "And then . . . ?"

Richard sighed. "And then there were no other times. She disappeared. She was stolen away."

He was fantasizing. The obsessive image of the princess. Had his parents interfered? Had hers? Was it just her refusal to deal with this clumsy boy? "Stolen?" she asked.

"Yeah. Stolen. Bought."

Bought? What did he mean by that? Bought off?

"I began to hunt for her."

"Where was she taken? Did you find her?"

"I . . . I . . ."

"Yes, Richard?"

"I found a way to . . . *hear* her."

"Hear?" Voices? Hallucinations?

"Through the telephone."

"The telephone?" Again, this use of technology in support of his system of visions and voices. "Where had she gone?"

"New York. Connecticut. Massachusetts. Washington. California. London. Rome—"

"Did you go to her?"

"Only once. I called her up and she laughed at me. Once I saw her. She laughed at me . . ."

"When was that?"

"About five years ago."

"And that's the last time you saw her?"

"No. First, I saw her two weeks ago. She was dead. Then I saw her four or five times. She was alive."

Treat it as if it were real. Don't deny the vision. Find out what it means to him. "Where?"

"Here in New York. The same day they brought me in here."

219

"That was when she was dead?"

"No. Yes. I don't know. Something was wrong with me . . ."

"You seem to have it wrong, Richard. You said that she died, and then you saw her alive. Is that right?"

"Yeah. That's right. That's the way it happened."

"My mind is reeling, absolutely reeling. I feel as if I've looked into the pits of hell and seen the heights of heaven," Sidney Ficino said.

"A little more wine will restore the balance. The papers which bring together Metatronics and launch it effectively will be ready next week. There'll be a lot of papers to sign."

"The amount of work that has been done . . . I feel like I'm a student again."

"You'll catch up."

"One thing bothers me."

"What, Sidney?"

"Why can't I bring Carol into this yet?"

"She's doing something very sensitive. In fact her very lack of knowledge is a positive asset. Her skills are needed . . . her 'old' skills. Her gentle art of probing. She's not ready yet. How would *you* feel if the area in which you are making enormous breakthroughs was not the virgin territory you thought it was? A lot of research goes on that has already been done but has to remain under wraps. Someone discovers a new process and has an attorney make a search of the patent files. Nothing there. No one seems to have discovered your discovery. You're elated. You go and file a patent claim. You get back the word that there *is* a patent, but it's classified. Or you just have to lay off, no explanations, thank you. Military applications requiring a classification— something that you thought should not be able to come into existence for ten years down the line. In a sense, the things that you and Carol have been working on are put into a kind of abeyance, and it will seem that you will make enormously speeded up progress, and you will be able to get support, and you will not only invent what's been invented, but you have to go through it as if it all hadn't been gone through before."

They finished their meal. They moved on again into one of the lounges where they had coffee, brandy and cigars.

"Now tell me; I know that you've been rushed—"

"I must have read about ten thousand pages."

"You're exaggerating."

"No, I'm not. I've kept count. And anyway, I have an almost photographic memory."

"That's a help. All right, given that, what's your prognostication of the direction we should take?"

"It's not formulated well, Mr. Barnstable. But the problem is Distant Influence . . ."

"And Remote Assessment."

"That when one gets, on all cylinders, so to speak, a complete profile of a person, one can feed that profile back—with some variations, of course—to alter a person's belief system, emotional state, time sense . . ."

"Good."

"I mean in a variety of ways, all complementing one another. Drugs, food, sound, light, chemicals, electrical, and with the appropriate contents . . ."

Barnstable was grinning.

Ficino's face fell. "You're going to tell me that it's been done too?"

"It has, but that's not a reflection on your abilities, Sidney. Not at all. It's just that certain scientists have had help and many have had no help at all."

"I'm a little worried . . ."

"You're full of worries, Sidney."

"Well . . . it's what I see happening down the line, the ability to probe into people's minds . . . to control them."

"People are crazy beasts, Sidney. Think of it as an exchange. You give up some of your irrational attachments to freedom, you give up a little privacy, even some dignity. But what's the exchange? When people become linked up, then we can stop the craziest behavior patterns, the stealing, the murder, the lust for power.

"Look, I want you to pay particular attention, again, to the second case history. Start to really refine your findings. I think that some very important people are going to need your findings."

The second case history was Nikita Sergeievich Khrushchev's.

221

Khrushchev was beginning to make overtures through channels. Wouldn't it be a grand idea if the Berlin problem could be discussed man to man, as it were. What if Kennedy were to come on a state visit to Moscow? Or what if Khrushchev himself were to come on another visit to the United States? The feelers went their secret way. It would be another month before it would be leaked to the papers.

CHAPTER 25

"WHEN can we begin some feedback and input?" Keats asked the Metatronics engineer, Ziegler.

"You want to be careful. We don't have anywhere near a complete profile. It's too soon—"

"I want a little fugue. A marriage of two complex themes. Him and her. I want something agitating, something sexy . . . Figure out the cycles. Subliminal. You know what I mean . . ."

"The boys in the audio lab can compose something for you in the interim." The audio lab was in San Francisco, where new kinds of musicians were composing new kinds of music, playing with strobe lights keyed to the music, fluctuating, hypnotic, constructed out of the personality they were monitoring.

"You're getting her too?"

"Yes."

"Consulting the library of archetypes?"

"Yeah, but composing sounds and visions for it is not so easy. Give us time."

"There's practically no time. Mix them. Try and coordinate the two sets of readings as if they were one person." It was happening between the two of them. "Use the him and her theme as an underlying motif, then add some stuff. Heartbeats, variations on the heartbeats, recorded screams. The sound of Carol and Sidney fucking. The rhythm-beat of Richard's voice talking about Laura

. . . You know what I'm trying to say?"

"Sure. No problem. It's just chancy."

"I take the responsibility, not you."

Carol began to come late at night. She was avoiding Sidney as much as possible. He was rushing her on Richard. Each day he intensified the pressure. Richard was growing to trust her more; she felt it. At the same time she grew to trust herself less and less.

Three A.M. would pass and begin to crawl toward four. Even though Richard's room was cocooned under layers of floors and walls inside the hospital, the city's predawn silence began to reach even here, a wave passing through buildings and people, calming some, agitating others. Time slowed down. Words became clearer in the stillness. They grew closer. As the city fell into its deepest sleep, they became more and more awake.

" 'Stolen?' 'Bought?' 'Dead?' Those are strong words," Carol said.

But she hadn't seen Laura dead. She hadn't seen Laura alive in the streets, after she was dead. Maybe he was crazy. Was this Carol Rothschild just playing with his mind? Something I heard. The President talking. Something I know. People talking about the President. Someone wants it. Whatever it is, it's a catastrophe. He probed his mind when he was alone. Of the hundreds he had heard, who said what to whom? One set of people talked of war: another set of thwarting war. One person talked both sides. Familiar voice. All he could remember was the President's speech, Laura, and the rain of atomic fire.

Richard didn't have his notes. It must be in his notes, whatever it was. He would use Carol to help him to remember, but not tell her, not unless he could sell the information for his family's freedom, or trade it for a phone call to Ziggy.

He had to test her. Approach slowly and carefully. "Could I have one of those cigarettes?"

She laughed. It sounded natural. "I'm sorry. That's impolite of me." Unthinking, she held the pack out in the dark. His hand took it. "Can you see in the dark?"

"It's never totally dark. There's always some light. And anyway, I can hear you, smell you, feel you."

"I can't see a thing."

224

"I could always see good in the dark. When I was a kid I used to lie in bed and stare into the darkness and see things forming there."

She lit the match. His hand took her wrist and moved it closer. Their faces glowed. Bright and flickering; angles and planes. She had soft lips. He had prominent cheekbones. Her hair looked like a gleaming puff of delicate strands, and he smelled her perfume under the acrid smells of tobacco and match.

The remote sensors caught a tremor in her voice. A red arrow. Keats laughed and mated a yellow arrow with the red one. Richard's agitated touch agitated Carol as they talked about Laura. When are they going to finally fuck one another, he thought.

"But you said she was stolen." Go slowly, she thought. She had to unravel the threads. What did Laura really mean to him?

"At first I thought her parents were trying to keep us apart. After that day I didn't see her anymore. She stopped coming to school. I asked other kids about her. They didn't know anything. Finally I called her home. Her parents sounded funny; nervous, mad, scared . . . I don't know what. I wondered if I was going to be arrested for rape. They didn't want to talk to me."

"Why?"

"They had gone to college. They were schoolteachers. They thought they were better than us. They were ambitious for Laura, wanted her to be a doctor, a lawyer, a teacher . . . one of those things. Our family came from the wrong side of the tracks. They were in the junk business. You know the way people like that are."

Carol remembered the case history again. It was classic. Richard had reversed the roles. Made his family the poor family and her family the higher one.

"You said 'stolen.' Did you remember the stories about the princess your father used to tell you?"

"No. Those were fairy stories."

"Richard. Quickly, and without thinking about it. What does 'the princess' mean to you?"

The first thing that came into his mind was the word "knowledge." He was puzzled. Why? He said, "Nothing. It's just a story."

225

"But it involves your family, doesn't it?"

"That was hundreds of years ago."

Evasive or unconscious? "Richard, I'm trying to help you."

He made a move. "I know."

"Richard, let's go back. What happened then?"

"I just stopped going to school. It took a week for me to get the courage to go and ring her doorbell. Laura's mother opened the door . . . only a crack. The way she looked at me . . . I was dirt. She was a real witch. She was also scared. I said, 'What's the matter with Laura?' They said, 'Who do you think you are, daring to come here and ask these questions?' They slammed the door in my face. I rang the bell, and the door opened again. It was Laura's father. He said 'If you don't go away, I'll call the police.' I began to yell, 'Is she dead? She's dead, isn't she?' They both yelled at me. 'Get out of here.' Neighbors opened their doors. I kept asking, 'Is she dead?' and finally they said, 'Yes. She's dead.' "

"But she wasn't dead?"

"I didn't believe them. But there was no way I could find out."

"You could have gone to the police."

"No! You never go to the police!"

"Why not?"

That was a mistake. He shouldn't have shouted. His parents always told him; whatever happens, you come to us. But his parents never told him what to do if something happened to *them.* "In our neighborhood, no one trusted the police. Anyway, after about a week her parents moved away."

"Where?"

"I asked the movers. They were moving Laura's parents to Brooklyn, somewhere in Flatbush. They gave me the address. I waited around about a week and went out there. They bought a house in a good neighborhood. Trees. I asked myself; where did a pair of schoolteachers get the money to buy a house like that?"

"What did you do then?"

Richard paused.

The tape had a gap. When Richard began to talk, the analyzer showed a lot of stress. Obviously he was thinking out his next move, Keats thought.

226

"I listened in to their phone conversation."

"How did you do that?"

He had taken the leap; he was beginning to trust Carol. Now she could begin to see that they were talking about real things. Her line of questioning would have to change. Ficino wouldn't have to intervene so directly. He waited. The tape hissed. The telephone line bringing him the tape-sound from the hospital, routed via Cornell University, relayed back to St. Elizabeth's Hospital in Washington, crackled. Noise buildup in the lines. The thermal color images coming to him from MIT via Washington, quivered. The EEG spiked in peculiar ways. Why did the delta wave appear? The synthesized record showed enormous stress, but Richard's voice sounded calm. He would have made a good agent.

"You find the neighborhood telephone switchbox, sort out the line that goes to their house and hook into it."

"You wiretapped them?" That was outrageous, she thought. She calmed her voice. "You knew how to do that?"

"Yes. Her parents were very angry at her. They called her a slut, and worse. They screamed at her for running away from home, throwing away her life. Then, all of a sudden, she started to scream back at them. 'You think I don't know you sold me.'" He stopped. "How could people do a thing like that to their own daughter?"

Carol saw that Richard was spinning fantasies. He had been rejected; he was confusing, scrambling the facts, rationalizing what he couldn't face. Don't push.

"I found out where she was living."

"How?"

"I traced the number she was calling from. Then I got the address."

"How?"

"The phone company has a directory organized by phone numbers and their subscribers. It also gives the addresses of the telephones."

"You had that directory?"

"A friend got it for me."

"Where was she living?" Carol asked.

227

"She was living in an apartment building on Central Park West and Seventy-second Street. I went up there."

Richard took a walk from the Lower East Side and then the ride uptown on the subway. When he got to Seventy-second Street, and stood, his back to Central Park, looking up at the apartment house, he realized he had made a journey into a strange land. The people were different here. The building was an old, gloomy, rich house; strange corners and edges, rounded towers on top, slanted roof . . . a chateau. He imagined her, in one of those windows, somewhere, looking down, wanting to call out to him and not able to. After a few hours he got courage and talked to the doorman stationed in a little booth. A great iron gate, behind the doorman, enclosed a vast, dark courtyard. Little sunlight fell there and no birds sang. The doorman looked at him suspiciously and told him that no one of that name or description lived there. The doorman told Richard to go away. He waited across the street. He came back day after day, watched through the night a few times. Then, one day, he saw her.

He could see two figures walking through the shadowy courtyard. She was walking with a man. She was dressed—he didn't know how to describe it—like a little girl, and yet like a grown, sophisticated woman. The man was slender, pink-faced; his face looked porcelain-glazed. The man's eyes were gray, seemingly without pupils. Veiled. Seeming to see nothing at all, yet seeming to see everything. The man's face turned toward her. She seemed now to come alive and glow. It was an expression Richard recognized. Love.

"How do you know it was love?"

"I can't tell you. I just knew." His voice was trembling. He had seen that expression many times . . . in the movies . . . on television. He was in love with her, hopelessly in love, and she loved him. The man's face looked yearning, and then turned humorous, smug. White hair, neatly trimmed, came out from under the edges of the Homburg hat. Then Richard realized: he was an old man! They could be father and daughter. The girl said something again, and he came closer to her, embraced her and began to kiss her upturned face again and again. It made Richard rage. In his world only perverts screwed little girls. He fell silent.

Carol thought of it as the reliving of some traumatic scene, in

228

one of its many transformational guises. The Father has stolen The Mother. The Mother has been metamorphosed in the mind of the son into a girl, young enough for the son to love without feelings of guilt, set backward in time, before she was defiled by the father, and had given birth to the son who loves that as yet unviolated woman. The unconscious is clever and tricky. Was this older man Richard's *real* father—the rich trustee Sidney had told her about? And did Richard, unable to hate his father directly, hate the ultimate substitute, everyone's father, the President of the United States?

"What did you do?"

"I yelled. Their faces went absolutely blank. They looked right through me. I didn't exist."

He started to run across the street. Before he got halfway, he was intercepted. A huge man materialized from nowhere and blocked his way. A bodyguard, who began to walk backward, not even seeming to exert power, saying nothing. It was humiliating.

Richard was shaking. His body was strained, as if his muscles carried in them the memory of that day. Carol inched her chair forward. They were almost touching now.

"Richard . . . Richard." She reached out in the darkness. Her hand touched his face. It drew back suddenly. She reached lower and touched his leg. She reached again. This time she found his hand and held it. "Think back. When Laura talked to her parents, what did they say?"

"They called her a slut . . ."

"Are you sure you remember it the right way?"

"I heard them. She said 'Did you think I wouldn't find out? How much did you get for me?' They didn't answer her directly, they just got more hysterical. She said, 'You got enough to buy a house, didn't you? How much? I want to know in dollars and cents how much he thinks I'm worth. Since I was a little girl, all my fuckin' life—' "

"Richard! 'Fuckin' life?' "

"Yes. Those words. 'All my fuckin' life you told me about living the right way. Study hard. Become a doctor. Become a lawyer. And then you sell me, you pricks.' " He stopped.

"That doesn't sound like a thirteen-year-old girl, Richard."

He was staring into the darkness . . . toward where Carol sat.

229

He remembered now. The years dropped away. Her voice came back to him through the phone wires, through the tap. It reached an ugly crescendo. "And you thought *you* were selling me—the innocent virgin! That's what you thought he wanted. Pure virgin. I haven't been a virgin for years. And let me tell you something else. *You* didn't do a thing. *I* arranged it, from beginning to end. How much for you, how much for me. It takes practice to pimp. I'm going to go to school all right, all the way to college. The best in the country. And you're not going to get one iota of benefit out of it. I have a *contract*. You ever think of a contract? That's payment enough for taking that man's cock in my mouth, or up my ass, or in my cunt every night. And you know what? I like it. I love it . . ."

"Richard, I can't believe this."

All these years, he had never wanted to believe it. Everything reversed for him. He was saying it, facing it. He began to weep. His childhood was over. He was all alone now.

She heard the sobbing and reached out for him again. She held his head against her breasts and felt his body throbbing to each sob. "Richard. Richard."

"What did she do it for? Why did she take me up to the roof? Why did she make love to me? She was arranging that other thing. It was love, it really was. I know it was." His face was between her breasts, his arms were tight around her. She smelled his hair. Her body tingled. She was sweaty, moist, excited.

"All right, Ziegler, we're having a breakthrough, as they say," Keats said. "Hit it. Feedback. Make them feel it."

She couldn't believe his story. Everything had turned around. The ingenuity of the paranoid schizophrenic. "Richard, Richard, what was all that about? Listening in to the President? Laura. What you think you saw on that television screen? The atomic fire? You were making it up because you didn't want to face—"

"No. That was crazy. I know I wasn't really seeing the President. Something weird was happening to me, playing funny games in my head. But I *did* listen in to the President, before that. You'd be surprised who I listened in to. I listened in to

230

Laura, for years. I listened to the people she talked to. And then I branched out and listened to the people *they* were talking to." His voice was muffled.

"But the President? Where did he come into it?"

"Why not? Even he has to use the phone."

"And Laura?"

"Laura's high-class. That's what that old man made her."

"High-class?"

"A high-class whore. She will fuck anyone as long as he has money and power, and who has more power than the President?" He calmed down. Carol's perfume, her skin smell, was in his nostrils. He shook his head and breathed deeply to control his sobbing. His face moved left and right against her breasts. "The things you hear. The things you hear people saying." He was talking calmly now, almost entranced, half-lost in some little memory. "The dangerous period is initiated, the test of strength begins when Khrushchev proposes a meeting of minds, *mano-a-mano*—don't you think the Spanish is appropriate under the circumstances?—you and me, Jack and Nikita, two human beings, both fathers, both men of power and responsibility, who have the fate of billions in our hands. I heard someone say that Khrushchev will propose: pick your place. Pick it. Moscow? Berlin? Washington? Havana. I will go there. We will meet without the negotiators . . ."

Good, Keats thought. It was emerging. Richard was putting the message in order.

231

CHAPTER 26

HOLCOMB was hanging on by his teeth. He had a blizzard of paper work with a diminished staff. He recognized the symptoms —life was being made intolerable by his superiors. How long could he keep his network together without funds? He had Braunstein's people; Don Calogero had given him some help; Billington at FBI was helpful in searching out the files on Keats and the Aquilino family. But he was getting little more than he already knew.

Maybe there was nothing to do but arrange for a safe house, take Keats, and beat it out of him. Or let Braunstein take him to Germany. He didn't want to do the questioning himself, not after the way Keats had unnerved him with all that talk about *The Manchurian Candidate*. No. Just watch Keats a little longer and wait for him to make a mistake that would lead him to Aquilino and the whole family.

Holcomb left the Coffin. It was late, ten o'clock at night. There was a nip in the air. September. Autumn was definitely coming on. His car was waiting for him at the side of the Foundation. When he opened the door, there was someone sitting inside, in the far corner. He recognized the classic operation. And that was another sign that he had slowed up a step: in the old days he would have reacted before he thought about what was happening. Someone had stepped out of the shadows and pushed him into the back seat, next to KGB General Skuratov, the man they called El Supremo because of his tour of duty in Spain from 1936 to 1938. It was Skuratov who had personally interrogated him in Moscow. It was Skuratov who knew every part of his body intimately. Skuratov the survivor who had slithered through all the purges and changes of regime, even the killing of Beria and all of Beria's personal vassals. Holcomb recognized the angles of the Asiatic cheekbones, the lean body, the enormously wide shoulders, the huge hands, all radiating power. There had to be a gun on him, as well as on the others backing him up from the shadows.

"You used to be faster than that, my friend. But we all grow older, don't we? I doubt I could have done better if our circumstances were reversed. Don't fret—your chauffeur is a little indisposed, but unharmed. I just want to talk."

The door shut behind Holcomb and the car began to move. It made its way to the Franklin D. Roosevelt Drive and turned north. Holcomb's heartbeat was regular. His breathing calm. Good. He was still tough. They looked at one another. Figure out how long before he was missed. Skuratov's face went in and out of the light and dark of the street lights, a strobe effect. Holcomb remembered Keats's words. The white hospital room. The white bed with the piece of missing enamel, leaving the blackness underneath, like the map of France. And he noticed how an irregularity in his pulse . . . too strong, erratic. A glimpse of someone else, a medical technician . . . a doctor. The drugs . . . the hypnosis he had no memory of. Was Skuratov his control? Had he been doubled after all?

Neither one of them spoke until the car passed Ninety-sixth Street. Then Skuratov said, "Gholcomb, why are you going around killing my people?"

That moment when Richard remembered what Laura had said to her parents, and the way in which she said it, had freed him from his past. But it had thrown him into a kind of limbo. What did "they" want him to believe?

Days of isolation lead to fantasy. They ran tests on him. They hooked him up. Nothing happened. Would it be possible for him to send thoughts, minimal flows of electricity, back through the

233

machines that monitored him? Thoughts that would work their way through some system, to activate some phone—*the* phone—and call Ziggy?

The guards had become uncommunicative. Sometimes it seemed that a cycle of "day" and "night" came and went, sometimes two or three, when Carol did not come. Or was he merely sleeping in shorter cycles? Dreamlife became richer somehow, but the distinction between dream and reality softened. "Can't I have a room where there's a window?" Richard asked Carol.

"We think it's best for you here for the time being." She's lying, but at least she's troubled about it. Someone else was telling her what to do.

"Who's 'we'?"

"Dr. Ficino and myself."

"I'm a prisoner."

"No you aren't, Richard. You're disturbed. You've had an episode, but you are *not* a prisoner and you have to stop thinking like that. I'm trying to help you."

Her voice was angry, defensive. Remember that, he thought. Use her guilt.

Lately he was having erotic dreams, wet dreams. He was embarrassed. The attendants who changed the sheets in his room would notice and tell her. He hadn't had those since he was a kid; now he had erections at peculiar times. Was someone beaming vibrations at him through the walls?

When he remembered Laura's voice, the blackness flowed in waves. Electromagnetic frequencies connected him all the way to the High Places. To the *kether,* the crown. (Crown? The President!) A connection that went to a man the Secret Service codenamed Lancer: John F. Kennedy. And Lancer evoked again what Richard had seen on the television. Lancer and Laura. . . .

You have nothing left, he told himself. No friends. No family. Maybe you never even had those people and you've been crazy all your life. Carol's helping you to recover. A whole second existence, a Richard and a sort of Richard-prime who lived another life beneath his consciousness. There was something, or someone, that he couldn't remember. Are you someone else, he asked himself. He went back over his life, looking for some break in it, a false moment through which he could see this other being trapped inside of him. What is it that you think you must say to someone so awesome and distant as the President? "Listen . . . I have something to tell you—wait, don't hang up . . ." How would Richard reach out again to contact him? He knew the private phone number. All you have to do is dial. . . .

Memories emerged to combat the blandness of his room in the hospital. What had been stored in his mind, transmitting itself now to the surface? Magicians, politicians, knights, merchants, kings, bishops, emperors, cardinals, policy advisors, witches, poets, smugglers, gangsters, the mercurial crew of runners, warrior-monks in robes, the securely hidden castle that had to be reached—or fled from—and a princess. Royal secrets. *Kether,* the crown of all. *From what corners of his memory did such words come from?* Had they been encrypted in his father's ancestral memory-stories? Inside him was a hissing darkness, and beyond the galaxy's edge a hideous roaring, some kind of demon, a snake with tentacles, a nest of snakelike tapes, memory worms in his body, the twin sharing his body with him, Richard and Richard-prime uncoiling from one another in the darkness of his almost-memory, wet, slippery, working its way out of him, a thought being born, to emerge breathing the yet-to-be secret of thermonuclear fire.

The power of the awesome and distant figure almost overwhelmed him. God speaking: the three-fold Kennedy. The one who was a god, distant as a galaxy. Another that you heard on the phone, sometimes petty and perfectly human. A third, the one some others talked of with contempt. Someone to be maneuvered. A ring of evil guards surrounded him—soldiers, Secret Service men, the FBI, the CIA, the National Security Council, advisors, staff—the weavers of spells, making a thousand masques to entertain Him with tales of daring, alarm and national danger. Remain secure but alert against the perpetual onslaught of Russian demons who are always coming but never arrive. And there were fast rides pursued by cars, helicopters and the rattle of machine pistol fire, carrying away the secret, Top Secret, G-classification, royal, imperial secret documents, captured from some seemingly small and unimportant Viet Cong subofficer who happened to be carrying on his person the plans for world conquest. The plans are brought before the royal eyes. Look. You see? These are the marching order for the legions. Dates. Places. A tactical timetable.

No. The memories had nothing to do with one another. He had mixed it all up together—Laura, Kennedy, the stories his father had told him, his obsession with evil demons, the blond knight wearing the black armor. And yet Laura was a talisman, a key, a token of some awesome power. She was a code that started tangled pathways of memory and escape unravelling. Giggling. Love words. Memory. "When am I going to see you again?" Explosion. "Khrushchev will make his gambit, an offer of *détente*. Kennedy and Khrushchev must never be permitted to get together. Kennedy will be overwhelmed, as he was in Vienna . . ."

"Richard. Richard," Carol said, stroking his back. "Tell me what comes into your mind."

And then Richard saw it quite clearly: Does *He*, Kennedy, hold Laura in thrall? But the new Richard-prime wondered, is it *she*, whatever she is, who holds *Him* in her power?

The security viziers entice Him with bad advice, down into a dank cave deep in the earth called the Situation Room. From there the sensing threads of control reach all over the world. They spin out the scenario-tales—all that might be and all that never will have come to pass. Richard has overheard it all. The counselors fight to offer up women to him. Laura comes to him in a thousand disguises, miming a thousand women all clamoring for his Presidential body. He is dazed. Enchanted. Stoned. Aroused. His back is broken. The magic and vitalizing fluid is prevented from climbing up to flood his brain with knowledge. Ceremonially they approach the Presidential desk, under the Great Seal with its magical and enchanting symbols, the arrows, the wreath of marijuana leaves, saying reverently, "Mr. President." Mr. God, Mr. Emperor—he is mesmerized by the light of his power reflected back at him. They say: we have the wisdom of the gods here in a little seed, in a little powder, released by a magic mushroom trigger-button. This, they say, is what made the ancient rulers great. Be like Alexander. Taste and see visions. Accordingly, he knows less and less every day, descending the ladder of secrecy from Imperial, G, Eyes Only, to what are secrets no more but classified simply for general distribution. The great object of all knowledge has No Need To Know.

To whom should Richard bring his knowledge? Whom else but Kennedy? He must awaken him from the spell, break through the cordon of spell weavers and liars. First he'll have to get the help of someone he trusts completely, somebody older, wiser. Ziggy's been through it. Then, what magic words will Richard say to waken the enchanted President? He muttered: "When the Short, Fat Man who dances on his hands-wearing-shoes comes to you, don't reject him. You must listen. Take the offer of friendship. Make treaties. He will take the shoes off his hands and put them on his feet, uncoil out of the shell of his short body and rise to be ten feet tall, like you are. Listen to what he has to say. Don't let them lead you to the Apocalypse According to St. Kahn.

"No. Please listen to me. I'm not crazy. The scales have fallen from my eyes. I know what she's like. She tells you to exert your will, you to be a man-God, doesn't she? She whispers and her tongue makes words on your body—"

"She? What she?"

"Laura."

"Who's Laura?" he says.

Go back. Begin again. Start it from the beginning. You have missed magical steps in the ritual of activiating him. *First you have to reach him:* dial him up.

Richard imagines himself dialing the number Ziggy had given him. That's the first step of the ritual. Seven motions made in the air with his finger. He tries to change the levels of his energy and send out his thought. Arcs of circles. The gesture activates a phantom addressing system. His mind is a transmitter, activating the address-and-subscriber-searching switches to the President's particular and private phone, which will then ring.

The phone is picked up. "Who is this?" His voice was blurred, as if drugged or sleepy.

"My name is Richard Aquilino. You don't know me. You are in great danger."

"What is this, some kind of joke?" And the recipient hangs up. But it's Him.

He tries it again.

"Who the fuck *is* this?"

"You said . . ."

237

"How did you get this number?"

"... You said, 'What the fuck is wrong with Rusk?' You said it to Schlesinger. You said it to Bundy. You said it to your brother. You said it to Sorensen. You said, 'First he's ready for a strike; and then I can't get hold of him—and he's supposed to be the Secretary of Fuckin' State?'"

"And then your brother said, 'I think he's close to a complete physical and mental breakdown.' *Now* will you listen to me?"

"When did I say anything like that? I never said any such thing. Who is this? Where are you calling from? How did you get hold of this number? Mister, you are in big trouble." He sounded puzzled and angry.

"Task Force W. You said to Bissel, to William King Harvey, to McCone, to Lansdale: 'Why are you people dragging your feet?' You planned thirty-two actions against Cuba.'" Breakdown and chaos." Thirty-two secret paths of wisdom. *Sefirot.* Creation ... creation of the secret paths to the President. "... operational schedule for sabotage actions inside of Cuba ..." Thirty-two steps to creation: thirty-two paths toward total destruction ...

"How did you hear all this?"

Breakthrough. Okay. "You're being bugged. First tell me what you did with my family."

"What the fuck are you talking about?"

"I'll get back to you. Expect my call. Tell no one. You're surrounded by enemies. And you can't trace this call." Richard disconnected; he didn't dare to stay too long on the line.

No. Something was wrong. Then he remembered. It was something else he heard.

"Can we count on Rusk?"

"No, he's one of nature's fence sitters. He'll vote for a surgical strike, then an invasion, then diplomacy, and then nothing."

"What Richard had done was to invent a probable conversation out of the elements someone had put in his mind.

He interrogated his memory to see if all this was something outside of himself, like his father's voice, as he drifts off before sleeping ... "There came a time when the evil ones, cursed be their names, had captured us and thrown us into the deep dungeon."

"Us, papa?"

238

"Yes. It was really your great-great-great-and-so-forth-grandfa-ther, give or take a great or two—what matter—in fact all our fathers, and me, and their spirit is *in* you, the great briefing transmitted through the centuries. You remember what hap-pened to us in Cadiz and Cordoba, Massilla and Venice, Constan-tinople and Fustat, in Languedoc and Venice and Genoa, in Palermo and all along the ways to China and Sind, but you must protect us with your silence, though you are taken prisoner. The walls are damp. This is the great test, for he is about to torture us with strange apparitions. Confess! Convert! Debrief! They asked, in 1510 in Salamanca, 'And what did this President have to say?' Those who were once ours—apostates and *conversos*—came in to tempt you. 'Come over to the other side,' they whisper in your ear, using the sacred tongue of the fathers.

"They've got you strapped to the rack. Your flesh is torn. Every bone hurts. Some are no longer connected. They've beaten you on the genitals. They are swollen to the size of oranges. Whips? Of course. Clubs? It goes without saying. Thumbs desocketed? Routine. Needles in your gums. Electric shocks. How much can we bear? We long for death—*meth*. But such is their demonic way that now they feed the pain directly into your skull. Your flesh, though untouched, it *feels* bruised, but who shall say that the pain is not real? The walls are made of stone ten feet thick, yet you got out. Do you remember how?"

"How?"

"You walked through the walls. You began to vibrate, faster and faster, and you came apart, vibrating differently than the stone atoms vibrated, allowed you to float through the walls."

He's in a dream, in a room. An ordinary room, not the one in the hospital. There's an ordinary wood table with a telephone on it. There's no dial on the phone. A man comes in, a man as tall as he is. He wears a dark suit, with threads of gold shot through it so it glints with metallic highlights. The feet are shod in black silken socks which also glint. Black shoes like metal, elegant, also gleam. He has a bland face, hard to focus on. Handsome? Hard to tell. Blond hair. The man sits down. But there's only one chair and Richard is sitting on that. What's *he* sitting on? No, the man is only pretending to sit on an invisible chair. A trick. What strength, to hold that pose. The man smiles. It's an open, win-

239

ning, warm smile. On his wrist, there's a golden watch. Richard feels his stomach contract with hunger. His whole body aches.

"This is terrible, Richard. Simply terrible."

"Who are you?" His voice is a rusty croak.

The man shakes his head. "Savages," he says. "Barbarians. And yet, what can we do? You and I, we know the game, don't we? It could have been me there and you here. It's nothing personal." He shrugs. "The watch interests you, Richard?" The voice is melodious, singing, almost like a woman's. "It's very expensive. It shows you the second, the minute, the hour, the day. It can show you what the time is anywhere in the world. All you do is press one of these buttons . . ." Richard sees that the watch's rim is studded with small, precious stones, buttons made of ruby and diamond and emerald. "You want to know what time it is? All right, look if it makes you feel any better. We set it to subjective time. It's set to your time." The man holds up the face of the watch. Peculiar. No hands.

"There are people who have been taught the ancient tricks of avoiding pain. They taught you that, didn't they, Richard, when . . ."

"Who's they?"

". . . when they recruited and trained you. They told you that someone might catch you—small risk—and torture you. Where did they teach you that? In CIA Central? Which branch? Moscow or Langley? You see we have lots of time, Richard. It takes a year or five for a second to pass.

"Listen, why torment yourself? It's all over. You've had a good run. You gave us a hard time. You did your duty. It's turn-around time, Richard. Who holds out all the way anymore? When the situation is hopeless, you make a deal."

"Turn-around time?"

"Come on, Richard. Don't play games."

"I'm not a spy. I don't know what you're talking about."

"Look, there comes a time when reasonable men can talk to one another. Your own people have abandoned you. Your control has flown the coop. He's halfway to Langley now . . . or is it Moscow?"

"What's a control?"

"Don't play games with me, Richard. I'm on *your* side. You're

240

not worth anything to them anymore. All they can hope for is that you die, the quicker the better."

"I'm not a spy."

"Why were you listening in to all those people? You *have* to be a spy."

"All right. I'm a spy. Have it your way."

"Good. Doesn't that feel better? We're on our way. Look at the watch. See? Time is moving faster now. You're a spy, you're a courier, you're the route."

"Who am I supposed to be spying for?"

"You're regressing."

"Who am I spying *on?*"

"Dangerous backsliding. Soon the pain will start."

"What do you want me to say?"

"That's not the way it works. You know that. What's your code name?"

"Richard."

"What code name was your operation given?"

Richard didn't answer.

"Take your time. What was your mission? Who briefed you? Where was it done?"

He thought: to listen and bring the information to the President. But he said, "I didn't have a mission."

"Or were you Laura's control?"

Richard bargained. "Where are my father and mother . . . my sisters . . . the rest of them?"

The blond man's voice was changing. Getting higher. "One thing at a time. For the time being they are all right. We're protecting them from your employers."

"What employers? I don't have any employers."

"Richard, tell me what comes into your mind," the man said.

Richard didn't answer. He heard a scream from someone close to him. And the man said, "You don't know how it hurts me to do that to them."

Richard sat up suddenly in the dark.

CHRPTER 27

IT was going better than their wildest dreams for Ziggy, Tarzan and Marvin, yet Ziggy was troubled. Maybe it had gone too well. He looked around him, seeing through Marvin's description of the small convention. "They're here, Ziggy, thronging in from all parts of the galaxy, and from the realm of the supernatural."

Ziggy had tried to be careful. They were dealing with murderous criminals. And where the Mafia was concerned, the FBI couldn't be far behind. So their meetings had been intensive, moving from seedy restaurant to seedy restaurant. The Mafia were cautious too. They wanted samples of the work. First, could they detect police and FBI taps on Mafia operations? Second, could they bug selective sets of people? If the tests showed that the three could produce frequency scanners, debugging equipment, scramblers, listening devices responsive to key words, descramblers, on the large scale required by the Mafia, then they would expand the operation and spring Richard.

The sci-fi convention was not all inclusive. Only a hundred were invited in the name of the future. "Leap into Space: Men into Gods." That was the theme. The invitations to the conference dealt with the current danger: invasion from "somewhere in space" by a fabulous and totally alien race who were listening in to everyone's communications, preparatory to taking over everyone's lives. It was an emergency; the government had been taken over. The conference was the first in a series of far-ranging conferences which in time would be conducted through radio and telephony. Space was rented in a seedy hotel in the New York garment district.

People arrived from all over the nation. There, some of the conferees put on strange costumes made out of cloth, or elaborately constructed out of papier-mâché, metal, cardboard, plastic, depicting the planets they came from. Under the cover of the conference, Ziggy was particularly interested in talking to about fifteen people who had expertise with telephone and radio. Each in turn could round up another twenty or so in different cities. Then they could cover the whole country.

Ziggy began by addressing the convened conference; in fact eighty-five people. Marvin described the audience to him. Partly human, partly alien. Creatures with tentacles and cilia. Creatures that were in no way humanoid. Creatures that had somehow contrived to keep their bodies moistioned with liquid against the too-dry conditions of earth. Creatures that had to be accompanied by their anti- or pro-gravity machines to keep them in constant adjustment to earth's pull.

Ziggy began by talking about the developments that lay open for man in the future. Manlike gods. Immortality. But there were problems. The rich, the government, were going to monopolize the fruits of research. The technological breakthroughs were going to be only for those who could afford it. Most of humanity would be frozen out.

He then asked, why had things taken the turn they had? Simply enough, Earth had been invaded a long time ago by creatures from another planet who had systematically taken over governments and were turning the Earth into a colony. Now the aliens were engaged in consolidating their rule. What was required for the United States, for the whole world, was a kind of global First Amendment assuring freedom of communication. "Not only shall Congress pass no law abridging freedom to speak, communicate, listen, but this freedom shall not be abridged by any government executive order, any government bureaucracy like the FCC; neither shall it be done to us by any gigantic monopoly."

Ziggy was cheered.

243

During the breaks between the workshops and discussions, Tarzan brought together the fifteen. Ziggy swore them all to secrecy—and silence, as Marvin swept the room for bugs.

Ziggy began. He had brought them together because not only were they already men of the future, out of their time, but they all had technical abilities. They were on the one hand geniuses, wild talents, not destroyed by a technical-school education, but they were the kind of people who shouldn't be bound to working for the bureaucracies, the military, or business.

Now one of them, Richard Aquilino, had been captured by those alien forces. They wanted the contents of his mind, his skills. Possibly he was being tortured. It was up to us to band together, set up a network which would cover the country, to liberate Richard. The few who were gathered together in the room would have to find ways of getting in touch with trustworthy others. There would be some money for this, from others who were being spied on, and who were also interested in liberty.

The first job was the organization of the immediate network. The second thing was to get Richard rescued. The third job on hand was the bringing together of more radio and telephone people, who could listen in to every possible frequency and find their way into the switching and cable centers. The fourth priority would come in time . . . perhaps soon . . . when the great invaders made their final move to enslave the free creatures of the world.

They agreed to do it. And then came the nuts and bolts. For years the radio people had been compiling a list of secret government radio frequencies; the FBI, CIA, NSA, Secret Service, White House staff, Department of Defense. People started to exchange mimeographed copies.

From the Mafia, Ziggy had gotten a rundown on the conditions as they existed in the hospital. They had discovered a secret and enclosed area inside the hospital itself. It was not only guarded, but the area wasn't anywhere near the outside shell of the hospital. The area itself was too large to determine exactly where Richard was. Ziggy decided to get some inside advice—from Richard's parents.

CHAPTER 28

"IS it too much to ask, Harold? A little walk," she said.

He was short, thin and bald, and he smoked too much. Obviously she made him nervous. He hadn't seen her for—how long was it? Ten years? At least. "It's a fantasy, Lilly. If anything were going on in this hospital, I would know about it."

She was still good-looking, and still a little frightening. He looked for signs of fanaticism in her and found none. She looked pleasant, a big woman getting older—she should have been about what? Sixty? Sixty-five? Surprisingly attractive still.

"You've been out of practice, Harold. You've forgotten what people can do, how they can hide under our noses. You've become an important man, a leader in your field. Chief of neurophysiology?"

"Yes."

"We're proud of you. Success encourages comfort, but comfort encourages a little blindness. Look, it's not like I'm asking you to pick up a gun."

"Yes. Yes," he said nervously. It's not like you're asking me to pick up a hypodermic needle, or provide some fast-acting poison. He didn't even want to remember. He used to go home and weep for days after a job. He was getting old . . . well, not so old. He was only fifty-three. And yet, in a way the best years of his life had ended for him with 1938—and the Hitler-Stalin pact. He had

245

dropped out of the revolution and concentrated on his practice. He had become rich and renowned. He had contributed to their cause, at least. "You're trying to tell me that something has been going on here without my even knowing it. Impossible."

"How many times in the past were you, and others of us, able to be in place without anyone knowing you were there?"

He smiled at the memory. He had been good. "True."

She smiled. He had forgotten how beautiful she could be—and dangerous. He had seen her beat a strong man nearly to death. He had seen her kill. He had seen her hold a large audience spellbound. He had always envied her husband, Samael. How Harold—and so many others—had wanted her. What did that little shrimp have that others, much handsomer men, didn't have more of?

"A little probe, Harold. You're a big fish, an executive.

Who can question you? Perhaps you exhibit a little absent-mindedness. You know the geography of the psyche so well, all of its twists and turns, its corridors and blind alleys. So what are a few corridors and floors in a building? It's a big building, but it isn't infinite."

"I paid my debt. I gave time. I was dedicated. I helped you and your husband when you were on the run. I did other things . . ."

"You wouldn't be where you are today without us, would you? The International paid for your college education, it paid for medical school . . ."

"The Party is not what it was. It's corrupt, warped by bureau-cratic deformations. It suffers a dangerous senile psychosis."

"I said 'International,' not Party. You mean *them*, not us, Har-old."

How dangerous was what she wanted?

"You're thinking of expanding the hospital," she said, having done her homework. "A lot of planning and a lot of construction."

"Those discussions have been going on for a long time. It keeps me away from my work."

"How hard would it be to send for the ground plans? You've had a new idea. Read the plans and then go for a little walk. Take

246

a few students along for cover. You were always a great talker. Get involved in your discussion, so involved that you fail to see where you're going. Sooner or later you'll come to a locked-off area where even you, chief of whatever, cannot go. You will be turned away, politely. That's all. Just remember where you walked; remember obstacles, false turnings, blind walls, directions from all the exits to the outside. What's so hard? Tell us what's in there, and we'll do the rest."

"This is a huge hospital, Lilly. You must have someplace in mind. It would help to cut down the search. What's in this place?"

"The less you know, the better."

"If I do this, I'm doing it for you. And for Samael. Listen, Lilly, I want to tell you something. I was in love with you. I still remember the way you were . . . in fact you've hardly changed. Physically. But you've thrown your life away."

"Harold. Inside, I'm still seventeen."

"Maybe that's what's wrong."

"Is it wrong to feel young, alive, and burning?"

"Well, I'm doing it for old friends. I don't believe in the triumph of the proletariat, dialectical materialism . . . or any of that anymore . . ."

"What do you believe in?"

"In loyalty to old friends."

She leaned forward and took his hand and squeezed it. "The man whose place of operation we are interested in is a man named Sidney Ficino . . ."

"That pompous fool?"

"Does that narrow your search considerably?"

"It certainly does. What's going on there?"

"You're forgetting that you're an absentminded professor who has found a new and exciting way to lecture, Harold. What else do you have a need to know?"

She got up. She was tall, strong, with the body of a much younger woman. The thighs—he could see them outlined under her skirt—were strong and full. He stood up and put his hand out to shake hers. She leaned over and kissed him.

"I need a week," he said.

"No. Three days."

"You're a hard woman, Lilly."

"Better hard than dead, Harold. Give my love to your wife. How are the children?"

"In college, would you believe it? And yours?"

"They're well. Goodbye. In three days."

The name of Ficino disturbed him. Before he made his little journey he would check out the records. There had to be someone of Lilly's there, in that area. But that was not the kind of work Ficino was supposed to be doing.

CHAPTER 29

MR. Kelley was depressed. He was beginning to sense something in Keats . . . betrayal. It was almost as if he smelled it on Keats. A woman. Laura? Yes, Laura.

Mr. Kelley had flown to the Aegean for three days of intense meetings with the leading members of Parvus on a yacht cruising along the Greek Islands. Everyone had been helicoptered in. Kelley brought news of the unfolding events in the United States leading to a crisis which would evolve in October. There was a clear danger to their plans for the future. He presented his case to representatives of Parvus from the eastern bloc of countries, Mr. Helphand himself, father of it all; Herr Bindelmacher who represented a not-yet existent United States of Europe; Mr. Taira of Japan, who carried the burden of representation of East Asia; Mr. Sidvisias who represented his principals in the subcontinent, India and Pakistan; Mr. Phillips representing Southern Africa; Mr. Ortega who spoke for his principals throughout Latin America.

Everyone wore The Mask, which was a way of protecting one's innermost thoughts from being read as they sat there with faint and perpetual Buddhalike smiles. They were used to long periods of immobility.

Behind their shields, though, were the calculating machines, figuring the angles for themselves and those they represented, massaging the minute fractions of a percentage point of interest, monitoring the flow of money in and out of nations and enterprises, able to move the money entrusted to them (and their own money) in and out of mazes of entities, real and false. Sometimes it looked like the capital of which they were stewards appeared in a thousand places at the same time. But what occupied Mr. Kelley's mind, what bothered him most of all, was the effect his love for Keats would have on his judgment.

Kelley reviewed the situation:

Their plans were in danger. *Détente* between the United States and the USSR was in difficulties, primarily because of Cuba. There were elements in both countries that would not let go of the cold war. These elements perceived that their interests required a constant danger, or even an actuality of war, feeling that this insured domestic tranquility—and blocked Parvus's efforts at free trade.

Each time it looked as if *détente* would truly begin to be implemented, Kelley said, the spectre of hot war came out of the hat. He laid out the information he had received through a number of sources, including what they had gotten from Richard Aquilino, that the idea of a coming confrontation was now being advanced by the President himself, John F. Kennedy. He also laid before them the notion that possibly, just possibly, there would be an attempt, if the coming crisis was successfully managed by Kennedy, to create a kind of dynasty, a Camelot. John F. Kennedy followed by Robert Kennedy, followed by Edward Kennedy . . . Twenty-four years, more than time enough to create a social revolution which would go entirely against their plans. The very notion of a "royal" family, transmitting power to blood-related, family-united people, was inimical to their long-range aims. It was what they and their predecessors had fought for hundreds of years.

What to do in order to fulfill the long-range strategy of reconquering—for the general marketplace rather than for any specific country—those areas encroached on by the superpowers? Mr. Kelley proposed that the coming crisis be managed in such a way as to leave Kennedy beholden to Parvus (although Kennedy had never heard that name), and work to destabilize the Presidency itself. "We want to be able to get *our* man in there, not someone who decides to go off on his own."

On his own. The words echoed in Mr. Kelley's mind. What was he doing but going off on his own? What was he risking for his jealousy of Keats? For the first time in a long time, since he had been young, Mr. Kelley experienced a complete weariness, a loss of *Ch'i.* Had he thought he would live forever? He must do something about it; prepare for the future. He wanted a child, and the only way was to make Keats his inheritor—if Keats showed contrition—along with Laura. He knew her. She knew her ambitions. She would be a check on Keats. It was time to prepare for the adoption ceremony.

It had all taken a second. He could only hope none of the others noticed this little lapse.

There were a few immediate tasks, Kelley went on. Protect Castro, especially in the next few months. Protect and strengthen Khrushchev.

Now the counterarguments began.

The representatives of Parvus refused to be properly alarmed at the developing crisis, except for Mr. Helphand who had, after all, trained Mr. Kelley and understood it perfectly. No one else could believe that a confrontation—even a nuclear one—would lead to an actual exchange of nuclear weapons.

In the end it was a standoff. They agreed to meet in another two weeks to evaluate the level of the emergency. Everyone would consult with his principals.

Mr. Kelley reached a decision after a talk with Mr. Helphand. He would break discipline and go off on his own. Perhaps he would, through Keats, use Richard in another way.

Mr. Kelley also took back with him a report provided by Mr. Helphand on the Aquilino family, their history and mode of operation. It was Richard Aquilino's father's interest in Cabala, coupled with the sudden disappearance of the family, the past possible intelligence background—that had alerted him to an ancient enemy. The Cabalists, like the Taoists, had been an invisible trading empire and intelligence operation that concealed itself behind mystic practices. He shook his head in admiration and despair. The Aquilinos were of the darkness battling Parvus, the merchants of light. As young people they had joined the Bolsheviks, and participated in the Revolution. Later they had been sent out of the Soviet Union. The mother, Lizaveta, and the father, Samael Samelovich, had both been assigned to work abroad between the period of 1925 and 1936, going from country to country, setting up networks. She was an activist, had trained operatives in crash courses of agitation, sabotage, assassination, setting up networks of sleepers. The father had originally been a linguist, a Cabalist, descended from a long line of mystic scholars tracing their ancestry back to the rabbis of Italy and Spain of the twelfth century. They were a people used to cover, concealment, the ambiguous statement and the recursive riddle.

They were working Italy in 1936 when the Moscow Trials began. Evidently the Aquilinos had seen which way the wind was blowing early, changed their names, assumed a string of new identities and fled with their two daughters and the money in their charge, presumably to the United States.

In America they had dropped out of sight. It was doubtful that they retired entirely from revolutionary activity. The Aquilino's network and Mr. Kelley's circle still confronted one another across the chasm of ages.

Yes. It was clear. In intelligence jargon, Richard Aquilino was a sleeper. In Cabalistic terms, a *golem* waiting to be woken up to its task. But what *was* his task? Listening in to people in high places? The long history of his family, its flights from country to country, what was that all about? A briefing coded as a family saga that wound through different countries through the ages? If so, Samael and Lizaveta must have trained their son indirectly.

And now Richard Aquilino and Keats, the next generation in an ancient struggle, faced one another. That meant that Richard Aquilino, using that inner resource, had somehow spotted Keats for what he was, just as Keats had spotted him. And to complicate matters, off to the side stood this boor, Holcomb.

If Richard was indeed a sleeping *golem,* could he be activated to perform a task entirely different than the one planned for him by his father, or, for that matter, by Keats? Keats had told Mr. Kelley Richard's story of the stolen princess hidden away in the castle, the blond knight, the fortunate son doing impossible tasks with magical helpers, fighting his way into the magical center. In other words, Richard had overheard Excom's . . . what? Delibera-

252

tions? Rehearsals? Plots to generate a crisis? The people who were generating the confrontation over Cuba were the most likely to be convened into a body, a committee of senior statesmen. Now there remained only the task of making Richard actually, physically, geographically replicate the trip he had taken through his unconscious via the telephone system, guided by Cabalistic principles, to nullify the fire-breathing dragon—in the person of Kennedy himself.

Would Keats change Mr. Kelley's plans? He was in a position to do so. Supposing Keats had Richard deliver the wrong story? Supposing Keats went to Kennedy himself and exposed Parvus? Keats was arrogant. Keats didn't love him. Keats was using him, playing with him, tormenting him. Was Keats going to betray him?

Mr. Kelley sent for Vassili Oprichnik.

CHAPTER 30

THE car was passing the north end of Welfare Island before Skuratov spoke. "First there is shock. How could *I* have been caught? Was I betrayed? You curse your relaxation of vigilance. Then the mind recovers and begins to think of a way out. What shall I do? Where am I being taken? Will they try to rescue me? Am I important enough, or am I a sacrificial pawn? And after all, your people haven't treated you very well, have they, Gholcomb, my old opponent?" Skuratov sounded almost affectionate. "How many years have you and I opposed one another, hated one another? Fifteen? How many times have I wanted to kill you, and could have? How many times have you wanted to kill *me*, and could have? No. We were more valuable to one another alive, we knew one another's moves. We were comfortable like husband and wife. So how can I convince you of my good intentions? I am going to plead with you in the name of the burning hatred I bear for you; it is one of the pure things in my life."

Holcomb tried to suppress the doubt Keats had planted in his mind. *Had* he been doubled, turned into a sleeper without knowing it? Was Skuratov here to waken him? Would he even know the moment when he passed from one state to another and became the enemy of his own country? "Which people of yours am I supposed to be killing?"

Skuratov told him. Holcomb knew all about the death in Times

254

Square, but that was more than even—Morrison and Corson were dead too. The reports of Morrison and Corson's subordinates assured him that no one on his side had killed anyone on Skuratov's side. So who had killed Skuratov's man for Keats? "Your people killed two, in fact three, of mine."

"We killed no one," Holcomb said. "You won't believe me, but . . ." and he told Skuratov just a little of what he knew. A small offering. What would Skuratov offer in return?

Skuratov sighed. "Then we are dealing with the third force here. One of yours and one of mine in alliance, working for Parvus. I know who yours is but you don't know who mine is. They want this Aquilino for themselves because he was not only penetrating your communications, and ours, but Parvus's. So who did Aquilino work for? We set a watch on him but found that he was already watched by you. We thought; find out who's running him, and how, and bring him in. We were led to you.

"What trick am I pulling? Listen, you know my style. You know the marks of my craft. I am not another James Jesus Angleton lost in a wilderness of Chinese boxes and literary interpretation, who says always to himself, there *must* be another deeper meaning. I am going to offer you something; the name of the man in charge of my operation is Vassili Oprichnik. You know the meaning of that name? No? Well. It turns out that Oprichnik is not *nash;* he is *chuzhoi.* What do you offer me?"

Holcomb sighed. Again, this Parvus. His head was tormented. He couldn't bring himself to offer up an agent yet, no matter how much he hated Keats.

The car was passing 103rd Street, shifting over to the left lane. Was it going to go across the Triboro Bridge? Could Holcomb make his move at the toll booth?

"We have about an hour. Then you and your chauffeur will be missed. You will be back within that hour.

"Gholcomb, a change in world policy demands a change in our relationship. I have something for you to look at." Skuratov reached into his breast pocket and pulled out an envelope. He pulled out a picture and handed it to Holcomb, and the interior carlight was switched on. Holcomb looked at it. Three men were standing in front of a building. The two younger man looked respectfully at the older one. "You recognize them?"

Holcomb looked carefully. He knew one, Yuri Andropov. Holcomb nodded. "I recognize that one."

"And the tall elegant one, that is Poniatowski . . . French. You know the name?"

Holcomb recognized him now. He nodded.

"There were also meetings with certain British and West German entrepreneurs, one South African and some others. I can get you pictures. You don't know the other?"

Holcomb shook his head.

"We will get nowhere with one another if we are not open."

There was silence. The car did not turn onto the approach to the Triboro Bridge, but continued north toward the point where the East River narrows and separates Manhattan from the Bronx. He couldn't make his move. Too few cars there.

"The third man is your boss. Your real boss. Edward Kelley. You work for an opposition."

Holcomb said nothing. His mind worked fast. Kelley. The lawyer for The Coffin. "The Coffin is very big. Our unit's contact with the regular staff is minimal—"

"Very well. But where is this unlikely trio standing? This photograph was taken a few weeks ago, the day my man was killed. They are standing in front of the Century Club. What is such an unlikely trio doing together in the middle of Manhattan?"

It was the day Richard Aquilino had escaped Keats's surveillance and disappeared. Lights on the oily water were passing by, a barge moving south. Holcomb could make out Skuratov's crazy Russian face; his hair almost white-blond; the heavy, dark suit didn't fit him so well.

"In the UN, your bosses and my bosses came together on the issue of a unified Congo while appearing to confront one another bitterly. Who really opposed who over what? Who was it who managed to oppose the mighty and sovereign powers of the United States and the USSR? You know the answers. Your subordinate . . ."

"Keats."

"Thank you. Keats and Oprichnik. We are even and the world has not collapsed around your ears."

Had the moment of activation and turning taken place already? Had his offering of Keats's name been the signification of

256

his acceptance of Skuratov's control? It was an anguished thought, worse in some way than the electrodes, the indignities to the private and secret parts of his body. Was this what the double felt like? Who were they working for now, he and Skuratov?

"Keats was in the Congo. Who ran that operation in Times Square? Keats. How did this 'amateur,' this 'bungler' we were tailing and chasing, this Aquilino, manage to listen in to your and my operations without help? How did this Aquilino manage to escape two highly trained teams?"

"Keats and Oprichnik?"

"And those who run them. You're interested? Another photograph?" Skuratov handed Holcomb the second photo. They were coming to the end of the drive and would turn off soon into the Manhattan side streets. They would be in city traffic; maybe he could make his move when they stopped for a traffic light. "Look at the photograph, Gholcomb. Please. Don't distract yourself with thoughts of escape. You will be free again in perhaps forty-five minutes. You have my word. If you will think over what I'm saying, you will see we have mutual interests.

"How do we convince one another of our bona fides after so many years of combat, you wonder? But in fact, if you refuse to believe what I am showing you, it would be simpler for me. Things would be as before. If you accept what I'm saying, then the real difficulties will start, not only for you, but for me too. We will think: how can I trust this man? That is the thought that will obsess the both of us. Here, look at the next picture."

It was a shot taken from the air and blown up. It wasn't clear. It could have been a clearing, and on it was what could have been, or could not have been, missile shapes. Launching cradles? He wasn't sure. He knew enough to recognize what he saw but he would need an expert aerial photographic analyst to verify it.

"Yes. It's just what you think it is. A missile launching site."

"Where were these photographs taken?"

"Call it Cuba."

"You want to defect?"

"Gholcomb, Gholcomb! I am not offering you information for asylum. I am talking about an alliance. Our beliefs are being perverted. Comrade Khrushchev, it is not *nash*, but also *Chuz-*

257

hoi, a man of the west. He has sent out feelers to President Kennedy, asking for a mutual meeting of minds, informally, and off the record. A summit beneath the soil, germinating noxious seeds. Peaceful coexistence. What do you call it? That pernicious doctrine of 'convergence.' The cold war is to be wound down. Settle the Berlin question. Settle the Mideast question. End Israel. End the conflict with Cuba. Wind down the involvement in Indo-China. There will be collaboration in many spheres; in fact it has already started. Already we allow your overflights by the Strategic Air Command. We are informed where the U-2s go. We were also informed which one to shoot down when Gary Powers was captured. You allow our overflights. Sometimes the commands exchange flight plans with one another. Informal military missions are meeting and sounding out one another's capabilities. Low-level technical and scientific missions meet regularly to exchange data. There is discussion about cooperation in space. The president of your Westinghouse will shortly be in Moscow. Siemens sends us diplomatic missions. Anglo-American sends emissaries. DeBeers Consolidated controls the marketing of Soviet diamonds. Who are these rootless merchants to send *diplomatic* missions, as if they were sovereign states?

"Gholcomb, we are being replaced by traders and technocrats. Human beings, the differing aspirations and national destinies of our two countries, are being perverted. 'It is a sign of the decay of nations when they begin to have goods in common . . . When the same conceptions of good and evil become prevalent in several nations, then these nations are dying, and then the very distinction between good and evil is beginning to disappear . . .' the sterility of a world bound together only by technology and money. A single-value world. As much as I hate you, as much as I hate your country, Gholcomb, you are a *human*—misguided —but a human. You have the dreams of a human; you are the receptacle of your people's destiny. So it is with me. We are destined to compete. What is to become of us, of the planet itself, if we don't contend? Contention makes us strong. What is America? What is Holy Russia? What is Germany? Parvus would have there be no America, no Russia, no Germany, no England. Your fanatical friend from Berlin, Braunstein, knows all this. He was the first to see it. These Parvus internationalists have penetrated

258

both our organizations and are replacing us. What will happen if one of them rises to the top, takes over our military, our intelligence, our political apparatus? Global charade, a vast theatre, puppets dancing from two hands of the same puppeteer.

"Gholcomb, I propose an alliance, a pact to restore things as they were. I will give you these photographs and more, no strings attached. I have more shots of the bases in Cuba. You will know how to verify them, informally. If you accept, I will provide the coordinates for your U-2s to fly over. You will find that they are not fakes. We should meet again in a week."

They had crossed the upper tip of Manhattan and were on the West Side Highway headed south. On the opposite side, the dark mass of the Palisades. Ahead, the string of lights shaping the George Washington Bridge. "The three of us—you, Braunstein, I—should sit down together in about a week. An opportunity is presenting itself soon, probably in late October. You must introduce those photographs into the proper channels and they will flow upwards. With this evidence, your people will not be able to draw back, nor can mine."

Should he reject Skuratov's offer? What if he were picked up as soon as he left Skuratov? What story could he construct to show how he got hold of the photographs? He sighed. Skuratov knew that he would at least have to see if the photographs checked out. He was *already* involved. "My chauffeur. I'll have to explain what happened."

Skuratov shrugged. "If he were to die, it would contribute to the war effort."

Holcomb sighed. The sigh was agreement.

It was the sign of their alliance.

They were passing under the bridge and were almost passing near the massive pile of Columbia Presbyterian Medical Center.

CHAPTER 31

THEY had just come back from dining with Laura and Vassili. It was clear that Sidney Ficino had fallen in love with Laura. He hadn't been able to stop babbling. Barnstable pretended to finish reading Carol Rothschild's typed-up notes. She was clearly holding back a lot.

"At this rate, Sidney, we will have the answers we're looking for in about two years."

"Well, I'm pushing Carol—"

"Fucking Carol isn't pushing her. She treats the whole thing in that typical way of all psychoanalysts. Everything is in the mind. You have to speed things up."

"She says she has to win his confidence."

"Her notes don't show it, but she's already won more than his trust. And as for your idea that you're pushing her, Sidney; whining at her to speed things up—whining and fucking—*that's* persuasion?"

Ficino had never heard Barnstable sound so harsh. "You're *watching* us?"

"Why do you have to state the obvious?"

"I'm overloaded with work, plus—"

"I don't like excuses, Sidney. Our company, Metatronics, yours, mine, ours, doesn't like excuses either. We have to get this kid on his feet, find out what information he's stolen from his father and

260

what he did with it. Then the Foundation will open its coffers and confer legitimacy on us. We're going to be big, Sidney, but it hinges on the kid—and the other profiles. I would say, wouldn't you, that the prime subject of our remote analysis, the little fat man, is quick to shoot from the hip? A man of extreme temper, even when it comes to the lives of millions."

Ficino was glad to change the subject. "But not wholly irresponsible."

"Ah, then there is a measure of usable restraint, and the temper may be theatre? He's capable, if the world isn't watching him, of extending the hand of friendship in a genuine way? Trustworthy, but only out of the limelight? You can build a case for that? Maybe we should be ready for any contingency and have two reports—one that shows he's reasonable offstage; the other that he's intractable."

Barnstable was whipsawing him back and forth. "There's nothing in her notes that—"

"Believe me, I know."

"I guess that's what . . . what do the shrinks call it? Transference?"

What Barnstable really wanted to know was, will they make love soon? "And she's reciprocating, but she doesn't quite know it yet. That's transference too, isn't it, Sidney?"

"Well, if she's so involved, she shouldn't be doing the questioning."

"Wrong, Sidney. The newest theories say the shrink *should* get involved. She is *exactly* the one person who should be doing the questioning. But maybe she should make it more intimate. To reverse our traditional sexual metaphor, she holds the key to that particular lock."

"I don't know what you're getting at."

"Come on, Sidney, don't act like such a completely dense shithead. They want to fuck. They have to fuck. Then he's going to trust her completely and the transference will be complete."

"Wait a minute—"

"Wait a minute, wait a minute," Barnstable mimicked. The delicious moment was coming for Barnstable when the subject, having felt violated, passes into another state. The expression on the face would be surrender, hate, fear . . . and a kind of love

261

. . . all over having an intimate secret revealed to the world. "Come on, Sidney. What's a fuck? A little body contact, some moisture, some screams of pleasure? I thought you were a scientist. From a scientific point of view, I'd think you'd be interested in seeing her in someone else's arms . . . or even yourself in the act."

"I am a scientist, but . . ."

"Sidney, you're moving into the big time. Life is a little different up here. I mean this middle-class possessiveness, mine, yours, that's just petty. Are you afraid that the kid is a better fuck than you are?"

"No, it's just that—"

"What? You're not going to tell me you love her?"

"Well, it's not exactly that, but—"

"You have to be clinical, Sidney. Clinical and detached. You have to persuade her."

"I can't do that!"

"You have to do that." The tone of Barnstable's voice changed now. Instead of being harsh, insensitive, he pitched his voice to become warm, confidential. The tone said, "I know your secret . . . it's just between the two of us. But if you do the wrong thing . . ." Barnstable had been right. It wasn't the fear of being watched: it was the fear of being thought inadequate . . . "Sidney, Sidney . . . I understand. Growing up is hard. If we don't change, what are we? We're like all those little people out there. Each move upward, Sidney, changes our vision of the world. You've already suspected what I am. You know I'm not just a funding officer for the Coffin, or an officer of Metatronics, but have you really faced the implications of what you know? You know state sectets. You know that you were given that sensitive material for a purpose. That was the first test. You passed it, and asked for more. You're quick, even brilliant. You showed you could do the job. Each stage of knowledge brings both liberation and at the same time a new set of responsibilities. You weren't born yesterday, Sidney. It's time to let go. You don't want to be a second-rater all your life."

"But my God, Mr. Barnstable, what you're asking—"

"Isn't it time you called me Bob?"

262

"Bob . . . You're asking me to act like a pimp. For the woman I love. For someone else to fuck. How can I do that? And what about her?"

"*How* can I do that, not how *can* I do that. Sidney you've been working up predictive profiles of our two prime candidates . . . you know who I mean. You didn't think it was just an exercise for your ingenuity. There may come a time, perhaps quite soon, when that profile will be necessary, I mean vital. Perhaps a crisis will arise, perhaps not. Perhaps it will be a matter of national security. If so, certain very important people on the highest level will be fascinated to know how those people will respond in a crunch. Will one of them panic? Be hardline? Will they back off? You can see the value of knowing in advance what the competition will do, knowing them in ways they themselves don't know. And when the time comes, if you, yourself, were to present that assessment to the people who have the greatest need to see it, your reputation would be assured. This is going to be a big business, Sidney. People are going to want to know everything about their rivals."

"Yes, but . . ."

"You've asked yourself how I got that material?"

"Yes, but . . ."

"What if I told you we got some of that material from—" And Barnstable thumbed his hand over his shoulder, in the general direction of where Richard was—"him."

"Jesus. That kid?"

"Now what's a half-psychotic kid doing with complete profiles of people who are *that* important? Your President *and* the Russian Premier. Maybe, you follow my drift, the kid's 'father' isn't just a businessman and trustee of the Foundation. You see the importance of what I'm saying? See why they have to fuck? See why you have to let go? Sidney, you've been up to your ears in your work. Tell the truth now; you haven't had the time to do much fucking, have you? Fact is maybe you're a little bored with her. And as for Dr. Carol Rothschild, she's interested in him."

Ficino sighed. "How can I begin to ask her such a thing? All right, Bob, maybe it isn't a question of morals, but it'll take getting used to."

263

"Sure, Sidney, sure."

"But how do you say . . . How do you say . . . Do I just tell her? I mean . . ."

"No. Not yet. She has no need to know. Not yet. You just isolate her a little more. She'll make the right move. Get into an argument. Drive her. Threaten to take the case away from her. She'll hold on."

Ficino sighed again. He had a thought. "Laura? She's married? She's certainly a dynamic person."

"One of the brightest. That's one tough lady."

"Yes. And she's beautiful."

"She sure is."

"Bob. Have you ever . . . I mean do you think she could . . ."

"Sidney, you'll have to do it yourself. And you're not at the point where you can turn around and throw at me what I've thrown at you. But she is moved by successful men."

CHAPTER 32

THE battle for influence over the direction of foreign policy intensified during the months of August, September and October 1962. The coin of influence was knowledge, delivered in packets flatteringly marked For Your Eyes Only. And its value was expressed in knowing what few other people knew.

As the Congressional elections of 1962 approached, some Democrats and many Republicans became vocal about Cuba and the administration's inability to take a firm position. The "loss" at the Bay of Pigs was like a deficit that had to be balanced. Senators Smathers, Keating, Javits, Dirksen, Goldwater and Capehart fulminated, increasing the pressure on the President through the media, to which "secrets" were leaked. There were struggles to gain audiences with the President, and if not the President, then with his more trusted advisors, Ted Sorensen, McGeorge Bundy, Bobby Kennedy, his friends, even members of his family. If the President distrusted the CIA, the CIA had other ways of reaching to the President.

U.S. intelligence operations had become like redundant and overlapping nervous systems, some parts of which were semiautonomous—CIA, State, Defense Intelligence, the Office of Naval Intelligence, NSA, the FBI, the U.S. Reconnaissance Office, the special unit set up by President Kennedy after the Bay of Pigs, the intelligence agencies of other countries, the intelligence gathering and covert operations systems of various large corporations, domestic and foreign, were in conflict. And inside each bureaucracy, personal and ideological conflicts raged which were resolved by subtle paper moves, gossip and back-channel operations . . . or sometimes even more drastically: by killing. Actions were launched which were designed to commit the administration in ways it didn't want. The administration complained that the CIA's Directorate of Plans was operating on a freewheeling basis in highly critical areas—in Cuba; in Vietnam—sometimes in direct conflict with, say, State Department diplomacy.

The sensing tentacles of the agencies reached everywhere. Raw data was gathered up in a thousand places by thousands of agents. Overflight information poured in, nervous stimuli and sensoria to activate the mighty muscles of nations. But the data, the stimuli, didn't always originate at the point where they were gathered. The system appeared to *feel* that something was happening on the nation's skin, or beyond, but sometimes the data was just made up at the center. Thousands of items were constantly being collated, linked, associated, summarized, refined, edited, analyzed, gamed before they were passed on. And at each station of ascent, the mass of data was again examined, tightened up, re-edited, analyzed by somebody else. This process created difficulties. It was possible to intervene and insert information anywhere along the line.

There were short circuits built into the system. Robert Kennedy and Pierre Salinger kept meeting privately with Khrushchev's personal back-channel to Kennedy, Georgi Bolshakov. They were passing information to one another about the intentions of Kennedy and Khrushchev, trying to bypass the unwieldly bureaucracy.

All this material, an absolutely unmanageable flow, was seen by a very few people before being passed up to its ultimate peak, the Chief Executive. Millions of items compiled daily struggled for attention; only the most dramatic could survive. The daily product had to be short enough to be read by one person in a reasonable amount of time. And now, in September, these reports were also seen, assessed, argued over informally by a free-floating sort of proto-committee which would be called formally the Executive Committee (Excom) of senior statesmen, working under the aegis of the National Security Council to be assembled when the expected crisis broke. Keats's assessment, based on monitoring Richard's wiretaps, proved to Mr. Kelley that Keats was right. The minutes of the not-yet-existent Excom validated what Mr. Kelley already knew: that the arguments which would be acted out in council had already been rehearsed and were moving toward some end which would unfold in late October. Keats wanted Aquilino to influence the outcome.

Now, if you knew enough, as Keats and Mr. Kelley did, thrust and counter-thrust were clear. Did Khrushchev extend, through informal channels, an invitation to meet with President Kennedy in order to settle world tensions? Perhaps to achieve truce, nuclear arms-limitation, an end to testing, even peaceful coexistence? How genuine was the move? There were those who argued in the proto-Excom that the move was a sham. Don't meet with him. And there were those who argued in the proto-Excom, why not take a chance? What can we lose? Those who argued for the meeting produced a psychological assessment of Mr. Khrushchev which concluded that in such off-stage moves, Mr. Khrushchev was 85% certain to be sincere. Others countered with other psychological assessments.

Another response to Khrushchev's initiative was a raid on Cuba by Alpha-66, a secret group of Cuban exiles with more than a little informal operational assistance by the CIA. Alpha-66's raid was an extension of Operation Mongoose. Operation Mongoose was an extension of the fruits of National Security Action Memorandum (NSAM) 100, "Contingency Planning for Cuba," which had been generated by a Special Group convened in October 1961 by President Kennedy. The Special Group consisted of McGeorge Bundy the Security Advisor, Alexis Johnson, Undersecretary of State, Roswell Gilpatrick, Deputy Director of Defense, John McCone, Director of Central Intelligence, and General Lyman Lemnitzer, Chairman of the Joint Chiefs of Staff, and the National Security Council Staff. The object of this contingency planning was the removal of Fidel Castro. The operational arm of NSAM was called Operation Mongoose; "to use all available assets . . . to help overthrow the Communist regime . . . culminating in October 1962."

At the operational end, where humans live or die, the exiles mounted their raid in the struggle to liberate their homeland from communist tyranny. The purpose, known to the raiders, was sabotage. A purpose not known to the raiders was to prevent the meeting between Khrushchev and Kennedy from happening. The raiding party was gunned down almost immediately. It was as if they were betrayed, as if the knowledge of their mission preceded them. They were mutilated and left as a warning; photographs were taken. The people who gunned them down immediately disembarked and made their way back to Florida, where they reported what Fidel's goons had done to Cuban patriots. A wave of outrage swept through Miami, transmitted all the way back to Washington.

One practical effect was to slow down the negotiations for the release of the Bay of Pigs prisoners. It also alarmed the Cubans and their Soviet advisors. Were these skirmishes preliminary to a full scale invasion and war? All the signs were there; an embargo was in the offing. Marines practiced amphibious operations on the beaches of Virginia and North Carolina. There were jungle exercises in the American territories of Panama. The alarm, like a headache, was transmitted back to Moscow Central and passed on to the party hardliners, such as Mikhail Suslov, who mobilized other hardliners to put pressure on Comrade Khrushchev. No meeting with Kennedy; not in the face of such an affront. Khrushchev then had to reconcile conciliatory messages coming from Kennedy through Georgi Bolshakov, with hostile signals coming from the mounting number of small strikes against Cuba.

Alpha-66 swore revenge once again.

The intelligence and counter-intelligence effort to win American hearts and minds wasn't the only way the battle went. There was the opinion-molding media to be considered. Mr. Kelley launched his own media assault. Think tanks generated studies. The missile gap was explored and denounced as a fraud. Attacks were made on the General Dynamics TFX cost overruns. Those who were for peace fought back by pushing strategic arms limitation talks . . . asked for an end to the unreasoning fear of the Russians. Editors and columnists were lobbied, taken to lunch, invited to fashionable dinners, briefed in a hundred forms, were at the pleasing center of a blizzard of gossip, rumors, leaks, backgrounders, the not-for-attribution throwaways . . . Senators, congressmen, security advisors were invited to lunch at the *Times, Newsweek, Time, Life,* etc., to air their opinions and ideas. Committees were formed to fight for detente. European papers speculated about the high-handed methods of the Americans. Committees were formed to alert the nation to the present danger. Publicists were deployed. Items were exchanged in bed, in homosexual bars, in whorehouses . . . Leaks found their way into domestic newspapers: "A senior advisor said today . . ." On . . . background. On deep background. Items were disseminated to foreign newspapers in order to be picked up by American papers. *Le Monde* reported . . . *Corriere Della Sera* stated . . . The *Times of London* noted . . .

CHAPTER 33

NIGHT, or what passes for night. Room. Bed. Bathroom without a door. A chair. Books. A table. Smooth walls. Richard tried staying awake for long periods of time. He didn't want to wake up as Richard-prime in the "dungeon."

No clock in the room. As he would fall asleep, but before he had gone under deep, there was a faint hum. A faintly pulsating light. Both seemingly keeping time to his heartbeat. Like conversations . . . rhythm of light . . . falling asleep . . . rousing faint memories of overheard conversations. Should he tell Carol? Places. Numbers. He woke suddenly, as if to surprise the light and sound in the act. They stopped suddenly. Caught them. Does Carol already *know?* She must. He got up from the bed. He was not feeling tired. He got down on the floor and began to do push-ups. Five, ten, twenty, twenty-five. And he heard the sound of his own breathing becoming heavier and heavier; a slight sweat. Was there an echo of his endeavor coming back at him from the walls, the floor, stronger than the sound of his own breathing, just a little out of sync? He stopped flat on the floor to listen, and heard one last panting breath that didn't issue from him. There. He had caught them again.

Did he dream? Did he fall asleep? He was rolled up on his side, his arm under his head. Carol was there. He smelled her. She said, "Richard, what are you doing on the floor?" And then she turned on the light and it was "daylight."

"What month is it?"

"September."

"What day?"

"The eleventh."

Therefore, Richard remembered, the President was in Huntsville, Alabama, meeting with Dr. Werner Von Braun on schedule. Later he would fly on to Cape Canaveral to inspect the Launch Operation Center. Mercury, Atlas, Titan II . . . missiles. What was it about missiles he should remember? Warning to the world. Operation Sandgrain. Like a tumor growing, growing into a pearl. A Pearl Harbor. Sandgrain? A Pearl Harbor in reverse. Who said that, in reverse? America making a Pearl Harbor?

How many stories had his father told him? How much of it had the walls whispered to him in his sleep? The President goes on to Houston. Couldn't get through to him. Richard remembered the first thing the President would do; he'll order an embargo of Cuba. Someone will say that "quarantine" is a better word than "embargo." The word implies the disease that suppurates in the boil that Cuba is, which must be contained, or lanced with a surgical strike—Lancer. Kennedy's code name. Electioneering, Kennedy will then go on to Minneapolis. Maybe there . . .

In his mind, Richard stepped out of a crowd, stepped up to the President, and began to talk. "I'm Richard Aquilino. I've been talking to you on the phone. Look what you people have done to me." Everyone dreams of such a moment in which he can talk to the President. To Jesus. The President listens, nods, and is amazed by his wisdom. "My God, I had no idea," he says.

"My parents, my family, your people have stolen them away. Give them back." Somehow he's going to know what to say when the moment comes. Then, the President will change his plans, order an investigation, and punish the guilty.

Can't do it that way. The Secret Service would hustle him away and he'd be back in "their" hands. There must be another way to reach him. Between New York and Huntsville, Canaveral, Houston, it's only a few seconds by telephone. But he might as well be light years from the nearest telephone. Ziggy will have to do it for you. Maybe Carol . . . "Please go outside and get to a phone booth and dial this number. When someone answers, you say . . ."

How could he do it? A telephone call? The White House switchboard? The command and communication center travels wherever he goes, and he has his own private phone, in order to talk to whomever he wants to, unheard . . . he thinks. All his women. Laura.

Carol sat down, composed as always, her notebook on her thigh, pencil ready. Flat board on a soft swell. Deep breathing. Her breasts heaved outward. What would it be like to stroke them? He smelled her perfume. A slight erection. He turned downward and resumed his pushups. This time there was no echo of his heavy air-intake coming out of the walls.

"Richard, can we begin talking?"

"What's the weather like outside?"

"It's raining. Are you avoiding me today?" she asked.

"Just a second." He was in good shape. Everything in him felt more alive than it had felt for months. "Turn out the light. I feel better talking in the dark."

He herd her get up and walk. The light went out. He stayed there on the floor. He heard her heels clicking on the floor, a scrape of a chair being pulled along the linoleum. She was sitting down.

"I'm free," he told her.

"What do you mean?"

"I'm free of her. Laura. Thanks to you."

"You can only free yourself. Do you want to talk about that?"

He rolled over on his back and sat up, clasping his knees, staring into the darkness toward where her voice came from. "What was I looking for all those years?"

"Something in yourself that you interpreted as a princess?"

"That came from my father's stories. That wasn't it. She sold herself . . ."

"She was only . . . what? Thirteen? Fourteen? A child. Richard, relax. Why don't you sit on the bed, lie down?"

"I'm comfortable here. I want to feel something hard."

"All right. *Now,* what does the imprisoned princess really mean to you? You never faced it . . . the deeper meaning."

272

"No."

She paused. She wanted him to understand something.

"Even the way you talk about . . . what did you say? Tracking her? Laura. The telephone. *Listening* in. Not facing. Not seeing. Not wanting to *see* . . ."

"What do you mean, 'the way you talk about her?' That was real. Real phones. Real wiretapping. Real."

The words frightened her. After the argument with Sidney . . . she didn't want to face that reality herself. "And that's what I mean when I ask what does the imprisoned princess . . ."

"Witch. Bitch. Whore."

"Princess or bitch . . . the two sides of a woman . . ." And what was she; something to be driven toward Richard by Sidney? A whore? "Do you have to think of her in those extreme terms? Angel or slut?"

"Was. She's dead."

"Was? Is? You say you saw her later, after she supposedly was dead."

"Demons can die and not die."

He was mad. "Is her 'death' what you wished on her? For rejecting you? And what did you see later—when you were being chased—a whore? Maybe in your bitterness and obsession you saw Laura in every whore . . . if you really saw a whore. She's a person. It's not a question of what Laura is, but what you feel about her and what she represents."

A demon who could be alive and dead and alive.

". . . people do things . . . sometimes they are forced to do things against their will, forced by circumstances, people, pressures of all kinds . . . she was only a child."

"She was dead. Dead. Carol, I touched her body. That was real. She was . . . slashed to pieces. Blood. Shit, Carol, there was *shit*. They say you shit when you die." He shook. "My hands . . . her face . . . her eyes . . . it was her, Laura, her . . ."

"But then you saw her again. And what did that mean?"

"Maybe you're right. I was mistaken. You're thinking I had a hallucination, right?"

Carol didn't say anything. The other Richard, Richard-prime, the other and broken body, hovered on the edge, pulling him back into a universe of pain.

273

"You're still fantasizing about her."

It was true. Laura, it seemed, could be everywhere, dead and alive, at the same time. Newport. Harrisburg. Wheeling. Where the President was, she would be there. And so would He. More speeches. Off to the side would be the Situation Room. He thought of it as a dark room with a glowing map on the wall, with illuminated lines and numbers in pairs. Coordinates. Fleets of ships and planes: armies. Lining up in the Atlantic athwart Cuba. A room deep in the earth where men debated, argued, cursed, maneuvered to move President Kennedy step by step to some devastating end. If he remembered now, they could drag it out of him. How could he conceal these things even from himself and yet remember them, save them until he got out of this place? Carol was the one forcing him—or helping him—to remember. He got up and went softly to her side of the room. His hands reached out in the dark and his palms found her face. She jumped a little. "Don't be afraid," he whispered. "I'm not going to hurt you."

She half-sighed, half-sobbed. His hands felt so good. If only he weren't so disturbed. If only Sidney hadn't . . .

His palms pressed into the sidepieces of her eyeglasses. He took her glasses off and leaned forward, his lips searching the darkness for hers. Her hair tickled his face. Forehead . . . soft skin wrinkled in a frown, eyes, cheeks, nose—lips. Her mouth opened, their tongues met.

His hands ran down her body. His penis thrust against the cloth of his pajama pants. She rose, muttering, "No, don't. We shouldn't . . ."

"It's dark," he whispered. "No one can see us."

"Richard, it's wrong. You don't know . . ."

"Help me," he whispered. "I'm scared. I need you. I want you, but I'm scared." His hands felt for her. His hands had eyes. Her breasts under her clothes, pliant where they had appeared rigid. His hands moved up and down her sides, brushing over the swell of her thighs. Ridges for the garters, one hand moving upward, bunching the cloth between her legs, feeling behind the cloth. She moaned. Her arms were around his neck. Cheek to cheek. A woman. He had never slept with a woman. Only girls. He tasted tears. Why was she crying? "Why—"

274

"Shh . . ." she said. Her hands were unbuttoning the pajama jacket, pulling it off, as his hands kept moving around, looking for the zipper, or the buttons of her dress. He was afraid to be clumsy. He swung his arms free one at a time so he could keep touching and stroking her as his pajama jacket was slid off. His penis ached now. He was afraid he would come. The drawstring of the pants was jerked loose and his pants fell around his ankles. He found the zipper at the back of her neck and pulled down while he stepped out of the pants. He pulled the dress off her shoulders, feeling skin and nylon, brassiere and slip. Her hands traced the muscles of his neck and chest, feeling each muscle there, moving sideways and down his rib cage, chilling him.

He pulled the dress forward and down. It was stopped by her belt. He unbuckled it. Her other hand was down at the small of his back, beginning to trace the jut of his behind. The nailtips tingled his skin. The dress slid down. He wanted the lights on; he wanted to look. But he was glad the lights were off; he didn't want to be seen. Her other hand moved in small dartings through his body hair, on his belly hair. She took his penis in cool, moist hands. She was surprised at how big he was . . . his hardness. Her breath sucked in, noisily. She gulped. He had undone her brassiere straps. Her hand slipped down the length of him and, palm upward, slid beneath his testicles. He jumped, then pulled brassiere and slip downward, stopping when he got to her waist. She moved against him. He bent and his mouth was all over her. Rigid nipples were against his palm and lips. She let go of him and slithered out of the rest of her clothes while his mouth was all over her. Richard tried to visualize her. The motion moved her body forward as it bent, yielding her breasts entirely into his hands. She bit at his chest, mildly, harder. He wanted to squeeze, to grasp, to have his fingers meet through skin and flesh, to feel every possibility of her flesh. She took one of his hands and moved it downward until it was between her legs, and closed her thighs on his hand. His fingers found soft flesh, moistness . . . and her body shook. He thought: I did that. They sidled clumsily through the blackness, toward the bed. She sat down and pulled him gently forward on top of her. He hoped he wouldn't come too soon, that he wasn't being too eager and clumsy. They were on the bed entirely and then she guided him partway in. The heat of it shocked him. She moved wildly. She raised her legs and grasped him with her thighs, arched her back, thrust her hips forward, let him a little further into her . . . it was big, it ached . . . and pulled at him hard, stifling a scream. He was in. They lay still. Thirty seconds passed . . . a minute . . . an eternity . . . and she began to move.

He started to groan.

"Shh," she whispered. "Don't say anything. Don't make a sound." He understood. Body to body, in simple, uncomplicated movements. Everything was unlocking in him. All the futile years were passing away. Each moment made him feel stronger and prouder.

She was shocked by his size and vigor; her shame began to drop away and she thrust in return, forgetting why they were here and who had brought them together . . . what that bastard had made her do. She'd had no idea it could be like this. Uncomplicated, unlike being with Sidney who kept dreaming up new things to do. Sidney was nothing like Richard, whose seemingly simple thrust and withdrawal was infinitely varied, providing new discoveries of pleasure. She felt a flutter inside her. So soon? She moved faster. He felt her flutter and moved harder and faster, straight and sideways, leaning backward, trying to see her face in the blackness of the room. He felt her thighs grip tighter and tighter, squeezing his hips, his waist, his rib cage as she began to move, getting out of control now but making no sound other than the passage of breath. She planted her legs on the bed and arched, suddenly, lifting him and pulling him, as if she would throw him off, over her, while her hands held him, not letting him move, pulling at his hair, clawing his back. It came again. A second time. Stronger. His hands slipped under her, holding her behind now. She let herself go now. A third time now, on the edge of being excruciating. He stared into the darkness for a second, trying to hold himself back, and began to come.

And then he pulled out and rolled off. She emitted a choked-off groan. The air chilled his wet body. He snuggled close to her. He smiled. Was she smiling too? He looked into the blackness. Who cared if it was night or day?

His eyes played tricks on him. It was not so much the blackness but it seemed as if a kind of light filled the room . . . pulsing colors

276

. . . reds and blues and yellows, whites . . . some bits of black . . . flickering . . . like curtains . . . shells . . . shells of color . . . a massive black shape outlined in the colors . . . a shadowplay . . . shoulders . . . waist . . . a man . . . no head . . . No. A head. A head of pure light. Light, white light where a face would be . . . a yellowgold smudge where hair would be. It was he. The blond knight in his black armor . . . and he knew what that face looked like behind the white lightmask . . . He had seen it across the abyss of time and back, seen for him by his father and his father's father . . . he had seen it for one or two minutes, across the abyss of space, Times Square.

Carol's hand reached for him. She traced the shape of his testicles, his penis, above, beneath . . . it closed around the penis. Nothing happened. The black shape seemed to turn. The back of the head . . . black . . . a headshape . . . the face was not to be looked at . . . and through the headshape he saw the stars and beyond the stars, the faces of the gods, huddled around their table, and the stellar lights on the map of the situation room . . . It, the shape, he, moved into the curtains and shells of colored light . . . growing larger and larger till the blackness obscured the flickering light and the room was black again, as if they were inside of him. Then Richard's penis began to harden again and wax . . . and he was surprised. Richard turned to look at Carol's face, as if expecting it to be illuminated. It was dark here, where her face was. Did she see it? If she did, she gave no sign. And they began to make love again.

CHAPTER 34

THREE aging men, not so fast on their feet anymore but still strong, sat around a table. The table was in a cube, ten by ten by ten. The cube was transparent, suspended in air. Holcomb, Braunstein, Skuratov. They looked at one another. It was a change of history that brought enemies together. A change that threatened their countries, their beliefs, their way of doing things.

The first problem had been: whose territory would they meet on? They couldn't count on backup; they were doing this on their own. None of them would have anything to exchange if he was taken prisoner. Within Holcomb's territory there was a little fiefdom belonging to Skuratov. A container ship, built in Japan, brought by Ecuadorians under Panamanian registry, but owned by the Russians. It was both container ship and electronic spy ship.

Braunstein had had to weigh coming to New York. Holcomb couldn't provide protection; he could be caught and sent back to Russia. Braunstein held back until Skuratov arranged, through Holcomb, to talk directly to Braunstein. Skuratov didn't bother to plead with Braunstein the way he had with Holcomb. He merely recited a list of names: Braunstein's people in the Soviet party, in military intelligence, in the KGB. Skuratov knew them *all!* "You see, we are already married," Skuratov said. Braunstein

278

got the point. His network had been in place too long. They had families. They had power. Whether they liked it or not, the very nature of their jobs insured that they had in fact become what they pretended to be a long time ago: Russians. Braunstein was in shock. Had all the years of intelligence out of Russia, which he had sold so profitably to NATO, been disinformation? And what was more shocking; Braunstein realized that it was not disinformation, but good intelligence. He agreed to come to New York to hear what the others had to say.

The ship was in New York Harbor. After taking the usual steps to shake any tails from, say, the Parvus Game, or the CIA, Holcomb and Braunstein arrived about ten minutes apart and walked into a container on the dock beside the immense ship. The container was fitted up as a room. When they were both inside, the container was lifted by a huge crane and lowered into the hold of the ship. The door opened. Skuratov was there to welcome them. They looked around the hold. It was enormous, piled with containers arranged in a complex loading pattern: an abstract cubist nightmare. Floodlights cast odd shadows. There were open areas, narrow corridors that went far, far into the distance. Beyond, there was blackness.

"Comrades, this is a historic occasion," Skuratov said and began to laugh. The others, seeing the joke, began to laugh with him. "Comrades." The metal sides of the ship multiplied and boomed back each peal of laughter. When the echoes died down, Skuratov said: "Old friends. Gholcomb. Braunstein. We must trust one another. We have no choice. There will be no recording and no pictures of this meeting to haunt us later. Please, follow me."

They walked down long twisting corridors between the piled-up containers to an open area where, above them, suspended by wires, hung a large, transparent cube. Looking up, they could see the bottoms of a table and chairs. A ladder led up to the cube. They climbed up, one by one, into the cube. The door was shut behind them. A humming noise started. A white-noise machine. They sat down. There were glasses and bottles on the table. "A little schnapps, some vodka, bourbon to oil the discussion. Absolutely surveillance-proof. If you have any lingering doubts, then inspect the plastic and see if you can see any kind of bug at all. I suppose microphones could be in the wiring that holds the cube

279

in place. And even if you decide to your satisfaction that there are no listening devices, we may have long-range directional microphones and so on and so forth, until there is no satisfying you. But at some point there must come risk and trust. In short, there is no assurance."

Braunstein nodded. "It is a shame that three old men are called upon to save the world."

"Not so old," Holcomb said.

"Let me chair this meeting, friends," Skuratov said. "We have a long night ahead of us. I propose this. You, Gholcomb, will give us a brief rundown about the conditions that led to your calling on Herr Braunstein for aid. The case of this vanished Richard Aquilino, seemingly eavesdropping on high places and important people. Tell us your suspicions, what you did, what you think went wrong when you lost him. I will then take up the story and tell of my intuitions; how I think my people were brought into the case and used—namely, that one of our agents, Vassili Oprichnik, to protect or take Aquilino, betrayed us, not to the United States, but to someone else."

"The Parvus Game," Braunstein said.

"Exactly. But more, an internationalist game inside of an internationalist game."

"Yeah," Holcomb said. He was accepting it for now.

"Then Herr Braunstein will give us a briefing on the history of Parvus, his vision, the growth of the Game, the seeding of our countries with our people. Parvus—Helphand—is still alive, you know."

"Not really!" Braunstein said, already excited.

"In his nineties, but his mind is still alert," Skuratov said. "He'll die soon, but he's trained others in preparation for that day. When we have had Herr Braunstein's summation, we will pool our knowledge and decide on a course of coordinated action. I think that our interests lie in supporting the most reactionary and conservative elements of all countries. But that will come later. The thing to ask ourselves now is, why is this Aquilino so important, to whom, and for what purpose?"

If it was dawn or daylight, no one inside the container ship could tell. They had been talking and drinking for hours. They had moved closer but still had not decided on a course of action. The discussion had begun to tail into reminiscences of past probes, encounters and shoot-outs. Skuratov spoke:

"It's getting very late. Our minds are flagging. I have a suggestion. This much is clear. Gholcomb is in an unfortunate position; he is still rounding up a network among his colleagues, but he is being watched. Who do you have, mostly CIA people?"

"A few FBI. Some others."

"This is no time to hold out. Who?"

"Mafia. Contract people."

"Untrustworthy. Who else?"

"Cuban patriots."

"You're working with Harvey in Florida? Never mind. Dangerous. Fanatics. Penetrated top and bottom by Comrade Castro's intelligence."

Holcomb had his reservations about what Skuratov was telling him.

"That means only Braunstein and I have reliable networks in place. But outside New York, the American terrain is not so well known to us. We will need some of your people as guides; they don't have to know what role they will be fulfilling. Then we can provide backup by keeping Oprichnik under surveillance. Harkavy, the radio and telephone technician, is in our hands. He swears he was forced into this position by Oprichnik. He claims he thought he was working for us. He will cooperate. It would be helpful, Gholcomb, if you could make available to Braunstein and myself your telephone company list of those eavesdropped upon. You've been watching Keats but you're hampered; let us do it for you. It would be better if a few of Braunstein's people watched instead of mine and yours, who can probably be spotted. Aquilino is salted away somewhere, being prepared for something. His role is not yet clear. He is being intersected with the developing crisis. Cuba, late October, he will emerge with some startling piece of news. Military units are being moved into jumping off points in Florida. Marines. Army. Paratroopers . . . we read their communications . . ."

"It will be war?" Braunstein said.

"If Parvus has its way, there will be no war, it will be pure theatre. If we have our way, it will at least be cold war again.

281

Keats will run Aquilino; we can only follow Aquilino through Keats through Oprichnik until the action is clear. Then maybe we will take Aquilino, or take over the running of him, when we see what must be done. In the meantime we will begin to circulate the aerial photographs to interested parties. They seem to have difficulties in finding what's in front of their noses. What is it one of your great capitalists once said? 'Send pictures and I will provide the war'?"

"Hearst."

"I suggest we get a few hours of sleep. Our minds will be clearer. There are, among this wilderness of boxcars without wheels, sleeping quarters, quite comfortable. Some food will be brought to you. A little entertainment will be provided, if you have the strength." Skuratov began to laugh again. "No photographs of *that,* you have my word of honor."

"The word of an intelligence agent is written on shit," Holcomb said. "Isn't that what this meeting is really about?"

"I want to show you something. Come this way."

They got up from the table. They were stiff. They stretched, but they remained wary. Skuratov led them to one wall. Holcomb felt peculiar standing on a transparent floor, and the alcohol didn't help.

"Look that way," Skuratov pointed.

In the distance, Holcomb and Braunstein saw, half-sticking out from behind a wall of containers, a neat pile of cone shapes.

"Missiles?" Holcomb asked.

"So to speak."

"What range?"

"Intermediate."

"What megatonnage?"

"None." Skuratov laughed.

"None? They're empty?"

"No. It's just that the triggering mechanisms are . . . shall we say, in a safe place."

"You don't trust the Cubans?"

"You don't trust the Greeks or the Turks?" Skuratov mocked. "Never mind. You are victims of an optical illusion. You think you see missiles here, but in fact they are somewhere else. In the middle of the Atlantic, being moved southwest, very slowly indeed, perhaps ready to be intercepted by the American fleet. They must be in a certain place at a certain time, and that's one of the things we must determine."

"You cocksucker," Holcomb laughed.

"No, that's Braunstein," Skuratov said. "Don't confuse us. It's time to sleep."

CHRPTER 35

"WHAT was it like to sleep with him?" Keats asked Laura. Keats had three "hims" in mind, three aspects of the same problem: Richard, Kelley and John F. Kennedy. Of the three, Keats was most interested in Kelley. He had to know, if it were possible to know in their world, how loyal to Kelley she was.

They lay on the bed, covered in red satin, naked and bathed in sweat. They savored the cool air playing on their drenched bodies. Perfume, cigarette smoke and body odor beginning to emerge from the masking scents. On the wall opposite the foot of the bed, a man and woman's dim, flickering images were projected, Richard and Carol locked together. The images were relayed here, to the safe house Keats was using, from the hospital after a trip around the country. There was another panel to the side of the main frame, not a picture as such but rather the representation of a brain in action, taken directly from the instruments monitoring their bodies. Keats thought there was something unexpected in the image. There should have been concentrated brilliance in those centers of Richard's brain where pleasure was registered, surrounded by darkness, but the multicolored glow was spread throughout. That meant Richard was thinking furiously. Something was wrong there.

A small movement of the bed under him; Laura must have shrugged.

284

"Do they know they're being observed?"

"He'd have to be a wizard." Although Keats was discovering that Richard was beginning to show peculiar talents. "There's too much between us and them. A wall full of sensing devices, infra-red light. Some stuff like radar. Thousands of miles of wiring. Relays and switches, amplifiers, processors, step-up and step-down transformers, vital-sign monitoring machines . . . all the kinds of things that our little business Metatronics is acquiring. You and I, we take surveillance for granted. But not him or her. God, look at that. He has big hands."

"Yes. I remember the hands."

"You remember the hands?" Keats asked.

"You don't forget your first time."

Her first? Was Richard lying or was she? Everything he had heard Richard say about Laura turned around for him.

"What were you like when you were a kid?"

The question made Keats uncomfortable. "Not happy."

"As a young man?"

"Not happy. We were poor but proud."

"What a monotonous life. Mr. Kelley brought you happiness?" She was mocking him, her voice low, throaty; a contralto. He didn't look at her. He stared at the images. He felt a stirring. Slowly he could feel his body rhythms begin to resonate with the pulsing lights, beginning to excite him.

He turned to look at Laura in the dim light. Long legs, slender, almost muscular thighs, athletic, but the muscle was hidden beneath. The hips swelled slightly; the shoulders were wide. The breasts were on the small side, with no extra flesh at all. Black, black hair. Her face flickered as the light from the projection was reflected. Only the gray eyes were steady, like ice. She was preparing herself to resist. Or perhaps she was looking inward. His eyes, his gray eyes, stared at her body. It was almost too perfect. No flaws. What made her exciting for him was the way her flesh was dappled in black and white, and colored by the reflection of the brain scan . . . as if she were under the shallow waters of a clear, refractive tropical sea. Tight, absolutely unwrinkled, a harlequin's skin. Her nipples were large and stood up. He bent over and kissed them. When he lay back, he left one hand resting idly, palm tickled by her pubic hair, fingers slipped between her legs.

285

Absentmindedly, he played with the flesh there, timing his movements to the pulsebeat from the images.

A long time ago Mr. Kelley had taken Laura under his wing, away from Richard Aquilino if she could ever have been said to be anybody's. But instead of discarding her after a night or two, he had sent her on to college and kept her around. What was special about her that might enthrall a Mr. Kelley? That he would keep her around and send her on to college? She was more than a high class whore: she was an instrument of policy. Had she beguiled him with body stories, being variable and intriguing ... an infinite subject? A thousand and one nights; a thousand and one positions; a thousand and one personae? She was one way to probe that shifting cloud, Kelley, for its true identity, for her body retained memories. Obviously Kelley had been heterosexual in those days? A consumer of little girls? What had changed him? The only role Keats had seen Kelley in was that of an aging, but powerful empress, with pretensions to Chinese magic, choosing to be fucked by one of her young and vigorous warriors. Kelley, as 'she' let herself metamorphose into an older woman, hopelessly in love, with passions appropriate to a romantic girl; desperate, Mr. Kelley had almost lost command. Queen Dido of Carthage and young Aeneas on his way to found the Roman empire. But Mr. Kelley knew his history; he knew he moved in a world full of changes and betrayal. And if the empress tired of her new toy, Keats would be finished. What would have happened in history if Dido didn't let Aeneas go? The Romans would have written the story anyway; it was propaganda in the first place. The Romans fucking the effeminate Phoenicians. Sex, policy, intelligence, money, power ...

Keats sighed. They, he and Laura, had finally come together. Two such people? That much was almost destined. But while their passions enjoyed, their minds had not been engaged. It was a skirmish; prelude to a battle. A thought began to form in Keats's mind.

"How was the other one in bed?"

"Which other?"

"The Chief Magistrate of our land."

She laughed. "You're curious?"

"Childish curiosity always remains."

286

"Sometimes that's the only thing that remains, isn't it? You're jealous?"

Her large, strong hand reached for his penis. She wrapped her fingers around, squeezed, and then moved it slightly up and down. Muscles rippled beneath the smooth skin of her forearm. He wanted to trace the slight bulges and indentations with his tongue. "I could tear it off," she said. "I learned that trick."

"You could tear it off," he acknowledged. "Did you practice the trick?"

"Yes. Three times. Once for myself. You want to know if you're as good as the President? Men . . . shit."

"Couldn't you just see someone asking some ravaged virgin, 'And this Apollo, he's a good lay?' "

She laughed. "You have a nice body. He has a bad back. There's not much tenderness to it with him. He depends on his exalted position. I told Mr. Kelley I didn't think we could get much information out of him. He's charming, but only up to a point. No mysteries, really. Smokes a little grass. Takes an LSD trip, but very hush-hush. He doesn't share secrets of state with the women he sees. He thinks he's under surveillance. He's obsessive about it. The FBI, the CIA and whoever are on his tail. On the one hand that makes him cautious. On the other hand that gives him some kind of incentive. He's showing the buggers what kind of man he is. He thinks his virility has something to do with the potency of his policy. They're quite primitive down there. You know the way politicians are."

"You've been listening to Mr. Kelley."

"Maybe Mr. Kelley has just been listening to me. He's not God, you know."

"No, he's not God."

"You've been fucking him?" she asked.

"Listen, Laura. What binds us is the color of our eyes, the shape of our bodies . . . and his fucking the both of us. But there's something else. Something deeper that's ours and ours alone."

"What?"

He leaned over and kissed her lips, the tips of her breasts, her eyes, and his tongue kissed into the cloud of black hair between her legs. He licked her ankles, the place behind her knees. He ran his tongue up one thigh and crossed over above the line of

287

hair and went down the other thigh. He did it lightly, affectionately, but keeping to the rhythm. He leaned back. "I don't know how to express it. We are—twins. It's not on the surface, but deep. I felt it as soon as I met you. You did too."

"You've been hanging around Mr. Kelley too long. That Taoism. He feeds on—"

"Us."

Keats nodded.

"Have you ever been raped?"

"I guess I have been. Yes. I'm here. You're here." He said it slowly, sadly.

"Before Kelley, I was in high school. I was popular. I was good-looking. My parents drove me toward a career, but that was all right. Then one day something began to happen. I didn't know what it was. Someone was watching me. Then I sensed that my parents changed; they were disturbed and I didn't know why. It was a tough neighborhood, so I learned to sense trouble before it developed. Danger was coming, but I didn't know from where. My parents turned harsh. They had lost something; moral superiority, although I didn't know that. Something else had replaced it. Greed. Shame. Without knowing what was going to happen, I decided to do something about it. I finally overheard my parents talking. They were sitting there in bed every night, arguing, bargaining, discussing, agonizing like a pair of pushcart peddlers. How much money would they get for *me?* Would there be enough money for them and enough left over for me to go to college after . . . After what? And what was so bad, they asked one another? What was so bad. Do it one time. Get paid. That would be the end of it. Do what? And how they would invest the money. Well, you know what happens in situations like this."

"Yes."

"No. You're not a woman."

"Men get seduced, raped too. In another way."

"It's not as if I didn't know about sex. At least as far as talk was concerned. It became clear that the person my parents were doing business with wanted a virgin. It's a weird taste. But I wouldn't have thought so then. Virginity was an 'it,' a 'thing,' a value." She looked at the images of Carol and Richard. They were exploring one another's bodies with their mouths, kissing and licking. At one point, Carol's mouth was opened in a sound-less scream of pleasure. Laura shook her head.

"She's not making a sound. They think they're bugged for sound. Still, there's always some very low level sound. I could amplify it and get the scream. Or use someone else's scream."

"Later. Never mind," Laura said. "I decided that I wasn't going to give whoever it was what they wanted. So . . ."

"So you had sex with Richard?"

"He was my first. I thought I was going to give him something that Mr. Kelley wanted—my virginity."

She thought about this for a little while.

"Then Mr. Kelley did take you away," Keats prompted.

"He humiliated me and he uplifted me. I held on to Mr. Kelley for a long time. I made him need me. And I got him to send me on to Radcliffe. And then I went to work for him. But in the long run I can't inherit power up there in Parvus's higher circles. They're against family . . . afraid of dynasty."

"That could be changed."

"You'll be changed yourself, Keats, or you're out. I don't know how my parents arranged the deal, the pickup, but it was made to look like a kidnapping. They were covering themselves. A car pulls up. Someone jumps out of the car and grabs you. The limousine windows had no handles inside, nor did the door."

"A Mafia special," Keats said. He put his arm around Laura while she was talking, kissing her face, her shoulders, her breasts, taking care to keep each move timed to the movements of the partners in the projected wall image.

She paused and stared at the images of Richard and Carol. Keats sensed that her body was beginning to come alive, in part stirred by memories, in part excited by what she saw happening on the wall. He lay on his side, turned toward her. She was on her back, looking toward the wall. He emanated vibrations of sympathy, love, tenderness.

"Look at her," Laura nodded at the images of Richard and Carol enjoying one another. "She's learning, but she's learning out of love. So's he. They change, willingly. They don't know what's in store for them."

Keats decided it was time to plant the suggestion. "You know, between the two of us handling Richard, with your access to the

289

President, we could have a significant impact." He had become rigid. Holding her gently, he slipped himself into her. Her muscles contracted around him. It was almost absentminded, affectionate. As they lay on their sides, facing one another, moving minimally, Keats brought her into the rhythm of the two on the screen.

"Look at her, the innocent doctor; would you like to be her?" Keats whispered.

"You can orgasm, but something holds back. A lot of men get their kicks out of seeing the woman completely out of control. But that memory of Richard is what I use to hold on to my control. The memory of us on that roof."

"And the memory of them, there, you almost being Carol now."

"The memory of that last time of innocence. Every time I was alone I practiced; I summoned up that memory. I remembered how I felt . . ."

"Like Carol feels now . . ." Keats increased the intensity of the movement.

"I remembered the tenderness, I remembered how it felt when he entered me, the shock, the pain, the joy. And finally I got to the point where, whenever I brought that memory up, it threw me into a kind of trance that enclosed and saved a part of me from violation."

For the first time in years, Keats felt a twinge of jealousy. "And what if Richard dies? Will your spell still work?" he whispered. And now Keats began to time the patterns of his strokes to Richard and Carol's rhythms more boldly, as they enjoyed, devoured one another miles away.

Laura was beginning to respond. She had almost "become" Carol. Keats made his thrusts simple, powerful, naive.

The four of them were intricately bound together for a moment. It seemed as though the energy and pleasure of their sex kept switching from body to body as they became a single couple. The experience went on and on for a long time, reaching toward a different kind of climax. And as they got close, Keats called out, "They're going to kill me. They're going to kill me. Save me, Laura, hold me."

The effect on Laura was unexpected, shocking. Keats had got-

290

ten by her guard by letting down his own. On the deepest level, and for the first time in his life, Keats actually felt fear, terror, need. And Laura sensed it and held him. And they began to orgasm . . .

What Keats didn't see was Richard, turning his head, his face distorted in passion, looking over his shoulder in the direction of Keats and Laura, his face transfigured, ecstatic, puzzled.

CHAPTER 36

CAROL was in love. Carol was terrified.

Sitting in her apartment, she couldn't sleep, though her body was tired. Morning sunlight slanted through her window. Night was their time; she didn't want to go in to work until it was time to talk to Richard again—and she couldn't bear the thought of seeing Sidney. It was a beautiful day. Autumn was coming on fast. The world had changed for her. She could never have believed that people had such capacity for love and sex. She was risking her whole career and she couldn't stop herself. She had caught Richard's psychosis as if it were a communicable disease. Now she looked behind her all the time to see if she was being followed. A plot against the President, leading him and the country into war? Madness. Possibility.

She wished it were all over and Richard were here with her, nothing on their minds other than making love. They could sit across the room from one another, perhaps naked, perhaps partially clothed, looking at one another. Body would hunger for body. Then they would get into bed, or do it on the couch, or on the rug. It didn't matter where. The thought of new places to have sex excited her; she felt released, wanton. What had happened to her? She had to get him out of the hospital. If what Richard was saying was true—they were once again communicating by written notes which she destroyed as soon as she left the room—they were in real danger. There were powerful people after him—and whoever they were, whoever Sidney was working for—they wanted to know what he had heard. Then they would silence him. She had no one to turn to. Sidney had made her distrust everyone . . . the police, the government, her friends, her own lawyer. And if it was all *not* true? Then, at best, she was in love with a madman.

Where was safety? Reach the President, Richard's notes had said. Personally? Why not just telephone the President, she had scribbled back. No. The people manipulating the President had already been alerted when they discovered Richard listening in. He wanted her to do something different. All she had to do was to place a phone call to Richard's friends. A certain number. Remember it, don't write it down. Someone would answer and identify himself. Then she should follow any instructions she received.

But worse than *not* having the phone answered was *having* it answered. She would be more entangled in this world of spies, bizzare deceptions, eavesdropping, betrayal, murder, torture. Had Richard really *killed* six people? It meant that some of the nation's most respectable leaders were steering the country into war. Richard named Presidential advisors. She recognized the names. He mentioned certain plans, something called Operation Mongoose, and Operation Sandgrain . . .

He also mentioned another group, a certain bargaining procedure, trade-offs if there *wasn't* war. He didn't understand it completely himself. All of it would have sounded insane except for those "cases" Sidney had shown her, the ones they had worked on. And the influx of money and equipment . . .

Once she made that phone call, *she* would be in danger, dependent on Richard's friends, whom he described as if they were almost mad scientists, people like Richard himself. And she was supposed to depend on people like *that?* Neurotics? Paranoids? The kind of people she once might have treated for delusions of grandeur?

The phone was there. The day grew brighter. She couldn't decide. She should sleep on it a little. She wished Richard were here, beside her in the daylight, playing with her body, kissing her, beginning to excite her. Could she ever give that up?

They lay, linked, arms entwined, barely moving at all. Keats was revising his estimates, thinking of how they might work together, when Laura said, "Can we save Richard?"

"If there's a way, it's to use him to reach the President with a warning. There's protection. The way we planned it, Mr. Kelley and I, we would guide him, planting the information he had to the message we wanted delivered, changing and supplementing what he already heard. But what he heard was dangerous to us. He knew about Parvus, although he couldn't have named it. We had to make him forget Mr. Kelley, me; you had to become, in his mind, nothing more than a simple whore with expensive lovers. We did some of that by interdicting his taps with our own voices; actors. Before we could really do a good job, we were forced to kidnap him to get him out of Mr. Holcomb's hands. But there's the very real question of his family. Who got them? Or did they leave on their own steam? We were going to do more 'briefing' in the hospital. We had to improvise fast. It didn't work out neatly. What Mr. Kelley and I wanted was a guided missile, so to speak, someone we could control. But I and I alone wanted someone who could deliver whatever message *I* wanted to have delivered.

"Mr. Kelley was dubious, but I persuaded him: Richard gets to the President after overcoming a series of horrendous obstacles. The timing is important. The drama of his appearance at the right moment alerts Kennedy and his closest advisors—his brother, Sorensen, people like that—to his manipulators, and that in confronting Khrushchev over Cuba he's not only on the verge of a great political mistake, but war. Maybe we say that the Russians are for real. Kennedy's suspicious enough after the Bay of Pigs fuckup. He's inherited a series of bureaucracies who not only feud, but have their own internal wars. Some of the factions *hate* him. He set up his own intelligence unit, headed by an admiral, loyal only to him. If that wasn't enough, the content of Richard's message might include the news that there was an actual plot against him. He's got enough enemies. However we framed the message, what Mr. Kelley wanted was that Kennedy was being steered into an invasion of Cuba . . . maybe he was even doing the Mafia's work for them—recover their lost investments —and maybe Mr. Nixon's work. We could even plant the right

294

documents to back Richard's story up. Mr. Kelley would supplement Richard's work with the media and public relations, bring pressure from the British, the French, the Swedes. Mr. Kelley doesn't trust melodrama. Sometimes he thinks that politicians are rational."

"But an invasion *is* one of Kennedy's options."

"He told you that?"

"There are no secrets in Washington. Half the Capital knows what's going on. Kennedy hates Castro personally—who has the most *machismo*. The rest of it I learned working for Mr. Kelley, who does *not* want confrontation—and certainly not invasion or worse, a surgical strike—to happen. Kennedy, on the other hand, almost *has* to have this confrontation, or the appearance of a confrontation. He is being forced into it by the Republicans, among others. For that matter, I wouldn't be surprised if Kennedy even wanted the invasion himself.

"Mr. Kelley not only wanted the whole drift stopped and reversed, he wants the nationalist and war faction among the Russians discredited. That's Mr. Helphand's job. The purpose is to erode the power of those who oppose Mr. Kelley, the Parvus Game. He wants an end to the cold war. It stands in the way of business."

"I think he's changed his mind," Laura told Keats. "He's going to change the mission."

"How? To what?"

"Mr. Kelley never told me. I have no need to know on that level. But I think some of the people he and Parvus represent smell a quick profit out of a confrontation with Russia and Cuba. You diversify your holdings. You hold shares in uranium, steel, grain, defense industries, construction, automobiles, media, communications. A crisis comes; policy develops; what's in the wind? If you managed the crisis, you can sell off the losers, acquire the winners. The people in Parvus sometimes find that their interests are in opposition to Parvus's strategies. They can't stand short-term losses, no matter how big they are, and that means that Mr. Kelley has to give a little. A confrontation between America and Russia will set Parvus back. But when you brought Richard into the picture—"

"Richard brought himself into the picture, and he can really help me . . . us, skew the game. I told Mr. Kelley that Richard could be run, be made into the ultimate agent, the perfectly controlled missile," Keats said. As he had told Holcomb the same thing. Now he would have to switch his operation around, enlist the help of Holcomb in order to deliver Richard to the President.

"I'm not even sure Mr. Kelley believed you could deliver, but he's in love with you, Keats."

"He's jealous. Mr. Kelley is jealous of us, Laura."

"Then we're as good as dead." She hugged him and leaned her head on his shoulder.

"We're far from dead, Laura. This is what must have happened to Adam and Eve in the garden. They fucked for themselves, not for God, His design, His economy. They they found out they were being spied on, because the archangel appeared on the scene."

"The serpent," Laura said. "That's a pretty serpent," she said, handling Keats's penis.

"The serpent was God's agent-provocateur. He tempted them to eat of the tree of intelligence . . ."

"That's tree of knowledge."

"Knowledge, intelligence, same thing. Our motto in the CIA is 'And The Truth Shall Set Ye Free.' If we can spring Richard, we can chart our own course. We can set Richard loose, start him running again to reach the President. You prepare the way."

"I don't have that kind of control."

"The President is in a bind. He's faced with a crisis. In part he's helped manufacture it, in part he's been forced into it. His first and foremost thought is to stay in power. On top of that, he has to go along with an overwhelming consensus of people who have contributed to his power, and they want a first strike against Cuba, want to go against the Russians eyeball to eyeball. That's the kind of stuff Richard heard. An emergency will develop. Kennedy will assemble this invisible government. They'll debate. Tactics and strategy will emerge. To retain power, Kennedy will go to *war.*"

"Richard, on the other hand—he's a voice from the outside. That represents great dramatic power. As an innocent, he carries weight. He's nobody's man. Can you imagine what it will do to Kennedy, in the middle of all this, when this kid reports that on such and such a day he heard Dean Acheson, or Averell Harri-

296

man saying such and such to one another about him? If he escapes out of that hospital then Mr. Kelley can't touch him. He can make Parvus work or he can shoot it down. And as such, he becomes a bargaining chip."

"Can you control him that perfectly?"

Keats said, "Yes," but he wasn't sure. "I think the first thing is to move fast. Get Richard out of there."

"How?"

"For that I think I have to pay a visit to Carol."

"You're going to fuck her, Keats?"

"I hope it isn't necessary. I hope you're jealous, because, I must confess, I'm not too thrilled about you and Jack Kennedy."

Tarzan hung up the receiver and turned to Ziggy. "She did it."

"Who did what?" Marvin asked.

"Richard's doctor, the person who's taking care of him. She made the call," Tarzan said. "Only trouble is, she made it from her own apartment."

"We can only pray that the phone isn't tapped," Ziggy said.

"Other than that, she followed Richard's instructions. She was told she would be gotten back to. We can check to see if her phone's bugged."

Ziggy groaned. "My legs are killing me. And now I have to move. Help me. We have to get to a phone booth. I've got to get to our friends."

"What friends?" Marvin asked.

"Our Mafia friends, who else? It means that now the lady's willing to help us get Richard out of there."

She had done it, gone through with it in a fit of panic. The morning had evolved into afternoon. The sun disappeared behind a wave of thick clouds borne eastward without rain. Then the doorbell rang. So soon?

She began to tremble. Richard's friends? Control yourself, she told herself. She walked to the door. What would they look like? She looked through the peephole. All she could see was a man's head and shoulders. He was wearing a coat and tie. He was smiling gently. He had blond hair. She had never seen anyone as handsome in her life, outside of a movie. "Who is it?" she asked.

"I'm a friend of Richard's."

She was confused. Did Richard have friends like this? She opened the door. He stood there and smiled at her. He motioned to her. "Step into the hallway for a second," he said, and she did. She was a little overcome. He was almost beautiful.

"I can see that you don't have much experience," the man said.

"What do you mean?"

"You should never take anyone for granted. You don't know who I am. You're lucky that I'm a friend of Richard's. I asked you to come out because I didn't want anyone to hear the two of us talking."

"You mean . . . what *do* you mean?"

"I'm working under the assumption that your apartment is bugged."

Carol's hand was over her mouth as if to take back the words she had said over the phone.

"What's the matter? Oh. You placed a phone call to Richard's friends."

"And you're not from Richard. You're not Richard's friend."

"I'm not from Richard, but I am Richard's friend. I'm from the CIA, the Central Intelligence Agency." His wallet was out and he was showing her identification. "Don't panic, Carol. Don't be afraid. We both have Richard's interests at heart. Look, this is what we'll do. We'll go back into the apartment. You'll put on a jacket. You won't say a word to me. Then we'll go out the back way, just in case, and have something to eat, maybe a drink and have a little talk. I'll explain. You'll be back in an hour. It'll be all right."

She was in it now. She decided to get her coat and see what he had to say. He wanted a one-hour session, in effect. Well, maybe she could learn what was really on his mind. She decided to start watching him carefully, like a patient.

Ziggy was uncomfortable in the phone booth. They were in a tobacco store, with Marvin outside in the street. Tarzan lounged near the booth. Ziggy kept the door closed. "His doctor called," he told Samael Aquilino. "He's all right. He's been confiding in her. What now? Do we try and rescue him?"

"You're sure it's not a trap? You trust her?"

"I think it's worth a try. I think if they had really broken Richard and she was working for whoever grabbed him, they would have found a way to get us before this."

"Siegfried," Samael said, "we'll deliver the plans to you. Send your little friend, Marvin, to my Mafia capo. I'll have given him a sealed envelope containing money and the layout of the hospital. Then you'll decide how to rescue him yourself. We'll arrange it so that Marvin and Tarzan—what a name!—rescue him. We'll have our people there, protecting you. It should be simple. You'll get in touch with this doctor, this Carol, and try and persuade her to come along. If she doesn't, just take her. Persuade her it's for her own and Richard's good. Scare her a little. Tell her of the danger from Richard's enemies. If necessary spin her a tale of Russians, but only if necessary. Then you have to find out what Richard knows."

"There's only one danger, Samael. She telephoned from her own apartment. Her phone might be tapped."

"So you'll have to work very fast, Ziggy."

"You're just going to have to go along with him when he makes his escape. Look, he's in danger. But he's also very . . . well, sick isn't the right word for it," Keats said. "He's had a lot of drugs pumped into him and one doesn't know what the effects are. You're a doctor—"

"I don't know what to do if he has an episode."

"Tranquilizers and comfort. I've tried to explain to you what's riding on him. Right now he's one of the most important men in America. We have to find out what he knows and what he thinks he wants to do. He trusts you completely. I'm sorry, but that's the way it is. Really, think of it as an adventure, Carol. It's not all that dangerous. And you'll keep in touch with me all through the event. There will always be someone close to you, watching over you, protecting you and Richard."

He leaned forward and took one of her hands over the table. His startling gray eyes looked into hers. "What I'm going to say is going to sound fatuous to a woman of your talents and education and sophistication. But Carol, your country needs you. It needs Richard. What Richard has been telling you has sounded as if it came out of some spy movie, but it's all true. In some ways the boy is a genius. Let me put it to you this way: perhaps unwillingly, you have begun working for the Central Intelligence Agency and there's a lot riding on you. I'm not even going to ask you—"He pressed her hand. She felt shocks going up her arm. What was the matter with her?"—Whether you'll help, because I know you will."

She sipped her drink. The cocktail and a night without sleep combined, to intoxicate her.

"Richard's friends will contact you in a day or so. I suppose they'll have a plan to get Richard out of the hospital. We'll help from our end as much as possible. There's no danger."

"I think I can handle it," Carol said, hoping she could. Wondering if she should.

CHAPTER 37

THE escape was easier than anyone could have anticipated; the problems arose only afterward, when they got away with a Richard who was quite different than the one who had been driven half-mad and captured.

On the morning of the last day of September a telephone truck parked at the Columbia Presbyterian Hospital complex. Two people dressed as telephone company technicians got out casually; they were wearing the usual regalia of repairmen hanging from their belts. They carried toolboxes. One of the technicians was very tall and bulky, the other small and animated—by fear. They entered the hospital and moved toward their destination without being challenged. They knew which direction to go; what elevators to take; what corridors to use. They were met by an attendant who by now was used to seeing telephone and communication personnel, and let his gun stay underneath his white attendant's uniform. He said, "Hey, you guys are in the wrong wing. You must have made a right instead of a left at the double doors. That's where all the wires are. Go back to the end, turn again and—"

And at that point Tarzan pulled a gun and told the attendant to lie down on his face. Tarzan took the attendant's gun.

"Jesus," Marvin said. "Jesus, Jesus—"

"Shut up, stupid," Tarzan said. They tied the attendant up with

301

wire and gagged him with electrical tape.

"I don't get it," Tarzan whispered. "There should be another one around." He didn't want his voice recognized. "Knock on the door—you remember the signal?" Marvin nodded. "I'll stay here in case anyone comes. Now remember, when the door opens, don't go in. Just stay in the doorway. No good having your picture on record."

Marvin walked to the door and knocked the way he had been told to. The door opened. It was Carol, with Richard behind her. Marvin, to whom every second was an eternity, waved them out, hopping up and down. "Richie—" he started to say. Richard put his finger to his lips and they fell in behind Carol who assumed her most authoritative doctor's stance to lead the little procession. Inside, she was trembling and feeling oddly exhilarated.

They walked past the bank of elevators to the staircase and began to walk down.

They came to a floor and turned off. It was too early for anyone to be there yet. Carol was wearing—for the first time in a long time—a white coat. The party separated. Carol led Richard to a stretcher and motioned for him to get on. She swathed most of his face in bandages and covered him with sheets, then rolled the stretcher to the elevator and rang the bell. After what seemed an hour, the elevator came. She wheeled the stretcher onto the elevator and told the operator to go all the way down to ambulance intake.

Tarzan and Ziggy had gone down and out another way and were back in their truck. No one seemed to be looking at them.

"Jesus, that simple?" Marvin asked.

"Don't kid yourself, Marvin. There are people all around, watching."

Marvin started to turn. "Where? I don't see anyone."

"Christ, how stupid can you get? Don't *look*. Just act normal like any repairman would. *You don't know anything.*"

"Have you done this before?"

"Yeah, three times a week."

They drove away.

The hospital ambulance service got a phone call. There was a serious burn patient who was to be transferred to another hospital. An ambulance was to be ready and a stretcher would come

302

down, accompanied by a doctor, and they would then take the patient to Cornell Medical Center downtown. The stretcher was wheeled onto the ambulance, which was started. What no one saw was the battle that had taken place near the exit. Three men had been pulled away and thrown into cars. There were no pursuers.

When the driver got to Cornell Medical Center, the patient and the doctor were both gone.

They had gotten out the back at a stoplight and into the back of a telephone truck that was following them.

The phone truck drove down Broadway, then West End Avenue. In the Thirties, they all got out and went up the stairs of a loft building.

Ziggy was sitting there, facing toward where they would walk in. He said, "Come closer. I want to 'see' you with what little sight I have. How are you, Richard? It's been a long time. Are you all right? We have so much to tell you, so much to talk about."

Richard came close to Ziggy. He bent down. Ziggy looked with whatever sight was left to him. His hands reached out and his palms were on the sides of Richard's face. They were frozen this way for a moment. Richard straightened up. He went back and took Carol's hand and brought her to Ziggy. "Ziggy, this is Carol. She called you. Dr. Carol Rothschild." He turned to her and said, "See? I was talking about real people." He kissed her.

She said, "I stopped doubting you a long time ago."

With the tension released, Marvin began to hop up and down. "Richie's back. Now we're really in business." Even Tarzan was at ease. He had gone and gotten a bottle, glasses, and poured bourbon into them. "We can celebrate. Man, we can get stinking drunk now. You realize we've outwitted the whole government of the United States?"

"Yes, drink," Ziggy said. "Give me one too. But we have to talk. We have outwitted them, but for how long? You weren't followed?"

"I'd swear I wasn't followed," Tarzan said.

Carol's head swam. She still hadn't taken in the enormity of what she had done. Had she cut all her ties with the past? Thrown away a whole life? She was in danger but she was protected. Or

303

so the CIA man, Keats, had tried to assure her. She would not only be protected, but she had been promised a job after this was over. Either way, it was supposed to be for Richard's sake. Damned if you do, damned if you don't. She was damned uncomfortable.

These three strange people. This crippled little blind man with his accent—from what country? The little one with his jerky movements and his constant babble. The giant, somehow menacing . . . the way he looked at her. Richard was the only one who seemed to be in any way normal. These were his friends? His helpers? His—what had the man called it—control? The surroundings, this huge, partly empty loft. "You're a trained observer," the man had told her as she observed him. "Observe like you never have. See everything. Remember. You'll get better at it as you go along." The pile of equipment running along the side of one wall. Radios. Wiring everywhere. An old couch with faded brocaded material. Two overstuffed easy chairs of the same material, shiny with use. The high industrial windows, encrusted, making the blue sky look evenly gray. Chairs around a table. A stove. A living area in the middle of an industrial neighborhood. Off to the side she could see a bed and mattresses on the floor. What had she gotten into? She hadn't thought the consequences through clearly. Grotesques, that's what they were.

"Who's after him?" she had asked Keats as they sat in the restaurant.

"Russians."

"But what has he done?"

"It's not what he's done so much as what he's heard. It has to do with a mole in high places."

"A *what?*"

He laughed. "Trade talk. A mole is an agent who's penetrated our network and appears to be on our side. If the mole is placed in an important, decision-making position, you can see what trouble that can cause."

"And that's what Richard heard?"

"Yes."

"Why didn't he tell me?"

"He doesn't know. I mean a mole doesn't announce who or what he is, even when he talks to his contact."

Love had made her cross some terrible line and enter into the nether world. It was frightening and exciting. In Ziggy's loft, she sipped her drink as the enormity of it hit her. There had actually been guns. The excitement of the escape had not let her really think about what she was doing. That man, the attendant, lying there, tied up, a gag in his mouth. But the other one, the one from the government, with his piercing gray eyes and his blond hair, had said it would be all right.

Marvin was saying: "We did it all by ourselves. Hey, it was easy. We sure don't need the Mafia—"

"Not so fast, not so fast. Richard doesn't know anything about this. Sit down. Calm down. Let's discuss all this. It's really good to have you back. You're all right? They didn't mess your mind up, Richard? You were pretty sick, crazy."

It was true, Carol thought. She didn't even have a change of clothes. That was an excuse to call someone if she needed to.

"Getting away is actually the easy part. It's what comes after," Ziggy said.

"What's so hard, Ziggy?" Tarzan asked. "We got an organization to protect us, don't we?"

"What are you talking about?" Richard asked.

"We're in business, man. We're going to the top. We're going to be rich," Tarzan said.

And Ziggy began to fill Richard in . . .

A few hours later, the situation had become acrimonious. Richard had listened to what they had done. Their operation. The organization of the network. The help they had promised the Mafia.

He said, after a long while, "We have to do something else first. I have to reach the President."

"Of what?" Ziggy asked.

"The President. John Kennedy. The President of the United States."

"Why don't you give him a call?" Marvin asked. It confirmed for Carol that there was some truth to what the blond government agent had said. Could she trust the CIA man? Was he really CIA? Richard had been telling the truth. She couldn't let herself distrust everyone.

305

"You're crazy," Tarzan told Richard.

Ziggy sensed that there was something new in Richard. A sense of authority and purpose radiated from him. He knew what he wanted to do, and he had become transformed by his ordeal. "All right. Richard, Tarzan, Marvin, we must be calm. We can't shout at one another. Tell us why you want to get to see the President, and how you propose going about it. And what you think you want us to do to help you. Then we can decide."

Richard began. He calmed himself. He organized his thought and how he would present it. "In the first place, it involves nuclear war with the Russians. Over Cuba. In the second place it involves danger to the President." And Richard began to tell *his* story.

After Richard had finished, Ziggy said, "Look, let's take a vote on this. But before we do that—" He turned his head to Carol " —I am going to ask a painful question. Carol, you're a professional, a doctor, a psychiatrist, a neurologist. Is Richard . . . all right?"

"You mean, am I crazy?" Richard said.

"Richard," Ziggy said, "you've known me for years. I'm your friend. But you can't expect us to go charging off without getting all the information we can."

Carol thought for a while. "When Richard was brought in," she said carefully, "I thought he was severely disturbed. There were real signs. Those were probably drugs. I couldn't believe that the world he was telling me about could be real."

"Oh, it's real, all right," Ziggy said. "I used to be a citizen of that underground world. It cost me my legs and my eyes. But the question gives to the validity of what Richard is saying. I mean how he's putting it together. Is he sick?"

"I found," Carol said, "that what he was talking about was real enough. I wasn't doubting that. But the drugs wore off. His talk became more coherent. I felt," she blushed, "that there was a basis of reality to everything he had to say. He's healthy enough." Although he had to be taken care of, the blond man said, and you have to go along with him. He might experience drug . . . relapses. She didn't tell Ziggy that, yet.

306

They sat there for a while, not saying anything. "All right," Ziggy said, "I'm for it."

"And me," Marvin said.

"I'm against," Tarzan said. "I don't see risking our lives. How is the Mafia going to look at this? We're double-crossing them."

"Don't worry about that. We'll come back after this little trip and finish our business with them," Ziggy said. "You're outvoted, Tarzan. Will you come with us?"

Tarzan shrugged. "Okay. I think it's stupid. Who cares about the President?"

"A nuclear war, Tarzan?" Richard said.

"I think that's bullshit."

"But you'll come along. Good. All right, Richard, how do you propose reaching the President and, if what you say is true, staying alive?"

CHAPTER 38

"JESUS Christ. Jesus fucken Christ. So Aquilino didn't escape. You took him and salted him away in the hospital. Wy didn't you tell me? Lives would have been saved. I ought to kill you, Keats . . ."

"Those were my orders. I tried to hint. You wouldn't listen. I grew suspicious. But instead we'll work together, won't we, Mr. Holcomb?"

"I have some choice. That lying fucker, Skuratov," Holcomb said. "One day I'm going to kill him. Slowly."

Revenge. What was it, Keats wondered? Underneath all the experience, the knowledge, the lessons, the years of cross and double-cross, was there still an innocent? "I have a little of that kind of business myself," Keats said.

"This Oprichnik?"

"Yes."

"And what about the counsellor, Kelley?"

"He was deceived. That's been straightened out."

"So what do we do?"

"We help this kid, Richard Aquilino, reach President Kennedy. You're in a perfect position to do that, working with Skuratov."

"Maybe I'm dumb, Keats, or old-fashioned. I mean, explain it to me in simple terms. Why don't we just grab the kid, find out what it is he has to say, and if it makes sense just get the message

—or whatever it is—to the President ourselves?"

"The way he's been worked over, and the way his instructions have been planted in him, he has to move closer and closer to the President for each part of the message—what he has heard—to become clear. If we start questioning him now it might scramble what he knows. We have to let him run. Through Aquilino, we get Skuratov and his network.

"I could have delivered Skuratov."

"I wasn't sure you could be trusted. I'm not sure now. But once in a while you have to take a chance."

"Not trust *me!* What the fuck are you talking about?"

"What happened to you when you were a guest of the Russians in the Lubianka."

That never happened, Holcomb thought. He said it to himself again: *That never happened.*

"Mr. Holcomb, let's make the best possible case. Let's say we know where Aquilino is. We move in and take him. He tells us what he knows. And in the right order. We then go to the President. But what if there are people of considerable power who *don't* want us to relay any message if it changes the course of events? If we go through all the levels of command, being debriefed at each level, what do you think is going to happen?"

"Nickeled and dimed to death."

"Or killed."

"So who're these people in place? Russian moles?"

"Look, Mr. Holcomb, we just have to move. Aquilino, you might say, is in some space where we can't get to him. But I think he will, so to speak, materialize. We know where he'll materialize: where the President is. In Washington, Covington, Cincinnati. October 5. Detroit. Hamtramck, Flint, Muskegeon, St. Paul. Chasing after him doesn't even take into consideration some of the things we're up against; the normal procedures and personnel devoted to the direct security of the President . . . Secret Service, local police and the like. Can you imagine being in a position where we have to gun *them* down to keep him alive?"

"I don't think that would trouble you, Keats. This is crazy. How do you know he's going to do all this?"

"He was probably fed the President's schedule and itinerary subliminally. But we don't know if the conditioning has taken. I don't know *how* he's going to do all this, but I'm sure he's going to try. I'd stake my life on it."

"You are."

"If we take him too soon, we lose Skuratov and his people. If we take Skuratov, we lose Aquilino. So you and I work together.

"And Mr. Holcomb, why don't I take you up on that offer of a drink."

Holcomb reached into his desk for the bottle. Silently, they had a stiff drink from the bottle itself. The liquor warmed Holcomb and loosened him. Keats was beginning to look quite human to him. But, he wondered, how long could he keep Keats from finding out what he had done with those aerial photographs of the missile emplacements in Cuba?

PART III

CHAPTER 39

OCTOBER 1, 1962

After the spring and summer and autumn of 1962, there would be those who would say that something fundamental had changed about the country. Having faced total annihilation, something had broken loose. A sense of permanent despair and cynicism had set in. Everything was coming apart and it would never be the same again.

That spring, a small group of students, some academics and some politicians had got together in a Michigan backwater called Port Huron. After a hectic conference, they issued a long, reasoned call for social change called the Port Huron Statement. It went much further in its vision than President Kennedy's program for sweeping reforms. Indeed, by implication, it called for a total restructuring of the country's entire destiny . . . and an end to the cold war. SDS had begun to move.

Massive civil rights unrest continued throughout the South. There were voter-registration drives for Negroes, calls for integration of all public facilities, compensatory education for Negroes. What had begun in 1954 in Little Rock was being escalated; violence mounted.

The Ambassador to the UN, Adlai Stevenson, and his retinue, continued to assure Africans—behind the scenes—that President Kennedy's domestic reform program, *vis-à-vis* civil rights,

313

demonstrated that the United States was committed to social justice and an end to racism . . . which was the sign of their good faith in opposing colonialism in Africa. It was not the time to issue public and official declarations; things moved slowly in the United States.

At the end of September and into the first days in October, the Governor of Mississippi, Ross Barnet, continued to oppose the admission of the first Negro, James Meredith, into the University of Mississippi. The National Guard, the Army, had to be called up to insure order. Apprehension rose throughout the South. The end of a way of life was coming and there were those who were determined to fight by any means possible. A sense of hatred toward the President, his brother, his advisors, was steadily coming to a boil. Not only was he a Catholic, he was almost a Communist.

In Washington, there was a conference of ministers representing the Organization of American States. The major issue before the conference was the question of Cuba, Castro and Communism in the Western Hemisphere; potential Cuban subversion in Latin America, and behind the Cubans, the Russian backing. American delegates used their muscle to get support for a possible embargo of Cuba. The Latin American ministers hemmed, hawed, backed and filled, hesitated. It's not that they didn't believe in Cuban subversion; what their maneuvers meant was "what's in this for us?" They knew how to use the Communist issue. Aid programs, loans, military aid, development money were mentioned, to say nothing of bribes.

In the meantime, Premier Nikita Khrushchev went public; he extended an invitation to President Kennedy to come to Berlin for a summit conference where they would be able to hammer out issues of substance concerning the question of Berlin. Perhaps it was even possible that the Berlin Wall might come down, certainly the tanks just on the other side of the Wall would be withdrawn. What had been offered secretly before was now floated in newspapers and the administration would have to respond. Privately, Kennedy was advised that the concessions on Berlin meant a raising of the ante in Cuba and possibly Laos.

After the first of October, 1962, they kept moving around, living in unused warehouses and safe houses. Right now they were in the industrial wilderness between Canal Street and Houston Street. Richard insisted that they *had* to get on the road and reach the President. "It has to be in person. You know as well as I do how many ears and bugs might be between him and us if we use a phone."

"Do you have any idea of what stands in the way?"

It was a tense conference. Richard, Ziggy and Carol were doing all the talking. Marvin and Tarzan felt left out, jealous. Carol always backed Richard up, and the presence of a woman was causing trouble. Ziggy could see that she wasn't used to living this way. Love was not enough. How long before she wanted to get back? Did she realize that there was no going back?

"Richard," Ziggy said, "I'm trying to be fair. The people who caught you listening in, the FBI, the CIA, the Secret Service, the telephone company, the Russians for all I know, are all after you. You always got your news from the headlines and the radio and television; now all of a sudden you're an expert."

"I had an education in foreign affairs just listening in on the telephone."

"You have to give me more. I have to know that what you're picking up on is a sign of these events."

"We have to be in Covington or in Cincinnati on the fifth," Richard said. "We have to set up contact."

"How do you even know he's *going* there?"

Richard sat there, thinking. The disjointed and fragmentary conversations he heard over the past years began to fall in place, a timetable of events leading to that ultimate burst of nuclear energy, after which there would be silence as it had been before the earth was created.

"I know he'll be there on the fifth in Cincinnati. Then Hamtramck, Flint, Muskegeon, and then on to St. Paul. But we can't wait that long for you to see I'm right. We have to move."

"There's another way, Richard. We have friends who work for the phone company in Cincinnati, Detroit, St. Paul. We can find out if they're laying wire for the White House party. We've got people who can scan the radio frequencies. They've got some navy surplus AN/URR-35cs, Collins R-278s, that kind of stuff. They can monitor the White House Communications Agency, the Secret Service, see where he will be staying, what alternate routes are considered. I just need time to figure out how to put it to them."

"Ziggy, we have to move. Everything is being orchestrated toward an air strike at Cuba, or maybe an invasion, or even all-out war. I know the whole itinerary up until October 19, but I don't quite know all the signs that show I'm right. After the nineteenth, it's a blank. The campaign tour will be suddenly cancelled."

"Richard, you heard all that on the phone?"

"That and much more."

"How do you know you still haven't got it confused?"

"We have signs, I keep telling you. If someone says to someone else something like, 'And then we get him to announce a quarantine' six months before it happens, that's a sign. It's not the President himself who's doing it. He's being maneuvered. I'm telling you it will escalate. They'll commit him and the country. There's no stopping after that. You know that."

"I know that. But what makes you think that it's not the President himself that's orchestrating the whole thing? Or the Russians? And if that's the case, how are you going to prevent it from happening? Tell the Cubans? Tell those fucken Russians? What are you going to do, go to the newspapers? Demand time on the radio, or television?"

Go to the newspapers, Richard thought? Get on radio? Get on television? Yes. That was a way. But how . . . It could be done . . . but it would have to be . . . yes . . . he was getting excited now. Something completely new, daring . . . Patch in . . .

"Look, Ziggy, it goes like this. On about October 15 or 16, he will have been maneuvered into the position where he is going to convene an executive committee of senior statesmen, top people in the defense and intelligence—what do they call it?—communities: Excom for short. They are going to argue the pros and cons about Russian troops and missiles in Cuba. There will be those who argue for a first strike, and those who argue for an invasion and those who argue for a limited exchange of nuclear weapons. There will be those who say, take the diplomatic route.

316

The first-strike group or the invasion group is going to win because the President is going to be offered limited choices, so limited that he's going to have to act the way they want him to. It's obvious, isn't it, Ziggy? We're going to have to make sure that he understands what we tell him, that he believes it. We have to convince him not to convene that executive committee at all." He paused. "If the people knew . . . Patch in, Ziggy, that's it, isn't it? We need insurance . . ."

CHAPTER 40

IT hadn't taken much to break Harkavy. It was as though he expected that his escape from Hungary would end in recapture, if not by the Hungarian AVO, then by the KGB. He wished now that he knew which one it really was, so he could figure out what they wanted to hear and tell it to them.

After they worked him over, he was dragged into a room, if that was the word for this peculiar collection of linked-up containers, big as truck trailers. Where was he? He smelled oil, salt water. Must be some warehouse by the ocean. Make a deal, he thought; hold on to just enough to maintain a bargaining position for the future. But they moved him along too fast. He could barely walk.

There was a table in the room. With some chairs at which five people were seated. There was an empty chair in the middle, heavily lit, for him. Everyone else, including some guards, he thought, was in semidarkness.

One of the five at the table was a low-level telephone company employee, a linesman, essentially. The second was a district manager, the business end. The third was an engineer who worked for the labs in New Jersey. There was a doctor, a psychiatrist, to see that everything was going all right. And Skuratov.

The people who knew about the telephone equipment were fidgety. They had stuck to asking technical questions, consulting

318

with one another to see if Harkavy's answers were correct. So far, they were. It was the others who kept applying more persuasion. They had been at it for two days.

"Harkavy," Skuratov said at the end of the second day. "To begin. Who brought you into this operation?"

Harkavy breathed deeply and answered as honestly as he could. He didn't know the real identity of his employer, so he described him. Skuratov was satisfied that it was Vassili Oprichnik.

"Comrade—" Harkavy began.

"Who are you calling comrade? You forefeited that right a long time ago."

"Sir, I honestly thought I was working for the KGB. Is it permitted to ask now who I *was* working for?"

"No, we're wasting time. Next question. You succeeded in penetrating this Aquilino's network?"

"I tried to reconstruct what he did, but I saw after a while that the process might take years, and my 'employers' were impatient. Then I began to work on another possibility."

"What was that?"

"The telephone company has mechanisms for tapping any phone it wants to. They listen to subscribers, cooperate with police or intelligence, monitor their employees. I thought it should be possible to automate, from the outside, a tap on anyone's phone. I decided to work on that."

"Is this true?" Skuratov asked the technical people. They said it was.

"Even listen in to, say, the CIA, the President, the Cabinet members?"

"So long as they use the phone and go through the main system. There are areas which are direct-wired and totally outside the public phone system, but not many. And, of course, they can scramble their phones, but then these children designed some descramblers. They're very ingenious, a peculiarly American phenomenon, communications enthusiasts, fanatics, fans, amateurs in every sense of the word, except—"

"Except?"

"Well, their expertise is first-rate."

"And the second thing?"

319

"About this Aquilino, I never met him, but this leader of theirs is something of an elder statesman."

Skuratov knew now about Ziggy. Siegfried Schweik. One of their own, once. A double, working for both the Communist International *Rote Kapelle* and the Nazi *Schwarze Kapelle*.

"This Ziggy seems to have other contacts, another—how shall I put it?—another program."

Skuratov was pleased, even though his face showed nothing at all. When this present crisis was resolved, he would have something left over of special value. A sure way of penetrating the communications of the U.S. government.

She appeared in Washington again. She got invited to diplomatic receptions, showing up on the arms of important men, English, French, German, Italian, but never American. Her escorts were always on A-lists. It had been a while, and her reappearance excited him. She gleamed, her body sheathed in glowing and shiny black. He had forgotten how beautiful she was. She seemed to catch his eye for a few seconds at a time, and then turned away, as if not interested. He remembered the grayness of the eyes, the black hair, the white skin . . . and her lips. He tried, as unobtrusively as possible, to signal her. She seemed elusive, or obtuse; she didn't pick up on the signals. People kept getting in the way. Finally he had to ask an aide to see that she was steered close. When she passed, he greeted her, shook her hand, applying Presidential charm, but she didn't seem interested. That fired him up even more. When she was close, he remembered her body. He said, "How'd you like to run away with me and take a little tour of the Midwest? You could meet me in Ohio and then we'd go on to Detroit."

"It's hardly the Riviera."

"Listen, your President calls on you to give service to the country."

She laughed. It was a laugh designed to sound out-of-keeping with what they were talking about. He appreciated her tact.

"We could slip away for a few minutes."

Her eyes turned toward him, a touch of mockery behind their childlike look. Her shoulders were smooth, white, exciting against the black. The light blazing down from the chandelier

320

delineated every muscle beneath the skin. He liked that. An athlete. He remembered her vigor and inventiveness, and the intense pleasure he had given her. "I haven't forgotten," he told her.

"What's my name?"

"Laura."

"You're a good politician. You did that without your remembrancer whispering in your ear and I don't even seem to have any political value at all to you."

"Remembrancer? What's that?"

"Medieval. Every king had one. They reminded the king of what he had to remember."

"Not only beautiful, but educated. Well, I'd love to hear the story of remembrancers from your own lips, close up, without all this babble."

"Your wife's coming this way. Doesn't she look beautiful tonight? She sees us together and senses the opposition, you know."

"We're both grown-up. How about it?"

"I have a prior engagement cementing relationships between two great and sovereign countries." She turned to one side as if thinking it over. The President's wife was working her way toward them as casually as she could. Laura turned back. She would accept, he thought. Tonight, or on his swing through the Midwest.

"One thing, Mr. President . . ."

"Jack."

"I get around. I meet people in, as they say, all stations of life. I hear a lot of things. People brag. There are no secrets. You know how it is."

"I know how it is. How is it?"

"It's not much of a secret . . . Berlin . . . the Congo . . . Cuba . . . Laos. Troops, a rumor of missiles, nothing really positive. Diplomacy, or perhaps a lovely little war . . ."

"Who said that?"

"I heard a crazy story. Someone quite unimportant managed to get hold of, some way or other, some vital information. For Your Ears Only."

"That's *Eyes*. Why doesn't whoever bring it to my people?"

"In this case it *is* Ears. And the word has it in certain circles that he's trying to reach you to tell you this piece of news. But reaching you is like climbing Purgatory. Tormentors and bureaucrats and advisors on every level. There are those, I don't know who, trying to stop him. Something to do with a cobra."

"A what?"

"Or is it a mongoose?" She smiled to see his face change suddenly. Her information was good. "Or is it about a grain of sand? No, I've got it reversed. The grain of sand is the irritant, isn't it, that harbors the pearl?"

Harbors the Pearl. She had reversed Bobby's words. First strike in Cuba. A reverse Pearl Harbor.

"A woman wants to feel wanted for herself, Mr. President," she said suddenly. "Goodbye."

"Wait—"

"You know my number. Or your remembrancer does. There are too many ears around here."

CHAPTER 41

BY 12:15 A.M. on the morning of October 3, 1962, they were almost ready to leave. They had finished loading the new truck Tarzan had stolen. Greene Street was deserted. A few lights cast some illumination. The truck had an electrical generator powered by the truck's engine to run the radio equipment, and external jacks to plug into telephones. They had decided to move to New Jersey, where one of the network was going to put them up.

Tarzan was still dead set against getting involved with this venture. "Look at the equipment we're leaving behind, Ziggy."

"We'll get back to it."

"Instead of making money, we end up running out on the Mafia, taking on the U.S. Government, the Russians, the telephone company and who knows what else."

"If there's the kind of war Richard is talking about, money and equipment is not going to mean a thing."

"You really think we're going to reach the President? You're dreaming."

Tarzan was dreaming too. He was clearly jealous, and Ziggy could tell that Carol was the weak link. It would cause trouble to keep her with them, but she had, after all, taken a terrible risk for Richard and had thrown her life over. More important, Ziggy thought, he needed her in case Richard really was sick, or had a relapse. Gently probing, he tried to find out what made her tick.

After a while she began to talk, reluctantly, about her boss, Sidney Ficino, her betrayal, the sudden influx of equipment, telephone hookups. Now Ziggy began to understand why there had been strange signals going in and out of the hospital, all over the country. It was that cybernetic revolution in the making that he and the others had been dreaming of so long. Only it was in the wrong hands.

"What's wrong with his memory?" Ziggy asked Carol. "He seems to know roughly what's going to happen up to October 5 or 6 as if he's *remembering the future*. Why, though, doesn't he remember what's going to happen all the way to the big crisis?"

"I don't know. He must be blocking out what he's overheard about the next few days because he's frightened or feels he must protect himself."

Talking to Ziggy put Carol in touch with the qualities that were inside her, qualities she had never even dreamed about. She had broken loose. Something in her had longed for a life of action, longed for adventure, longed to do things, and she had never even realized it. And the sense of immediate danger had diminished and begun to add spice to her life, and spice to their sex. She closed her eyes as she thought about it. There was Richard. A changed Richard. To make love in the middle of danger, to be watched, that aroused her. What had been inside her all this time?

By the end of the day they were near Newark. They put up at a friend's house, a peripheral member of their network who was barely aware of what was happening. It was a decaying, Victorian wooden house with a porch, on a quiet street. A small stand of trees in the back. New York was a distant hum in the day, a glow at night.

The owner, Stanley, had loaded up his house through the years with so much radio equipment that they would have to sleep on mattresses on the floor in one of the empty rooms. Marvin went out for groceries and they cooked a meal which they ate around an old table with an enameled top.

The day's news bought another sign of Richard's predictive powers. Stirrings on Cuba. Senator Javits asked President Kennedy to air his Cuba policy. "That's a move toward war,"

Richard said. "What are we waiting for? Look, Ziggy, on the sixth he'll be in Detroit. If we can set it up to maybe intersect with him there, or in St. Paul . . ."

"Patience, Richard, patience. You can't meet him without establishing contact first. You can't run out in the middle of the street, during a parade. You'd be gunned down. He has to expect you. The first thing we do is to get in touch with our contact in Cincinnati."

"And Covington?"

"We don't have anyone in Covington, but that's just across the Ohio River, and radiowise it's in Stanley's backyard. So maybe by tomorrow night—"

"*Tomorrow* night?"

"—we'll know something more. If Kennedy is really going to Cincinnati and Covington, we'll check out Detroit and all the other places. If the signs you predicted are there by late tomorrow, we can begin with the first contact. I feel like an astrologer. We have to be careful."

By the evening of October 3, they had gotten reports from Cincinnati and Washington. Two of their network had begun to listen in to the crucial radio frequencies; in Washington they monitored the White House Communications Agency's traffic and Secret Service, especially the escort frequency, FBI, and 162 megacycles, the President's personal staff. Most of the channels were scrambled, but the increase in the amount of traffic told the interloper that something was happening. Frequently a communications came across the bands in clear. In Cincinnati, they listened in to the bands assigned to the local police, the local FBI, the State Bureau of Investigation, and the State Police. They pieced everything together, including the route and the arrangements made to protect the President. He would give his speech in Fountain Square. Calls to working buddies in the telephone company ascertained that one-time wire was being laid, and they got the assigned temporary phone numbers the President and his staff would be using. This—in addition to newspaper and radio reports that there would be a unilateral effort to blockade Cuba —finally convinced Ziggy that Richard was right.

Something else happened. One of Ziggy's Washington people,

Moe Allerdyce, reported that he had gotten a strange signal on several channels, stumbling on it almost accidentally. Conversation. People talking in several rooms. Men. Even some sounds of sex. It could only be a tap that was then picked up, routed to a nearby transmitter and rebroadcast to some receiver. "I got three channels. That is, three American channels. One is assigned to the Department of Agriculture, another to the Immigration Service, the third to the Bureau of Mines, but you can bet that Mines, Immigration and Agriculture aren't the ones using them. Probably the FBI. And there's another one which is still unassigned by the FCC. Probably foreign. Ziggy, I swear, one of those voices is the President's. Isn't that wild?"

"Do you have a tape recorder?"

"Sure."

"Get lots of tapes." Who else was taping the President, using those bands? A plan had been gestating in Ziggy's mind since the convention of earth-bound space voyagers. What if the public could hear what the great figures of history said behind closed doors? . . .

They sat there, the two of them, looking at one another across the table. The small man looked a little shamefaced. He couldn't look directly at his wife.

"You turned your son into an agent," she said. "I'm never going to see him again."

"I wouldn't say that, Lilly. We'll see him. It will take a few years, but—"

"You're running him. He doesn't know what to do. He will be killed."

The man sighed. "We've lived with that possibility for years. But I doubt it'll happen. He's coming into his own now. He's passing every test."

"You had to give my child to this revolution of yours, didn't you? I told you he should be left alone."

"Of *mine* . . . *My* revolution, Lilly? It isn't *ours*? You mean what was alright for *us* is not all right for *him*? As if we didn't know that it was going to take generations of fight? And what was right for our daughters and their husbands was not right for our son?"

"Women are tougher."

326

"*You* are tougher, Lilly."

"We should never have had children. It's not right for people like us to have children."

"Lilly, for generations, centuries, my people have fought the vampires, the demons, the *gilguls* in their earthly phases and on their astral planes. Father to son. Parents to children. You tried to protect him. You *did* protect him. But for how long?"

"We should have retired, Sam. Just paid attention to business."

"He's coming along fine. He's beginning to read the signs and the symbols and the sacred codes of the life-aspiring and the death-denying. He hears the old voices calling him to action. Do you think I love him any less than you?"

"You wanted a son in your image—"

"Our image."

"The image of your ancestors. You wanted a son, a magician, a Cabalist. You had to recruit him with your devious ways, whispering those stories into his ears?"

"That is the way. It is written. The recruitment is done that way in our family."

"Not in my family." She sighed. "I should be there with him."

"Lilly, you're too old for that kind of thing."

"How old does one have to be to pull a trigger?"

"Lilly, you're forgetting. The crouching, the crawling, the sneaking, the running, the aim . . . you know it's more than just pulling the trigger. We have to think now of retiring. Fading into the background. Being advisors. Richard will be all right. And there are greater things in store for him. He will be a fully wise man. This is the initiation to full maturity. He will be a master of the letters, the words, the numbers, the codes, the channels to the top. He will tap into the energy and he will use it to penetrate the secret places of the men of Parvus who live in their false heaven."

CHAPTER 42

SIXTH Avenue to the common people; Avenue of the Americas to Nelson Rockefeller. It was being torn down and reconstructed. It had started to happen after the Second World War . . . slowly, and with resistance. Great plans were in store for this street. Great corporate towers would rise here; Radio City would be expanded. The rows of old brownstone apartment houses, the pawnshops would all be torn down in time. The old, squat and dirty buildings mingled with the newer towers, and everywhere there were cranes, trucks, wood-beam platforms to receive debris. Keats had arranged to meet Vassili in one of the old bars in the high Fifties, in a building that still hadn't been torn down. Keats had taken the precaution of secreting two guns in the demolition equipment bracketing the building in which the bar was. He carried a throwing knife in a holster between his shoulder blades, another knife tied to his leg under his pants. He liked the knife. It was intimate. He was good with it. One never expected a knife when you had blond hair, good American looks, and gray eyes. And, to heighten the illusion, tonight he wore glasses. The meet was for nine o'clock. Oprichnik would arrive in the role of a somewhat drunken construction worker.

Maybe this *is* futile, Keats told himself. There was no deal he could strike with Vassili if the game had changed. Kelley or Skuratov, which one was Vassili really working for now?

If he could convince Vassili, and *if* he had persuaded Laura to follow his plan, and *if* he could control Richard, he would be in good shape. The three of them could do it, and *he* would be able to take the credit with the heads of Parvus. Richard was in motion, perhaps a little too soon. Ficino was being channeled upward to make his little report on Khrushchev's psychology-in-a-crisis. The combined pressure would flow to the President. Kelley would be presented with a *fait accompli*—and might even end up admiring Keats. The only serious problem might be warding off Holcomb.

Holcomb had put Skuratov's photographs of the missile emplacements into the pipeline. The photographs, duplicated and reduplicated, were making their way up to the proper end-customers—newspapers, congressmen, various intelligence sectors —coming to the President. JFK would be forced to act on the evidence, falling neatly into the trap that was planned for him— another confirmation of what Richard had overheard. Kennedy would then *have* to convene a prestigious body—the Executive Committee of the National Security Council—within which there would be a tight little caucus devoted to its inexorable agenda of confrontation. There was a high degree of probability that Kennedy would be moved, step by step, to that moment when the counsels of moderation would fail, the talk would turn to an invasion of Cuba, a first strike, a limited war—and those in Russia and America who wanted to break loose from the cold war would be defeated, maybe for another ten years.

It was 9:10. No Vassili. What had gone wrong? Five minutes more. He sipped his drink. The five minutes went by. Execute the fallback at Third Avenue and Seventy-third Street, a brush-by in the street in fifteen minutes. Time to walk it. He went out.

The air smelled wrong. Damp, yes. Mold and plaster smells emanated from the gaping buildings as he passed them, going north. He passed a truck parked for the night, reached down in a pile of refuse by the truck to pick up his gun as he passed, planning to forget the other. No gun. A setup? He looked between the construction piping supporting the platform, toward the night traffic. They would be out there, in front of and behind him. How many people? Had they spotted his movement to pick up the gun? Of course. He turned. There was a thunk in one of

329

the wooden beams alongside his head. Bullet. Silencer. He slipped into the half-demolished building.

He felt good. After weeks of minimal moves, of planning, now there was some action. Crouched, his hand trailed as he moved, quietly, searching for the stairs. He hoped they were intact. His hand was pricked by the jagged splinters of some broken wood. He moved up the stairs.

They had missed the first run and lost the advantage. On the second floor now, he came to the point where the building ended and the next one began. The wall between the houses turned inward at right angles, going toward the back. Go on or turn? He turned. His vision now commanded the whole interior, the part that had been demolished. Noise of traffic. Cars running, horns honking while he was trying to listen for small noises, the kind that were masked to the ordinary person. He concentrated. It was like picking out one particular conversation in the middle of a roomful of people talking. He heard, finally, the sound different in quality from the jagged susurration of the unending traffic. A creak. There. He saw him. Emerging from the blackness, looking around, outlined in the city's faint skyglow. The man moved cautiously, a big, silenced pistol in his hand, not looking up.

Keats, half-crouched, moved, practiced the way he would throw, only with his body swing. Once, twice. He would use a brick, not a knife. To get full force, poised so precariously, he would have to turn after he had thrown and fall full-length along the wall. If he missed, it would be over.

Keats threw, and got him, a noise, masked by the unending city sounds, slammed into the man's head. He fell, thrown sideways and full-length. No, wait, something was wrong. The man started his fall a fraction-second *before* the brick reached him. Who else was out there?

330

CHAPTER 43

ZIGGY returned to the house after a few hours. The first thing he said was, "All right, Richard. It's happening as you predicted. The news from Cincinnati and Washington is that he's going to Cincinnati. And they're preparing for him in Detroit, at least the police are. The Detroit telephone man doesn't know anything about it yet, but that's not unusual; the order to lay wire doesn't come in till the last possible minute. It's time to call him up."

Tarzan was going to drive to a phone booth from which Richard would place his roundabout call to the President. When they got into the car, he turned to Richard and said, "All right, buddy. You ready?"

"Yes."

"And what if they try to pick us up, what do we do?"

"Fight. Try and escape."

"And if they got guns?"

"Give up?"

Tarzan pulled a pistol from under his jacket. "Here. You know how it works?" It was a .45 automatic. "See, you cock it this way. Slides the bullet into the chamber. Now it's ready to shoot. Don't forget to take off the safety. Then you point that thing. Hold it steady, aim. You squeeze the trigger. Do it again's all there is to it. When it's empty, you put in another clip. Here are two more."

"Is this necessary, Tarzan?"

"We're not playing games here. There's killers or worse out there. That's what you've been saying, right?"

"But I mean, what if they *are* Feds?"

"Shit, Richie, they're killers and they're not disposed to listen to the likes of us. Am I right?"

"Yes, I suppose so."

Tarzan started the car. "If someone tries to follow us this time of night, it'll be easy to spot them. You ready?"

They began to drive. Tarzan turned the car radio on to hillbilly music. Tarzan turned on a scanner in the seat between them. "Move the thing through the frequencies, Richie." And he read off some numbers. "Local police and FBI. We'll be able to tell if we got company." They drove through the deserted streets. Tarzan made frequent turns. "We're clean." They were soon in Newark.

"Richie, are the Russians after us?"

"I don't really know. Russians. The Feds. They're the same, aren't they?"

"That's what Ziggy says. But Ziggy isn't always right, Richie. I mean he's brilliant. I know a lot because of him, but he did have a bad time back there in Europe, didn't he? It might have warped his judgment, at least in that area."

They drove silently for a few more minutes.

"Listen, Richie, I've been meaning to ask you. You and that woman . . ."

"Carol."

"She's a sexy lady. A doctor and all, right?"

"What's that have to do with anything?"

"But it just shows you, don't it? A whore, or a society lady, or some lady lawyer or lady doctor, when it comes down to fucking they're all alike has been my experience. She just ups and gives her career up for you. I mean, you must be really good."

"What are you getting at, Tarzan?"

"Is it good with her in bed, man? That's what I'm getting at."

"That's none of your business."

"I mean maybe it's better, more experimental with older, educated ladies. They get frustrated. Hard to satisfy."

"Drop it, Tarzan."

"Just curious."

332

"I said it's none of your business."

"You're fucking her in the same room and it becomes my business. It's hard to sleep. It makes a man horny. I have to listen to—"

"We're not making any noise . . ."

"You're funny, Richie. Lots of guys, they would want to share the experience. I mean, do you like to go down on each other? We're all in this together, we're buddies, right? We're laying our lives on the line for you. Am I right? What's it feel like to put your face between those tits?"

"What are you saying this for, Tarzan?"

"How's it feel to have your cock in her mouth? Share a little of that with the rest of us is what I mean, Richie. I mean, think of what it's like on that poor perpetual horny fool, Marvin. Don't a day go by without he has to have his sex, and it's been a few days now."

Tarzan heard a loud click and knew what it was; he didn't have to look.

Richard said, "I cocked the gun. The round is in the chamber. The safety is off. And I'm pointing it right at your head. Am I doing it the right way, Tarzan?"

"Well, you don't have to get so huffy and righteous about it, Richie. It's only man-to-man talk. That's all it is. Put that thing down. I don't know if the trigger is sprung hard or soft. I mean, one bump might blow my head off. You got bigger things to do, don't you?"

Richard put the safety on and stuck the gun in his belt.

They finally found the phone booth along Route 9-W, along the Palisades, half-hidden behind a gas station that was shut down for the night. Tarzan parked the car behind the station and acted as lookout. Richard got out and went to the phone booth and closed the door behind him. The light went on and he disconnected the bulb. He sat down. The gun cut into his stomach, so he took it out and put it on a little shelf beneath the phone. He dialed . . . to Washington, to Kansas, to San Francisco, back to Washington, ultimately, 202-659-6787 . . . 202-OLYMPUS was ringing. The President's private phone. Where was it? In his bedroom? He hoped the phone wouldn't be busy . . . and he hoped the number hadn't been changed. What would they do then?

A delay before the final, signaling ring. The dialing and redialing mechanisms working—the switches, the relays, the repeaters picking up and amplifying the fading signal, the call going through great tangled mazes of wire and cable. Little traffic this time of night . . . switching station signaling to switching center, activating those switches which had been planted in phones to bypass them . . . one number activating yet another . . . a maze of delusions and false leads . . . recipients who were not aware that their phones had been enlisted for other purposes . . .

One ring. Two rings. The tension almost drove the memory of what he was to do out of Richard's mind. Would the President be sleepy? Grumpy? Or did he sleep always half-alert, ready to respond in a crisis?

The phone was picked up. "Hello," the voice said. How ordinary. "Hello?" The President of the United States. Just "Hello?" The voice was a little fuzzy. The sound of the voice triggered something in him, and a wave of violent hatred swept over him. He was trembling with rage. Laura. His free hand jerked and closed around the gun on the ledge before he realized what he was doing. Where did *that* come from?

"Mr. President," Richard said. "I'm going to tell you something of great importance. Don't hang up. Hear me out. I have news that is important to the fate of the country . . . and yourself."

"Who is this?"

Richard ignored the question and mentioned, as quickly as possible, some conversations he had overheard Kennedy having. One of the conversations had been with his brother.

"Hey, wait a minute," the President said. "Who is this? How did you hear that?"

Richard didn't stop to answer.

The second conversation was with Robert MacNamara; it had to do with the power of the Department of Defense, the opposition, intransigence, resistance to MacNamara's budget-conscious, cost-efficiency policy, the need to end cost-overruns . . . cutting down the power of the military and the resultant fury of the Joint Chiefs of Staff. " 'Air Strike Scenario.' Mr. MacNamara is going to be worried about retaliation if we use nuclear weapons. General Taylor, or General LeMay, is going to laugh at Mr. MacNamara's fear that we might have nuclear weapons used against us in retaliation. This conversation should take place some time after the nineteenth of October . . . unless . . ."

"Unless what?"

"Sir, you'll find that out in a day or two. And one more thing. There are two or three strikes against Cuba being mounted every day out of Miami."

The President said, "Who are you? How did you get this phone number? Where are you calling from? What do you want?"

"I have to see you in person." He was shocked at the brusqueness of his reply to the President.

"Who are you?"

He had done it! The anger, the nervousness, was receding. He was beginning to feel sure of himself. There was no going back now. His free hand jerked up and he waved the gun above his head. He wondered if Tarzan was looking at him.

"My name is Richard Aquilino." A nobody and the President of the United States. Did he hear the scratch of a pen, or a pencil, on a notepad? "A-q-u-i-l-i-n-o. I used to live in New York City. By accident, I happened to listen to a number of your conversations and the conversations of others as they talked about you, and about what was going to happen this month. I heard those conversations in July, August . . . I was caught listening in. Some people thought I was a spy. Nothing I could say would convince them I wasn't. I have been chased, beaten, drugged, thrown into an insane asylum. I escaped. My family—my mother, my father, my sisters, their husbands, their children—has been kidnapped. You're in danger too."

"Who's after you?"

"Your people."

"Who? The FBI? The CIA? What makes you think it's *my* people?"

Richard didn't respond. "I think they are trying to get me in order to stop me from telling you what I heard. You're being led into a war with Cuba and Russia, an atomic war. There will come a point where you can't back out. If you try to avoid war . . ." Richard paused.

"That's where the danger to me comes in?"

"Yes. I'll explain that later. I don't have much time left. In

335

about a week, or maybe two, you are going to be presented with what looks like strong evidence of a Russian troop buildup in Cuba, including aerial photographs of missile launching sites there. This will force you to act; otherwise you won't get that congressional majority in the elections. If you try to track me down, Mr. President, you will have to alert the people who are trying to stop me, those who want to maneuver you. And anyway, it will take too long—if your people can even do it—to find this phone, never mind me. I'm calling from everywhere and nowhere. This phone call comes from San Francisco, but that's not where I am. Tomorrow's call will come from somewhere else. I have to meet with you alone to tell you what I heard. I don't trust anyone else. Please wait for my call . . ."

"Who are these people? Please keep talking . . . Richard . . ."

Richard hung up. He sat there for a second, staring at the phone. His heart was beating strongly, shaking his whole body. His hands were trembling.

He stood up and went out of the booth. The air smelled moist, green, fresh. He felt strong and alive.

"Put that thing away," Tarzan said.

Richard put the gun back in his belt.

"How'd it go?" Tarzan asked. "We in business?"

"We're in business, Tarzan. He certainly listened. He accepted some of it, I think. I told him not to set his people after us."

"That's what I was afraid of, Richie. We're really in the shit now. Let's get away from here."

The President hung up the phone and turned away. She was lying on the bed, naked. She was on her side, her head propped on her hand, facing toward him. One leg was thrust out, long, slim, relaxed. The other was bent, knee drawn up, calf pressed against the back of her thigh. It was a graceful, enticing pose, and yet, there was something mocking about it. The posture displayed her vagina. The blackness of the hair there, flanked by the muscles of the inner thighs . . . and the folds of the labia shone through the hair, pink, glistening, attracting him. He was thinking of what he had heard and what it meant, and yet, at the same time, his penis was becoming tumescent. "You were right, Laura. This is wild. Richard Aquilino. Is that who you meant?"

336

"That's him."

"What's this all about? Who is he?"

Her voice was low, soft, caressing. "I'll tell you as much as I know. Do you want to hear it now, or . . . later, Jack?"

"I . . . I have to call someone first . . ."

His brother, she thought, or maybe someone else in the inner circle. A close friend. She turned. Her back was to him. He stared at her buttocks. No fat at all. Perfect, each cheek round, perfect . . . "But first," he said.

But first we fuck, she thought. Well, it isn't going to take him long. "How's your back? Why don't you just lie down and let me . . ."

CHAPTER 44

KEATS had been waiting for an hour now. No one moved. The body was still there. Dead or unconscious? He could wait until the demolition workers came back on the job at daylight. If nothing had gone wrong, Richard would now be moving toward Cincinnati, Detroit, starting his guided journey with everyone in pursuit, but it would be hard to set up a private meeting with the President. There would not only be all of the President's security forces to contend with, but also the team sent by Skuratov, Holcomb and Braunstein, who had obviously figured out that Richard's message was not the one they wanted delivered. As for himself, who was after *him?* It didn't matter whether Vassili was working for Kelley or Skuratov. Just stay alive.

The theatres would be emptying soon. No one would shoot in a crowd, not unless they got very close. He began to inch toward the shadows in the rear of the building. Were there back stairs? Were the fire escapes intact? They would know by now that the man they sent in after him was dead.

He crept toward the back until he came to the part of the building still standing above the second story. Torn floors, beams hanging down. How solid? Could he climb them? He turned and saw the body still lying there. He began climbing upward. The rim of the torn wall between the buildings was on a slant, not vertical, slow climbing but not too dangerous. He hoped the wrecker's ball hadn't loosened any chunks of the wall. Good, he was on the third floor. Part of the apartment toward the back was still there. He tested the floor by tugging on it. Still solid. He pulled himself up and was in what remained of an apartment. The window frames were gone. He moved to the opening and looked down. He could see the backs of buildings opposite, across a space where there had once been backyards. He watched for some motion when the waiting got on the watchers' nerves. In this case the hunted had a small advantage. To keep the initiative, they would have to move around. Five minutes passed. Ten. Fifteen. He was losing his attention too. He now began to work on himself, a kind of trance. Ignore itches, the burning of the scraped hands, the need to kill. Negate yourself. Be only eyes and nerves, recording the blackness.

There. A quick little move . . . an infinitesimal flicker. The stalker was back as far as he could get against the opposite side, so he could scan four or five half-gutted buildings. Perhaps the movement was generated by an itching nose, a twitching eye, or the need to shift the weight of the gun. And there. A responsive move off to the side. Someone else was stalking the combatants. A three-sided war.

Keats reached down and pulled his pants leg up to take the knife out of the leg holster. He stuck it in a little clip on his belt. What was down there in the shadows, in the remnants of back-yard fences, the rubble thrown down by the demolition crew? Which one was his protector?

He backed away from the window. He bent, found a grip on the flooring, swung himself down and hung there. How high? About nine feet to the floor below. He dropped with extended legs, making almost no sound. He was not far from the dead man. Should he get the gun? No, they might have marked where he was, waiting for that move. He moved toward the back window again, feeling for the knife.

339

CHAPTER 45

THE next day, the fourth of October, proved Richard right again. All the signs he said would be there were there. Ziggy prepared again for the next night's telephone routing, and set it up for the next three days. He also got in touch with his Washington contact. "Moe, did you get anything?"

"Hey, it's wild stuff, man. High-level. Just about everything the President does or says. Must be the Russians; wouldn't put anything past them. I taped some. Man, if the people only knew."

"Play me some."

"I got a lot of tapes here. Where should I start?"

Ziggy thought a second. "Listen, you keep a log of when you made them. Have you got anything for about four o'clock yesterday morning?"

"Let me see. Oh, yeah, listen to this. This'll drive you wild. About midnight he gets a broad and spends his time in bed with her. Boy, wouldn't you like to be like that, have them delivered to you like you order up hamburgers? And she, she keeps on telling him what a great lay he is. Oh, and yes, get *this*, Ziggy. They were smoking grass. Mari-Ju-Wanna. Reefer madness in the White House. Listen."

The tape ran for about fifteen minutes, then there was an interruption. A phone call. It was Richard. Confirmation. Ziggy listened to the whole conversation. Good. Good. After Richard finished, an outgoing call was made. Bobby Kennedy was summoned to a meeting first thing in the morning. Something important had come up. Then Ziggy heard the woman, Laura, give JFK a rundown on Richard Aquilino, whom she had known as a girl . . .

Mr. Kelley looked into those maddened, exhilarated eyes and knew that you cannot reason with death, and Keats was now death's emissary. He prepared to die; he tried to soothe his rebel body.

His ever neat clothes were disarrayed. Terror excited him. Keats held a bloody knife. Kelley smiled. He closed his eyes. He intoned a Taoist prayer, to prepare himself in his mind. He wanted to suffer the coming pain and die with dignity, like an Adept who was beyond the body's needs. The grip on his collar tightened, more cruel, more cruel. Keats wasn't going to let him die the way he wanted to.

"Open your eyes, look into my eyes. You're always interested in the way people die . . . the way they feel at the exact moment . . . look at me or I'll rip your cock out slowly . . ."

Mr. Kelley opened his eyes.

"You lied to me. You tried to kill me. You set me up. I'm going to slice you up, piece by piece." The bloody knife moved closer.

"You're going to destroy everything? For what? For mere revenge? And what will you do afterwards? You'll be alone. I die, but Parvus lives. Parvus won't rest until it gets you. You will be at the mercy of all, Mr. Holcomb and his insane patriotic friends. Worse. You will leave yourself outside the gates of paradise forever, and I, *I* am the gatekeeper . . ."

"I don't give a shit. I'll manage. You'll be dead. Don't give me more of your mystic bullshit . . ."

Bloodcrusted, the knife came closer. Whose blood was that; who had he killed? Vassili? The knife-edge was close now to his neck. Kelley sensed the cooling-off life energy emanating from the knife . . . the knife had soaked up the life of the killed, and it radiated a wave, a scream, like a gravitational or an electrical field . . . Soon his own blood would mingle with the blood of whoever Keats had killed. A whole life destroyed by a whim. Ego. What knowledge, what power. Think of something else. Think of the past. Think of what might have been. Think of Laura . . . That bitch. She had betrayed him. She had made the invincible Keats fall in love with her. She was getting back at him; she had learned nothing, nothing at all. Love. The love of males for females, females for males . . . it destroyed all possibility of ascending to the higher realms . . . Mr. Kelley's *Ch'i* would escape, unsaved, uncaptured, ejaculated, a spurt of blood, piss, sperm, power, waste. The knife's edge touched him and his body throbbed; he almost came, or pissed, he couldn't tell the difference. Balanced along his skin, the knife turned sideways. Keats wiped the blade on the skin of Mr. Kelley's neck.

And yet their eyes never stopped looking into one another's.

Suddenly Keats took the knife away and dropped it on the rug. His hand let go of Mr. Kelley's neck. He reached out and took Kelley in his arms and said, "I can't do it. I don't care. I can't do it. I love you, Edward. I don't care if you kill me. I need you . . . It's worth it."

"It's my fault," Kelley said. "I was jealous. I only meant to frighten you. Have you roughed up. Drive you back to me . . . They weren't going to kill you."

A joke? A practical joke? There were three dead men . . .

They kissed.

Later Keats told Kelley the story. How he had been trapped. How the first man had been killed. How he had exfiltrated slowly out toward the back of the building, the whole thing taking half an hour. A few yards, a half hour. There he waited, sensing, tasting, smelling the air, trying to see in the dark, moving incrementally toward the man and his opponent, lying in wait for him and the other.

They were on Mr. Kelley's bed now. The sheets were covered with plaster-dust mingled with their sweat. Keats lay on his back, his head on Mr. Kelley's forearm. Propped above him, Mr. Kelley looked down lovingly on Keats's face as he told his story. Mr. Kelley felt the death now; Keats emanated the killing from his body. Mr. Kelley received two souls.

When Keats had got to within five feet of one man, he waited. He sensed and tasted the man's energy flows and ebbs, and waited for a low point. When the traffic noise increased . . . maybe five minutes, maybe ten. Slowly moving his body into a crouch, becoming a ball, his legs doubled under him, frogtight, he exploded at the right moment and launched through the air, hand sweeping in a tight arc, catapaulting the knife into the body, and his own body hurtling after, while his other hand reached for the gunhand. The watcher never even had a chance to move. He was perfect. When he was finished, swearing revenge, he had come for Mr. Kelley.

"Two men were mine," Mr. Kelley said. "Who was the other?"

"You tell me. Vassili's?"

Kelley was annoyed. "I told you that Vassili was reliable."

"Edward, you have to rethink your whole arrangement. The trouble with doubles is that they may be just that. No loyalty supersedes any other loyalty. My impression is that Skuratov has prevailed on Vassili to rethink his loyalties. There's nothing like a little electricity on the dental nerves or testicles to make a man thoughtful."

Or was the outside stalker another player? If so, from where? Richard's parents and their network, protecting Keats because to guard Keats was to protect Richard? Perhaps he should make some contact with Samael Aquilino and work out some *modus vivendi?* In the short term their goals were the same. "I'll have to think about that," Mr. Kelley said.

Kelley decided. Keats was lying. The selfish impatience of the young. But that didn't matter anymore. The trouble was that Kelley was in love with him. He would put up with lies. He would risk everything. He would never again question Keats too closely. The world's politics were going to change because he had fallen in love with a willful child. He was going to gamble. In time his love, or Keats's love, might fade. That would be the time to kill Keats. Or adopt him. He needed Keats. Mr. Kelley was changing the game for his love, but even that was going to keep the world's forces in balance. Indeed, All was The Way. It was a beautiful move on Keats's part, to give up his power of the knife, just at the point of triumph. Something inside of Keats had assessed the situation with incredible rapidity and his instinct had led him to come up with the right move. He was going to risk everything and put himself in the hands of the enemy. He was pretending

343

he was overcome with love, and that love conquered all.

All this means that Aquilino's use is also negated. Vassili will know Aquilino's moves. Keats argued; but Holcomb had now changed back again.

Kelley bent his head and kissed Keats lightly on the lips. "You are nature's Adept. But what nature and an accident of genetics have done are not enough. Not enough. My dear, you're still a child. You have not given up your ego, human pride. In order to gain something higher, you will have to give up that little failing. You think you know everything, but you have much to learn before you will be fit to be where I am.

"I was like you were once. There aren't many like us in the world. Maybe a few thousand. What are we? The world's regulators, demons. Together we are the Demiurgos who are recreating the world. What is it we regulate? The ebbs and flows of power and energy . . . We try to control that flow and slowly, incrementally, with ever increasing velocity, we gather it together for ourselves. We seem to work at the service of temporal power; we work, those of us who are truly initiates, to some greater end. The trappings of power are nothing in themselves. The regulation of power is a beginning, but it isn't the substance of power. We work to control those who have the power . . . mere animals. But we have our limits.

"A man like JFK mistakes regulation for substance. He, like many businessmen and politicians, doesn't understand that they are the mere guardians, the vicars of power. When they become counterproductive . . . JFK spends from moment to moment, thinking he has an infinite amount of this nation's energy at his disposal. You have been that way. But because he's blinded by his own reflected brilliance, he doesn't see that he's embedded in a system and he is impotent, subject to forces, surrounded, imprisoned. Thinking himself a man, he is a woman. Petulant, changeable, dangerous. How wise he would be to understand what he is, what his limitations are. Eisenhower was like that; he knew his limits; he was perfect. And you are like JFK; you think you know everything. And you make the mistake of placing yourself in the center of the universe, whose nature you don't understand. Everything around you seemed to reveal its secrets. But then suddenly, the flows of power changed. And everything around you

344

told you lies, and you didn't know it. And when you realized it, you tried to force the flow back into its old channels, all directed at yourself.

"The game changed, darling. You didn't know that. We planned to stop this dangerous conflagration before it began. We couldn't. Now the momentum is carrying events farther than I like. It's going to be the same event, but the meaning will come out differently. But the people whom I regulate, and the people whose servant and master I am at the same time, wanted the game to change. I have to bow to their will in order to keep hold of our control and our triumph later on. *If there is a later on.* That's the risk we have to take. And you thought you could control what you didn't even understand by controlling me. You played too many games.

"The Presidency must be weakened to a ceremonial office and, in particular, *this* President must be controlled. The mission is scratched, wiped out, and you must undo what you have set in motion . . . undo that beautiful structure. I could have others do that, but if you're to learn . . . I know that you won't regret the lives, dear. They don't mean much to you. But you will regret the aesthetic game structure which you love more than anyone's life . . ."

"Richard Aquilino is launched. He's on his way . . ."

"Recall him, stop him, or kill him. Be as simple and as efficient as possible. Don't think up another masterstroke . . . I know you engineered his escape, and you did that beautifully . . ."

"I didn't engineer his escape at all."

"Who did? He had to have help, didn't he?"

"Probably Vassili . . . I wonder who's running him now," Keats said.

Mr. Kelley laughed. "Poor Vassili. Lost to us. He'll rot in their prisons for a long while. No matter. Do the job. No frills. You know where Aquilino is going to surface. Do the job. The wise move in their tiny, incremental steps, and court invisibility. The turn of a hand. The nod of the head. A computation of a point or two of interest reveals the world.

"I think we may have lost this round. We have to salvage what we can. The short term gains have overridden the long range gains. Now we must do the opposite; even let there be a limited

345

nuclear exchange . . . low yield. When they see what happens as a result, they'll be scared out of their wits. They will turn from that destructive path, because we'll launch the biggest propaganda campaign ever. We'll discredit both the Russians and the Americans."

Keats listened, his face composed, his eyes half shut, as if in a hypnotic dream. Was Kelley setting him up? Or was Kelley really inviting him into the inner circles? Were there inner circles or a higher mystique? Let go, he told himself. Take the chance. Do nothing and follow orders. Give up the smaller game for the larger one. He shuddered and his body relaxed completely. And he almost felt the edges of his body dissolve. He began to drift off. He was tired. He hadn't realized how much the hunt and the escape had taken out of him. He had acted too soon. He had almost lost his life.

Keats didn't regret the people he would have to give up. Richard, Carol, Richard's friends, Vassili; and he didn't regret Holcomb, that fool Ficino; he didn't even regret the possibility of JFK. But he wanted one thing out of it: Laura. He had to prime Richard to deliver to Kennedy a message Kelley didn't want delivered. Then, he would come to Kelley, and . . .

It was very early in the morning and they were walking in the Virginia woods, not far from Robert Kennedy's house. Secret Service men all around them, were discreetly out of sight. "How real do you think this thing is?" John F. Kennedy asked his brother.

"Jesus," Robert Kennedy said. "I don't know what to say."

"I get the feeling sometimes that we're surrounded by a fuckin' bunch of wolves. I mean, who do we trust? The military? The CIA? Or the bankers and businessmen, legitimate and otherwise? We can't let it paralyze us."

"Look, we have to get the few people we trust together and sort out what's happening. Who *is* this joker Aquilino? He calls you out of nowhere and tells you things I've said to you, things you've said to people in strictest privacy. Obviously we have no security. Who else is listening in, Jack?"

"All right. You round up Ted Sorensen, some of the others. When I get back from St. Paul, we'll hold a war council. Should

I see this kid alone, the way he wants?"

"I'd like to run a check on him but I don't even know how you can do that securely."

"Listen, we don't have much time. We have to open up a secure backchannel to Mr. K, fast and direct. You have a little talk with Georgi, what's his name?"

"Bolshakov. He wants me to be ambassador to Russia."

"Bolshakov is Khrushchev's mouth. Find out what's really on Khrushchev's mind, what he's going to say in public versus what he's going to say via his ambassador—and then what he *really* means . . . what kind of pressures are on him."

"I don't think they want war, but Mr. K has his own problems."

"We have to contain this thing, but at the same time we have to look to the voters as if we want this—what is it they call it in Russia?—the final struggle. Because if the Russians push us too far in Cuba, we're going to have to give up all those programs. Forget civil rights. Forget welfare reform. Listen, I want our own plan of action drawn up, step by step, with all the protocols worked out. What they give up and what we give up. And, oh yes, I want someone to sit on those pistol-packing Cuban fanatics down in Miami. No more actions. Sit on them, Bobby, and if there has to be blood, so be it. That's the way it's going to have to be. Jesus. What is that kid going to tell me next?"

Ziggy decided to abandon his truck and divide up their group. Carol and Richard would start in their pursuit of the President, while Ziggy and Marvin would man a floating command post in New York, changing the dialing configurations from day to day, changing the routes the messages to the President would take. They would gather more and more information from the network around the country, feeding it to Richard.

Ziggy arranged a sequence of telephone call number changes with Richard. They would shift each day according to an already worked-out pattern. When the contact was arranged, they would come together again.

Ziggy, Tarzan and Marvin drove back to New York. By now, Ziggy had confirmation from Samael that they were not being tailed. Manhattan. What better place to hide? When they were absolutely sure they weren't being followed, Ziggy and Marvin

347

were dropped off. They were on their way to a half-rented office building, where Ziggy had set up a terminal. He sent Marvin out for food, and then contacted Spectre (original name, Spector) in Washington, an old friend. Spectre, as Spector, supported himself by being a manager of a small radio station.

"You know, Spectre, if we were invaded by the agents of another world, and the government knew, they would never tell us, would they?"

"Ziggy, you know it. Not until they saved their own asses."

"But supposing we found it out? It would be our duty to inform the American public, wouldn't it?"

"Everyone has the right to know. No more secrets."

"No, no, nothing like that. But we have to test our capability and ingenuity, don't we?"

"Short wave? What channel? What power? I mean who would hear it aside from a few nuts like ourselves?" Spectre asked.

"Well, it's a problem of money and equipment, isn't it? We can't afford a 500,000 kilowatt station, can we? No, I mean we want to inform the whole world? Piggyback onto the system as it is. Let all America know at the same time . . ."

"Network radio or TV?"

"Right. How might we do that?" Ziggy asked. He knew the answer.

"What have you got in mind, Ziggy? Tell America to wake up? Or tell our government to go fuck itself, live and coast to coast?"

"Something like that."

"Radio's got problems. The networks are broken up. Television has other problems. I mean, will you use visual stuff?"

"We can't afford that. Maybe our audio along with their video."

"Unless there's some kind of national hookup, because of an emergency . . . you know, President addresses the nation, there's the time zone factor. You have live shows, like the Saturday football game, or like the Ed Sullivan show, only that covers half the country. The other half, in the west, gets a re-broadcast. The show is relayed by coaxial cable . . ."

"Telephone company?"

"Right."

"Now with something like the Ed Sullivan show, if you cut in with your audio, you'll hit the east, but when they get the kine-

348

scope out there, they'll know something is fucked up, and so they'll just redo the show . . ."

"Redo the show?"

"Sure. If there's a fuckup on the recording, they have to do it all over again. *Then* it goes out again on the coaxial cable for the west . . . relayed out there and probably broadcast live . . . at least I think that's what happens. We could check it out."

Ziggy said, "Say it's Ed Sullivan. You mean to say he keeps all those entertainers hanging around in case they have to do it all over again?"

"I think I know what you're getting at. I love it. Come on, Ziggy, give. What're you thinking of doing?"

"Let's just say that I always hated Ed Sullivan . . ."

Richard and Carol drove west through the night, along the Pennsylvania Turnpike toward Pittsburgh. It was one o'clock in the morning, and the highway was almost deserted. Richard was driving fast, above the speed limit. He turned to look at Carol, asleep beside him with her head on his shoulder, her left hand lying relaxed between his legs. The radio played softly. They had lost the New York stations; nothing out here but hillbilly music. What was she dreaming? Was she scared? How different her life had become, dozing there with a map on her lap. She was doing this for him. He took one hand off the wheel and put it on her thigh. Maybe they should stop again; could he ever get enough of her?

When the occasional headlights ahead of him came up, they had a hypnotizing effect. He felt that the world was watching him with eyes and wires that crisscrossed all over the country. They were heading for Johnstown, Pennsylvania, the next step along their underground railroad, a small town whose only claim to fame was a great flood disaster. Friends were there, people like themselves, a couple with two children. Would those lives Richard touched be killed? And when it was all over, would he and Carol get married?

He glanced at his watch. Almost two o'clock. Time to start looking for a phone booth, a gas station, a diner . . .

349

CHAPTER 46

THAT day, October 5, John F. Kennedy made stops and speeches in Covington, Kentucky, in Cincinnati, and then flew on to Detroit. He was campaigning hard for a Democratic Congress. Surrounding him, to provide security, was the visible line of the Secret Service, the cold-faced men who faced outward toward the cheering crowds, looking for the one, or two, or three people who might mean danger. There was a second visible line of defense provided by the local police, and a third provided by the FBI.

Unknown to the President and the President's protectors, however, were two invisible entourages, a fourth and fifth encirclement. The fourth was the combination of Germans, Russians and Americans put together by Braunstein, Skuratov and Holcomb, looking for Richard and possibly Keats.

The fifth line, commanded by Vassili Oprichnik, had been set up by Keats to protect Richard and help him reach the President alive. Vassili used KGB men. But something had gone wrong. Vassili had gotten word from Skuratov that he was to terminate Richard when he appeared and withdraw his forces. The mission was being scratched. What was he going to do? If he disbanded the people in his charge, then Skuratov would get him. It was classic. Unless he could create a diversion . . . even a shoot-out? Get himself captured? Defect?

He could ignore the orders for one, maybe two days, while he made his decision.

They pulled off the road at a gas station. She woke up, stretched and yawned. "Where are we?"

"Gas station," Richard said and leaned down to kiss her. His hand had slipped between her thighs.

"Don't do that, Richard. Not here."

"Ever make love in a car before?"

"Not until tonight. I don't know if I like it. I kept feeling that someone would come to the window and look in."

"Didn't you do stuff like that when you were younger?"

She shook her head and looked at him sadly. "My head was always in a book. I was shy."

"So was I."

"I waited for someone to take the lead. They never came until . . . well, you know all that."

He leaned over to kiss her again. "We should pull off the road somewhere after I make these next phone calls, and then we should make up for all those lost teenage dreams. Better late than never."

"Why is it better in a car?"

"You're really innocent in your way, aren't you, even after listening to all your patients spill their secrets?"

"You're making me regress, Richard, into the adolescence I never had."

They got the gas tank filled and drove a few yards to the line of phone booths. Richard parked and turned off the lights. "Look, Carol, what are you going to do if something happens to me?"

"What can happen?"

"If *anything* happens, I'm going to give you three telephone numbers to Ziggy. Don't write them down." And he spoke the phone numbers twice. She repeated them. "Now comes the hard part." He sat up and kissed her again, his hands cupping her breasts, then held her away from him and looked at her. "I don't know how to say this." He reached into his jacket and pulled out a small automatic, a Beretta. She stared at him, wide-eyed. He began to explain how it worked. He worked the slide; the bullet slid into the chamber. He showed her the safety.

351

"Richard, you really expect me to use that?"

"I hope not. But you should know about it. Supposing you have to get away."

"Richard, I can't."

"You say what they did to me?"

"I can't do it."

"Is it better to die? At least take it, just hold it."

"Richard . . ."

"Carol, think that the person in front of you is Sidney . . . He's part of it all, isn't he? If they told him to torture me, he would have done it."

She was horrified, but she took it. The gun was warm from Richard's body.

Richard put his hand on her face. "I've been thinking while you were sleeping. We could just drop out of this, forget the whole thing."

"What do you mean?"

"America's a big place. It goes on forever. There are thousands of towns, big cities. We could get lost. There are millions of people living out there, sleeping in bed together right now, living normal lives. Why can't we be like them?"

"Because we know too much. There are your parents, wherever they are, and then there's the possibility of war. A horrible kind of war."

"Sometimes I think it's crazy, Carol. You and me, Ziggy, Tarzan, Marvin, some nuts scattered around the country, *we're* supposed to stop a war?"

"And then there's the President."

"Yes, and then there's the President. I can't believe it. *I* know more than he does? *I'm* going to save him? *Me?*"

Richard got out of the car. He went into the phone booth and began dialing.

The first contact was with Ziggy, for the day's report. The news bothered him. Military tension was secretly building. Was the President lying to him and going ahead? Was the President being lied *to?* Alert-status of the air force movements of troops to Florida, combat exercises by marines, stepping up of CIA activity in Florida, plans for raids on Cuba. And something new and strange. Internal squabbles in the intelligence community down there—even killings. Ships of the navy, supposedly on routine exercises near Key West, Mayport, drifting out to sea.

Richard realized what bothered him. *Ziggy had too much news. Things that would never be reported in the papers. Was his network that big, that sophisticated?*

"We should plan," Ziggy was saying. "Where? St. Paul? Buffalo? Baltimore?"

"No. I'd rather see how it goes, what arrangements the President can make."

"All right, Richard. When you decide to make your move, tell me. You should know something, though. Somebody both in Detroit and in Cincinnati is on the lookout for you. We monitored channels."

"Government channels?"

"So-called, but that doesn't mean a thing. Whoever it is is near the President. You have to figure out whether he's playing it straight or setting you up."

Richard hung up and began to dial again. Detroit. This time the phone was picked up instantly. Again, along with the awe, he felt the wave of inexplicable hatred seep over him. He couldn't talk for a few seconds.

"Hello? Hello?"

"It's me."

"I was waiting. I thought you might show up here today. Then I realized I don't even know what you look like. Well?"

"I tried. I got close. But there were people lying in wait for me."

"How do you know that?"

"We—I monitored the security channels."

"My people?"

Who are *your* people? Richard wondered. "I don't know. The fact is, we have to meet, Mr. President. Alone."

"It isn't that easy, Richard. A President isn't as free as people think. My security forces have a mandate to protect me and it overrides what I might want. I can't go wandering off alone. You're here in Detroit?"

"Mr. President, it's not that I don't trust you. I don't trust the people around you. I'll get to you. Just look for me."

"Where?"

353

"St. Paul. Indianapolis. Buffalo. Look for me."

"Why don't we do this in Washington. At least there I can arrange to have someone meet you and escort you in. Why don't you talk to my brother, or anyone else you think you can trust. I don't know who to suggest. Listen, did the people you monitored sound like the FBI? The CIA?"

"You tell *me* . . . sir."

"Why don't you tell me some more of what you think is going to happen."

"Let me think about that for a moment."

"How will I know you? What do you look like? I have some trigger-happy men around me. I've got to tell them something, who to let through."

"I'm six feet tall. Black hair, dark brown eyes, you might say almost black. I weigh about one hundred and ninety pounds. I guess that's it."

"Richard, you have to give me a little more than that. How am I supposed to distinguish you from a hundred other guys?"

Richard paused. Was he good-looking? Ugly? "I don't know what to give you."

"Richard, this isn't the time to be modest. I have to be able to recognize you. For God's sake, man, you look in the mirror when you shave, don't you? You go to the movies, watch television? Can't you think of someone you look like who you've seen in the movies?"

"Have you ever seen this actor, John Derek?" Or maybe it was like Tony Curtis, or was it Farley Granger? He smiled at himself. At a time like this.

"I've met him, in fact."

"I look something like that."

"How are you going to get to me?"

"That's my worry, sir."

"Listen, be reasonable. Let's arrange a meeting in an area I know. I'll send someone I trust implicitly to bring you in. I'll send my brother. Personally. It can't be me. I can't just disappear for a half hour."

Richard said, "No, no, I'll connect with you. Wait for me."

"Don't hang up yet. What else is supposed to happen?"

Should Richard give him anything? "On the fourteenth you

354

will be given hard evidence that the Russians have put missile sites in Cuba."

"What kind of evidence?"

"U-2 photographs. They'll also be leaked to maneuver you into calling together a group of advisors, among them some of the people I overhead talking. They're the ones who have been planning to push for an invasion of Cuba, a first strike."

"Richard, are you saying that these photographs are *faked?*"

It had never occurred to Richard to ask himself this question. Since the plotters were attempting nothing less than to maneuver the country onto a war footing, Richard had assumed the photographs had to be real.

"Richard. Are you there? Are they real or fake?"

He made a decision. "Real. Real. They can be confirmed by more U-2 flights."

"You're sure?"

"I'm sure." He hoped he was right.

"What else? Who did you hear talking about this?"

"I'll give you one name. I don't know many of the others. Never heard of them before. Dean. That was one name."

"Dean *Rusk?*"

"Dean, that's all I know."

"Give me another name."

"I can tell you one other thing, Mr. President. There are hit teams being sent to Cuba. When everything begins to heat up, they go into action. And, among them, there are Mafia button men."

"Jesus, Richard, Jesus and Mary Mother of God. I have a hundred thousand spooks and they have to depend on some torpedo?"

"I'll see you in a day or so. Look for me in St. Paul."

Richard hung up. One thing was certain, he was not going anywhere near St. Paul.

355

CHAPTER 47

VASSILI figured he could disobey his orders for only one or two days, no more. His only hope was to provoke an incident that would allow him to escape, then reemerge later to sell his knowledge. He knew enough of the Parvus Game to make it worthwhile to *some* government. He knew enough of its agents in place all around the world, had a sense of its overall operations and strategy. Who would buy?

Not his own people. Why buy when they can sweat it out of you? And anyway, he had betrayed his country. They were paranoid back home.

To go to the Americans, though, was risky at best. Who was Parvus and who was not? America was a sieve, not a country at all. The English? That too was risky. Too much like the Americans. The French? Ah, the French were serious; their nationalism would be just made to order.

Where? When? He would have to make his move in St. Paul or nowhere. He would just have to improvise a lot of shooting.

When Kennedy got to St. Paul, a curious incident happened. Four students entered the Leamington Hotel, where the President was meeting with Hubert Humphrey, local politicians, businessmen and fund-raisers.

A crowd was standing around outside the Leamington, waiting

for a glimpse of Kennedy, perhaps for a chance to shake his hand, when some of the younger people—not the four student prize winners, who weren't due for an hour—began to talk. Why not just go in and ask to meet the President? Or even go right up to the floor where they were staying? But what floor? An older man, in his thirties, said, "I couldn't help overhearing you. Why don't you just go in. He's on the fourteenth floor."

"Oh," one of the students said, "we can't do that."

"Why not? I mean, he's not an ogre. He likes young people. He's just a man. Means a lot to you?"

"Oh boy, sure. But the FBI'd stop us."

"You mean the Secret Service. Listen, why don't you just go in and pretend you didn't know you weren't allowed in. See how far that would get you. I have an idea. Why don't you pretend you're foreign exchange students. French. German. I mean, you'd look perfectly good that way. You didn't understand that you're not supposed to do things like that. Don't ask for the President. Just go up to the fourteenth floor and ask for the Senator."

"Senator Humphrey?"

"Sure. He's the kind of man who's ready to meet his constituency."

"Well," one of them said, a tall boy with curly brown hair, "I don't know . . ." Four of them had gathered around the man.

"Just sail in like you own the place. Worst that can happen is that they'd turn you back, right? Tell you what. I'm a plain-clothesman . . . St. Paul police. There's a password you could use when you get up there." And he told them.

They decided to pretend that they were German exchange students, because two of them had German grandparents. They could just speak English with a German accent.

When they got to the lobby, they went to the elevators. They were stopped and asked where they were going. They said that they were the high school students, German exchange students, who had been invited up to see Senator Humphrey. They had won a high school essay contest on American Democracy. "Hell of a note," the Secret Service man muttered to himself, "when foreign students waltz off with the prizes." He took them in the elevator to the fourteenth floor.

The security was, as always, heavy on the fourteenth floor.

Suited men, some with machine pistols. Keeping up the pretense, acting politely, never hesitating, they walked down the hall, past the Secret Service men. They stopped only once to ask, using the German accent, saying that they had been invited by Senator Humphrey. What room was he in? They were told the room number. They were ushered into the room where the Senator and the local Democratic politicos were talking to the President. The air was heavy with smoke. They came forward.

The President glanced at them, did a double take, and jumped up. He came toward the tall dark one with the dark eyes, sticking out his hand: "Richard, you did it. How did you get past all my people?"

Hearing this, three Secret Service men jumped up with drawn guns and started to surround the President. "Jesus, put those fuckin' things away," Kennedy said. "Some security. I could have been dead ten times over."

The tall dark student said, "Sir, *I* was supposed to say that to *you* . . ."

"Say what?"

" 'Richard.' "

Now the President looked puzzled. "Okay. You're home safe. You can drop it."

Someone said, "Mr. President, we're running late."

"We're going to run later." He pulled the tall dark one forward. "Come on, let's go into the other room, Richard."

"But sir," the young man said, "my name isn't Richard. I was just told to say that word."

"What word?"

" 'Richard'. That was supposed to get us in to see you and Senator Humphrey."

Senator Humphrey, beaming, detached himself from the others and came to them. "What splendid initiative. We here in Minnesota are nothing if not enterprising, Mr. President."

"Who told you that?" Kennedy asked.

"I don't know. We were standing around downstairs, a bunch of us kids—gee, it's really a great honor to meet you."

"Go on, go on. What else?"

358

"And we were talking, sir, about how we might get to meet you, shake your hand, and . . . well, you know, that kind of thing . . . and some of the others were saying, I dare you—"

"How did you get to use that name. Richard?"

"Well, this guy, I guess he must have heard us talking, he was standing there in the crowd and he says . . ."

"What did he look like?"

The four of them looked at one another. One of the other students said, "It's hard to remember. A guy with sort of brown hair."

"Brown? Real dark brown?"

"Yes," one of the students said. "No," the student with black hair said. "I don't remember," the third said. "Ordinary kind of guy. He said he was a detective. Plainclothes, and he knew the password."

"How tall was he?"

"I would say he was about five feet eight, maybe nine, shorter than me, sir."

"What did he say, do you remember exactly?"

"He said . . . well, I don't remember exactly. There was a lot of noise, a lot of people talking, but he said that it was easier to see the President than you think. All it takes is a little courage. And then—"

"Did he say anything like Richard sent me, or for you to say that I come from Richard?"

"No . . . I don't think so . . ."

"He might have . . ."

"I think that you're all splendid boys." Hubert Humphrey said. "Fine young Americans with a lot of spunk. But boys, you are taking up the time of the busiest man in the world. Say hello, shake hands, and then we'll have to—"

"He said to use the name, Richard?"

"It was, what do you call it sir, a password."

"That's just what it is, boys. A password." Jesus, he thought, they walked in just like that. Richard had used a cut-out. Did that mean that Richard was near and was testing him? How many others were working with Richard? Or was it someone else? If they could walk in that easily, who else could do it? And his security, they just sat there with their fingers up their butts. Suddenly, and maybe for the first time in his life, he felt very vulnerable. "Could you recognize this man if you saw him again?"

"Oh, yes sir, sure."

Kennedy turned aside to one of his security men. He was whispering fiercely. "You taking all this in?"

"Yes sir."

"When this is finished, some heads are going to roll, you know that? Your people fouled up. You take two or three of your people, go down with these kids. Find that man or it's going to be your ass. No strong-arm stuff." He turned to the others. "Boys, I'm honored to meet young people like yourselves. You are the hope of America. Please go with this man and see if you can pick out the man who spoke to you."

A small Secret Service team emerged from the Leamington Hotel, loosely grouped around the four students. From his vantage point, a little back in the crowd awaiting the emergence of the President, Vassili saw them coming. Now was the time. He pulled the small walkie-talkie out of his jacket pocket, put it to his mouth, pressed the on-button and said, "There he is. The tall dark kid in the sweater and jacket. Move in. Drift over there, don't run. Get him. Take out the others. No gunplay."

Vassili's people began to surge forward, shouldering their way through the crowd. The Braunstein-Skuratov-Holcomb people, seeing the movement, began to edge through the crowd too. The small group paused in the entranceway of the hotel. The young students came forward to scan the crowd. Vassili turned toward his bodyguard; he hadn't heard his message . . . the crowd noise was too strong. Vassili pulled out his pistol and shot the young man. He then unscrewed the silencer. He wanted noise. He was counting on panic.

The people at the Leamington's entrance were scanning the crowd for him, when he fired a second time. The bullet missed and ricocheted off the entrance wall. People were screaming as both teams surged forward. The Secret Service men were overwhelmed. Before he turned to leave, Vassili saw that someone had grabbed the tall dark student and was dragging him away.

More screams. Someone yelled, "They got the President." It would take at least ten minutes, probably longer, to find out that the person they had taken was not Richard. A fight had broken out between the two team members.

Now Vassili had time to disappear.

CHAPTER 48

SUNDAY, October 7 in Johnstown, Pennsylvania, depressed them both. Maybe it was because it was Sunday. Maybe it was the waiting until night, when Richard would contact the President again, this time in Washington.

They were staying with a family named Griggs. A radio ham, a man obsessed with the toys of his hobby. Every extra cent Ed Griggs made went into his equipment. He had a huge antenna over his house and his transmitter was powerful ... in fact, illegal. More watts than the FCC regulations allowed. Came the weekends, Ed Griggs was dead to his family. He was in contact with a constellation of ethereal friends all over the world. Ed Griggs had two navy citations for helping in a disaster, spending twenty-four hours at his set, relaying news to rescuers. The government would have taken away the citations if they only knew how many times he had interfered with government transmissions, or what he managed to listen in to.

The cover story Richard had worked out with Ziggy was that they were engaged in writing, and acting out, a sci-fi drama. Creatures from another world were in hot pursuit of them. Flight from the invaders who had taken over the world ... secretly, and how the hams rescue the world. Carol and Richard had stumbled on the aliens' presence. The invaders looked like ordinary people. But they wanted to take over Richard and Carol's bodies.

362

Well, there was a sort of truth to it, wasn't there? Everyone knew it was a joke, a kind of scenario, a preparation for writing a serial for *Fantasy and Science Fiction*. There was a possibility of movie money. The thing was not even to mention it to anyone; a game. Make it like real life. After all, the invaders were telepathic too, weren't they?

Mary Griggs was just as much a nut as her husband was. She didn't play with equipment: she was a witchcraft nut. She cast spells. She was a health food fanatic. She was convinced that she was a weredeer. Nevertheless, on Sundays, they went to church in the morning. After church their two children went to play with their friends. Sunday afternoons Ed Griggs disappeared into his "control room"—that's what he called it—and sent his tentacles out. Mary would go off with a few friends of hers and do whatever it was that witches did.

Richard and Carol felt constrained. They couldn't bring themselves to make love; the house was too small and they were afraid they would be overheard. In the morning, they were too tired from their all-night trip. They got up late and found the family tiptoeing around the house. There was a peculiar stillness in the air; the stillness of Sundays in rural areas; the stillness of small populations. Living in a large city had gotten into their bones.

Seeing Ed and Mary raised questions for Carol. It became an unspoken, barely formulated question in their minds, growing, gnawing, undercutting their relationship. In the long run, what did they have in common besides sex . . . and danger? How easily they had accepted Richard and Carol; no probing questions. Ziggy had recruited Ed without beginning to tell him the way he fit in. Security measures; Ed had no need to know. It bothered Richard.

Later that night, Ed was to contact another member of the network by radio in St. Louis. From there, Richard would be patched into the telephone network.

The afternoon weighed heavily. The sky was overcast. There was a chill in the air. "Sometimes snow comes early out here," Mary said. "It didn't used to be that way. All this atomic testing has definitely upset the balance of the earth. Changed the weather. Our spells don't work as good as they used to. And now they're talking about going to the moon. Know what that's going to do? Affect our bodies. Our bodies," she said to Carol, "respond to the moon. Our life cycles are moon cycles . . ."

Was she really that superstitious, Carol wondered.

"You can't stop progress," Ed said.

"No it isn't. Same principle as your radio. We're receivers. The moon and the planets send off vibrations. It's a man thing to want to destroy us, destroy our cycles. We make magic." Mary said. "We'll keep them off the moon."

What kind of world had Carol stumbled into? Connections she didn't understand yet had been severed. She missed something. The intensity that had been generated in Richard's room, the room he had been imprisoned in . . . Paradise . . . the world kept out. She didn't know it, but their love had begun to erode.

Late that afternoon they rode out to the woods outside Johnstown. Rain or not, snow or not, they couldn't stand being cooped up. Would this be their life? For how long? They went to a picnic ground the Griggs's told them about. They would take a walk in the woods. When they got there it looked gray, forbidding, chilly. The leaves were falling from the trees. The air smelled acrid, chemical. Factory smoke? Hand in hand, chilled, they wandered through the woods. They both felt watched although neither one of them said anything to one another. They walked silently for an hour. Here in the woods, following a path through the trees, what they had been through slowly began to seem like a dream. They avoided looking at one another. They began to talk. They probed at one another, learning more about their lives. What would they have been doing if they were leading ordinary lives like Ed and Mary's? What would they have been doing if they hadn't been thrown together? Carol frequently came into the laboratory on Sundays to catch up on the records of her experiments. Frequently, Sidney Ficino would come in too. A lonely time, she admitted: a lonely hunt for the ultimate stuff of the mind. Lonely . . . exciting.

They decided that they would make contact with Ziggy about ten o'clock that night. Before that there was nothing to do but sit around and listen to small-town gossip with Mary. Ed was in his "control room." Richard went with Ed after a while. Ed was proud of his rig and Richard was afraid he would hurt Ed's feelings if he didn't join him. "I got more stuff in here than a spy ship. Upgrade it all the time."

In the evening Mary turned on the television. There were some shows she never missed. But when the Ed Sullivan show came on, something peculiar happened. A strange kind of interference. It wasn't much, but it made Carol sit up, startled. The interruption of voices. "The reception's not good here," Mary said and tried to fiddle with the dial. Someone said, "Listen, America." What was it? A conversation. *Richard's* and John F. Kennedy's voices talking to one another. But it wasn't clear unless you knew what they were talking about and what it meant. None of it registered on Mary. Three minutes of it, drowning out one of the acts, and then a resumption of the usual audio. When Richard came out of Ed Grigg's control room for a beer, she took Richard aside and told him what happened. His face lit up; he was excited.

When Richard was ready to radio to Ziggy, Ed agreed to leave his room, but clearly he didn't like anyone fiddling with his equipment. "I won't touch a thing," Richard promised him.

"You're at Ed Griggs's?" Ziggy asked when Richard came up on the radio.

"Yes."

"Hi, Ed, how are you?"

"Ed's gone into the other room."

"Good. I can't tell you how relieved I am that you made it there, Richard. I thought something might have happened to you. Maybe we better find another way of doing it. Come back."

"What do you mean?"

"I mean, it's ridiculous to think you can reach the President in person."

"Why? What happened, Ziggy?"

"I'm not sure. Something in St. Paul. I thought you got to St. Paul and made your move. I was worried. I thought you might have gotten hurt."

"What made you think that?"

"One of our people there was listening to the traffic, police, FBI, Secret Service, White House communications . . . There was gunplay in the street in front of the Leamington Hotel where he

365

was staying. Six casualties, yet not a word in the papers or on the air."

"What happened, Ziggy?"

"I'm not sure. Everything was going fine. We hear Lancer this, Lancer that, Lancer will come out at such and such hours. When all of a sudden the airwaves are just full of panicky Feds and police. Someone took a shot at someone. A lot of milling around, some people arrested. They had guns. But nothing in the news. Richard, they're laying in wait for you."

"Who is 'they'?"

"Richard, are you crazy? You're forgetting the hospital? You're forgetting what you went through? Don't you see what this means?"

"No."

"They *know* you're trying to reach him. Why do you have to talk to the man face-to-face? What can you do in person that you can't do by phone? You could even talk to his brother. There are ways of setting up truly secure lines."

Richard didn't tell Ziggy that he was beginning not to trust anyone. He didn't even know if it was the President he had talked to.

"All right," Ziggy said finally. "Richard, we can do it from here if you're dead set on it. He's going to come to New York. He'll be staying at the Carlyle Hotel . . . It's our ground."

"You have to tell me what else is happening. What's the news, Ziggy, the news? What are the moves? If you don't tell me, I'll just leave right now."

There was a long pause.

"All right. Before I begin, when you make the contact, you have to ask him what happened in St. Paul. But don't tell him he's being bugged."

"Why not?"

"Because he'll stop talking to you."

"Sure, Ziggy, sure." But by now Richard was certain that he wasn't going to make that contact from this place. He would leave as soon as Ziggy gave him the news.

CHAPTER 49

AT three o'clock in the morning of October 7, Robert F. Kennedy picked up Georgi Bolshakov and drove him out to Virginia. Bolshakov was acting as Nikita Khrushchev's personal emissary to John Kennedy. They would talk in the limousine. After their talk, Bolshakov would be dropped of, picked up by another car, and brought back to Washington.

Earlier, after Richard's call, Robert had another conference with his brother. "If I could only talk to Khrushchev directly, without the whole fucking world listening in . . ." JFK had said. He had been nervous, irritable, impatient. Robert recognized the signs; he had a woman waiting. "This is crazy. I have to be my own intelligence agency *and* State Department."

"Is this kid crazy?"

"I don't know. He won't tell me much over the phone, but he's said enough to make it sound all too damn real. You have to get Bolshakov to tell his boss to set the ground rules. We can't control it and we can't head it off. The momentum is too strong. Neither I nor Khrushchev can reverse it without a lot of people wanting to impeach me—worse if you accept what the kid says. As for Mr. K, he'll wind up against the Kremlin wall. The irony is that politically I *need* a confrontation like this, and so do the Republicans. If I don't accept the bait, I think there's a fallback plan which ends in my . . ." He shrugged. "What are the options going

367

to be when we have to assemble the advisors? I'm depending on you to get your course of action clearly spelled out for Bolshakov to transmit back to Khrushchev. I don't know how well they know the limits of our system, but doing nothing will be unacceptable. We can use warnings, diplomatic pressure, bargaining, maybe close the missile bases in Turkey and Italy—but don't mention that at first—in exchange for their removing the bases in Cuba. There *are* bases in Cuba, aren't there?"

Robert Kennedy paused and thought. "We're going to be sending over confirming flights. Those launching pads had better be there, or we're going to be caught with egg on our face. Then what do I tell Bolshakov? 'Set up those bases so we can demand that you remove them'? They'll be there."

"So," the President said, "if the missiles are there, I'll have to at least set up a blockade."

"Quarantine."

"Okay, quarantine. And the next option they'll suggest will be an air strike."

"An American Pearl Harbor is what that's going to look like," Robert Kennedy said. "Can we get Krock or Reston to float the Pearl Harbor analogy in the *Times*? I can use that in our arguments. Americans don't do that kind of thing."

"Maybe you'll have to. Because the only other option, short of general war with Russia, is an invasion—for which almost everyone is in place if we believe what the kid tells me. You'd think they'd inform their President before they go to war."

"Which leaves us what?"

"We level with Khrushchev, then make up a tight set of bargaining protocol which will make us both look good. I wish I had a hot line, situation room to situation room, me to him. Your friend Bolshakov is the hot line for now. God, all the equipment we have and we have to use smoke signals and tom-toms. Be candid. But nothing in writing. Voice only. Meanwhile we have to open something else too, for insurance. Another backup channel."

"Who?"

"Someone forward-looking in the business community."

"Who? Cyrus Eaton?"

"No, he's practically a Commie to the kind of people we're dealing with."

"Armand Hammer?"

"Same problem."

"Not McCloy. Anybody but McCloy. Nelson Rockefeller? Forget it; he wants two hundred million bomb shelters. David? Same trouble. Knox of Westinghouse? A possibility. Harriman has gone to the well too many times. Andre Meyer? Another possibility. Kelley?"

"Well, at least he's Irish. If McCloy or Dean find out, they'll cut our nuts off. Just start on the low road with Bolshakov."

John Kennedy was on his feet and headed out of the room.

They left Johnstown on Monday, October 8. It was a question of where Richard would make his move to intersect with the President. But he had made up his mind. He no longer trusted the situation. He would do it himself, on his own terms. Random motion. Wild card. On his own. Harrisburg, York, Reading (because it was near Philadelphia), north to Scranton so they could easily drive to Buffalo, or to New York.

He and Carol were seeing America. Or at least a part of America. It slept beneath the threat, unaware, even uninterested. "It's our honeymoon," he told her as they drove eastward again, through Pennsylvania. This time they kept off the turnpike. Small towns, past hills, through the eroded mountains (hills really), the Tuscarora Mountains, up and down the hills and ridges, through the fertile valleys, a dreaming land, concerned with small things. Past farms and factory towns, through the dying foliage, the bare trees jutting up on the hillsides, partitioning the fringe of sky in an intricate lacework. He was beginning to fall in love with it. Now and then they passed dumps piled high with abandoned cars. They stopped in small dreary hotels in the small towns, hardly used. Motels. A loneliness on the land. No signs here of the intricate maneuverings in the small spaces that were called, by some, the great world.

The country Richard and Carol drive through remained unaware. Of all the events, only the uneasiness of what would happen with Cuba penetrated here . . . That much seeped through,

369

and always in the context of the great Russian menace. They began to lose touch. What they were doing began to become dreamlike.

There were those who would call the land they drove through America's backbone. Carol didn't like it. Civilization had not reached here. Nothing to do. Boredom setting in. They were losing their love. It began to evaporate, drain off into the air.

At first, to compensate, they tried to live as intensely as they had in the hospital, grasping at one another, trying to fuse bodies, become one, escalating their love-making until it seemed that the flesh could take no more. It wasn't coming easy. It became harder and harder to reach the climaxes. Was it only a few days ago, perhaps a week, that they had lived on the heights of passion? Now they experimented. The old and simple ways didn't work. The experimentation began to seem contrived. And beneath, a fear was setting in.

After each time they lay there, gasping, drained, unsatisfied, with the afternoon and the night ahead of them. Could it really be possible that someone was after them? Could it really be that Richard had intelligence so important that the fate of a country hinged on it? Here, here, in a decaying town, with its half-empty streets? Here, in this hotel room, with its cheap furniture and its smell of mildew, peeling walls, in a hotel that had never been fashionable, partially inhabited, having lost its business to those Howard Johnson type of motels on the major highways—originally built for easy access for cars and defense—that bypassed the small towns? The people talked slower. Their interests were narrower. What did you talk about if you didn't know the native language—even though it was English—of the natives, didn't know their interests, what gossip excited them? What could you do? Go to a roadhouse? See the monuments of the Civil War? Drive down to Gettysburg?

To Carol the people here were devoid not only of the things that interested her, they were another breed. They made her doubt the very universality of psychoanalysis. Did their brains even function in the same way as the brains of her experimental subjects? Peasant mentalities.

370

On the 8th, Cuba protested the blockade and appealed to the court of world opinion. On the 9th, a slightly distorted version of what had happened in St. Paul—not mentioning violence at all —appeared in the papers. The three students who had managed to meet Kennedy were mentioned. Nothing about shooting.

At night, Richard again telephoned Ziggy.

"Where are you calling from? Why didn't you go to one of the places I set up?"

"I'm just outside of Baltimore," Richard lied. "He'll be here on the 10th. I'm going to make my run."

"Where? How? You need help? We can set up the monitoring, see if they're expecting you. No. Listen. We picked up something. Someone phoned in a bomb threat. The security is being beefed up."

"They're trying to keep me from him."

"Richard, there *are* nuts in the country. Come back. We can get to him from here, New York. The Carlyle. That's where he'll be staying. Are you going to talk to him tonight?"

"Yes."

"What are you going to tell him? Find out his reaction to what we did on the Ed Sullivan show. Warn him that there are other things we can do . . . much worse . . ."

"What, Ziggy?"

"Cut off part of his whole defense communications' system, and send through confusing messages. Cut in on national radio and television. Let America know . . . let the whole world know . . ."

How could they do that, Richard wondered? Ziggy . . . Ziggy . . . there was so much he wasn't being told. The ability to organize a network of crazies, communications' nuts was one thing . . . but to play games in the higher and more secure channels? The special equipment required . . . not stuff you picked up at the surplus stores . . . hard to steal stuff . . . The telephone, ham radio . . . all right. But what else? There were thousands of radio channels. Richard had a good idea of what was required. Not that it was impossible . . . Could a few hundred people, even if they were disciplined, and parceled out the spectrum, really do so much? Amateurs, no matter how brilliant? No, all that took power . . . too much equipment. And yet . . . The birth of an idea was taking place in his mind . . . but it would take years of experimentation . . . Something smelled bad. Ziggy.

He came into the hotel. He was silent. He had to think it out. Draw his strength again. He was sure. The center of his certainty. He had put it together. He knew what was going to happen. He knew it.

She was lying on the bed, fully clothed. She was looking up at the ceiling. He sat down on an easy chair. The minutes of silence passed. He could sense the resentment. It poured out of her now, a palpable wave. He watched her. Suddenly he realized: he suspected *her, her* too. Carol. To stifle that feeling, he got up, walked over, bent down over her, to kiss her breasts.

"Don't, Richard, please. I don't feel like it."

They waited in silence. She was tense. She had finished talking to Keats about fifteen minutes ago. She had reported where they were, but she didn't know where they were going next. Richard was acting erratically, deciding where to move at random. "That's a sign of training, Carol," Keats had told her.

"I keep feeling as if I were betraying him."

"You're not. You're helping to save him."

"I wish this were over," Carol said.

"Soon. I think soon. Things are coming to a head," Keats said. "He's working on a timetable. Late October. Carol, you have to find out more. Look, if he's difficult, you have to apply some pressure."

"What kind of pressure?"

"Use your imagination."

She knew what Keats meant. It upset her. "Listen, I'm not . . ."

"You're not a whore, if that's what you mean. You love him, right? Husbands and wives argue, don't they? Don't they apply pressure on one another in a variety of ways? You're practically married, Carol."

And this upset her even more.

"Keep in touch. We'll be waiting and watching over you.

There's a lot riding on you, Carol, a lot. The destiny of a whole country," Keats had told her.

"Everything seems unreal, Richard."

372

"Except that we're here, in bed, together . . ."

"Even that's becoming a dream. The memory of what I had . . . what I was doing, that's becoming realer . . . ?"

"What are you saying? That being in an insane asylum was realer . . . ?"

"It wasn't an insane asylum, Richard," she said angrily, "Sometimes I think that when you get on that phone . . . I mean I don't really know who you're even talking to . . ."

"Ziggy. The President . . ."

"I mean, I don't even know if you're talking to anyone."

"I could be talking to a recording?"

"No."

"I'm talking into a dead phone, pretending that I'm talking to the President?"

"No. I don't mean that. I don't know what I mean . . ."

"Carol, what are you trying to say?"

"I don't know. It's just that . . . well, it's being here, in the middle of nowhere. These people . . ."

"They're ordinary Americans. They're all right. Places like this . . . quiet, nice. There are trees. You can breathe. Maybe we could settle down in a place like this . . . have neighbors, you know? Leave that crazy world . . ."

"Are you mad," she screamed. *"Here!* I hate it here. Don't confuse what you've seen on television with reality." And they got into an argument, the first they had ever had. The thought of living in a small town upset her.

Richard stopped himself. "We're tense, Carol."

"I don't understand how people live like this, in the middle of nowhere."

"That's real scientific, lady. I mean you won't even let yourself study them and understand them."

"I don't know what I mean . . ."

"You can't return, Carol. You forgot what your boss, Ficino, did . . . Carol, I told you what happened to me before I ended up there. Remember that. How did I get to that place? Someone brought me. I think what you were supposed to do was to get things out of me . . . what I had heard. I've been thinking about it. You were supposed to question me . . . interrogate me without knowing what you were doing. You were set up. But you did

373

something that no one counted on. You fell in love with me. That upset things, but it was still possible for you to do things . . . get me to talk . . ."

"Richard, how did they know, how did Sidney know I fell in love with you if I didn't know it myself?"

"Maybe it didn't take much of an eye?"

"That's ridiculous."

"No it's not. When you helped me to escape . . . you put yourself on my side. They might get me. Throw me in prison for the rest of my life. Try to kill me. But Carol, you don't think they're going to let you go, return to your job because you say, 'all right, I made a mistake, I'm sorry'? They don't think that way. They *have* to figure that I told you things you shouldn't hear. Our fates are tied together now. Our only hope is to reach someone powerful enough to get you back your job, get me back my family, powerful enough to be convinced that we're not spies, or agents. And I don't think Ziggy made things easier when he played those games with the Ed Sullivan show.

"Carol, *I heard all those things.* That's not fake. What they did to me is not fake. You saw the bruises. You found traces of drugs. *I heard those people talking. I heard them.* We have to hold on to that. I couldn't have made those conversations up. What did I know about foreign policy? I never even heard those names before. Through Laura . . ."

"And that's another thing, Laura."

"What is she but a high class whore with connections? She's nothing. It's her connections and where her connections led . . . Wait a minute. Are you saying that . . . Laura . . . that it's all my crazy revenge on her?"

"I don't know what to believe. Richard, what if I went back and tried to find out . . ."

"From who? Your old boyfriend? That little fat man . . ."

"Oh, Richard."

"You know what they'd do to you? Strap you into a chair and begin to question you. And they wouldn't be nice about it. I mean it isn't psychoanalysis. There would be torture, Carol. Torture. And you know the first thing they go for, don't you. Sex. Right for the tits and cunt."

"Richard!"

"Well, don't be shocked. I didn't make the world."

"Maybe if I knew a little more . . . of what you have to tell him . . . the President . . ."

The suspicion rose. Don't tell her. Don't tell anyone but the man himself. "Look. I'll tell you what. Let's take a nap. Tonight, what we'll do is go to the phone together. When I telephone the President, you just listen in. You'll hear for yourself. I'll even tell you how the connections are made. You'll hear his voice. Tell you what else. I'll even let you ask him a question. Will that satisfy you?"

"This just has to end soon, Richard. I don't know how much longer I can take this." Richard lay down beside her and, after a while, they dozed off. There was going to be no sex that evening.

CHAPTER 50

IT was an ordinary middle-class house in Kew Gardens, with a small plot surrounding it and trees in the streets. The eight people who came there seemed ordinary enough. The four older men seemed to be retired workers, maybe the kind who had run a dry goods or hardware store. Everything about the woman said housewife; probably a grandmother. Of the three younger men, one of them looked like a construction worker; the other wore a sleazy, shiny suit and the jovial air of a salesman, everyone's friend; the third young man, a shame, was on crutches. A friend brought him in and then left.

The younger men were waiting outside in separate rooms. They would come in, one by one, to make their presentation to this committee of five. The first was Georgi Bolshakov. When he finished, there was a moment of silence. One of them whistled.

"A peculiar request to ask of us. *Us!?* You want *us* to act as go-between for Khrushchev and Kennedy? You know our position on those butchers. You want to use our channels to transmit and receive messages? That's not acceptable. Our channels are living people. You know we'll have to know their contents—you understand that, don't you?"

"I understand that."

"A question. How do you even know of our existence?" Samuel

Aquilino was the one who asked the question.

"My father was one of you."

"He shouldn't have told you. You don't believe in his principles?"

"I believe. I just chose another way to work. From within."

"But why us? You know we are opposed to both sides, and above all to Parvus, which is worse than both sides put together."

"You have the most effective network for what I want to happen . . . those of us who have chosen to work from within . . ."

"And that is?"

"The continuation of the thaw. Liquidation of the bloody past. Opening our society up. Business. The bourgeois—democratic stage of history . . ."

"That's NEPism. Parvus's bloody nonsense."

"What's Parvus?"

"It's *who's* Parvus. Helphand. A dead theoretician who had a disastrous effect on the revolution. A middle man. A *handler,* a fixer, a broker hiding behind a theory."

"You've begun the job of opening things up. Contraband, smuggling; American goods, food, clothes, records, drugs, art, some writings smuggled out. You've been running guns to the Georgians and backing the Ukranian National Movement. It has to accelerate.

"The situation is this: I have direct contact with Nikita Sergeievich Khrushchev. He truly wants some of the things we want. But you know the way things work. He's surrounded by many eyes and ears. When I transmit, I have to use KGB couriers, KGB equipment. You know how the message can be garbled or twisted. I must appear to be fulfilling a limited mission. Kennedy wants a direct contact. This means that he doesn't trust the people around him, either. I thought of using your network to convey the messages of the highest sensitivity so that neither Comrade Khrushchev or President Kennedy mistakes one another's intentions. If it has to be this war of deceptions, penetrations, liberation movements, shifting sides, why then you are perhaps the most fit to survive, triumph in the long run. That's what you've been doing for almost thirty years with both the west and the east after you. But to do that you need to help me do what I want to do."

"That's it?" another one of the older men asked. "Why don't you wait in the other room for us."

The second man to appear before the committee was Vassili Oprichnik. He came in the custody of two armed guards, because he had come to them seeking asylum. "How did you find us?" one of the committee asked.

"I learned of your existence, oh, way back, in Russia. Vague rumors. I was interested. I asked some questions, checked out some files, all low level, personal. I brought some people in for interrogation: traders, profiteers, moneylenders, black marketeers. Among them there were some who did business with the outside, with your networks extending into Europe and Asia."

"Which directorates of the KGB did you work in?"

"That's a little tricky to explain. In reality the section I belong to doesn't appear on anyone's table of organization. It's a separate little duchy run by a man named Skuratov, an old chekist. Ring a bell?" Vassili smiled. "The section's purpose was to combat secret organizations and societies all over the world, those whose functions might be aimed, directly and immediately, or in the long run, at the Soviet Union."

"Such as?"

"Oh God, there are dozens. Masons, Jesuits, Rotarians, certain Mormons, Birchers, religious Jews, evangelists, such as the Triad societies, the old Macedonian underground organizations which have flourished for hundreds of years, the Mafia, the Unione Corse, people like yourselves, Nazis, the militant Buddhists, the Moslem brotherhood . . . and especially Parvus. But also I was recruited by Parvus. After training in the Soviet Union, one of their American villages, I was assigned to the United States."

"So we were one of the targets?"

"You were one of Parvus's targets. But I'm not here to penetrate your organization. I'm not schooled in Cabala, nor do I speak Aramaic."

The committee members looked at one another.

"Sure. I figured it out for myself. In investigating my prime target, and in doing other jobs, bits fell together and finally began

378

to form a pattern. You know how it goes. I began to see, dimly, I'll admit, and using a lot of guesswork, the shape of your organization and its operational pattern. And while you didn't seem to be a high-priority item for Skuratov, Parvus was, for some reason, very interested."

"So you want asylum from who? The KGB?"

"Yes, from Skuratov, but also from Parvus, organization I penetrated and ended up joining wholeheartedly."

"All this mystery."

"Please bear with me."

"And why are you running away?"

"To keep alive. Nothing more."

"You're not coming to us on ideological grounds?"

"I'll level with you. I've seen too much. I don't think I ever had any ideology. It was a job. Anyway, committment and belief is hard to keep, working for the KGB, or the CIA for that matter, or any organization of this nature. The CIA, the KGB, they need one another to perpetuate their empires. That's all there is to it. It's just that I'm on the run and I want to live to be a moderate old age, preferably here in this country. Get married. Have children.

"You slow down. I have the usual skills, but they're useless as you get older. I also have administrative skills . . . but I was never in a position to do the requisite bureaucratic infighting. Unlike in this country, you don't end up teaching at a college, or working as a journalist when you retire. What should I become? A courier with a small apartment and a large family in Kiev or Moscow? But now there are people looking to dispose of me. Well, you know how it is. You can't go to them and say, at some point, 'I've had it. Enough. I'm ready to retire.' They kill you. That's retirement?"

"In short, you're looking for the highest bidder?"

"I don't have very rich tastes."

"What can you give us?"

Oprichnik laughed. "I can give you Skuratov. I can give you a Hungarian technician who *inadvertantly* blew your operation and led me to you. I can tell you what's going to happen in the next few days—Cuba, missiles, the whole thing. I can give you someone named Richard Aquilino, the man who heard too much, to whom we listened in to, and upon whom much hinges. I can give you the ultimate plum, Parvus."

No one moved a muscle.

"I'm beginning to hit pay dirt? I can sense it. You're beginning to read me? Parvus. Mr. Parvus himself, Alexander Helphand, and part of his network, called, in this case, the Parvus Game, also some of his associates in high places, a lawyer, for instance, called Edward Kelley, very highly connected around the world, yes indeedy, and a man named Keats, who ran the operation to run Richard Aquilino, and a woman named Laura Geroyavich . . ."

"A Russian?"

"No, an American."

"Parvus is alive?"

"Oh, he sure is. Very much so. He's very old, but he's built out of iron, that man. He's alive, all right. I mean, he's not immortal, but he's still kicking and planning and organizing, and there are plenty of others to carry on the work he began . . . oh, in the 1890s."

"Let us think this over," Samael Aquilino said. "Why don't you wait for us upstairs? It will take some time."

The third man to report was Ziggy.

"You heard all that?"

"Yes."

"How does it correlate with what you know?"

"It fits."

"And what is the message Richard is bringing to the President?"

"It must be something like what's going to happen in the near future. This plan of Parvus's, their group, and a great danger. Something directed against the President. It also tells us why the President wants Bolshakov to do things in this way. But Richard won't tell me what it is he has to say to the President in person, and why he wants to do it that way."

"You can't recall him?"

"I've tried. He's dropped out. Tarzan is following him, but he avoids the safe places we tell him to go. He's become his own man. He doesn't trust anyone. He might take a chance and try and surface anywhere the President might be in his campaign itinerary. We don't have much time. As I figure it, the cutoff point is on October 14."

"Why the fourteenth?"

"Because by that time, certain evidence—aerial photographs of missile emplacements in Cuba—will be delivered to the President. I don't know how they did it, but the first photos weren't taken by a U-2; they were gotten some other way and inserted into the proper channels, appearing to come from their surveillance. Then the CIA confirmed them. Already our informants tell us that they have started to print typescript for the military maps . . . which means they're preparing for an invasion or an air strike."

"What about the woman?"

"Carol Rothschild? The doctor? I don't know. They were running a complicated mind-altering project at the hospital, part of a deeper and more extensive national project, highly secret. She was part of it. We always thought their escape was too easy, even with the help you gave us. In all of this, Richard is the wild card."

"All right, Ziggy, why don't you wait too. We have to talk this over."

The committee was silent for ten, fifteen minutes. They sipped tea, gulped coffee, made fresh tea, and another pot of coffee. Some pastries and coffee were delivered to those waiting in the other rooms. The air had become thick with smoke. And yet, they all knew what was on one another's minds. They had worked together too long.

"You know, this is work for younger people," one of the men said, his hair utterly white.

"I'm not happy with the idea of doing their work for them," the second man said. He was bald. His nose was broken. He had false teeth, the originals knocked out leading a strike so many years ago in Poland. But his body was still strong.

The third man looked like an ascetic. He was, in public life, a language expert; he spoke twenty of them quite well. He was a chain smoker, lighting one cigarette from another.

The woman, Lilly Aquilino, stirred. She lifted her cup and banged it down. "Come on. Time's passing. Make decisions."

"By the time we get a complete story, it will already be two

381

new stories past the original one," the man with the white hair said.

"I lost a father and grandfather in the struggle." This statement was a reference to the Aquilinos' son.

"But your sons know nothing about your work, and have become doctors," Lilly said.

"Actually, dentists. It's one of my great disappointments in life."

They all laughed. "It's my daughter who's the doctor, but even she is only a PhD., in comparative literature. You wouldn't believe how many times the CIA has approached her . . ."

"It never occurred to you to have her infiltrate them for us?" Lilly said.

"You're trying to spare us," Samael said. "I am punished for my pride, for trying to play two games at once with myself, my wife, my son. Being afraid to train my son to follow in the family business." He smiled. "I trained him indirectly to be one of us, but with peculiar results.

"We all know the story of the *golem*. The clay brought to life by words. And what are intelligence agents but *golems?* Activated by partial truths. Semblances of truths, and falsehoods that people take for truths. *Emeth.* Truth. But what is truth? The people, the ordinary people, they are as clay. Life and words have been breathed into them. The wise ones duplicate the work of God, creation and activate certain clays and bring them to life with this truth. There are many versions of the legend. In one, the word *emeth* is written on the forehead of the clay shaped as a man. It then comes to life or, as we say in our business, he is activated. But if we question what is truth, then many kinds of truth, many kinds of *emeth* can awaken many kinds of golems to life. My son. Our son. This *golem;* I made him that.

"In another and more sophisticated version of the legend, perhaps what we can call the coding, or cryptographic version, combining the sacred letters, or numerical equivalents, with the secret names of God, is imparted in a ritual and in a sacred dance. The *golem* comes to life. According to the legend, if the ritual is not done correctly, then the spell doesn't work. But, on the other hand, if there is, as the teaching has it, the possibility of a plurality of worlds containing a plurality of truths, put together by differ-

382

ent combinations of the sacred letters, then the clay we would wake can be woven by many rituals into many worlds. American, Russian, French, multinational corporate worlds, partly American, British, French, etc., and against their own countries of origin. Who knows what world my son lives in now, but he does live, armed with a truth, but it may not be the truth we believe in, yet it will have an effect in the world as if it were the only truth.

"Yes, the intelligence agent is indeed the *golem.* Our wisdom, passed on, in many forms, into many teachings. Combined with Gnostic, hermetic and secret Christian teachings, it found its way into the Gospel According to St. John. 'In the beginning was the word and the word was made flesh.' There is also another verse from that Gospel. '. . . and the truth shall set ye free.' This is the motto of the CIA, not lightly chosen. Free from what? Free from death, nothingness, the great anarchic scramble of pre-existent letters, or numbers, freed through knowledge, truth, *emeth.* But St. John promises the Apocalypse, just as my son foresaw it. The Apocalypse brings the ultimate ignorance . . . and so the CIA are the bringers of the ultimate ignorance . . . and so the CIA are the bringers of death, and that's the price for their life. The KGB displays the emblem of a sword cutting a snake. The dragon. St. George and the dragon. The serpent. The snake is life. It is the male principle, the bringer of life, light, knowledge, revolution. So the KGB is also for ignorance and death.

"Now, it was by the bringing of knowledge, by the recombination of the words, it was Marx who brought truth and began to breathe life into the clay . . . the proletariat . . . and this too follows the legend.

"If I believed in sin," Samael said, "I would say I sinned. I made a great mistake. By not talking directly, by whispering the teachings into my son's ears according to our ancient practice, by telling him of his role *indirectly,* he was recruited. I indeed said the letters and the numbers, and played the combinations, as required, but I reversed everything and they came up scrambled. He woke to life, armed by *emeth,* not on his forehead, but behind his forehead. But others were also putting other 'truths' into his mind. It is said that the *golem* is the servant of his creator; and I suppose, in modern parlance, the creator is the case officer.

383

"The *golem* has developed dangerous powers. My son is a patriot. *A patriot.* He grows stronger from day to day and in order to keep him from overpowering the members of the household, he must be returned to dust and ignorance by removing or erasing the *aleph* from his forehead . . . leaving *meth,* death. Deactivation.

"You want to spare me, us, Lilly and I.

"Lilly and I aren't sure what it is that Richard has to impart. I suggest that we agree to help Bolshakov, in case whatever matter Richard wants to deliver, some plot against the President, can throw the balance off, nullify everything we agree to do. We can't take a chance. Let's take a vote on it. Lilly and I, we have to abstain, of course."

They nodded. The three of them would vote.

CHAPTER 51

LATE the night of October 10 in Baltimore, frustrated by his inability to find a way of setting up a foolproof meeting, Richard decided that he would have to agree to a meeting with Kennedy on less than ideal terms. He would have to put himself into the hands of others. He would arrange a meeting and get Ziggy to monitor the channels to see if he was being set up.

The President was going to be in New York on the 11th, making campaign films for television. Then he was going to swing west and north. After another talk, Kennedy thought he might cut part of his itinerary short and fly back to New York on the afternoon of the fourteenth and they would meet at the Carlyle. "All you have to do is to call me up there, late in the afternoon, and tell my operator, or whoever answers the phone, that it's Richard. I'll leave word for you to be put through to me right away. Then we'll arrange the meeting any way you want it, within certain limits."

Richard agreed. The fourteenth.

Bolshakov had begun to transmit to Khrushchev. He sent messages from Kennedy through the Russian Embassy. But at the same time, he used the channel opened for him by the old Comintern Cabalistic and commercial network. Bolshakov was never told how it was done. He had no need to know. All he had to do was to get to a different telephone, preferably a street phone booth, dial a certain number—different every time—and begin talking.

His message was translated into the ancient Cabalistic Aramaic. Then it was sent out by shortwave radio, different sections sent using a variety of frequencies . . . a primitive sort of scrambler. The transmission was low powered, sent skipping across the Atlantic, relayed from cargo ship to cargo ship, into the Mediterranean, finally picked up in ports in Sicily, Turkey, Russia. Odessa. In port, the message was written down—still in Aramaic—and carried to Moscow.

If one knew in advance exactly what frequencies were going to be used, and in what sequence, one could have monitored the entire message. But what would the monitoring agent then have? A communication in Aramaic, of highly mystical import, which only a student both of Aramaic and Cabala might unravel. Even then, what would he have? A song to God, part of an incantation, an interpretation of the end of the world when all history, emanating out of a blinding light, reversed itself and went back into its pre-Creational darkness. The sign of a god, one god among many possible gods, who created one of many possible worlds, mentioned in one possible Old Testament out of many Old Testaments, each suited for different possible worlds, the many secret and the many public worlds, created and destroyed, out of the primal scramble of letters-numbers, which pre-exist everything, and out of which the material worlds are assembled, grow, live, decline, break up and return again to the everlasting anarchy of scrambled letters-numbers. In order to understand it the scholar would have had to think of it as an intelligence or diplomatic code or cryptogram.

The message, duplicated, flowed toward Moscow through a variety of smuggling routes; from Palermo, Sofia, Odessa, Istanbul. To Soviet Georgia, until it was finally hand-delivered to Moscow by black marketeers who flew every day bringing in fresh vegetables, bribing all the way.

Eleven men assembled in an apartment in Moscow. The eleventh man read the message out loud at a prescribed pace. The others began to do a Hasidic dance. Included in the message was a certain number which announced what dance was to be danced. They also sang. To the outsider it was a song and dance of holy ecstasy to God, but in fact the men were a human decoding machine. The rhythm and pattern of the dance broke the message into blocks of letters. The pattern of singing drowned out certain decoy portions of the encryption. When the dance was complete, the new message stood out in clear Aramaic. Now it had to be translated into Russian. The final message was dead-dropped near the Kremlin where it was picked up by the contact between Bolshakov and Khrushchev.

Thus the bargaining positions between Kennedy and Khrushchev flowed between Moscow and Washington. It was clumsy but effective, almost foolproof. And it was faster than one would have thought; the transmission from beginning to end never took more than twenty-four hours. And it was as Bolshakov suspected. There *was* a difference between the messages he transmitted through these two channels. Someone was subtly altering the messages that were going through the Soviet Embassy. He felt better. They were saving the world from madmen.

The next thing Richard did was to telephone Ziggy and tell him what he had done. Richard wanted backup—Ziggy's network to monitor the security frequencies, police, FBI, Secret Service, to determine if he was being led into a trap.

"At last," Ziggy told Marvin after hanging up. "Some action. Help me downstairs. I have a phone call to make."

Marvin helped Ziggy down to the street and they found a phone booth. Ziggy called up Samael. "He's coming to New York to meet the President on the fourteenth. The Carlyle Hotel. What now?"

"What Kennedy should know has been debated at length. We know the content of Bolshakov's messages so far between Kennedy and Khrushchev. We think there's a chance the crisis will be a complete fraud. Theatre. Kennedy will emerge looking very strong, heroic and determined in front of the world. They'll be horse trading. They both want maximum political advantages in their own countries. In effect, Khrushchev is helping Kennedy get elected by playing the villain. The price is the removal of American missiles from Turkey and Italy. India definitely passes over to the Soviet sphere of influence; there will be no invasion or attack on Cuba. A complete sellout—a recarving of the world.

"This is an unexampled opportunity. A direct voice in the President's decision-making. Since we don't know what it is that Richard is going to say to him, whatever he does say might tip the balance in a direction we don't want it to take—either war, or a peace engineered by Parvus."

"I can't just *tell* Richard what to say."

"And do you propose to wait until he comes to political wisdom? There's no more time. You have to tell him, Ziggy, the next time he establishes contact. But you must keep our name out of it."

"How is Lilly taking it?"

"She's not happy, but she's a good soldier. Of course we're going to do everything possible to save him. But she understands the risk."

"And if he doesn't listen to me?"

"He doesn't listen to you."

Ziggy could almost see Samael shrugging his shoulders. A death sentence. And how are *you* taking it, he wondered?

Richard and Carol drove at night and made it into New York City just before dawn.

"Doesn't making a decision make you feel better?" Carol said. "We're finally going to meet him."

"I'm going to meet him. It's too dangerous for you."

"Richard, don't you trust me?"

"I trust you, but—"

"Richard."

"All right. You can come along."

"And then we can try to live some kind of normal life."

They were approaching the great glow that was New York, already fading in the sky as dawn came. It was October 11.

They registered in a small hotel in the Thirties, one used mostly by prostitutes. It made Carol feel ill at ease, even though she was relieved to be back in the city.

The first thing Richard did was to place a phone call to Ziggy. It was almost as if Ziggy was sitting by the phone, waiting for him. "Have you established contact yet?"

"Yes."

"How is it going to work?"

"We haven't decided yet, Ziggy. I'm going to get in touch with him on the fourteenth."

"All right, Richard. Now listen carefully to me. I've been thinking about your meeting. Do you really think that some of his top advisors, famous, reputable, important men, the great decision makers, are going to double-cross him and push him toward a war?"

"That's what I heard."

"Richard, think of your position. It's unique in history. You will have a few hours of the President's undivided attention. You are going to be the most important man in history for a few hours. We have to use that meeting—"

"*We?*"

"You. Me. Tarzan. Marvin—"

"Tarzan? Marvin?"

"This is what you have to do."

"Ziggy—"

"Hear me out, Richard. You have to tell the President that Georgi Bolshakov and Khrushchev are double-crossing him. The fact that this secret diplomacy is being practiced, using Bolshakov as a conduit, will be leaked to the world media."

"Who is this Georgi Bolshakov?"

"Just listen to me. What will happen is this. The crisis will begin in about a week. Kennedy thinks, from what you've been telling him, that what will happen is that the United States, that is to say, he himself, will show great determination to withstand nuclear blackmail by the Russians. But at the last moment the Russians will threaten to leak the secret negotiations and use that threat to wring *more* concessions from the Americans. They'll go public and accuse Kennedy of double-crossing them. That Kennedy even held secret negotiations, and possibly made a deal with the Russians, bypassing Congress and his most important advisors, will look very much like treason. The Republicans will sweep the elections, Nixon will win the governorship of California and be in a position to become president in 1964. That is, if Kennedy isn't impeached, or worse."

"But . . ."

"All right. The next question you will get will be 'How do you know this?' Your answer is that you have overheard all of this being planned on the phone. Bolshakov was in place a long time ago, cultivating Bobby Kennedy. Yes, you will say, it was all chaotic, you heard all of this in bits and pieces and you don't know what it means. Let him put it together and figure it out. All you have to do is to drop the names. Especially Bolshakov's."

"Ziggy, what the fuck are you talking about? I never heard that name. None of this is true."

"How do you know the meaning of what you heard? And anyway, the truth has nothing to do with it, Richard. It's the question of how it comes out. It's what we want."

"Ziggy, who is this *we?*"

"I told you. It's the three of us, and it's you, and it's also the people in our network around the country."

"You meant those space fanatics, ham radio operators, telephone nuts? *They* know about international politics? The only one who knows such things is you, Ziggy."

"Richard, you're very young. You never even had a proper education. What the fuck do you know about international affairs?" Ziggy yelled.

Richard was still for a while. "Ziggy, are you working for the Russians?"

"How dare you say such a thing! The people who crippled me? I hate them. You have to trust me. You have to—"

"No! You do it *my* way! Give me the backup. Tell me if you can hear them planning anything on the government frequencies. I can't tell a story like that. It's not true." And he hung up.

While Richard was out, Carol Rothschild telephoned Keats. She could visualize him, tall, blond, concerned, handsome . . . no, beautiful. She had watched his slightly full lips moving and could see them again as she shut her eyes in order to make the call more vivid to her. "We're in New York . . ."

"At last."

"The meeting is on the 14th. It's at the Carlyle."

"You've done a great job and you've saved his life. I might add that you've saved the lives of his parents. What's he going to tell the President?" Keats asked.

"I haven't been able to find out."

"You haven't listened to my question in the right way. The question is rhetorical. What Richard thinks he knows is all nonsense. It's all garbled in his head. After all, how can you listen into literally hundreds of people, talking, to all intents and purposes, a language you don't understand, and make sense of it? He doesn't have the training. We've been working, putting the pieces together, translating raw intelligence into a coherent picture. You need a framework for that and he never had that. He's only an ignorant kid and that makes him dangerous. We have to help him.

"Listen, Carol and listen carefully. What he has to tell the President is that *yes,* he *is* being maneuvered into a confrontation with the Russians over Cuba. That *is* indeed what he heard. The President does not make the decisions by himself. It's just that these people are themselves being manipulated. And who is handling them? The Russians. How? They have put in place a large ring of spies—agents of influence, we call them; they're not, properly speaking, spies—whose task is to influence policy. These people are planted in defense, intelligence, in key corporations —banks, aerospace, defense—and the State Department.

"You would be shocked at how much in American stocks and bonds the Russians hold through dummies. *Especially penetrated —listen to this now, Carol—are a variety of right wing organizations. The superpatriots, such as the Birch Society.* The American intelligence services and the FBI always look toward the Left for spies, so the Russians have taken control of those right wing organizations. It's a brilliant stroke. Now their purpose is to foment a crisis . . . a crisis that may lead to a small war. There's always that danger isn't there? Now if the President rises to the bait, all right, that's what they want to happen. If the President backs down, then they have every motive for pushing the extremists to stage a coup. A right wing coup that will be controlled by Russian agents. The name of the operation—and this too is important, Carol—is called *Parvus.* Remember that name. I know the name of the leader, but I'll tell you this if you can persuade Richard that this is what his information amounts to and this is the message that he must deliver.

"Why? The target is Khrushchev himself. The Russian financial managers have invested so much of their money in American growth stocks; defense and aerospace. Khrushchev is out. *Détente* is over. The stocks go up. If Richard agrees—can I put it that way—I'll tell you more. I'll guide you."

She was confused. "How am I supposed to do that?"

The voice in her ear was purring. "You've heard enough details. Richard told you an awful lot while he was in his psychotic phase. Do you think he knows what he said and in what order? Do you think he understands who links up with whom?"

"You were listening in to us."

"We had to, Carol. To save him. I told you that. He's an innocent who's in far over his head, as you are too. We had to prevent him from falling under the wrong influences. And what's more, Carol, do you think *you're* in a position to assess what Richard was talking about? I'm just putting things in perspective for you.

"Carol, we're almost finished. It's been a nightmare, but once the message is, so to speak, delivered, then you can not only go back to your work, but you'll find that my organization is very grateful. Many doors will be opened to you. You'll have the most astonishing facilities put at your disposal. Assistants. Equipment. Yourself as the head of a lab. And you and Richard will be able to live a complete life, free of worry and danger . . . It will be nice to have a long talk . . . maybe over a dinner . . . get acquainted . . ."

On October 12, Kennedy visited Newark to make campaign speeches. There was a bomb threat, and an air gun was taken away from a child by the police. The police, the FBI and the Secret Service were especially cautious about the Cuban refugee organizations. The Ecumenical Council opened up in Rome. Trouble continued in Mississippi and all through the south. The British shipowners remained adamant about their right to trade with whomever they wanted to, including Cuba, and Sweden balked at what they called a de facto blockade. The *New York Times* editorialized: James Reston wrote a thoughtful little piece on Cuba and Pearl Harbor; an attack on Cuba would appear to the world like a reverse reprise of the Japanese sneak attack, mounted by the Americans.

Keats scheduled an emergency appointment with Mr. Kelley in his office.

"Dear boy . . ." Mr. Kelley began.

"Edward," Keats said, sitting down in what he presumed was the client's chair, across the desk from Mr. Kelley. "I'm afraid I have bad news."

Kelley looked at Keats for a while. "I think I know what you're going to say."

Keats was silent.

"Very well. You're going to tell me that Richard Aquilino cannot be located; that he is going to reach President Kennedy, but with a message that will upset, rather than further, our plans. Is that it?"

"More or less. I have the feeling that Aquilino is inclined, at the present moment, to blame Parvus for all his sufferings and the country's troubles. He's likely to name names, repeat certain delicate conversations, and embroil a lot of Parvus people. Worst of all, I suspect Kennedy will shut his mind to the blandishments of all sides and strike off on his own. This might lead to results we don't really want."

"Such as bombing and invading Cuba?"

"Such as bombing and invading Cuba."

"And you don't know where Aquilino is?" Kelley asked.

"Regretfully not. He's ingenious. All I have is word from a contact in the Secret Service that he will connect . . . in fact, he already has."

"All right, John, you control Aquilino. What's the bottom line? What do you want?"

"A leading policy-making position in Parvus. A hand in the decision making. A high position in the CIA as a cover, a position close to the Presidency, and Holcomb out of the way. Maybe deputy director in charge of clandestine operations. Certainly the handling of funds. I have a few operations of my own in mind. I want to be close to you, Edward, when you meet important leaders."

"What I told you before has no meaning to you?"

"Edward. Stop the mystic bullshit. It's time to stop playing mind games. I'm not going to spend time going through your

393

initiations, getting wisdom slowly. I don't intend to be aged when I reach the pinnacle. I want the crash course."

Keats leaned forward in his chair.

"There's something else I want. Laura."

"Are you sure Laura wants you? And what would you do—settle down domestically? How silly."

"Come on, Edward, do you think I'm the domestic type? I have other plans for the both of us. But first, in order to assure Parvus's well being, I want to come along when you have your meeting with President Kennedy. I want to hear everything that's said. I want you to praise me as the man who unraveled this whole thing from beginning to end and saved my country."

"And Aquilino?"

"At the point where I'm satisfied that what I—we—want is going to happen, that's going to be the moment when Aquilino gets terminated." And Carol Rothschild, he thought.

Kelley sat staring at him.

"Come on, Edward," Keats said, getting up. "Don't look so sour."

CHAPTER 52

ON October 13, a Saturday, the President campaigned in western Pennsylvania where Richard and Carol had just come from. He made whistle stops in McKeesport, Monessen and Pittsburgh, then was on to Indianapolis. He returned to Washington and prepared to go to Buffalo the next day. That night he was told by his brother that the aerial photographs of missile emplacements in Cuba had surfaced, just as Richard had predicted. They would be made public in a day or so. John Kennedy had to act fast before there was a leak. They needed more confirming photographs. More U-2 activity was requested. "Invoke whatever you have to, Bobby. Plug all the leaks. Lean on *all* the media. Lay it on heavy. Issue guidelines about the dissemination of news considered vital to national defense. The DOD is to release nothing. Unofficial sources have to be blocked too. No tales about plans for the employment of strategic or tactical forces, no second-guessing, estimates of U.S. capability for destroying targets, details of U.S. forces, details of command and control systems. . . . I want a curtain of silence."

"They'll scream."

"Let them. As long as they do it after it's over."

"Then what?"

"Well, you might as well begin assembling the National Security Council and that executive committee. We want to be able to go to Congress with a bipartisan *fait accompli.* I'm going to meet with that kid. I'll cut my trip short to Buffalo, come to New York and meet him at the Carlyle."

"Too many people."

"We'll work something out."

The pretense offered to the media for the sudden departure from Buffalo was that certain problems had risen over the Congo-Katanga issue again. The President had to consult with Adlai Stevenson. Kennedy also arranged to meet with Mr. Kelley and brief him on his mission to Mr. Khrushchev. With Richard's missing pieces and the initiatives he had set in motion through Bolshakov, and with Mr. Kelley and his principals as insurance, the President would be able to handle whatever contingency arose. He was reasonably sure now that he would be able to get some mileage out of the crisis.

On the flight back to New York, Laura was sitting next to him on the plane. She told him, "I'm getting tired of this moving around."

"We'll have a few hours in New York. Why don't you come back to Washington with me?"

"I don't want to. I like New York. Everyone's boring in Washington."

"We'd have more time together."

"And what do I do, sit around and wait in some little house for you?"

"I would get you an appointment on my staff."

"And we have sex with the Secret Service looking on? No thanks."

"You're becoming an obsession with me."

"Pull an Edward VIII for me."

He laughed.

"You see, darling, it's not true love."

"But in the meantime, it's going to have to do. You know, I can have you detained."

"Without due process?"

"I can have you . . . terminated."

"That's life."

CHAPTER 53

A long shriek came floating up faintly from somewhere below. It went on for a minute before breaking into a cackling laugh. Richard and Carol looked at one another. Where did it come from? "What kind of place is this?" Richard asked. They were on the eighth floor of the Madison Avenue Psychiatric Hospital, across the street from the Carlyle Hotel, waiting for the President. He had seen Laura on the street again, walking into the Carlyle. Crazy premonition generated out of torment and drugs, when they were chasing him? If Laura was with the President, then it was war. His inner prevision had been right. He said nothing to Carol. He no longer trusted her. Who was the girl who had been killed in his loft? A stranger?

Carol was in a state of excitement. They were actually going to meet the President. It was all true. What a strange place to meet. She had imagined a palatial suite at the Carlyle; a movie dream. Her feelings about Richard were changing again. She felt warmer now. She felt she had helped in this enormous undertaking. "It's a place for the rich to dry out," she said. "From drinking, drugs. It's very discreet. Psychiatrically speaking, it has a bad reputation. They're very practically oriented. Use a lot of drugs, vitamins. It's been rumored that they use shock therapy too . . . and I've even heard of lobotomies. I've never been there."

It made Richard nervous. He had had enough of psychiatric hospitals.

They were waiting in a suite; three rooms. The apartment was ordinary but the furnishings were obviously expensive. Tables, sideboards, bookcases, leather-inlaid coffee tables, the wood giving off a rich, red-brown sheen. The curtains, made of heavy brocaded green stuff, were drawn across the windows. There was statuary and paintings. Real paintings.

"Not *this* apartment. It's a safe house," Richard said. "The whole building above the fifth floor is made up of safe houses, rented out, kept furnished and stocked with food and liquor, kept empty for people to hole up in. Spies. Executives with a need for privacy. Someone wants to get laid secretly . . . a boy . . . a girl . . . or more . . ."

"Richard!"

"You don't think important people have those tastes? The rich know how to live, don't they, Carol? Not like all those people out there."

"What people? Where?"

"In the streets. Where we came from in Pennsylvania. The ordinary slobs. They don't know about conspiracies. They live their lives, worry about bills, think about their problems; maybe now and then they worry about total annihilation."

The faint cackle-shriek continued with piercing regularity. A call for help from another planet. "DTs. I'd hate to see what he's seeing," Richard said. Maybe I'm seeing worse, he thought: I did. "Where the fuck is he? He's late."

"Richard!"

Earlier that afternoon, Richard made the final arrangements to meet the President. He decided after two days of indecision and torment. He would take a chance and do it on Kennedy's terms. He telephoned the Carlyle on the morning of the fourteenth, asked for the President, was asked who he was. Richard gave his name and was put through to an aide. The aide told Richard not to come to the Carlyle directly but to go across the street to a place called the Madison Avenue Psychiatric Hospital on the corner of Madison and Seventy-sixth Street. "Just walk in the front door. We'll be watching for you, covering you. We've been told what you look like." Richard was to arrive at eight o'clock, go to the eighth floor and wait. The President would come to see him as close to eight as he could. "Don't be afraid. It's a safe house," the aide told him. "You'll be alone?"

"No. There's going to be a woman with me."

"Who's that?"

"Her name is Dr. Carol Rothschild. She's a doctor. She's been sort of taking care of me."

"What's the matter?"

"Hey, listen . . ."

"All right. Just remember. Eight. Don't be late."

It was all over. In some ways, although he felt as though he had complete control of himself for the first time, Richard had been going through another kind of hell for the past two days. This hell was indecision; too much conflicting knowledge. It began with Ziggy's instructions. Mention Bolshakov. Say it's a communist trap. He had denied—when he was in the hospital—that he was an agent, or being run. Now he didn't know. The hell was compounded by Carol. Mention Parvus; say it's a Presidential trap.

When he got back to the hotel after talking to Ziggy, Carol began to act as if she had missed him dreadfully. She was affectionate. She hadn't been that way for days now. He was about to tell her what Ziggy said, but she began to get him excited. They had almost torn one another's clothes off and made love.

Drenched with sweat, spent, relaxed, lying on the bed, Carol began to talk. She had been thinking. True, she had been abstracted, distant, even cold for the last few days. Partly she put it down to being out of her environment. Partly there were other reasons. Fear. Guns. Danger. Being on the run. But the major reason was that her mind had been working on the puzzle Richard had presented. She began to rehearse for Richard the many things they had talked about, and asked, what was it that Richard had *really* heard? She remembered everything he had said when he had been at his most disturbed. Some things he was sure he had never said. The whole pattern was beginning to make sense to her, she said, and scrambled Richard's pattern. "I went over the notes again and again. It was a jigsaw puzzle, but then that's the way dreams or the mind of the psychotic work, and you have been through very bad times, drugged . . . I tried one way of

399

putting together what you talked about, and then another, and still another. But each time I came up with a picture, dear, something was wrong. Then this evening, while you were out, I saw it." And then Carol proceeded to give Richard a coherent version, Keats's version, of what she thought he had heard. Parvus. Agents of influence in important strategic positions, aides manipulating their bosses, penetration of America's right wing, collaboration . . .

Parvus? Had he ever heard that name? No. He was sure. He had never heard that name mentioned. She was glowing now, relaxed from the efforts of sex, warm, triumphant, having overcome the puzzles that tormented Richard, imparting love and a solution. Parvus. Parvus. She mentioned the name over and over again as if trying to drive it into his head. And then she made love to him again. Had he heard the name? Maybe.

Something was wrong. Ziggy and Carol were both lying to him. But instead of getting tense, Richard's body began to relax completely. He was calling on something inside of him. He felt each block of muscles yield, a relaxation deeper than the tiredness that comes after sex. Beneath it all there was a kind of alertness. He was detached and watching. Time slowed up so that each word, each event, left a space and time between the fragments . . . time to send feelers into his memory, time to sift through vast amounts of material . . . Ziggy. Carol. They were both lying to him. That's why it had been so easy to escape from the hospital. It had been a setup.

"Richard, are you listening to me?"

"Ummm . . ." he said.

"You're not falling asleep."

"No, I'm not."

"Does what I said make sense?"

He was drifting into a trance. How had the notion of reaching President Kennedy even gotten into his mind in the first place? His senses were now acute, sensing better, beyond ordinary eyes and ears. She was lying to him now. She hadn't before. Someone had gotten to her. All the "theys" were trying to use him to deliver messages to Kennedy. A war of conflicting messages. How many sets of "they" were there? He heard Carol, talking, snuggling, stroking his body, persuading. There had been a change in her. Her caresses were now instrumental, persuasive, and she was being excited by his yielding.

Tap into yourself. Beyond the short-term memory, the babble of voices and conversations, he was getting deeper into himself, to the long-term memory and beyond that to the memory stored up in his body by his fathers. A tangle of neurons, a collection of enzymes, labyrinthine corridors that lead to the true princess, the inner intelligence. His ancestors had the magical ability to smell out lies and evil. Evil lay like the spoor of another man on Carol's body. He tasted it. The blond man in the black armor. No, the blond man hadn't fucked Carol, not in the ordinary way. His seductive voice had penetrated her body.

He felt a touch on his penis. He opened his eyes and saw Carol, but as if from a great distance. She had bent down and was kissing his penis. Don't yield, he thought. Stay in this blissful calm, and remember. Her lips murmured love, and they kissed with love, but they transmitted poison. Lies.

Everyone was interpreting the conversations for him. Everyone was trying to turn him into an instrumentality, a telephone, a conduit, trying to push his buttons, using him, using him, controlling him. With the information he now had he could spin a thousand variations of which only one was the true one.

He woke in a while. Carol was asleep. He got quietly out of bed and looked down at her sleeping there. Her naked body did not move him now. He wrote a note saying he was going out for a walk. It was almost dawn of the thirteenth of October, Saturday. Tomorrow he would be meeting with Kennedy at last. Now he knew what he had to say.

And he was out in the grimy morning streets. The sky was gray. Almost no one in the streets. He began to walk. At first he strolled randomly. Maybe he should just walk away from the whole thing? Forget it. Leave them all. No. He couldn't do that. So much depended on him. He thought of the countryside in Pennsylvania, and the people. He thought of the trip he had taken cross-country. Cities and plains, the desert areas, the West Coast. He thought of the network of innocents Ziggy had assembled. Ziggy had made spies out of all of them without their knowledge. And Carol? Was she his control, or was she an innocent too?

He was walking now, still casually and without purpose, northward, walking up Fourth Avenue till it turned into Park Avenue South. He approached Grand Central Station. He looked at the buildings, watching the few people in the streets. Would he see them again after tomorrow? He passed under the overpass and ramp that led up to and around Grand Central Station and underneath the Vanderbilt Building. And then he was out on Park Avenue. New buildings going up and old buildings being torn down. Park Avenue and Wall Street, symbols of extraordinary wealth. And beneath his feet, now and then, he could hear the rumble of trains coming in and going out of Grand Central Station. Tunnels. Tunnels under tunnels. A vast complex. Gloom and trains and train headlights, snaking here and there, backing and filling, coupling and uncoupling. You could wander around down there for years.

He walked up to the Fifties and past. Here were the stately apartment houses and some mansions. He realized now what he was doing. He was going on a scouting mission. The castle is the Carlyle Hotel. The maiden. The princess. Kennedy. Ignorant. Tricked. Knights. Armor. Arthur, the cuckolded. Camelot. The fucked king. Was Kennedy still there, or had he departed on his campaign swing again? It was a symbol of their chase, always missing one another. The trains rumbled under his feet, bouncing across the switches, the metal joints on the street corners shaking. Still too early for the people in these great apartment houses to come out on the streets. The rich slept late. Should he take a chance and appear before the President at a time when he doesn't expect . . . Become invisible. Go into the Carlyle without anyone seeing him? How had those old-time magicians his father used to tell him about become invisible? He could never think beyond the real, the material. Obviously those magicians had found tunnels into the interiors of the castles, appeared to go through walls. You could fake it with radar. You could fake where you seemed to be but you couldn't fake yourself . . . or could you? There must have been secret passageways for escapes. There had to be a way out, and in, in case of a siege. Trapdoors. Tunnels. Tunnels everywhere in New York. Here and there he saw black and yellow signs with the letter *S*. Bomb shelters. Shelter from an atom bomb? That was a laugh.

What do you look like, he asked himself? He stopped and looked into a plate glass doorway to an apartment building. Windbreaker. Pants. Shirt. Quite ordinary. Tall. Black hair. You look like a messenger boy, he told himself. He saw a face peering at him. The doorman behind the glass staring at him suspiciously. Fuck you, he thought and raised his middle finger out of his clenched fist. You could never just walk into the Carlyle looking like that, he told himself. He was now in the Sixties. Fool, he thought. He kept looking at his image in spite of the doorman. He brushed his hair back and straightened his clothes and kept walking. Carol, Parvus, and a network of spies and agents. If he presented that version to the President, what would it mean? Peace? Why did whoever was controlling Carol want that message passed on? Ziggy, Bolshakov, the Russian betrayal, the news of Kennedy's secret diplomacy leaked to the media. If he presented that message, did it mean war? Why did whoever was controlling Ziggy want *that* message passed on? Or was Ziggy his own control? And what was the truth? The truth? The truth? Did it matter? Get out of here. Just leave. Leave them all. It was not Carol or Ziggy's truth; he was arriving at the truth and he hoped it was right.

He crossed Seventy-second Street. Broad street. It was almost like crossing a border into the land of danger. The atmosphere changed, but Richard couldn't have said how. Watchful eyes all around him. Plainclothes cops, Feds, no doubt, Secret Service. He looked up. Did someone withdraw from the ramparts of a building? Sniper? Be careful of how you walk now, appear ordinary. Ordinary? He was.

Get to Seventy-sixth Street and turn left toward Madison Avenue. And here there were more visible manifestations of security. The guards in and out of uniform ringing the sacred body. Camelot in a modern hotel. Wooden police barriers. Cars. Loungers. Strollers. Uniformed police. People standing around waiting for the sacred body to appear . . . perhaps autographs. If you're stopped, what is it you're supposed to be doing, he asked himself. He saw the sharper-dressed young men with icy eyes. You're on your way to the park, that's what you're doing, he told himself. That's the story. Apartment houses with their ubiquitous *S* signs. The rumble of trains underneath. He turned left and began to

403

walk toward Central Park. He would bypass the hotel and see what it was he could see.

He was halfway down the block between Park and Madison when he realized something. He had the pistol stuck beneath his windbreaker! What if someone stops you? He kept walking without a break and hoped they couldn't sense a change in his attitude. Stupid! Sweating? Keep walking. Control emotions.

He made four passes before he saw something he had been seeing all morning; a way into the Carlyle castle, or, for that matter, a way out. He walked west, past Madison to Fifth, and then turned north and walked east to Seventy-seventh and Park, turned south to Seventy-fifth and walked back to Madison Avenue and bypassed the Carlyle on Madison. He saw Laura but controlled himself. He hoped she didn't see him. He didn't dare try another bypass. The tunnels. The shelters. That's what he saw! The complex of bomb shelters and normal tunnels that burrowed beneath the city and interconnected! There *must* be a tunnel that leads into the Carlyle from the New York Central tracks. After all, where and how were you going to evacuate people to in the event of a bombing?

He went back east, got the Lexington Avenue train, went down to Forty-second Street, walked through the Grand Central complex, and began to find his way onto the tracks leading north.

"I think he just passed by," the man reported to Keats. "Fits the description."

"You just keep your people in readiness. He's slated to contact the President tomorrow, but he might just make a pass." He turned to Holcomb. "It's happening. He's coming up from ground."

"We'll be ready."

"And Skuratov?"

"He and his people are around. How are we going to know when the meet will take place?"

"The good doctor. She'll let us know."

"Is she going along?"

"She's ours. It's not going to be easy to get Skuratov and his people that close. The place will be swarming with security."

"There might be shooting. You should warn her, Keats."
Keats shrugged.

It was late afternoon. Richard was coming back to the hotel where he and Carol were staying. He stepped into a phone booth and called Ziggy. "All right," he told Ziggy. "I've been thinking it over. You're right."

"Richard, I can't tell you how happy I am that you see it this way."

"I don't understand it, but then, what do I know? Maybe I heard it all wrong. I thought it was his *own* people who were plotting against him. Bolshakov? How did you get that name?"

"Richard, we've put together one of the finest listening posts the world ever saw. And they're all people like ourselves. People on the outside. Outlaws, renegades. I'm telling you that there isn't a move they can make without our hearing it. We're listening in by every device thought of. I mean, we know what's happening all over. Whether Kennedy likes it or not, there *are* Americans who want Cuba back. And there's the Russians. They need a test of strength and will, but they have to load the dice in their favor. We picked up—get this, you'll love it—a transmission from the Russian Embassy. It was this guy Bolshakov receiving his instructions. Play Kennedy along. Every contact he makes with Khrushchev plants a nail in his political coffin. But the beautiful thing is that we didn't pick up the transmission directly, but through a tap the FBI is running on the Russians. We heard it all."

"In *Russian,* Ziggy?"

"In Russian. I talk Russian."

"Not in code?"

"No. That's the sign that the fix is in. They're transmitting in clear. *In clear.* You know what that means?"

"No."

"You transmit in clear for three reasons. The first is when you're panicked and have to move fast; you don't have the time to encode. The second is because you're careless or sloppy, or think you can get away with it once in a while. *The third is because you want someone to hear you.* Richard, why don't you come over and I'll explain it to you . . ."

405

"No, Ziggy. I know enough now. I think it's better. I'm feeling paranoid. I don't trust anything or anyone. When I listened in they found me, right?"

"Yes."

"Supposing they're on to *you?*"

"That's impossible."

"Listen, when you broadcast those tapes and overrode "The Ed Sullivan Show," you think you didn't get them to hunting? I don't want to take any chances, not when I'm about to do it. I'll connect right after I've had my interview with Kennedy . . ."

"Richard . . ."

Richard hung up.

The President was at a party on October 14. It was on the floor above the Presidential Suite in the Carlyle. It was getting raucous. The rooms in which the party was being held were perpetually rented by a holding company that owned a number of major Hollywood studios. People were getting tipsy, laughing. There were politicians, bureaucrats, advisors, diplomats, stars and starlets. If things continued this way, it would end in a drunken rout. The only sober people around were the Secret Service agents. Someone was playing a piano. Men and women were drifting off to bedrooms. But there was one bedroom they couldn't go into without permission. There were two guards in front of it and the President was seated inside.

Mr. Kelley was shown in. He was accompanied by two people, a man named Keats and a man named Churchman, who was Mr. Kelley's political advisor; his secretary of state, so to speak. Churchman was a banker. Kennedy wondered if he had time to go out and spend a little time with Laura. She was outside having a good time. She was becoming an obsession with him. She had been with him in Baltimore, New York, Buffalo, Pittsburgh . . . Was he falling in love with her? No. He couldn't leave. Mr. Kelley was here. Couldn't keep a man like Kelley waiting. He was an emissary of what was practically a sovereign state whose parts were all over the world and whose capitol shifted with its capital.

Kelley shook the President's hand. "It's an honor, John," he said.

No "Mr. President?" It irked Kennedy. "Edward." He almost

said "Mr. Kelley" but he remembered: *he* was the President, not Kelley.

"This is a trusted and highly valued associate of mine, John Keats. And this is Emil Churchman, *my* security advisor."

The President nodded. "Why don't you sit down." Kelley sat across the coffee table from the President, about four feet away. The others sat to the side, one on the bed. A secretary was taking notes. "You sent for me?" Mr. Kelley asked.

"No one sends for Mr. Kelley, do they? You *request* Mr. Kelley to appear . . ."

"Mr. President, Jack, I'm always honored to serve my country and the Presidency. What can I do for you?"

Kennedy noted the way Kelley put it; "the Presidency," not "the President." He glanced at the others.

Kelley interpreted the look. "These are close and trusted associates of mine. Their discretion is a byword in the international community. Nothing that is said here will ever be repeated outside of the precincts of this room."

Kennedy laughed. "Edward, once again the country needs the services of someone extremely well-connected like yourself. You know the Premier of the Soviet Union?"

"We're not, as they say, kissing cousins, but . . . he's a perspicacious and progressive man."

"It's a delicate mission; so delicate that many close to me don't even know of it."

"Jack, I'd appreciate it if this were off the record. You understand. I've never courted the limelight. I'd rather not crop up as a subject of someone's memoirs in years to come."

At Kennedy's nod the secretary got up and left. "Your modesty . . ."

"Come on, Jack. Cut the shit and let's get down to cases. You want me to go to Moscow and see Khrushchev. You and the Premier want to know what's going to happen when the shit hits the fan. You want to handle this crisis so you get your Congress elected and come out looking good. That's it, isn't it?" They looked at one another.

"You're well informed."

"That's why I'm hired. I and some of the people I represent are not sure we want your reelection to happen in two years. What's in it for us? I mean the economy is stagnating. The securities market is in a slump. Investment money is just not flowing. Tariffs are too high. As for taxes . . . Too much government, John. Too much nationalism. The barriers and borders have to open up."

A burst of laughter came floating through the door.

"Well, that's going to play hell with my social programs. But if you don't help me, who're you going to get yourself? Dick Nixon? Jesus Christ."

"Everyone sells Nixon short. He understands the way things work. He's flexible. He's come up the hard way."

"Fuck him, that creep. I would also want him to lose in California."

"You shouldn't let personal considerations get in the way of statesmanship. He'd love to be sitting where you're sitting right now, riding out his seventh crisis."

"He'd bomb the shit out of Cuba and incinerate the world."

"Don't underrate him. He'd come out with a Russian contract for Pepsi, concessions for Chase, and sell them that turkey, the TFX bomber too."

"He has no style. Your mission . . ."

"Before we get to the mission, I want your agreement in principle on several items. *Détente.* Business. We win the war through business. An end to the strategic materials ban to the east. Loans to the Soviet Union, from us and from the Europeans for development and joint ventures. No invasion of Cuba. Similar *détente* in the Far East. In turn the Cubans will stop proselytizing for revolution throughout Latin America. Accelerated decolonialization in Africa with gradual autonomy for *all* localities. A gradual phasing out of the embargo, allowances for foreign investments in American industry, even permitting controlling interests. A movement toward a world standard currency and a loosening of currency flow . . ."

"And if I find that unacceptable . . ."

"Jack, there's lots of money to be made; for you, for your family . . ."

"There's my country . . ."

"Jack, Jack, we're not in front of the public now . . . Perhaps a decent interval, another President, and then, why just then it might be Bobby's turn . . . Camelot, Jack, Camelot. Camelot and

King Arthur stood for order, peace to a country riven by factions and robber bands . . .”

"All right. I'm inclined . . .”

"Now a second matter. You'll soon be going across the street to meet someone at the Madison Avenue Psychiatric Hospital?”

"You know about that too?”

"People will talk. We're all concerned about you. We don't think that a President should descend to talking to agents far down the line. It's undignified. Richard Aquilino, that's the name, isn't it? Before you go rushing off, I think you should listen to something Keats here has to say about that. He's quite a man and he has quite a story to tell. We owe it all to him and his alertness.”

"How long's this going to take?” Kennedy asked.

"As for whoever it is, she'll wait. And Aquilino . . . a little delay might save you a very long wait indeed . . . in the grave.”

In his reconnaissance of the previous day, Richard discovered that a tunnel did run from the tracks of the New York Central to the Carlyle. There were many other tunnels branching off. Many escape routes. When the meeting place had been changed to the Madison Avenue Psychiatric Hospital, Richard found there were three ways to get there. Through the front door, through a tunnel that connected the Madison Psychiatric with the Carlyle and the tunnel to the railroad tracks. There were three staircases leading up and one bank of elevators. One of the staircases led from the subbasement to the tunnels.

They were getting fidgety. The President was a half hour late. They heard noise in the hallway. Richard got up to look. He opened the door. He saw a man standing at one end of the hallway. The man turned in his direction and put his hand into his jacket pocket. Richard raised his eyebrows. The man nodded. Richard returned the nod and came back into the room, closing the door behind him. "I think he's on his way. One of his Secret Service types is out in the hallway.”

"Then we're finally safe,” Carol said.

But Richard wasn't so sure.

Keats, a tall, slender blond man, leaned forward and started to talk. "The man whom you've been in contact with, Richard

409

Aquilino, and whom you're on your way to meet is ingenious, elusive. A technological genius when it comes to telephones. He is also insane and homicidal. His one dominating obsession is to kill you. He's what you might call a guided missile. You might be more familiar with the concept of the Manchurian Candidate. Aquilino's been conditioned, or brainwashed, instructed to go off at certain signs and stimuli. *You,* sir, are such a stimulus . . . the final stimulus in a long chain."

Kennedy whistled. "Why? Who did it?"

"Jack, I want you to understand that we're not giving you this knowledge merely out of the goodness of our hearts," Mr. Kelley said. "Keats has done a brilliant job at considerable risk to himself. What he's going to tell you is very much linked to what you want me to do for you . . ."

"For the country, Edward."

"Jack, Keats is still young and impressionable. I don't want you poisoning his mind with such talk."

Keats said, "It goes back a way; it's a mind-control program run by the CIA. It has several code names. MK-Ultra is one of them. After the Second World War, when the cold war was heating up, the thought occurred to certain people that agents could be conditioned to perform certain kinds of missions. If they were discovered it would be useful if they had no idea who sent them, or what their purpose was so they couldn't confess even under torture, couldn't be doubled, without going mad. Perfect deniability. The need became pressing after the Korean conflict when it seemed that the Russians and the Chinese could do such things. Funding was secured. Experimentation started. A massive program was set up. The U.S. Army runs such a program and so does the Veterans Administration. It's all based on notions developed by Pavlov. Techniques using drugs, electroshock, reinforcement, subliminal suggestion, sensory deprivation, and so forth were developed. There was limited success. Sometimes it works and sometimes it gets out of hand. Some subjects have proven superbly suggestible. Aquilino is such a person."

Laughter came flooding in from the other room. There was a sound of breaking glass. "They're having a lot of fun out there," Kennedy said, almost wistfully.

"A number of people went permanently insane. Others be-

410

came sort of generalized time bombs, waiting to go off . . . like the dud bomb that goes off twenty years later. Still others have been reduced to idiots and thrown out into the streets. There have been many buried mistakes. The science is in its infancy.

"On the surface, Aquilino was an ordinary kid. Came from a lower-class background. By some quirk of fate, he had a series of wild talents. He was a communications genius. He thought it would be interesting to listen in to the rich and powerful, see what they had to say to one another . . . sex, money, that kind of thing. He held a job with the telephone company and figured out a way to do it. He rigged up devices, connected them to the switching mechanisms, fiddled with the cables, routed calls through his own apartment setup, gained access to unlisted numbers, and began to listen. Well, sir, you can imagine what he had to hear. Business, politics, intelligence, whores and whorehouses, sadism and masochism, homosexual arrangements, payoffs, bribes, state secrets, the great talking to the great, movie stars, both male and female. Raw intelligence. He worked his way up the chain to higher and higher circles till he finally found the way to listen in to you.

"Aquilino is naive. Brilliant with technology, but an idiot in the serious matters of life. It was gibberish to him. The major thing that interested him was the personal gossip. People would, of course, pay a lot for that kind of information too; it would make the whole Profumo affair look pale. The sex revved him up. And maybe a touch of jealousy came into it. He had no thought of taking the stuff and selling it. In the process he was spotted. The CIA, under a cover, tapped into *him* and heard who and what he was listening to. It was assumed he had to be a spy. They looked for his control. There was no control; no drops, no microfilm, no radio. They couldn't believe that. It had to be something very deep. The man who ran the operation was my immediate superior, Mr. Holcomb. Holcomb thought they could bring him in and turn him without his knowing he had been turned, but not against his masters—who were assumed to be Russians—but against you."

"Holcomb. I've heard that name."

"One of the Company legends. Close friend of and very like William King Harvey."

411

"That asshole . . ."

"Holcomb works under cover of the Coffin Foundation, which is one of the conduits that funnels money for mind-alteration and control projects. In particular Holcomb worked with people he rounded up and suspected of being spies, deconditioning them in order to double them . . ."

Holcomb entered the Carlyle Hotel. There were two men with him. Some action at last. He was going to round the whole thing up and roll back Skuratov's operation. They walked unchallenged through the lobby, and turned off toward the staircases. There was a door that looked like it led into a utility closet. It led downstairs to the basement. The men went downstairs.

At about the same time, Skuratov was coming through the tunnel from the New York Central tracks to the Madison Avenue Psychiatric Hospital. He had four men. Keeping careful watch, they climbed the stairs to the lobby. It was Saturday. There was only a receptionist and a security guard on duty. One of the men turned to watch the entrance. The others pulled out silenced guns. The receptionist's face turned white. The security guard said "What the hell is going on here? Is this a holdup?" Skuratov said, "The keys to the front door. You are closing up business. Please." The guard was foolish enough to reach for his gun and was shot down. The guard's body was thrown backward against the wall. He was already dead. The receptionist was trembling so hard she couldn't find the right key. Skuratov took the ring of keys from her hand and tossed it to the man at the front door. "Find the right key and lock the doors. Get the body out of the way and stay." He turned to the receptionist. "This is regrettable. There is no cause for alarm if you keep your head. How do we get to the eighth floor?"

"But there's no one up there now."

"Then what are you worried about? Please."

"Take the furthest elevator on the left . . . it goes to all the floors above the fifth . . ."

"The elevator on *your* left or mine?"

"I . . . mine . . . I mean yours . . ."

412

"Why don't you come with us and show us. Don't be afraid. You're not going to be hurt."

Richard was becoming impatient. "Where is he?"

There was more noise in the hallway. The sound of a vacuum cleaner. Richard got up to look. "Let me," Carol said. She opened the door. Now there were two men standing on either end of the hallway. Moving in the center was an old, bent-over woman, pushing a vacuum cleaner. There was a housemaid's truck full of brooms, mops, pans, vacuum-cleaner parts, sheets, pillowcases. She was working her way to the door of their suite. The men all looked at Carol when she opened the door. They seemed tense. The old woman continued to clean the hallway, oblivious of the people. One of the men called to her: "Lady, go and work on another floor."

The old woman turned slowly and looked, not seeming to understand what he was saying. Another one of the men waved Carol back into the room. She came back saying, "There are more of them out there . . ."

"Security. He must be on his way."

"They seem very jumpy," Carol said.

"I suppose it's their job to be jumpy. Remember the bomb threats in Baltimore and Newark? What happened in St. Paul . . ."

Keats continued. "Holcomb brought Aquilino in and the shrinks began to work him over. They got everything they wanted out of the kid . . . everything he had heard. Then they began a crash program. They threw everything under the sun at him. Drugs, strobe lights, mild electroshock, subliminal instructions, sensory deprivation. Certain ideas were planted in his head . . . and an itinerary. Such as he had a special message to deliver to you and you alone, based on the stuff he had heard on the phone . . . including some things he hadn't heard at all. For instance, Operation Mongoose. The surface message was that you were in great danger and were on your way to becoming the victim of an enormous deception . . ."

"For what purpose?"

413

"To insure that you would be resolute on Cuba and follow through all the way. Certain people want Cuba back. They think you're responsible for the Bay of Pigs failing. They think you're soft on communism and you were going to avoid, at all costs, war . . . you are selling the country down the river.

"The events Richard would hear on the radio or see in the papers were kinds of linked triggers, confirmation of the news he had to give you. What gave additional urgency to the whole thing were his parents. Holcomb had them snatched," Keats shrugged. "But Aquilino didn't know that. He thought that *you* took them. That resentment was to be activated by the sight of you."

"If he thinks I can be in on every fucking little operation . . ."

"He's unsophisticated. He personalized it. It was you and him, just the two of you."

"Can they do things like that?"

"The mind is a fragile thing, sir. If you can make it plausible and it locks into already prevalent attitudes."

"Jesus, what else are they running out of Langley? The CIA wants me killed?"

"Let's just say that there are people among them who feel you're not doing the job."

"I'm going to wipe those bastards out, or get my own people in charge of that circus if it's the last thing I do."

"For that you'd need a counterintelligence operation inside of a counterintelligence operation. They allowed the kid to escape. He contacted you. He was going to save the country by warning you. He would be invited to come and see you. If the signs were that you were going to back down on Cuba, then he would trigger, or be triggered when he got to within a certain optimum distance from you."

"Why did Holcomb want to do this to me?"

"He wanted to affect and change your policy."

"Who's running *him?*"

"Well, sir, that's harder to ascertain. He's tied up to a network of superpatriots on the one hand. But on the other hand he was taken by the Russians in Berlin. They had him for a few months and probably did the same kind of thing to him that was done to Aquilino. *Certain Russians* also want confrontation. But Hol-

414

comb could never have done what he did without backup . . . right inside the Company itself. People helped get him placed in a key situation, working at the Coffin."

"You're saying that the CIA and the KGB are in collusion?"

"No, Jack," Mr. Kelley said. "It's just that certain people in our government and certain people in their government see eye to eye on the way world politics should run, and so they collaborate. It's the opposition that keeps them in business."

Keats said, "Aquilino contacted you. He recounted certain of your own very private conversations. That a total outsider was telling you these things represented—aside from the shock—a sign of the highest verification . . ."

"I almost shit in my pants."

"You set the meeting up yourself, finally, right across the street. He was going to tell you about the plot. He was going to tell you how you were going to be maneuvered by the deliberations of a body that does not yet exist, but which must shortly be called into existence because of the crisis; the Executive Committee of the National Security Agency, or whatever name you choose to give it, which will debate on how best to respond to the presence of missiles in Cuba. Once the news of the missile emplacements is out, your options become limited. Holcomb had the shrinks feed some of the terms of the debate to Aquilino."

"Then it's all faked?"

"Only part of it is faked. Aquilino did hear some of those people talking about how they could wake you up to the present danger. The odds are that when the committee is convened, people will say the same sorts of things they have been saying for years; bomb Cuba, invade Cuba. You got the news that committed you yesterday, or today, didn't you, sir? Aerial photographs of missile emplacements. U-2 stuff?"

"Yesterday. Everyone and his mother seems to know about that. Senator Keating . . ."

"Well, what everyone doesn't know, sir, is that those photographs were not taken by the U-2 at all, but by the Russians . . . those certain Russians. On the basis of those photographs, our U-2 will find confirming evidence."

Keats now changed his tone and his emphasis. "But a President has the option of accepting or refusing the peace or com-

415

bat gambits. Let's say that the President accepts the position hammered out by his advisors. War. But the Cubans could retaliate. Some of those missiles are in place. One strike at a major city . . ."

"If it has to be anywhere, I vote for Miami," Kennedy said.

". . . would be enough to plunge the world into a very short, intense and final war. But let's say that a President refuses and wants to negotiate, diplomatically, in front of world opinion, and squeeze the whole situation for points. There's that possibility. But people would have in mind the unfortunate events of the Bay of Pigs . . ."

"Don't remind me."

"There are those who already consider you to be an agent of the Russians, or the devil, or both. We believe that the people who run Holcomb don't want to give you the chance to negotiate and squeeze out of the confrontation. Your death is their insurance. The new President, Lyndon Johnson, might be the perfect person to respond, say, if *he* were running the deliberations of the National Security Agency . . . A surprise attack would have public approval."

"Holcomb's a fuckin' traitor."

"I don't know about that, sir. It's a touchy point, a gray area. He thinks he's a patriot."

"Such patriots are better off dead."

The laughter floated in again. The pitch was higher now. "What the fuck are those fools laughing about?"

"If one has been made into—conditioned to become—a tool, is he responsible for his actions? If I were a lawyer, that's the line I would take. I don't think that such matters should ever come to the public's attention."

"Why didn't you go to your superiors and tell them all of this?"

"That's obvious, isn't it?" Mr. Kelley said.

"Jesus, there's no point in seeing the kid, is there?"

"There are others to consider. Holcomb. The people he used. After the kid goes into action, he'll probably be killed, as well as the psychiatrists who worked him over. There are maybe twenty people involved. Perfect deniability."

"Jack, why don't you let my people handle this . . . Keats . . ."

Keats stood up and smiled.

416

"I want you to know that your President appreciates what you've done. I'm going to need someone down there in Langley. Your idea about a counterintelligence section inside of our counterintelligence . . . that's a good one."

"Thank you, sir." And then Keats remembered how Abromowitz had been treated. As he was leaving he heard Mr. Kelley saying, "And now, Jack, I think we can get down to a little horse trading. I think of what we're trying to do here as a sort of treaty between *three* sovereign powers. I want to represent your interests to the best of my ability to Mr. Khrushchev and I'm sure he wants me to represent *his* interests that way too, and both your interests to my principals. We're all looking forward to a peaceful world so we can get on with the business of getting America moving . . ."

"You're an arrogant bastard, Kelley, but at least you're Irish . . ."

No, Keats thought. He's Chinese. He walked out through the party. People plucked at him and offered him drinks. The party was getting messy. He saw Laura. Their eyes met. It was enough. It had been done. All that remained was the killing and that was a small enough thing.

A man came into the room where Richard and Carol were waiting. A big man, perhaps two hundred and twenty pounds, wearing a rumpled black suit. Quite different looking than the FBI or Secret Service types. He was heavy-set and thuggish-looking. Holcomb. The man walked to the side of the door and stood, looking at them.

"Is he coming soon?" Richard asked.

The man didn't answer, but looked at them impassively.

Probably a bodyguard, Richard thought. "What's keeping him?" Richard asked. The man didn't answer. The face was completely blank.

Another man came in. This one was also big, but taller and leaner, about six feet four. He had white hair and he wore a brown suit. He nodded at the other man. Skuratov. Holcomb looked from Aquilino to Skuratov to see if there was the slightest sign of recognition. There was none. The two men looked at one another. Something passed between the two of them. An imper-

417

ceptible nod toward Richard and Carol? Suddenly Richard realized that the President wasn't going to come. Something had happened. Had the President betrayed him? He had trapped himself in the castle. Nothing smelled right. Richard saw them looking at one another. They were poised, but for what? Richard began to fiddle with himself, as if restless, loosening his jacket so he could get to his gun. Carol didn't see what was happening. There was a noise outside the door. One of the men, the one wearing the black suit said, "What the fuck is going on?" But he kept his eyes on the man in the brown suit. Richard was standing.

The President was more and more interested in what Kelley had to say. He listened intently. There was a loud noise in the other room. "What the fuck is going on?" And he got up to look, striding past Mr. Kelley. The party was reaching orgiastic heights. He opened the door and there was a blast of noise. "Just keep it down," he yelled. Someone threw glass; it exploded. A woman shrieked. The Secret Service man moved out to restore order.

One of the men, Skuratov, nodded toward the door. Holcomb shrugged his shoulders and shook his head slightly. He sidled toward the door and opened it. Someone who was standing just outside, or leaning on the door, crumpled to the floor. Carol gasped and started to rise. Holcomb jumped back into the room. Richard had his gun out. The man in the black suit had his gun in his hand. Outside there were the whisper and puff sounds of silenced guns. Carol stood there, unable to move. Richard was moving to get in front of her. They all stood there for a second, frozen. Someone else came into the room. They all glanced at the person. It was the old cleaning woman, straightened up now. She was carrying a silenced submachine gun, a wisp of smoke curling from the muzzle. Richard yelled, "Momma, what are you doing here?" The sound unfroze them all.

Holcomb pointed his gun in the old woman's direction. She was looking at the other man, Skuratov, staring at the white hair and his bony, almost skeletal face. She dropped to her knee, pointing her gun in his direction, as he shot. Lilly Aquilino shot the man with the white hair. He was lifted backward by the

418

weight of half the clip firing off. The soundlessness was eerie. Holcomb was raising his gun to shoot Richard's mother when Richard shot him. This sound was deafening. The .32 bullet blew the man's head apart; it exploded against the wall in a shower of blood and bone. Richard saw that his mother was wounded. He shrieked, "Mom!" His mother! His mother! What was she doing here? Where was his father? He jumped over to her. She was struggling to get to her feet. "It's nothing, Richard. Nothing. That bastard. That insect. He's hunted us for thirty years . . ."

"Who is he? Are you all right?"

"KGB. Don't talk. We have to get out of here. I can stand. I can walk. Get your girl friend, Richard. Come on. I can walk. It's nothing."

"Mom . . ."

"It's time to stop talking and dreaming. Move."

Richard went over to Carol. She was almost in a state of catatonia. "Darling. Darling. Come on. We have to get out of here. Come on . . ."

Her mouth moved. She couldn't say a thing. She closed her eyes. She wanted to wipe what she had seen out of her memory. She wanted to go to sleep, right there, on her feet. If she slept she would be protected. Her face was slapped. "Carol, come on, we have to get out of here."

"You killed that man. The President's guard . . ." she whispered.

"He was going to kill my mother. Let's get out of here."

Lilly was erect now. "Be calm. Move and think. Let's go. Richard, make her leave or forget her. There will be others . . ."

Seven men led by Keats went down into the basement of the Carlyle. They went through the tunnel under Seventy-sixth Street and started to come up the staircase into the Madison Avenue Psychiatric Hospital. They were all carrying machine pistols. As they came up the stairs, the first man was shot and tumbled backward. Keats and his people poured fire past the wounded man, up toward the entranceway and kept coming. The man who was guarding the lobby was riddled. As they came into the lobby another man fired at them and another one of Keats's people went down before the man, one of Skuratov's, was blasted aside. "Upstairs. Split. Elevator and staircase. Move. Move. Keep alert. There should be seven or eight of them. Move."

The hallway outside the suite was a shambles. Bodies lay strewn in the hallway. The carpeting was soaking up blood. Lilly led. They walked to the stairwell. She was moving slowly. "Mom. Are you all right?"

"I'm fine. It's age, not the wound. I got him. It took me thirty years. Come, down the stairs." She had put a new clip into her gun.

They began to walk down. Richard had to drag Carol. She was almost paralyzed. "Sweetheart," he kept whispering. "I love you. You have to move. Move or die. Come on. You can do it. You can do it. Remember, I love you. Are you all right, mom?"

"That's your mother? What . . . ?"

"I don't know, Carol. We have to get out of here. We can talk about it later."

"But I didn't do anything. He was going to protect me . . ."

"Who was going to protect you?"

"A man. His name is Keats . . ."

"Oh shit. Love, it doesn't matter. You'll get killed if you stop. Please, stay alive for my sake . . ."

"I was trying to help you, Richard, but I betrayed you."

"I know. I love you. I understand."

They went down the stairs. The light was dim in the hallway. He saw his mother hold up her hand. They stopped. They could hear feet on the staircase, running up toward them. His mother knelt on the landing. Two men appeared. She shot them before they could even get their guns up. Richard turned. Time slowed. There, standing on the landing above and behind him, il-luminated by the landing's backlighting, stood a man with no features, appearing as if his head were encased in a halo, gleam-ing like an angel's. Richard shot once, twice, three times. The sound was deafening in that small space. The man disappeared.

Carol screamed: "It's *him. Him!* He tried to kill me."

"This is not a dream, Richard. Come. We have to get out of here," his mother said.

They moved down the stairs swiftly. Carol was moving under

420

her own volition. They came into the lobby cautiously. There were bodies on the floor. A man who was looking toward the elevator turned. Richard threw himself forward, hitting him with everything he could; the gun, his hands. His hands were all over the man, hitting him in the face, the groin, the stomach, pounding, pounding, letting all the rage out now. The man was down and Richard kicked him in the ribs, the face, the head.

"Enough, Richard."

They went downstairs again and into the basement. He found the entrance to the tunnel and entered it. They ran eastward toward the New York Central tracks. If they could get into the tunnel complex they would be safe. Behind them they heard the sounds of running feet.

The men stood up. They shook hands. "It's going to take time, Jack. We don't expect miracles. But at least you know what you're in for when you assemble the committee. I'll accept the mission. When I get back, your people can sit down and talk to Emil and work out the details. Emil . . . that's what technicians are for. Sometimes I think they really run the world. You know, Jack," Mr. Kelley put his arm around the President's shoulders. "They always talk about the Roman Empire's decline. The Praetorian Guard was making and unmaking kings and emperors. Sometimes I wonder if we haven't created our own Praetorian Guard. But in spite of all that violence, its so-called decline took hundreds of years. Who was minding the store all that time? Who was getting the roads built and the aqueducts and the buildings while the high drama of killings was going on? Who was doing the paper work and the administration? People like Emil . . ."

And people like you, you old fuck, Kennedy thought.

They went out of the bedroom. The party was in the last stages of decomposition. Mr. Kelley leaned over to the President and whispered, "See. That's the kind of thing that was happening during the Roman Empire. Orgies, lust, blood. But people like Emil Churchman never get to go to parties like these . . ."

"Who are you kidding?" Kennedy asked.

After Mr. Kelley left, Kennedy called over one of his Secret Service men. "Harry, I want you to get about fifteen men and get over across the street to the Madison Avenue Psychiatric. There's

421

a kid I want you to pick up. Now you may run into trouble, so be careful. This is what you have to do. The kid's name is Aquilino, Richard Aquilino. He looks a little like John Derek. Now . . ." And he continued whispering instructions. He thought, fuck you, Kelley. I'm not going to let you put me over a barrel.

CHAPTER 54

"ARE you all right? If we can get into the big tunnel, we can get away. I found ways out."

"I'm fine. I'm fine. But listen. If for any reason I can't go on, you have to promise me that you won't stay . . ."

"Mom . . ."

"Richard, what good will three of us dead do anyhow?"

"I can't leave you."

They had come to the entrance through to the railroad tracks. Richard opened the door. The footsteps were louder. Someone yelled behind them. The sound of a shot reverberated through the narrow tunnel. Richard turned. "Don't stop. Keep moving," his mother told Carol and Richard.

"Turn right," Richard told his mother and Carol. His mother was panting. He saw her face in the dim lights of the train tunnel. They were spaced far apart. At this point the tunnel was about four tracks wide, bolstered up by steel pillars. They crossed the tracks to the uptown lane. At least that way there were pillars between them and whoever was coming for them.

"Don't run," Lilly told Carol and Richard. "It makes too much noise and it panics you. You have to be calm. Promise me. If something happens to me, you'll leave."

"You're hurt," Carol said.

"Yes, but not seriously. I have been hurt before."

Before. There were so many questions Richard had to ask her. A whole life. His father. His sisters. His brother-in-law. Who was she? Who were they? Who was Richard?

"He betrayed me. The President betrayed me," he whispered.

He could see her smile. It was a bitter smile. "If I can't go on, you have to get to your father."

"Where? How?"

"Through Siegfried . . ."

"Who?"

"Ziggy!"

They had walked about a block, as Richard figured it. From behind they heard a voice yelling, "Spread out."

"They're coming."

"If we can get downtown a few blocks, then we can get out. I know every exit. I scouted it out. You're sure you're all right?"

"Keep moving. Less talk."

The tunnel widened as another pair of tracks melted into the lanes. He knew that if they got down far enough, the tunnels proliferated into a maze. Lots of places to hide.

"Richard. I'm proud of you. It's in your blood, you know."

"What, mom?"

"Later. We keep moving. Is that the only weapon you have, that pistol?"

"Yes. But I have more clips. Carol has a gun and clips." But he was afraid she wouldn't use it.

As Lilly walked, she removed the spent clip from her submachine gun and put in another. She bent and carefully, quietly, laid the clip to the side of a track where it wouldn't be noticed easily. As she straightened up she groaned.

"Mom . . ."

"Richard. I'm an old lady. Old ladies groan a lot, *kvetch,* as your father likes to say. I sound like this every morning."

"You're sure?"

"Richard, believe me. This is my last fight."

Her last fight?

They heard firing behind them. The tunnel branched off. More tracks leading up here from Grand Central Station. Some of the tunnels branched downward. They followed the downward branch. "Good," she said. "They're killing one another."

"Who? For Christ's sake, who is killing who?"

She stopped and took a deep breath. He could see her face contorted. Pain. "Oh my God, where do I begin. We can't stop to talk, Richard. When we get away . . ."

"Who was that man you shot . . . thirty years?"

"His name is Skuratov. He has been trying to kill us for thirty years. KGB."

"Then they were all KGB? Russians?"

"No. No. When we get out. Listen, more shooting. Good. I don't know where to begin. This is no time for explanations. It's too complicated . . ."

They had tumbled into the tunnel and had been met by gunfire from across the tracks. Keats's people moved through the entrance to the tunnel, firing as they went, fanning out right and left. Keats came last. He didn't hesitate, but dived through and onto the tracks, turning in flight, landing on his shoulder, rolled, stood and crawled downtown, rose into a crouch, ran bent over, gradually straightening. The most logical direction. Toward Grand Central Station. More tunnels. More exits. He got to his knees, into a squat and began to run, weaving in and out of pillars, keeping low. He heard some shots whistling in his direction. Probably Skuratov's people. And some of Holcomb's. All shooting in the gloom, not even knowing what they were shooting at or what side they were fighting for. Just get to that little bastard Aquilino, Carol, and finish them off. Aquilino's mother. Where had *she* come from?

The police received a phone call from someone who had been walking on Park Avenue. "Are you sure?" the police dispatcher said.

"I'm telling you I heard shooting."

"And just where were you when you heard it."

"Seventy-second and Park. I heard it coming up through the grill. You know there are grills on every corner."

"There's no need to get sarcastic. You're sure it was shots?"

"Listen, I'm a veteran of the U.S. Army. I know firing, gunshots, when I hear them. Someone is doing a lot of shooting down there. Maybe they're holding up a train."

Oh Jesus, the cop thought, he thinks this is the Wild West. "All right, sir, we'll send a patrol car . . ."

More men were pouring out the entrance to the tunnel. Secret Service men. They fanned out. "Which way?"

"Come on. Come on. Come on. North and south. Remember who we're looking for. Jesus, what's that?" He had backed into a body. "Watch out," he said, too late as a shot slammed into the wall beside him. "Get help," he yelled. The second bullet hit him and he went down. They began to radio for help.

A roaring, coming up from the south, began to fill the tunnel. A strong headlight probed the darkness. The train was gathering speed. The engineer, who had made this run to Westchester thousands of times, was hardly looking, trained by this time to respond to red lights. Far ahead he saw some clouds of smoke drifting. A fire? He saw someone flit across the tracks. Jesus. Be careful. A few weeks ago one of the derelicts that used the tunnels for a flophouse had been killed.

Behind him a window of the train was shot out. There was no one sitting in the passenger seat; the train was mostly empty. A passenger went looking for the conductor to report it. The conductor said, "Fuckin' kids. I'll make a report."

"Do you realize I might have been killed?"

"I'm sorry. It might have been me too."

"You know, I never thought of that," the passenger said.

The KGB Resident was interrupted in the middle of one of his more pleasant experiences in New York. He reached for the phone and listened. The girl didn't stop her writhing and wriggling. "How should I know what he was running? El Supremo is a law unto himself. That's the trouble with legends. Off," he said to the girl. "Off! All right," he said into the phone, "I'll be right down. In the meantime get some people down there. There's an entrance there, at Sixty-third Street. We'll assemble there and get moving. What? About ten. You know who to get."

The girl had rolled to the side and looked at him. "What's the matter, sweetheart, don't you love me anymore?"

"My dear, now, more than ever, I love you with a passion I

cannot begin to put into words. I would like to spend the rest of my life here with you, but duty calls. Get dressed and leave. Quick."

She knew better than to question him.

There was more firing behind them, reverberating through the tunnel until it began to sound like vast armies firing at one another in the gloom. "Not too much further, Mom," Richard said. Carol was supporting her on the other side.

"Wait. Let me catch my breath."

"You're hurt."

"Yes, I'm hurt, but it's not the wound, it's age. Your father wouldn't approve. He doesn't like gunplay. For him it's always the last resort."

"Mom, what happened?"

"It was the first time in my life that I went against the committee decision, but you are my son . . ."

"What committee? What are you talking about?"

"Oh, there is so much to tell you. I couldn't let my own son be run like a common agent . . ."

"Mom."

"Your father has the answers for you, if anything happens . . ."

His eyes filled with tears. He fought the feeling back. Later. Mourn later.

"But whatever happens," his mother said, "don't blame your father. He's an honorable man and he loves you too, in a different way . . ."

"Where is he?"

"He must be worried sick about me. He always worried. I would say to him, 'Sam, why do you worry? I'm strong as a horse and I have a charmed life. Didn't we live through the revolution, the civil war and the starvation? What could ever be as bad as that?' Sometimes I think he lives through his mind too much. That's no good for a materialist, you understand?"

"No."

The police were listening to the firing coming up through the grating. "That sounds like a war going on down there," one of the cops said.

"Maybe that's where the Mafia is going to have its wars from now on. Listen, I'm not going down there. You think I'm crazy? Call in."

They went back to their patrol car and radioed their precinct.

Men were pouring into the railroad tunnels under Park Avenue, coming down through a number of entrances. But there was no line of battle they could join . . . the line was fragmented. It was impossible to find out who belonged to whom. Men shot at movements in the gloom, and the gloom got deeper and deeper as some faint tunnel lights were shot out. They were reduced to shooting at flashes of fire.

Keats, running south, came to a series of forks. Where should he go? He stopped, standing close to a pillar so he would present the minimum possible target. Behind him the gunfire was mounting in intensity. Don't think, he told himself. They could have gone in any direction and he was only one man . . . the others were behind him. Feel it. Feel it. Intuition. He moved toward his left and downward. He heard someone running in his direction. He stepped out and fired. The gun made no sound. It was silenced. The man went down. The man cursed in Russian. Other feet were running. Keats stepped out onto the track roadway and yelled in Russian, "This way. This way."

The men came around the bend. A small army. "Where is he? Where is Skuratov?" someone said. Keats pointed uptown. "There. Our people are in trouble."

"Are you all right?"

"A little wound," Keats said. "A scratch."

The men were running past him, guns drawn. "Get out of here and get yourself taken care of," one of the men yelled at him as they went past.

Police cars were assembling in the seventies. A police captain said, "I don't know what the fuck to do. We've been on the phone to the New York Central. The sons of bitches said 'I don't have to remind you, captain, that this is private property.' What the fuck is going on there?"

"Shit, it's nothing. It's just the New York Central and the Pennsylvania Railroad having a proxy war."

428

"Thanks, I needed that. Get hold of the commissioner, the mayor, whatever. I need advice."

Keats hunted. They were ahead. He knew it. He moved swiftly, silently. Richard had to be silenced. The other loose ends would be taken care of. There! He saw them. Richard, the woman he had called "mom," and Carol. He crouched and moved forward, and began to flit over the difficult terrain, crossed by railroad ties and tracks, worse than natural terrain, weaving in and out of pillars. The shooting was reverberating down from uptown.

By the time the Russians got there, the lines had stabilized although it was hard to say who was fighting whom. The Russians spread across the tracks and took up positions behind pillars, behind abutments, in niches designed to protect trackmen when trains went by. They were firing north and south now. The sounds now drifted up through the gratings on Park Avenue. Traffic had been stopped and rerouted. The street was swarming with police. Dwellers on Park Avenue were looking out their windows. Passersby were asking what was happening. There was a consultation between the representative of the New York Central and the police.

"What do you mean, we can't go down there?"

"It's a matter of jurisdiction," a man from the mayor's office said. "Look, sir, really, this is a police matter."

"Well, um, that is . . ." the New York Central official said. His instructions were to stall for time until this matter could be resolved on higher levels.

Three men came barging into the huddle. "We're from the White House staff. This is a matter of the highest priority, you understand? The President himself takes an interest in this. We have to be careful or this could lead to an international incident of the gravest proportions . . ."

"Shit," the policeman said. "There are people shooting at one another down there. It already is an incident of the gravest proportions . . . you mean graves, don't you, like for the dead?"

The man from the White House staff looked at the police captain, exasperated. "This is no time for joking."

"It isn't a time for dying, either," the police captain said. "Who are those jokers?"

"I'm sorry, officer, you have no need to know."

"Jesus Christ." He turned to the public relations official from the railroad. "Why don't you just run a few trains through there and crush them all?"

Richard turned.

"What's the matter?" his mother asked.

"There's someone here. Let's move to the side."

There. He saw something move. Flitting from side to side. A gleam of gold, caught in the light, flashing in and out of the darkness. Carol raised her pistol and fired. She had crossed a line. "I'll kill him, I'll kill him."

"Don't waste your bullets. Pistols are inaccurate. Wait. No matter how scared you are, wait. Patience will save your life. Now he knows you know."

Darting in and out of pillars, movement, coming closer and closer.

"That bastard," Carol said.

"Be detached. Don't think in personal terms, not now. Later you can feel. Alert. Patience . . ."

"Mom . . ." Richard whispered.

"Stay alive. Live. Live for me. Who is he?"

"The blond knight in the black armor . . ."

"Your father's stories . . . Who?" She stumbled back. She turned her machine pistol toward the north and fired off a clip, spraying the area. Bullets ricocheted off metal pillars and thunked into brick supports.

"Mom . . ."

"Leave. Remember me. Remember, this is not a dream. Revenge me. Revenge me."

"Mom . . ." he looked for the flash of golden hair. Carol fired again at a wisp of golden smoke: a flat crack.

"Leave. You'll be the death of me . . . you're eating my heart out . . . why don't you listen to your mother?"

"Mom . . ." Again. He fired. A bullet whizzed by his ear.

"I didn't bring you up to die. Live. Get out of here. Get married. Live. Get to your father . . ."

430

"I can't . . ."

"You can't compete with a trained killer. Run. Don't think of me now . . ."

Richard fired again. How many bullets did he have left in his gun? He got up, took Carol's arm. They began to run, weaving back and forth, his eyes filling with tears again.

Respective ambassadors of the Soviet Union and the United States were working things out.

The battle raged for another hour. No one could get close to the combatants. There were curses exchanged in Russian and English. It seemed to have become a personal matter. People tried to reach them with loudspeakers. Nothing seemed to deter the fighters; it was now a matter of honor. They insulted one another and fired. Now they were entrenched and no one was getting killed.

But after a long while, they were running out of ammunition. The shots became fewer and fewer. A calm began to descend on the underground battlefield. They began to detach themselves.

It was agreed between the Russians and the Americans that the whole event was unfortunate. High spirits and patriotism had led to certain deplorable events. It would hardly help to assuage international tensions to permit this to come out. The incident never made the papers. Besides, there were other, more pressing events that would soon be surfacing. It would hardly do to have this skirmish muddy the issues that would be debated . . .

It was about three o'clock in the morning when Keats appeared before Mr. Kelley. He was dirty. His hair was rumpled and matted with sweat. His face was smudged. Mr. Kelley raised his eyebrows.

Keats smiled. "The loose ends are tied up now. It's finished. He's dead."

"Were you close to him when he died?"

"No. It was a long shot, down a dank and dark tunnel. When I got to him, he was already dead."

"My warrior hero," Kelley said.

Keats looked at him to see if there was any irony to the remark. Kelley looked serious. "I need a shower."

"Do take one, my dear boy, do take one. You've done a good job."

Richard and Carol had escaped. They emerged from the labyrinth of Grand Central Station at four in the morning. Should he go back and get his mother's body? What point was there? Carol asked. He was numb. She held his hand. They walked in silence for a while. She started to apologize for what she had done. Richard nodded and said, "Later. Later. You couldn't help yourself. How could you know what he was?"

They passed a phone booth. Richard went in and called up the Carlyle Hotel. He was told that the President had returned to Washington. He dialed the Washington number collect. The phone was picked up. It was Kennedy. "You fuckin' son of a bitch. You set me up. You tried to kill me . . ."

"It's you. Richard, listen. I didn't do it. I didn't do it . . ."

"Fuck you," Richard said and hung up.

"What good did that do?" Carol asked.

"Just shut up," Richard said.

They walked again through the deserted streets. Where? Back to their hotel? Should he call up his father? Ziggy? No. No. His father had killed his mother.

They came to another phone booth. Richard called up the President again. It was answered immediately. He didn't say a thing.

Kennedy said, "Richard? Richard? Richard, I know you're there. You have to believe me. I didn't try to have you killed. I was told that *you* wanted to kill *me.*"

Richard said nothing.

"Richard, listen. You have something important to tell me. Why should I kill you? Use your common sense. Do you really think I have the power to have people killed without due process?"

Yes, Richard thought. "You were told I wanted to kill you? Who . . ."

"A man named Keats."

Richard sighed. "Call you back," he said. Never stay on the phone for more than three minutes. "You hear that?" he said to Carol.

432

"No. What . . ."

"Keats told the President that I wanted to kill him."

"That monster . . ."

"And that means if you were with me, you were part of the plan to kill him."

They walked in silence through the streets. A few times, seeing police cars coming, they huddled in doorways, pretending to neck. They found another phone booth and called again. And, without waiting for Kennedy to begin asking him questions, he began to tell the President what he had heard. Richard talked in three-minute stretches, hung up, and they walked to another phone, dialed, and began again.

Richard summoned up and summed up the fragments of fragmentary conversations. He talked about what should take place when Kennedy was forced to assemble his augmented National Security Agency, the powerful elders who would be likely to assemble. And he named those who had already decided for war, months ago, and those who would be for diplomacy. It was as if he were assembling a movie, giving the essence and then the already rehearsed pieces of dialogue, the dates when people would say this or that, the crucial dates from the fifteenth or sixteenth on up until the crisis broke. And he knew what the Russians would say, and what the responses would be and what courses of action were open to them. And this the President would already know, having used the Bolshakov conduit.

Richard began to mimic the voices he heard; Dean Acheson's aristocratic tones, contemptuous of compromise; Dean Rusk's almost-Southern drawl and his indecisiveness; George Ball's reasoned approach; Maxwell Taylor's hawkishness . . . Richard assumed the dialogue roles as if he were splitting into a number of people at the same time. He outlined for the President how these men had come to this position. And now he invoked the name of Parvus and told what it was, and mentioned that there were key aides in key positions. An enormous penetration had taken place. If the deliberations of Excom didn't lead to a clear decision for taking Cuba, then an "incident" would have to force the issue, a contingency plan devised by the hawks.

Now Richard came to the decisive incident that would inevitably lead to war. In the event of failure of the war party to get its

433

way, something might be arranged. "Go on. Don't stop," the President said.

"I'll be back," Richard said, hung up, and they moved to another phone.

There had to be insurance. Two things would happen. There would be a blockade, of course, to interdict Russian ships bringing missiles and launching equipment to Cuba. The Russians would sail up to the blockade line. The world would hold its collective breath. At the same time a task force of Cubans, CIA personnel and Green Berets would be launched out of Florida and near Mobile.

There were options; Richard wasn't sure which would be used. One of the ships bearing the missiles to Cuba might, in fact, not stop. It would be a container ship under foreign registry, but at the right moment its nameplate and true Russian name would appear, as if challenging the Americans. The ship was equipped in interesting ways. It was an electronic communications ship, much like the American NSA monitoring ships which had several additional capabilities. It had the ability to blank out communications between all other ships in the general vicinity, and be electronically invisible while jamming the sensing devices of other ships, radar, sonar, and the like. The ocean is a wide place in spite of the way people talk about the shrinking world. Even a huge ship could effectively disappear unless spotted by a human eye. By the effective use of electronic emissions it could appear to be elsewhere. It could do one of two things. It could disappear for a while and then reappear, having slipped through the blockade network, on its way to Cuba. Then it might be attacked by the air force or the task force launched from Florida and Mobile.

Or: what if it projected an image of itself to be picked up by other American ships in the vicinity? What if it *actually* or electronically appeared to ram an American ship, or launched, or appeared to launch missiles at an American naval ship?

"That sounds like very sophisticated weaponry."

"That weaponry has been sold to the Russians by Americans, sir."

"Who . . ."

Richard shrugged. "I don't know."

"Causus belli . . ."

434

"If there is an actual exchange of fire, then one of the targets of choice is the *Joseph P. Kennedy.*"

"Oh, that's neat. The *Joseph P. Kennedy.*"

"And that incident is an open invitation for the invasion, which will already be under way, a massive bombing, or an invasion. Hard to resist when it hits the media. The task-force strike will take place even before you give the order, sir."

"The Bay of Pigs again."

"I guess so," Richard said.

"So Bolshakov and Khrushchev are lying to us?"

This would be the moment, Richard thought. It was up to him and him alone now. He had no idea of the truth, or if there was even a truth but he had to make a decision. "Hold on," he said. "What do I do? You've been listening."

Carol looked at him and didn't say anything.

Richard took a chance. "No sir," he told the President. "No sir. They're telling the truth to you. They don't want war. But both countries are being pushed that way."

"What about the missiles, Richard?"

"I suppose they are there . . ."

"Suppose!"

"But I'll bet . . . I'm sure that they're not controlled by Cubans, but by Russians. Yes. That's it. They're for bargaining, not for shooting. Yes. That's it. I heard one of those people on your Excom saying that . . ."

"Who?"

Was it Dean Acheson who said it to Edward Kelley, or was it Edward Kelley who said it to an aide of Dean Acheson's? It didn't matter. "Dean Acheson's aide—I don't remember his name—and Edward Kelley talked about it," he said.

Richard then took it further. If Kennedy accepted the news of the incident as genuine, he would have to declare war. If he questioned the incident, counseled moderation, ordered an investigation to see if apologies and reparations were in order . . . if Kennedy decided to see what could be politically milked out of the situation, then his backchannel contacts to Khrushchev would be leaked to the media. Then he would have to contend with the military, who were ready to take emergency control. Kennedy would end up being impeached, called a coward and traitor. This would signal to the Russians that they could get away with anything.

It all took about two hours and he was finished. He had put the story together. He had done more than that; he had achieved a kernel of wisdom, made his own decisions, taken it all on his own back.

Kennedy said, "Richard, why don't you come down to Washington where I can have you protected."

"No. I don't trust any one of you. Just remember: the incident in the Atlantic . . ."

"Richard, I can help you get your parents back for you."

"Fuck you," Richard yelled and hung up for the last time. "Come on, Carol, let's make a life for ourselves."

Kennedy was totally awake now. He rang for an aide. "Get me Bobby. Get me Ted. Right now." He hung up. That old bastard. He was off the hook now. Kelley. There were going to be some changes made in command, never mind what Defense and the CIA said. It was going to come out *his* way. In his way, the kid had really saved the day. *His* day.

EPILOGUE

AFTER he talked to Kennedy, Richard and Carol fled. They disappeared into a limbo where no one would follow. They left their hotel and fled west and south. The spent a night with Ed Griggs, and were passed along to others in a chain, changing their names as they ran. They took on odd jobs, she as a secretary, he as a laborer. They acquired false identification. Now and then Richard emerged, wandering into libraries to read day-old papers.

In the days following the 14th of October, there was nothing of the Executive Committee, Excom. Certainly nothing he read in the newspapers indicated that he had told the President anything. Kennedy continued making his campaign speeches, doing the business of the day, right up until the nineteenth of October. On the nineteenth he returned to Washington hurriedly, cancelling his tour. He was said to have a bad cold. Lyndon Johnson came flying back from Hawaii, also claiming to have a bad cold. Though many of the newsmen suspected that something big was happening on the weekend of the twentieth and twenty-first, none reported, or even speculated about what that might be. The "curtain of silence" was effective. On the twenty-second of October Kennedy made his announcement, inaugurating what would become known as the Cuban Missile Crisis. The role of Excom would come out later.

On the evening of the twenty-second, Kennedy went on the air to make his announcement; the discovery of missiles in Cuba. Richard and Carol saw the telecast in a cheap hotel in Indianapolis. Deep down, he could feel fury. Kennedy had let himself be maneuvered in spite of what Richard told him. There was some interference. Voices cut in for a while. He recognized his own and Kennedy's voices. The quality of the tape was not good. He heard snatches of military orders. Ziggy. There was no sign on television or in the newspapers that anyone noticed at all. People didn't have the will to listen. Ziggy's plan was a bust. Richard stood there, looking at the set, mouthing Kennedy's words in advance. He knew what was going to be said. Hadn't he overheard it in advance . . . or almost all of it?

The crisis began. The terrifying possibility of nuclear annihilation was in the air now. And even this didn't reach Richard. He was drained, a shell. Reserve units of all armed services were called up and put on alert. A great terror took hold of the country. From that day on, while the crisis lasted, relatives called up their dear ones and said goodbye to them. A great national trauma developed and sank into the American unconscious permanently . . . despair and desperation. Why work? Why build for the future or save? Why have children? For what? The children suffered most of all, but that would come out in later studies, which were suppressed. No therapist seemed to recognize this event as a *psychic* trauma.

A number of versions of the events have been written. The story is there to be read. All too well known to be recapitulated. But of Kennedy's secret diplomacy, the Bolshakov connection, little was written till it was exposed by the Alsops. And then there were allegations that the Kennedys were traitors. But there was nothing ever written of Richard, of Carol, of Keats, of Kelley, of Laura, of Parvus or of the role of the network Richard's father ran, nor were the peculiar disruptions that Ziggy's network tried ever written about.

Richard monitored, as well as he could, what happened during the crisis. The days passed. The Russian ships came closer to the quarantine line. The twenty-fourth came, and the twenty-fifth. The Russian ships stopped in the middle of the ocean. The American navy lay across their path. The world waited; would the Russian ships try to break the line or would they back off? The event Richard waited for and feared the most was *the incident,* the exchange of fire between a certain Russian container ship and an American destroyer named the *Joseph P. Kennedy.* It never happened. And in a way Richard almost wanted it to happen, to relieve the burden of his sorrows. Fuck it. Blow the world up.

Had it been prevented? Or had an incident happened, but no one reported it? If it wasn't reported then it had no reality. Had he stopped the war? He? Himself? Alone? Somehow he had gotten through. Did he dare believe that? Carol said yes; she had to hold him together, get him out of his depression. If she couldn't do that, she would be all alone.

They had a little money. With judicious husbanding, it might last them for a few months . . . at least the way they were living. They would have to get jobs. Richard made no effort to contact Ziggy . . . didn't even know if he was alive. What could *he* do? He was sure people were still after him. He had seen his mother destroyed. What did it mean? Why had his mother appeared with a submachine gun in her hands, trying once again to protect him, her son? What kind of lives had his mother and father led? How had they concealed that from him? He didn't even know if his father was still alive . . . and he didn't care. He felt that his father had done something to him . . . crippled him.

"You should try and get in touch with him," Carol said.

"No. My father was responsible for the death of my mother. I'm going to close the door on those mysteries of my life."

To think about the past was to become curious and curiosity led to death.

Laura? Where was she? There was a corpse that looked like Laura and a tunnel full of dead men and there were dead men in some dusty office. Laura, she had tried to kill him too. And she had almost gotten it done. He had been used. Why? Why him? The blond man. Him! The man named Keats, if that was his real name.

Slowly he recovered. And, slowly, a slow-burning rage began

to sustain him. He should want revenge. He had promised his mother. But for weeks, for years, it was too much trouble.

Sidney Ficino had his moment of glory just before the crisis was officially announced. He was awakened on the 20th, Friday morning, 3:00 A.M. He was told that he must go to Washington immediately. He was to bring his workup on Nikita Khrushchev along with him. A limousine was sent for him. He felt important; he was on his way to the top. He was told to be at LaGuardia by eight o'clock. He would be met and flown directly to Andrews Air Force Base and taken directly to the White House. *Barnstable had come through!*

He was in Washington by ten o'clock. He was at the White House by ten-thirty. He was kept waiting for three hours. He rehearsed in his mind just what words he would say when he met the President of the United States! After three hours he was taken into another room. He was ready with the momentous words that would change the course of history. He was met, not by the President, but by a young man who said, "The President appreciates what you're doing for America, Dr. Ficino. You have the analysis of the subject with you?"

"Right here," Ficino said. Why hadn't he thought of getting a new and expensive briefcase?

"Could you please give it to me and it will be passed right on to the President."

"I'm not going to meet him?"

"It may be difficult. You appreciate that he's the busiest man in the world. What I'd like from you is just one more thing; could you, in a few words, give a kind of . . . well, an executive summary . . ." He laughed. "A summary for executives. My secretary will take it down and I'll pass it along with your invaluable report . . ."

"I don't know what to say . . ."

"Well, will the subject—we should refer to him that way—draw, or will he blink? In a nutshell . . ."

"In a nutshell?" I have a long, detailed analysis, based on my method of Remote Assessment Profiling, R.A.P., a new and totally accurate way of assessing people . . ."

"I appreciate it, but time is of the essence. Just a few words.

The President appreciates your painstaking work and will respond in due course. A letter of commendation is being prepared. You've done a superb job. Your report, sir."

Stunned, Ficino passed the report over and mumbled a few words to the effect that the "subject" would draw, as it were. The "subject" was a man of volatile temperament, unstable, ridden with pride, having a strong ego-problem, which had its genesis from having lived under the shadow of a certain other "subject," "Stalin . . ."

"Shh," the young man said.

Khrushchev was not to be trusted. That was the message he had been told to deliver by Keats. And he instantly regretted it. He should have told them something else. It was obvious. They weren't even going to read his analysis.

Ficino was asked to wait. Three minutes later the President himself swept into the room accompanied by some people. He came up to Ficino and said, "Dr. Finikio, I've just read your report. It's brilliant, perceptive, superbly written, a masterpiece of long-distance psychological analysis. It's the one piece that's been missing from the puzzle. Let me shake your hand."

"You read it? In three minutes?" He was jabbed in the ribs. Ficino's hand reached out as if it had a volition of its own. It was grasped. Flashbulbs went off. The photograph of the two of them immortalized Sidney Ficino.

The President was saying, "I want you people to understand that we here, here in America, have the best psychologists in the world. That's because we don't use psychology the way others do, for purposes of state and to suppress dissent. It's a free society and free enterprise at its best. Dr. Finikio is one of our most promising practitioners. His report is a model of incisiveness, insight and intelligence. He's making valuable contributions to the state of mental health in America."

There was a scattering of applause. The President left. The young man said, "We would appreciate it if you could stay here in Washington for a day or two . . ."

"But I have to get back to my work."

"You might be needed for another little consultation. We'll make it worth your while. We'll put you up in a hotel. Have someone take you out on the town . . ."

441

"I should get back . . ."

"That's impossible, sir. Your President needs you."

On the evening of the twenty-second, Ficino saw the reason why he had been detained. He was proud. He had played a key role. He had affected the course of world events. Unknown to Ficino, this opinion was shared by Dr. John Gittinger, who had developed a system called the Personality Assessment System (P.A.S.), and who had also been summoned to the White House to present his evaluation of Khrushchev. Ficino was happy. They provided excellent quarters, good meals at good restaurants. And the girl was lovely too . . .

He left Washington happy. Two months later, he met with a regrettable automobile accident.

As the crisis continued, there was dissension and infighting in Miami. It heightened as the crisis became more and more of a cliffhanger. Paranoia became a disease in the Cuban émigré community. Once again the Cubans believed they had been used and betrayed by the Americans, in particular, Kennedy. So many things went wrong that infiltration by Castro's agents was suspected. Small, preliminary invasions were launched; every one of them ended in disaster. Bill Harvey, who was running the station —another man with his gun always ready ("If you knew what I knew you'd carry a gun around all the time too") became more and more vituperative; he drank more than ever and accused the Cubans of being everything his fertile mind could think of: spics, Commies, cripples, crooks, faggots . . . He had just heard that his good friend and old drinking buddy, Holcomb, had suddenly died. Harvey took to carrying a second gun. The Kennedy pinkos and liberals were sabotaging the operation again. Internal security became a mania. An internecine war broke out among the Cubans. Miami was littered with bodies. The war spread to the case officers and there was transmitted upward, infecting the CIA, becoming a small civil war never recorded in the official histories. The disease was to be called *Mollulitis virulentus* by someone who retired from the CIA after the war in Vietnam. It would lead to accusations, years later, in which such retired agents as William Colby and James Jesus Angleton were directly or otherwise, bureaucratically and by leaks, accused of being

442

Soviet moles. The same sort of thing was happening in the Soviet Union.

Richard and Carol worked their way westward. They took on small jobs in order to keep alive and tried to figure out what they were going to do with their lives. They lived in fear. Slowly Richard's pain subsided and the rage seemed to fade, mutating into a cold and permanent hatred. They needed explanations but where were they going to get them from? Had it all been a game? A vast deception? Did it come from the President himself? Or was it a web spun by the blond man, Keats, the knight in the black armor? What was this Keats? An explanation was owed to them, but who did they dare collect it from?

Richard began to have fantasies again of reaching the President. He saw himself going up to the man and seizing him by the jacket lapels and shaking him . . . Carol kept bringing him back to earth. Through the years Richard would read everything he could get his hands on about the event. He was convinced that he had done it. He had saved his country . . . the world. *He* had averted the war. Carol didn't fight this fantasy. She saw he needed it.

But Richard was recovering. Week by week, month by month, they made their way westward; Chicago, south to St. Louis, New Orleans, west to Houston, Dallas . . . The rage waxed, waned, became part of his flesh. What he failed to notice was that as he got stronger, Carol began to deteriorate.

Certain changes seemed to flow from the crisis. There was a renewed commitment to *détente.* The next year John F. Kennedy made a speech at American University in which he said that certain dogmatic assumptions about cold war attitudes had to be reviewed.

The stock market, which was slumping for months, began to recover from October, 1962, and began its long climb again. New money instrumentalities began to find use; a vehicle which allowed money to flow out of the United States faster and faster; Euro-dollars, rumored to have been invented by the Russians. Joint ventures were begun with the Soviet Union but kept out of the papers. Russians, Americans, Germans, Swiss, Italians joined to build an automobile plant in the Soviet Union. Trade loosened and began to flow east and west to and through Russia. An oil pipeline was laid down; it ran from Iran through Russia, ending up in Berlin, where there was the Wall to contain people, but not trade. The hot line between Moscow and Washington was initiated the next year. Russia and America exchanged military missions and sent observers to one another's war games. An exchange program of scientific data and scientists was initiated. A few years later, after President Kennedy's death, a dedicated, almost enclosed system called the Federal Telecommunications System was initiated. Bell got the contract.

But the transition to the new age didn't go smoothly. Maybe the old forces fought back. In November of 1963, John F. Kennedy was assassinated in Dallas. Autumns are times of harvest. Time when the vegetation dies, goes underground. Burial of the god of fertility. King Arthur lies in Avalon, waiting to be revived, the sleeping prince awaited in Camelot. In October, 1964, Khrushchev was deposed bloodlessly. There were certain Russians who called Khrushchev's deposition "The Little October." The message was clear. "The Big October" was the Bolshevik Revolution. Therefore "The Little October" meant a return to orthodoxy. Khrushchev was blamed for his adventurism in the crisis. Had they found out, in Moscow, how he was using Bolshakov?

When asked about Kennedy's assassination, Mr. Kelley merely smiled and shrugged his shoulders. He quoted from the *Tao Te Ching* appropriately and mentioned the Praetorian Guard syndrome. The trail of the killers was muddied by a thousand explanations. The accepted one—at least for a while—was that it was the work of a lone assassin, perhaps a madman. But how many who had been experimented on, in the search for the perfect guided missile, had been turned into just such madmen?

Two years . . . three . . . four, Richard recovered. He had lost Carol. One day she had gone to work in Los Angeles—she was working as a secretary—and never returned. He waited a few hours and fled. He left and went north, to San Francisco. Had she gone back? He would never know . . .

He had been sleeping in cheap lodging in the Mission district

444

of San Francisco. He woke one morning, hung over. He stumbled out into the street and went to have breakfast. He began to feel better after eating. He thought about whether or not he should go to work . . . shaping up for a longshoreman's job. The day was beautiful, clear, spectacular. Not a sign of the usual fog. He checked to see how much money he had. Not much, but enough. He decided he wouldn't work that day. He would take a walk.

He walked from the Mission district to Market Street. He passed through the noonday crowds. He drifted through the business section. He caught glimpses of the bay. It looked clear and crisp. He walked up and down the hills. He came to the Mark Hopkins Hotel and paused in front of it and looked up. He had heard the view from there was spectacular. He would go there some day. He turned and walked away. By now it was late afternoon and the sun was beginning to set. He decided to go to the Golden Gate Park, walk through and go to the Pacific and watch the sun set. As he walked he felt something and turned. Coming out of the Mark, he saw two people. A tall blond man and a woman. Them. The knight in the black armor and his consort. Together. They were fashionably dressed. Their faces—he could see their faces clearly—were not so much cold, not even bored, but terrifyingly empty, as if they were not human.

He turned and walked away. He continued walking toward the Golden Gate Park. He came to a small cliff overlooking the ocean. The sun was low in the sky. Then the vision of the two of them, the blond man, Keats, and Laura, came back to him.

He was going to get them. He was going to get the people behind them. It was time to begin to get his revenge . . . begin now or never do it. One man? He would do it? It was going to take time. He was finished drifting. People like that devoured everything around them. They destroyed whole countries . . . worlds . . . his country.

He waited till it was night. The sky was clear. He looked up at the sky, looked at the stars, looked *through* them to something greater and deeper. Words came rushing into his head . . . ancient words told to him by his father, woven for him with old stories of the wanderings and adventures of his family. He had never understood those words. He seemed almost to understand them now. A strange intelligence flowed between him and what was

445

beyond the stars. The words, the ancient words, passed down from father to son through the ages flowed up and, for a second, seemed to order the universe. Someone was watching after him. The stars danced and changed their positions. They reordered themselves according to his magical injunction. They fused their power down, down, coming faster than the speed of light. He felt the surge of energy. He was sure he was glowing, gathering strength. He would have to prepare himself. Ethereal power needed to be translated into earthly power, and he knew the way now. Earthly power would come to him through the computer and telecommunications and a network of people, giving him the ability to penetrate anywhere he wanted to.

Enormous changes were going on in the world. The dream of ancients was being modernized, the old dream, visions and spells programmed into computers and telecommunications. People like Keats were trying to direct the flow of the world's power, laundering money, transforming it, investing in immortality. Cannibals. The world's electronic mind.

If the new world and the new world's electromagnetic technology made people like Keats and Laura powerful, it also made them vulnerable. Anyone could tap into that power if they knew how. He knew some of it. He would have to learn more. He had done great things with telephones. Ziggy and his people had done it with radio. He, himself, alone—he had affected the destiny of a nation. It would take years and he had to start all over, but he would do it. He had been beaten, drugged, tormented, his mind invaded, and they had tried to kill him, but he had survived. He was going to play with the world's mind. He was going to force the blond man, and those like him, out into the open. He was cured. He turned and left, walking through the night, back into the city . . .

Starting tomorrow . . .